I0646104

# LOST IN THE LAND OF MILK AND HONEY

## An Immigrant Saga

### By RW Holmen

Copyright 2022 RW Holmen

Cover design by Lance Buckley

ISBN: 9781005765477

# EPIGRAPH

It is my fate in this paper to swing constantly from optimism to pessimism and back, but so is it the fate of anyone who writes or speaks of anything in America - the most contradictory, the most depressing, the most stirring, of any land in the world today.

Sinclair Lewis

1930 Nobel Prize for Literature Acceptance Speech

And so the world watches America—the only great power in history made up of people from every corner of the planet, comprising every race and faith and cultural practice—to see if our experiment in democracy can work. To see if we can do what no other nation has ever done. To see if we can actually live up to the meaning of our creed.

The jury's still out.

Barack Obama

A Promised Land

# PREFACE

A man in threadbare woolen trousers staggered from the darkened saloon. His bum leg betrayed him, and he stumbled from the stoop into a heap in the dusty street. Dust caked in his bloody wadmal shirt. Rising to his feet, he lifted his face to the sky and shielded his eyes from the searing sun, as if surprised by the brightness of the day. He opened his palm but quickly looked away and tightened his grip around the mother-of-pearl handle of his bloody knife. He glanced back at the door, as if the dead saloonkeeper would appear, the man he left in the back room lying in a pool of his own blood. The murderer shuffled first in one direction and then another, dazed and aimless. His wits deserted him.

Just a year earlier, he had arrived as a hopeful immigrant, but America chewed him up and spit him into this dusty street: a cripple, a killer, a man who would be hunted all his days. In this moment, he felt empty: no guilt or shame; no fear of capture; only confusion. What had happened to him and why? What next? Where to go? What to do? Destitute with halting command of the strange lingo of the Americans, fate was having its way with him.

\*\*\*\*\*\*\*\*\*

*My father, a convicted killer, died without sharing his deepest secrets with anyone but me, and I never expected to betray his confidence; nor did I intend to reveal my own secrets, but as death* drew down upon me in the darkness of December, I saw things differently, and I required a listening ear, a confessor.

The red birds came to me in the twilight. When the afternoon sun slanted through specks of hanging dust, I flicked off the light and rolled my wheelchair to my window to watch and wait as darkness seeped into my room. I didn't see them arrive, but when the sun set, the cardinals magically appeared, perched in the low-hanging branches of the pine trees outside my nursing home window. By ones and twos, they flitted back and forth from their perches in the branches to the bird feeder filled daily with black-oil sunflower seeds. Fat snowflakes sifted through the still air. A white blanket cooled the ground and clumps of snow grasped the pine needles. Suddenly, in a flutter of beating wings and batted snow, the flock exploded away as an owl swooped over the ground and claimed a night perch in the pines.

The only sounds were my raspy breaths and occasional hoots from the unseen owl. My labored breathing was part of it, but mostly I just knew. The upcoming Christmas would be my last, my ninety-ninth. I have been blessed with a strong body that now grows feeble, but my mind remains clear, and a sudden epiphany of my mortality riled me up and prompted a change of heart.

I remained seated in the dark until my door opened and light from the hallway flooded into my room.

"Suppertime, Judge."

"Not hungry," I grunted without turning toward the voice, but I knew it was LaDonna, the African American nurse of the evening shift.

"I'll bring you a tray," she said, flicking on the light.

"Won't eat it," I mumbled after she departed.

An hour later, she returned to claim the cart with the untouched supper.

"You feelin' ok?"

"I'm fine. Just not hungry."

"Well, if you change your mind, come to my station, and we'll find somethin'."

"Turn off the light. I think better in the dark."

I'm not always such a grump, and I added, "please" as she closed the door.

Outside, the buttery glow of streetlights in the falling snow silhouetted the sentinel pines. The lights marked the curved lane that served as entrance to my swanky home for the elderly. Located in a wooded area of an affluent Twin Cities suburb, the nursing home claimed to be the finest around, and I suppose the boast was true. Until two years ago, I lived independently, except for a cook and a cleaning lady, in my Lake of the Isles Tudor that had been my home for nearly fifty years. I had stopped driving years before that, but a private car service allowed me to be out and about.

Hours later, I rolled my wheelchair toward LaDonna's desk, and the round clock with a stark white face and bold black hands said it was nearly midnight.

"I'll take a sandwich now, if you please."

LaDonna raised her eyebrows and peered over her pink-rimmed glasses that matched the beads in the crinkly ends of her corn rows. She shook her head in mock disgust.

"Why Judge Johnson, you eat when you should be sleeping. I suppose you were sleeping earlier when it was time to eat." She smiled broadly. "Never mind, I'll bring a tray."

"Thank you," I said, and I followed her to the kitchen and watched her slather mayo on marbled rye bread before adding a slice of ham and two slices of cheddar.

"Could I have a Heineken with that?"

*She again peered over her eyeglasses in mock disgust.*

*"Hold this in your lap," she said as she began to wheel me back to my room. She set the tray with the sandwich and a glass of milk on the bedside table in my room and turned to leave with a smile and a tap on my shoulder.*

*"Eat hearty, Hon'."*

*"Thank you, again, LaDonna."*

*Now that my mind settled on what I must do, my manners returned, along with my appetite.*

*"I have one more request," I said as LaDonna paused at the door. "Please leave a note for the day staff to summon Pastor Donald Johnson, my nephew. We have some things to talk about."*

*Pastor Don arrived late the next afternoon.*

*"Come in, Donald, watch the cardinals with me."*

*Pastor Don slowly removed his camel-colored tweed dress coat and gray scarf as his eyes darted out the window and back at me. As usual, he wore a light-colored cardigan over a dark dress shirt but without a clergy collar. He slouched into an easy chair with another glance at me, as if he wondered if I asked him here merely to watch birds taking their supper. I am a very old man, but he is surely an old man, too, a retired Lutheran Pastor. He is the only son of my sister Lena. I was the firstborn, followed by five sisters, but I will be the last to pass on. Lena was a middle child, born two years after me. Like everyone in the family, Pastor Don is tall, but he is also paunchy, taking after his father. Fortunately, that seems to be the only trait inherited from his long-dead progenitor.*

*Pastor Don is my oldest living kin, the first grandchild of Jonas Jönsson, my father, a Swedish immigrant, and the patriarch of our family. And a murderer, did I mention that? Confessed, convicted, and imprisoned in the maximum-security Stillwater Correctional*

*Facility.*

*Even though I had much to say, we honored the ritual of the red birds. We sat silently in the fading light, and when the cardinals finally departed for their evening respite, he seemed relieved and anxious to learn why I sent for him. I, too, was eager to begin. With my sudden decision to reveal family secrets came an urgency to do so, and I chided myself for having waited until now, when my time was growing short.*

*"There are things you don't know about your grandfather, many things," I said. "Papa confided in me, and now I will share his secrets with you. You will also learn some things about me, and about your mother, and about the rest of the family."*

*With that, we made our beginning, and Pastor Don perked up.*

# CHAPTER ONE: 1891

Each morning, his odyssey to the promised land began with a few steps over muddy ground to the two-hole crapper on stilts straddling Phalen Creek. They called this ravine *Svenska Dalen*, Swede Hollow, a mishmash of immigrant hovels on the east side of St. Paul. He holed up here, tired from his journey across the sea, yet eager, impatient, anxious, and hopeful like the other teeming transients who dumped into this slum, bound for somewhere else but lacking funds. His dream of a farm with a big red barn, spotted cattle, and sturdy horses remained alive even if his current squalor was not what he expected when he departed the motherland for the promise of America.

A steam engine rumbled up the tracks that followed the creek, shaking the outhouse and the young Swede inside. He fingered a crinkled photograph before returning it to his pocket. He drew inspiration from the picture sent home by an earlier emigrant depicting an endless field of wheat stretching under a cloudless sky; he could almost hear the gentle breeze whispering across a shimmering sea of tall stalks bending under heavy crowns of grain.

After arriving in New York City five months earlier in the spring of 1891, twenty-one-year-old Jonas Jönsson traveled by railroad west to Minnesota where thousands of his countrymen had settled before him. Many, like him, emigrated from southern Sweden, an especially impoverished region known as Småland, "small lands." After paying for passage across the sea, the rail transport depleted his meager funds. Not to worry, he had a strong back, determination, and a willingness to work.

The jibber-jabber of the bustling capitol city spilled from the streets into this wooded ravine cut into the Mississippi River bluffs. Permanent residents atop the bluffs dumped their refuse into the ravine, and the transients used the trash for building materials for their shacks with boarded-over windows and cracks between wall planks—less hospitable dwellings than the sod-roofed farm huts of the old country.

Jönsson lived in a single-room shanty, shared with three other recent arrivals from *Sverige*. Twin brothers Sven Anders and Per hailed from the isle of Öland just offshore from the old royal city of Kalmar and Arvid from a farm north of Lake Vänern. Arvid was due to leave soon when his sister arrived from *Sverige,* and they would join cousins in Meeker County in the center of the state. Arvid had been here the longest and had saved enough to head west to become a landed farmer.

Jönsson planned to follow a similar path, but first he needed to earn enough to buy his own stake in the land where virgin soil was plentiful and cheap. He would winter here, but come spring, he expected to continue his journey to the nearby prairie where he would plant his crops and his roots in the land of milk and honey.

With a glance toward the muted sunrise, he donned his sheepskin coat and pulled a woolen cap with a short bill nearly to his eyes. Drawing a deep breath, he was off to his American adventure.

"Yer the boss today, Jönsson," said the warehouse man. "Dis Polack will be yer lackey."

Jönsson had taken employment as a livery driver—he knew horses--delivering casks of fresh-brewed beer for the German owners of the nearby Hamm's brewery. Jönsson's command of the American lingo was not yet sufficient to understand, and the puzzled look on his face caused the German to slowly repeat the instructions while pointing to a raw-boned fellow with an oversized felt bowler hat that bowed his ears out like wings. Communication in America was a bigger impediment than Jönsson expected, especially because of the many accents from the various immigrant groups, and it made him feel stupid, helpless, and suspicious that he was being talked about when others chirped away, making as much sense as a flock of blackbirds.

Later that day, his lack of understanding would detour his journey to the American dream.

The Polack's bug-eyes looked away when Jönsson checked him out. Four months on the job, and already Jönsson had a promotion, and he wondered if he had been as pitiable as this dolt when he first started. Four-hundred gallons of Hamm's finest lager in wooden casks were loaded onto a cart drawn by a single strong gelding, a large draft horse of a breed unfamiliar to Jönsson.

With a *click, click* of his tongue and a light slap of the reins on the horse's haunches, the pair was off to Main Street on the east bank of the mighty river that sluiced through Minneapolis, an eight to ten-mile journey that Jönsson had travelled weekly, but for the first time, he was in charge. After unloading their cargo at the Minneapolis saloon, they would fill the wagon with sacks of barley from one of the mills that harnessed the waters of the Mississippi spilling over St. Anthony Falls. The falls boasted dozens of flour mills and made rich men of the Pillsburys and Washburns and Crosbys; this Minneapolis neighborhood laid rightful claim to be the flour milling capital of the world. One day soon, Jönsson promised himself, his own farm would help feed the enormous appetite of the flour mills.

The Swede and the Pole travelled in silence since neither understood the other. At least the fool Polack rearranged his cap to cover his ears in the brisk October breeze. A surprise early season dusting of snow had all but disappeared except for a few shadowed corners, and the breeze carried the scent of wet leaves that now lay as a mottled gold and brown carpet under barren trees.

"Florian," the Pole said, breaking the silence.

Jönsson's eyes flashed wide at the intrusive sound.

"Florian." The lackey grinned as he repeated the name slowly while jabbing his own chest with his pointing finger. "Florian."

"Jonas," Jönsson said, turning his eyes back to the road.

After skirting the state Capitol grounds, the road to Minneapolis progressed through the emerging German neighborhood known as Frog Town, which Jönsson didn't understand; if French-Canadians were called "Frogs," why call a German neighborhood "Frog Town?"

Jönsson was surprised to discover the Friday-fish-eating, mackerel-snapping papists--Polacks, Krauts, Frogs, and Micks--also claiming the promised land. The Swedish farm boy knew only the rigorous and insular piety of Småland where Martin Luther's claim that the papacy was the anti-Christ remained gospel truth for local Lutherans—which Jönsson didn't question.

Not that he was a religious man, and he had a prickly relationship with the local priest from the village back home, the representative of the Lutheran state church of Sweden. Korp, the tiny priest, cowed the young boys. The adolescents weren't sure whether the crow who flitted about the streets wearing a black frock coat and a three-peaked biretta was the vicar of Jesus or of Satan, but the distinction mattered little to Jönsson. Korp pinched ears and threatened hell and damnation whenever he interrupted the boys lifting the skirts of the girls or taunting Oskar, the cripple with one leg and a stump who hobbled about on a makeshift crutch.

Shop owners tolerated Oskar's presence on their stoops; he didn't beg, he spoke highly of the proprietor's wares, and his fingers whirred with sewing needles stitching rags into handbags or knapsacks, which he would exchange for more rags and a loaf of fresh bread or a potato or a *krona* from an especially generous patron.

Once, Korp grabbed Jönsson's collar and accused him of swiping an apple. "Why, it's for Oskar," Jönsson said with a smirk, and he tossed the apple with a gleaming-white-bite mark into the cripple's lap.

Jönsson alone, the tallest and strongest, and certainly the most irreverent, was not intimidated by the beady-eyed, beak-nosed Korp. Jönsson chafed under his mandatory catechism studies, and he doubted the supernatural stories told by the priest: Jonah and the whale; Noah and the ark; Samson and his long hair; Balaam and his talking donkey. Jönsson was never one for fairy tales, and Korp's threats of hellfire didn't bully him. In the end, the priest allowed Jönsson to take his First Communion even though he failed to answer many questions correctly during his confirmation examination. For the other boys and girls of Korp's flock, the sacrament was earned by memorizing Luther's small catechism. Not that it mattered much to Jönsson; his First Communion would also be his last on Swedish soil.

On the other hand, Jönsson saw God in the bloody after-birth of a newborn calf, he heard God in summer thunder, he felt God in his mother's caress, he smelled God in fresh-cut red clover, and he tasted God on the lips of a certain girl from the village, but he didn't see the image of Christ Jesus in Korp, the parish priest.

If God in heaven sat in judgment, he would surely find Jönsson lacking in proper piety; nevertheless, the immigrant assumed that Swedish Lutheranism was preferable to the superstitions of the papists. Within his tribe, he may have been a slacker, but it was his tribe, after all, and he never thought to question his inbred anti-Catholic prejudice, and thus he was suspicious of the fish-eating mackerel snappers.

The road to Minneapolis bustled with traffic and construction of shops along the new electric streetcar line connecting the rival cities.

*"Jävla skit!"*

Jönsson swore loudly as a clanging streetcar frightened the gelding who lurched sideways, nearly tipping the cart. That would be the end of Jönsson's employment if he spilled Teodore Hamm's beer on the street. Every penny and nickel and dollar Jönsson earned was stashed in a sock that he stuck under a floorboard in the shanty that was home; Jönsson saved for the day he would head west where the farmland was cheap for those willing to work it.

Soon the road passed by Hamline University where a small crowd watched helmeted gladiators wrestle on a grassy lawn. "Futball" Jönsson heard someone say, "Minnesota is smashing Visconsin." Jönsson shook his head and clucked at the foolishness. Travelling through the new brick buildings on the campus of the University of Minnesota, the gelding quickened his pace, knowing that a bucket of water and a lunch of oats awaited him at the nearby saloon.

Jönsson smiled at the sun peeking through the clearing clouds, what a fine day to be in America, he thought to himself, and then his thoughts turned homeward. He clenched his eyes and breathed deeply, remembering a little barn with Swedish red cattle chewing on fresh hay after the morning milking. *Fader*--Father--carried a wooden pail filled with warm milk in each hand as he made his way to the pump house where he would separate the cream.

Jonas and his siblings inherited the tall and lean stature of their parents, and the boys matched the square-shouldered brawn of their father, honed by bone-numbing labor on the rocky farm. Thick-calloused mitts adorned muscular arms, and sun-burnished cheeks peaked from beneath billed hats. Jonas chose a clean-shaven face, but *Fader* and Jonas' older brother boasted bushy red beards. Gray streaks flecked *Fader's* whiskers, and Jonas remembered *Farfar's*—Grandfather's-- pure white beard that remained thick until he passed, well- manicured to the end, unlike the unkempt beards of his son and grandson. Jonas' father and his two brothers—Alfrid, the oldest, who would inherit the farm, and Tomas, the baby of the family--boasted fine hair the color of wheat-straw and just as straight and blue eyes like the sheen of the farm pond in the noonday sun, but Jonas and his sisters, Elsa and Anna, favored their green-eyed mother with her thick auburn hair and the hint of a curl. Alfrid had always been the father's favorite but *Mor*—Mother--protected and defended Jonas, who was never able to match Alfrid in wit or strength, always lagging by two years.

When Jonas mentioned emigration to America, his father first ignored him and then shamed him.

"You will not go alone, for you bring your unborn children and grandchildren. Your descendants will never know the re- wards of your ancestors' toil, tilling this soil and piling stones on these fences. Beware your pride, boy. Forty acres is more than one man needs."

Jonas would not insult his father, and so he held his tongue. He did not speak of the hardscrabble farm with rocky fields—and tiny at that--and sod roofs that would soon cave in. What had passed from generation to generation was nothing to crow about, and the truth was that Alfrid alone—as the old- est brother--would be the beneficiary of the forbearers' toil and Jonas could only be his servant. True enough, homesteaded farms in America covered forty acres, dwarfing the meager plots of Sweden that had been divided and subdivided over the centuries, but what was wrong with that? America offered land aplenty and the opportunity to be more than a serf, tilling land owned by another, especially one's older brother.

Nor did Jonas heed the foppish parish priest who attempted to dissuade him of his folly.

"Dissenters and preachers of false doctrines run amok in a land filled with evil," Korp the priest warned. "America is the great Babylon where Towers of Babel are built anew. She violates the fourth commandment with her disparagement of the one true God and disregard of proper authority. Democracy? Hah! Godless anarchy is more like it!"

"*Skitprat*," Jönsson answered, and Korp's jaw dropped at Jönsson's reference to bull dung.

"I imagine God is just as pleased to stroll through the mountains and prairies of America as these rocky old ridges," Jönsson continued. "Could it be that the bounty of America reflects God's blessing and this depleted land his curse?"

"Humph," was all the priest could say and departed.

*Mor* understood the dreams of her second son. So did his sisters and young Tomas. *Mor* pieced rags together and sewed a knapsack and filled it until it bulged at the seams with the necessary clothing and sundries he would carry to America. What was essential and what would fit in the bag? Two wadmal shirts and woolen underwear and socks. An extra pair of thick, scratchy wool trousers. His winter sheepskin jacket was too bulky to pack so he would wear it, but boots, mittens, and a wool cap would be stuffed into his bag. A pot of soft soap, hairbrush, shaving kit, and various medicinal drops. A fork and a spoon. She tried to fit in a quilt, but it was too bulky, so she packed a thin blanket instead. Not that she expected he would read it, but she packed a psalter. He would also carry a willow basket with food for the journey: ryebread, honey, smoked sausages, a thick brick of yellow cheese, and a jar of Brännvin—distilled potato liquor.

Of course, his pen knife would be safely carried deep in his pocket. The folding knife had been his fifth birthday present from his father, presented during a rite of passage. On his birthday, *Fader* and Alfrid led Jonas to the stand of beech trees on a hillside on the far side of the pond. Sitting atop a gnarly base with partially exposed root tentacles firmly clutching the ground, the largest of the tall trees was their destination. Jonas spied *Fader's* name carved in the smooth bark, and beneath it was Alfrid's.

"Go ahead, son. Carve your name beneath your brother's," *Fader* said.

"I don't have a knife," Jonas replied.

"Try this one."

*Fader* reached into his pocket and pulled out a shiny new knife and tossed it to Jonas, who caught it with both hands, wide eyes, and a broad grin. He handled the pen knife gingerly, as if he would damage the white, mother-of-pearl handle if he squeezed too hard.

"Open it," Alfrid said.

"How?"

"With your thumb, stupid."

Looking closely, Jonas located the blade's slight notch and slipped his thumbnail into the groove and flipped the folding blade open. Once open, a second, smaller blade became available to fold out on the opposite end.

Jonas set to the tree eagerly, pausing occasionally to check for *Fader's* approval. The "J" was a little sloppy, the circular "O" more so, but the straight lines of "N" and "A" were easy, and the

"S" was again sloppy.

More than a decade later, *Fader* forgot the ritual for Tomas until Jonas reminded him. Alfrid was too busy to attend the ceremony for his kid brother, but that didn't lessen the boy's enthusiasm when he received his own pen knife from their father, and he carved "Tomas" into the beech tree.

Despite a decade's difference in age, brothers Jonas and Tomas were peas in a pod. Big-brother Alfrid was always too busy for ten-year-old Tomas, but Jonas taught *lillebror* how to bait a hook, chased frogs with him in the tall grass around the pasture's pond, rode the workhorses with him bareback, and-- with a great deal of laughter and teasing--instructed him in *kulning:* calling the cows for milking in a high-pitched, sing-song voice without words.

When it was time to go, older-brother Alfrid drove the wagon that carried Jonas to the port of Karlshamn and pas-sage on a three-masted schooner to Liverpool and the steam-ship liner that would deliver him to New York. *Fader* was busy in the fields when they departed, and *Mor* remained stoic, but her face was damp and red. When she said, "why do I feel like this is a funeral," Jonas nearly reconsidered as it dawned on him that he would likely never see her again. Younger-brother Tomas rode along.

"Be brave, *Lillebror*," Jonas whispered in his ear when they arrived at the pier. "One day, I'll send for you."

Tomas refused to look him in the eye or to alight from the wagon. Alfrid shook his brother's hand with an odd look that Jonas couldn't read. Envy? Or good riddance?

Just as Jonas stepped onto the gangplank leading up to the deck of the schooner, he turned for a last look and saw that Tomas had followed him halfway down the pier with shoul-ders shaking.

"Go back," Jönsson yelled together with a hand gesture, but the boy just stood and watched. Jönsson turned and stepped aboard the schooner without looking back.

Jönsson was not the first second-son who sought the new world, and he shared the aspirations of thousands of Swedes before him, pinched by the shrinking farmsteads of a frail, worn-out and decaying old world, who crossed the sea for the land of opportunity. Time stood still in the ancient cottages where generations passed and nothing new came to be, where all that happened had happened before, and where nobles and sheriffs and priests were lords and masters and second sons could only serve under the heel of others, including older brothers. Not so in the new world, Jonas expected, where there were no emperors or kings—or older brothers--and no need to bow down to anyone. Fresh and new and bursting with opportunity, the vast prairies that had never known a plow beckoned the daring, the resourceful, the nimble of mind and spirit, who would not be servants but masters of their own destiny. Oppressed in the old world, the immigrant would live life free in the new. Jonas would be such a one. He harbored no illusions of grandeur, and a simple farm, his own farm, would do. Well, maybe with a grand barn; after all, anything was possible in America.

What started as a trickle a couple of generations earlier became a torrent, and now the stream of Swedish immigrants was as deep and wide as the mighty Mississippi. It seemed there would soon be more Swedes in America than in mother *Sverige*! Everyone knew a brother or cousin or uncle or neighbor who crossed the sea, and the letters home told of rails of steel crisscrossing a sprawling land of majestic mountains, virgin forests, and always the rolling hills and grasslands awaiting the yeoman's plow.

And a barn. He always imagined a barn: an immense wooden structure with a fresh coat of flaming red paint. Much grander than anything Småland knew. At the front end of the pitched roof, a steeple-like cupola tickled the clouds, and at the far end, a weathervane danced to the whispers of the breeze that promised rain showers to freshen the earth. He smelled the fresh-cut clover in the hay mow; he heard cattle lowing, horses nickering, and hens clucking; he tasted warm milk fresh from the udder and thick with cream; and he felt the supple backside of calfskin gloves across his burnished face as he removed his straw hat and wiped the sweat from his brow. His fields would be hallowed ground and the grand barn his sanctuary.

Jönsson would be a yeoman farmer, but other immigrants dug the mines, laid the sinews of steel track, and chopped wide swaths of great pine forests. Immigrant labor fueled the economy of the new land that would soon claim her place among the greatest of nations. And so, they came, Jönsson among them, with nothing but a knapsack and a few essentials, filled with hope that pangs of nostalgia barely muted.

Jönsson climbed down from his seat and stood in front of the wagonload of lager as he urged the gelding to back the wagon up against the boardwalk at the front of the saloon. The Swede and the Pole had arrived at the saloon on the east bank of the Mississippi. With a gentle tug on the reins and one hand on the horse's rump for reassurance, Jönsson clicked his tongue against the roof of his mouth, and the gelding understood and slowly stepped backwards. Jönsson knew horseflesh, and the gelding reacted to his easy, confident manner.

The Irish saloonkeeper arrived on the porch and waved his hand, speaking in a thick brogue.

"Not there! I want the casks unloaded on the other side of the steps."

"Hallo!" Jönsson replied.

He smiled and waved back at the saloonkeeper. He had no clue what the Irishman with his lilting dialect said, and he continued with the clicking sound, and the horse continued to back the wagon toward the boardwalk.

"I said, I want it over there," the Irishman said with his voice rising.

"Yah. Hallo." Jönsson replied and waved again.

Jönsson was outside his element. The God dammit Polack was no help with his bowed-out ears and swollen bug-eyes. The Hamm's warehouse man made a mistake sending a Swede and a Pole who couldn't speak the language.

"Go back where you came from if you can't understand American, you stupid sonofabitch," came a cry from an onlooker.

Nearby, the proprietor of a new saloon that sold Minneapolis Beer from the Grain Belt brewery watched with a smug smile. His establishment was proving to be keen competition for the business of the millers from nearby St. Anthony Falls, and the Irish saloon keeper who sold St. Paul beer was becoming red-faced because a Swedish sonofabitch couldn't figure out how to get the casks of beer unloaded in the proper place.

That's when the saloon keeper stepped in and whacked the gelding with a broomstick. The beast lurched forward; the cart knocked Jönsson down in the mud; and the cartwheel rolled across his right leg, right above the knee. *"Focka! Jävla skit!"* Only the Swedes in the crowd, if there were any, understood the blue streak Jönsson unleashed at the saloon keeper, at the gelding, at the Polack, at Teodore Hamm, at God in the heavens. And then he passed out.

*A faceless girl with long blond hair wearing a lingonberry wreath of glowing candles came near.* Jönsson shivered as December winds whistled through cracks between the slats of the shanty wall in Swede Hollow, and snowflakes sifted into a small heap in the corner. God dammit, it was cold. He dared not dip into the ration of coal that belonged to his shantymates, and so the stove in the center of the single-room hut remained unlit until the others would return from their daily labor. Jönsson pulled his thin blanket close under his chin and dozed again. *The blonde girl in the white gown and red sash carried a tray of steaming fresh raisin buns, but he couldn't reach them. He stretched his arm as far as possible, but the girl kept the bread just beyond his grasp.*

He had become a charity case. The coins in his sock had long been spent, and he endured long days alone in the shack, hoping that one of the other Swedes would bring him a chunk of stale bread or a potato after they finished their day's work. He wasn't sure if the pain in his empty belly was worse than the throbbing in his thigh, bound tight between a pair of pine splints. At least he was past the indignity of soiling himself as a y-shaped tree branch served as a crutch for him to make his way to the outhouse.

He couldn't remember how Florian the Polack managed to get him back to Swede Hollow after he broke his leg under the cartwheel, but he remembered the sneering face of the Irish saloonkeeper. He couldn't remember which of his shantymates splinted his leg, but he remembered the taunts of the onlookers on the boardwalk outside the saloon. He tried to remember running and jumping in the meadows of *Sverige*, of hooting and hollering with his siblings splashing in chilly pond water, of the back of *Mor's* soft hand on his forehead testing his childhood fevers, but all memories were clouded by a recurring image of Oskar, the cripple with one leg who was the object of teasing by dirty-faced street urchins back in Jönsson's village.

\*\*\*\*\*\*\*\*\*\*

*LaDonna appeared at the door, tapping her watch. Pastor Don exhaled a large breath, shrugged, and gathered up his coat and scarf with greater energy than when he arrived hours earlier. As my storytelling unfolded over the evening, his eyes grew wider, and he sat up straight in the chair.*

*"What time is breakfast served?" he asked as he moved toward the door. "I'll be back for an early start, if that's ok with you, Uncle Andrew."*

# CHAPTER TWO: 1892

Jönsson survived his first Minnesota winter, owing to the generosity of his shanty-mates who provided him with enough sustenance to stanch the rumbling in his belly, but that wasn't all. As blizzard winds buffeted the hovel in Swede Hollow, anger churned his insides. He plotted and planned and imagined, and bouts of despondency were chased by the allure of revenge. Somehow, he would exact vengeance on the God dammit Mick saloon keeper. Somehow, the mackerel-snapper would be made to pay. Thanks to him, Jönsson's original stash of coins in his sock had been spent, his job lost, and a whole winter without income had passed--to say nothing of the hobbled leg that would be his lot for the rest of his born days.

He also recognized his own sin of stupidity. He must learn the language of the Americans if he had any chance of making it on these shores. His shanty mates brought him newspapers containing the strange American vocabulary. The photographs helped. When he could relate the picture to the words describing the picture, he made progress. Parsing a word here or there allowed him to associate it with other words. Each small breakthrough led to another. By spring, he had a rudimentary understanding of the strange tongue of the Americans along with a determination to improve. Making sense of the written word was one thing; speaking the lingo was another matter, and his pronunciation remained thick and deliberate.

Acute depression flared up in December. Jönsson received a Christmas letter from *Mor*. The optimistic tone mocked his sorry state. He had previously sent one letter home, and one only--soon after his arrival in Minnesota, but he could not take up pen and ink to respond to the Christmas letter.

"Have you purchased a farm?" *Mor's* letter asked.

"Have you taken a wife?"

"Tomas celebrated his eleventh birthday, and he misses you nearly as much as I do. *Lillebror* boasts about you and tells everyone that he will join you one day on your farm with many cattle. Oh, dear, am I to lose two sons to America?"

There were dark days that winter when Jönsson fingered the blade on his pen knife, a favorite possession carried from the old country. Should he slash his wrists? Plunge the blade into his chest? His throat? Each time, his anger saved him. Hatred proved stronger than despair.

As the spring melt muddied the pathways along Phalen Creek, Jönsson asked for a branch to whittle into a cane to replace the crutch. The pen knife became a carver's scalpel. With the mother-of-pearl grip in his right hand and a willow branch in his left, he swept the blade under the surface of the bark and stripped the branch bare, one slice at a time. The fine work around the gnarled knots required the second, smaller blade, but the reddish-brown, diamond-shaped whorls rendered his first willow cane a functional, practical, piece of art, and he carved a second and a third, and more. By the time the robins returned, he became a street vendor, selling his diamond willow canes for a dollar each from a downtown street corner where the bankers and the railroad men and the lumber barons passed by.

Two days before the summer solstice, midsommer back home, Jönsson sold his last willow cane. With the setting sun at his back, he limped back to the Hollow after mingling with St. Paul's high and mighty, and he emptied his coin sock onto his rickety bed. He counted twenty-three silver dollars plus odd nickels, dimes, and pennies--barely enough for a single acre. The western farmlands of Minnesota seemed to be moving farther and farther away and selling a few diamond willow canes was not going to accomplish his dreams.

Jönsson fingered the large blade of the folding knife after he sharpened it again. He drew a deep breath, held it for a second, and pushed out the rush of air with an oath: *"Focka,"* he said as if to stiffen his resolve.

Jönsson snapped the blade shut and slid the pen knife into his pocket. He returned all the coins to his sock except for a pair of nickels that he would use for streetcar fare for a trip to Main Street in Minneapolis and back. The God dammit Mick would pay for what he had done.

His plotting coalesced on the massive black safe with a polished brass handle in a back room of the saloon in Minneapolis. Even the gold-colored lettering hinted at the fortune within. On Jönsson's weekly deliveries when he had merely been the lackey rather than the driver, the saloonkeeper always paid for the wagon load of Hamm's beer with ready cash from the safe. Now Jönsson would take what the saloonkeeper owed him. If the safe held a large sum, he would be reasonable, Jönsson persuaded himself, and he would only take what was fair. Would that be $100? $200? $300 would be too much. He settled on $250.

The pen knife would be the larcenist's weapon. He would move up close to the Mick and threaten him with the sharp point of the knife in his face, and the rest would be easy. The saloonkeeper would open the safe--it was usually unlocked anyway--and hand over the cash. Maybe $400 or $500 would be fair; after all, the saloonkeeper had rendered him a cripple for life. The Mick would probably thank him for leaving the rest.

The electric streetcar raced past the capitol, through Frog Town, past the shops along the midway point, and slipped through the campus buildings of Hamline and the University of Minnesota without Jönsson noticing, and he suddenly found himself on Main Street, observing millers from the falls descending upon the saloon in late afternoon. Now was not the time. Jönsson limped around the neighborhood with the aid of one of his canes and finally found a grassy spot overlooking the Mississippi. He would spend the night there and surprise the saloonkeeper when he opened the next morning.

Whether it was the aching leg, mosquitos, or the anxiety, Jönsson hadn't slept a whit when the sun first struck the smokestacks and steeples of Minneapolis on the far side of the river. As furtively as he could manage, he slowly ambled past the saloon, but the door was shut, and the windows shuttered. The same was true the second time he passed by and the third, and it wasn't until mid-morning when he spied the saloonkeeper opening the door from the inside since his lodging was on the second floor above the saloon.

Jönsson sucked in a deep breath, stood as tall as he could manage, and walked straightaway toward the stoop. He left his cane propped against the stoop and ascended the steps, masking his limp as he was able. Stepping from the sunlight into the darkened saloon, Jönsson paused to allow his eyes to adjust. The sickly-sweet smell of beer-soaked-pine-slab floorboards curled up around him. As his eyes focused in the dim light, he saw that the Mick had his back to him as he mopped the floor. He was bigger than Jönsson remembered, with yoke-like shoulders and mitts that threatened the mop stick with strangulation. Jönsson stuck his hand into his right pocket, but the knife wasn't there! *Ah, there it is, in the left pocket.* Jönsson fumbled with his weapon as he opened the blade, and it clanked on the floor; he quickly retrieved it.

Without turning, the saloon keeper growled, "We ain't open yet, come back in half an hour."

Jönsson said nothing but came up behind the Irishman, tugged on his sleeve with his left hand, and jabbed the point of the knife above the thick black moustache straight at the man's bent nose.

"I'll take vot's in yer safe, you God dammit Mick." Jönsson had carefully rehearsed his lines in his best English.

He jerked his head twice toward the back room.

"Who the fuck are you?" the saloon keeper sneered.

"Make no never mind. Let's yust say ya owes me."

The saloon keeper's eyes narrowed, and the upturned tips of his mustache twitched.

"Go, go, or I'll poke yer foockin' eyes out."

The man moved toward the back room, and Jönsson stayed at his side, clutching the man's sleeve garter with one hand while poking the three-inch blade toward the man's face.

As Jönsson had hoped, the safe was slightly ajar, and the saloon keeper knelt as he reached inside.

"I know you. You're the fucking Swede who don't know shit about handling a horse."

And then it all went bad.

As the Irishman turned toward him with a Colt revolver in his hand, Jönsson knew he would never plough a field on his own farm; he would never bring his younger brother to America; perhaps he wouldn't survive the moment.

What a fool he was! He was a stupid sonofabitch, a failure even as a thief. Of course, the Mick would have a gun. Of course, it would come to this base, mean, amoral question of survival: to kill or be killed.

Jönsson grabbed at the gun with his left hand as he instinctively thrust the pen knife toward the man's Adam's apple where the three-inch blade found little resistance. The pistol's hammer slammed down and pinched the webbing between Jönsson's thumb and forefinger, preventing the gun from firing. Jönsson pulled the knife back as the man's unbelieving eyes turned black and blood gurgled from his throat onto Jönsson. In a second, or a minute, or a lifetime, the man's grip on the pistol went limp, and he slumped forward into a lake of blood.

Without checking the contents of the safe, Jönsson bolted toward the doorway and burst into searing sunlight.

**********

*"But I thought ..."*

*Pastor Don's cheeks pinched tight around pursed lips, and wrinkles creased his forehead.*

*"I warned you that Papa's secrets would be revealed."*

*"Yes, but why ..."*

*"No questions now, please. Let Papa's story play out. All will be revealed in due course."*

*I was just beginning with a long way to go, and I had my own doubts—not about the story but about my own health and longevity. I couldn't allow diversions that would slow me down.*

*Donald sighed and slumped back in the plush easy chair. When he left last evening, he was pumped up, anxious to continue with my storytelling. Now, he didn't seem so sure.*

# CHAPTER THREE

*M*idsommar: the earliest sunrise and the latest sunset of the year inspired Sweden's celebration of life, abundance, and fertility, but instead of *Små grodorna*-- dancing around a greenery-covered pole and gorging on strawberries-- Jönsson slept a fitful sleep in the back of an ox cart that creaked along under the June sun. Days without food or rest and chewed up by mosquitos, he fled the city into the Minnesota northland.

*He jumped over the fire, and the flames licked at his trousers. He must do it again, and again, but the flames leaped higher and higher. "No, no, I cannot," his limp leg shrieked, but shaggy green beasts, tall as the trees, pushed and pulled him, this way and that, as they danced around the flames that tickled the clouds. Fader and Mor, under a witch's spell, hopped around like frogs, and the children stuffed pickled herring into their bulging cheeks.*

*"Give me a taste," he pleaded with Tomas. "I'm starving. Yes, yes, a strawberry. Please a strawberry!"*

When he hobbled away from the saloon on the banks of the Mississippi, his aimless escape soon intersected with railroad tracks, and the piercing whistle of a passing locomotive cleared the jangle of his mind. He could not return to Swede Hollow to gather his sock full of dollars and other possessions. The law would look for him there. The willow cane left leaning on the stoop would give him away. He realized he had forgotten to steal from the Irishman's safe--cold cash that he could sorely use now--but he was glad of his panicked oversight. Thievery would render the killing of the saloon keeper purposeful and not accidental, at least in his own mind. True enough, his intent had been to steal, but chaos intervened, and to plunder the safe *after* ... if the wide-eyed corpse that lay in a pool of blood like a stuck pig was a family man ... Jönsson shuddered as a dark shadow of remorse clouded his thoughts ... but if he left a family ... pray God that the black safe with gold lettering held a fortune.

Lacking a clear alternative, Jönsson continued to limp along the railroad tracks without knowing where they might lead, until a stranger found him by the wayside and loaded him into the back of an ox cart.

Months earlier, he had embarked--not merely on a journey but an adventure—and he enthusiastically descended a ladder into a cargo hold between decks—*mellandæck*--of a great steamship. Reality quickly pinched him, and he spent a week wedged into a bunk too short for his lanky frame and squeezed into quarters too cramped for two, much less the six single men forced to cohabit a makeshift cabin in the ship's hold referred to as "steerage" by the American seamen. Six men, five languages, little communication, but plenty of stink. Sausage and cheese stashed in the men's knapsacks supplemented the meager ship's fare, and soon the boar's nest reeked of fart-smell, unwashed men, and puke.

In the bunk below Jönsson, a short, stout, and swarthy Hungarian vomited whenever the ship pitched and rolled in heavy swells. In the next double bunk, two brothers shared a language: serfs forced off the land and into a railway car factory who now escaped Czarist Russia. The fifth hopeful wanderer began his journey in the marble mines of northern Italy, and the sixth from a Bavarian *bauenhof*, which Jönsson learned wasn't much different than his Swedish *bondgård*, and they soon shared a common word, "farm." It was the German who best understood the Babel of their shared cabin and served as interpreter of sorts. Mutual suspicions soon gave way to the shared experience of seasickness, stench, and stale bread.

The one thing the six had in common was that they were peasants with meager prospects in their homeland, and the allure of America promised more.

When the ship steamed into the New York harbor, the Swede and the Hungarian stood alongside each other on deck as they passed the Statue of Liberty. The diminutive Hungarian, who had mostly muttered guttural gibberish during the crossing, flashed a toothless smile, raised both arms, and exclaimed with an accent as thick as the man himself,

"America!"

Jönsson's reply stuck in his throat, before a barely audible "yah" squeaked out.

The cheeks of the Hungarian, and the others leaning against the gunwale, glistened with tears. Jönsson's heart felt strangely warmed by the flaming torch the tall Lady lifted high. She beckoned to him and the other wretches aboard the steamer, and they believed her.

Lady Liberty first called to him from the cover of a pamphlet he scoured in dim candlelight inside the sod-roof hovel where his mother birthed and nurtured him, but those pinching walls could not contain America the idea, America the vision, America the hope; nor could they trap the man who believed the idea, imagined the vision, and dared to hope the hope, and so Jönsson fled the hardscrabble existence of a Småland peasant to pursue the adventure of his own life's journey. Was that not America's essence: the freedom to seek one's own way in the world, where wit and work would be rewarded?

Jönsson glided down the gangway, swept along by the full force of the idea of America: liberation from the tyranny of where you were born and to whom. In America, you had the same birthright as princes, priests, and older brothers.

"Amen," he whispered as the firm ground of Manhattan

rose up to greet his footsteps. He would find his way to Grand Central Station and board a train headed west for the final leg of his journey to the heart and heartland of America.

But Fate didn't dream the dream of America, and as Jönsson bumped along in the bed of the ox cart, the Hungarian's shout echoed as a taunt. Servanthood on brother Alfrid's farm now seemed the better choice but a lost chance; America was less an opportunity than a challenge, and he had failed. The sea crossing in steerage haunted as an omen. He hadn't fit in the cramped bunk in the tiny cabin amongst strangers from strange lands, and he didn't fit in America. A peasant he was born, and a peasant he would be. Worse, he expected to live the life of a hunted scoundrel. And lame to boot.

"*Sveglia*," the ox-cart driver said in a language unknown to Jönsson. "Wake up."

A black cassock covered the olive-skinned stranger from his neck to his ankles, bound at the waist by a rope. Grey curls peeked from beneath a broad-brimmed hat. The driver found Jönsson squatting by the side of the road and delivered him the final miles to the village of Hinckley.

Two competing railroad lines intersected in Hinckley, each with its own railway station. The Great Northern passed through from St. Cloud in the west and turned northeast toward Superior, Wisconsin. The St. Paul and Duluth Railroad station marked the halfway point between those cities, and the surrounding village boasted a community of fifteen hundred souls, three churches, eight saloons, a cigar and tobacco store, an opera house, a newspaper, and the Brennan Lumber Mill and Company Store supplying general merchandise to the town and the lumberjacks who worked at the mill and in the nearby camps.

Jönsson knew none of this; he merely followed the train

tracks and walked seventy-odd miles north of Minneapolis and St. Paul. Somewhere along the way, he shredded his blood-stained wadmal shirt and cast it into a river; he considered tossing the pen knife, but it was still in his pocket when he reached the lumber town.

"Here's a dollar, and there's a hotel. Buy a meal, take a bath, and get some sleep."

Jönsson didn't understand the man's generosity. He fingered the silver dollar as a train whistle covered the whine of the Brennan sawmill. Each step kicked up dust as he trudged toward the wooden sign of the Morrison Hotel that creaked in a slight breeze. He sucked in a deep breath and smelled the mixed scents of wood smoke and horse dung. He mounted the boardwalk and turned to his benefactor.

"*In bocca al lupo*. Go into the wolf's mouth," the man said with a grin. "*Buona fortuna*."

The Italian priest kissed the crucifix hanging around his neck and disappeared down the rutted street.

# CHAPTER FOUR

S awdust and sap. Crosscut saws and axes. Jacks and river rats.

Jönsson's escape led him to the primeval pine forests of Minnesota's north country. After spending the priest's dollar well--bathing, eating, sleeping, and spending the last two bits on a flannel shirt--he followed the advice of the hotel clerk:

"Check the Brennan lumber mill."

The Brennan sawmill dominated the north side of the town.

"No jobs here," said the foreman's assistant, "especially for a man with a bum leg."

"Vot about tending horses?" Jönsson asked. "I knows horse-flesh."

"Nope. Full up."

Jönsson turned to leave, but the man called him back.

"I jest remembered. They say the old bastard who drove the cook wagon at the McGregor camp kicked the bucket yesterday. Check there."

The lumber camp of Angus McGregor lay north of town and west of the St. Paul and Duluth tracks. At first, the camp floated logs down the Grindstone to the Brennan Mill, but as the jacks stripped the pine forest northward, the Little Kettle River became the preferred route of the river-rats who floated the logs to the Kettle River, then to the St. Croix River, and then to the Stillwater booms.

Just a few days after fleeing the city, Jönsson found new life amongst the tall pines north of Hinckley, sharing a log hovel with nearly forty unwashed, snoring, farting bunkmates: red-skinned natives, olive-skinned Frenchies, and pale white Finlanders, Norwegians, and Swedes, but after days, weeks, and months of burnishing by sun, wind, and cold, all the smudged faces would become the same.

If the law looked for him in Minneapolis or traced him to the shanty in Swede Hollow, he didn't know it. He hoped a lawman would never find him among the grimy souls who stripped the white pine forests for the benefit of the timber barons, and Jönsson joined the world of lumberjacks for ten dollars a week, plus all the flapjacks, beans, and venison he could eat and a roof over his head. Although Jönsson's crippled leg rendered him unfit for the rugged work, much less riding the logs downriver, he knew horses, and he showed up at the Angus McGregor logging camp the day after the old man who drove the lunch wagon keeled over and died. Another man's demise was Jönsson's good fortune.

"Louis," the Frenchie said, extending his right hand. "Louis Archambault."

Jönsson hesitated before accepting a handshake from the mustachioed man in the adjacent bunk. When Jönsson rose to his feet, he stood a full head taller than his bunkmate, but he winced at the grip of the short man who was lean and hard as an axe handle.

"Ole," Jönsson lied, dropping his eyes. He dared not use his real name. He had escaped from the immediacy of capture into a new reality. He was a murderer, presumably a hunted man, and the innocent immigrant who dreamed of a red barn died along with the saloonkeeper. With the death of the dream came a new motivation. Obscurity. He couldn't be somebody; he must be nobody. Or, at least, "Ole" not "Jonas." Nor could he be the bold, irreverent youngster who challenged the authority of Korp the priest. He must retreat to the shadows.

Little Louis Archambault was called "Pete," a bastardized version of the French word *petit*. Jönsson would soon learn that the small-in-stature French-Canadian was the biggest personality among the teamsters in the lumber camp, and he introduced Jönsson to the sorrel-colored gelding that pulled the lunch wagon and instructed Jönsson in the process of delivering a more-or-less hot lunch to the logging crew each day.

"He's an American breed called a Quarter Horse," Pete said.

The sorrel looked capable enough with a strong, well-muscled body, especially in the broad chest and powerful, rounded hindquarters.

Pete also accompanied Jönsson to the Brennan company store; on credit, Jönsson purchased a fur hat, hobnailed leather boots that nearly reached his knees with plenty of room for tiered layers of wool socks, wool glove inserts covered by buckskin choppers, and a couple of scratchy union suits and red flannel shirts. Cotton pants would be covered by thick wool stag pants and held up with suspenders. Later, he would don an oversized buckskin coat and leggings and waterproof the boots with tallow grease. The blistering cold of northern Minnesota barely slowed the loggers even in the dead of winter, but it was the place for Jönsson to lose himself from the world, even from the folks back home.

Learning and performing the duties of his new employment, while protecting his anonymity, occupied him during waking hours, but he came to know the terrors of the night.

Perhaps it was the snoring that kept Jönsson awake deep into his first night in the bunkhouse. As he sweated in the tangle of his woolen blanket, he saw a red barn overlooking a pond; he heard a slow-moving locomotive rattling the walls of the two-holer over Phalen creek; he smelled the stale beer on the plank floor of a saloon, and he felt the hot blood of a murdered man spurting into his own face. Choking in the stale cabin air, he rushed outside to suck in the cool night breeze. Green and yellow lights danced in the northern sky, lifting him high before slamming him to the ground where he collapsed into a gasping heap of remorse, regret, and longing for the life left behind and despair for the future that would not be.

*"Je vous salue, Marie pleine de grâce."*

At first the words intruded like a dream, but then Jönsson sat bolt upright in his bunk. Pete the Frenchie kneeled next to his own bunk and repeated the papist gibberish while fingering beads on a chain:

*"Je vous salue, Marie pleine de grâce."*

Pete kissed the crucifix on his rosary and crossed himself to conclude his Catholic ritual that grated against Jönsson's Lutheran piety. Jönsson dressed slowly while Pete preened in front of a small mirror; unlike most of the loggers who allowed unkempt beards to scrape their chests, Pete meticulously shaved his chin each morning before waxing the tips of his mustache.

Jönsson first visited the stable to throw hay into his gelding's manger. He stroked the Quarter Horse's neck and tickled the ears. The gelding seemed amiable. He lifted his muzzle and turned to eye his new master. Jönsson offered a handful of oats, and the horse exhaled fluttering breaths through his nostrils as a sign of contentment.

"Mimir," Jönsson called him, for the simple reason that was the name of the family's longtime favorite horse back home.

Finally, Jönsson headed to the nearly empty mess hall where scattered woodsmen filled their bellies with salt pork and flapjacks. Summertime was the off-season for the logging camps, and the sawyers and axe-men returned to their wives and farms or simply holed up in a nearby saloon until their winter's earnings ran dry. Only the river-rats who drove the logs down the river and the teamsters who hauled logs to be dumped into the river maintained steady employment through the heat of the summer. Winter's cold was more obliging for the hard work of the jacks than the mosquito-infested heat of summer, and so the rhythm of the camps slowed to a crawl when the temperatures spiked.

"Ole," Pete yelled and gestured for Jönsson to join his table.

All eyes followed Jönsson as he limped across the room.

"Meet Ole," Pete announced in a loud voice. "Ole Wobble."

Jönsson's pale face burned crimson as he reached the table and awkwardly took his place at the end of the pine-slab bench. The nickname "Wobble" would stick but allowed Jönsson to retain his anonymity.

Jönsson lingered over his coffee after the others headed out to the woods. The tables were cleared and cleaned by Ojibwe women, who lived nearby with their husbands in a cluster of *wiigiwaams*, domed lodges with sides of elm bark boards and a roof covered with birch bark, hugging the shoreline of a blue-water lake. A few of the braves worked as jacks alongside the Europeans but most remained hunters and fishermen who supplied the camp with venison and walleyes and northern pike they snared in their seine nets.

Jönsson heard the name "Hole-in-the-Lake" mentioned in hushed tones, but he remained a bit of a mystery to Jönsson. He was apparently the chief of the small tribe, and he didn't come around the logging camp, but he would soon cross paths with Jönsson.

The few scrub pines that survived the logger's onslaught barely shielded the rising sun as Jönsson returned to the stable and harnessed Mimir, his gelding. Their first task of the day would be to pick up a wagonload of supplies from Hinckley. Jönsson had barely said a word during his first day among the men of the forest, but he jabbered all the way to town, with Mimir, with the squeaky wagon wheels, and with the whispering morning breeze. The fresh air along a secluded forest roadway invigorated him.

Jönsson and his horse performed an assortment of camp duties, in addition to hauling lunch to the men in the field—jacks in the winter and river-rats in the summer. Three or four times a week, they would travel the six odd miles to Hinckley, with three regular stops: the St. Paul and Duluth train station, Brennan's Company Store, and the cigar store to keep all hands in the camp supplied with snuff or pipe tobacco. Jönsson himself picked up pipe smoking that first summer in the lumber camp. His return cargo would include logging supplies but mostly foodstuffs. On this day, he hauled sacks filled with flour shipped via train from the Pillsbury mills of Minneapolis.

"*Framåt*," Jönsson said as he flicked the reins on the horse's haunches, "*skutt!*"

They must make up time so they would not be late with the lunch for the men who drove the logs down the river. Whether Mimir was bilingual or not, he heeded Jönsson's command and scooted forward with the same glee that swelled within Jönsson as he inhaled the pine-scented air. Screeching blue jays and the raspy caw of crows somehow comprised a forest symphony. Away from the stink and the grumble of the city, Jönsson's spirits were higher than at any time since his arrival in New York a mere year earlier. Under a boundless blue sky, even the darkness of a Minneapolis saloon was dispelled—at least for the moment.

Toivo helped Jönsson load tin canisters of hot food onto the swing dingle. His soup-bowl haircut bobbed atop a mop-handle torso. Toivo was a widow's boy, not yet whiskered, whose

Finlander father had died when the tree he felled kicked back the previous winter. Toivo worked in the mess hall as a *cookee*, and he accompanied Jönsson on his daily lunch-time deliveries to the crew in the field. When the ground froze in late fall, Toivo would serve as a water monkey to ice the trail for the wooden runners that transformed wagons into sleds, keeping the tracks clean and clear of manure. He would also sprinkle straw over sloping grounds to slow the speed of the fully loaded sleds that skidded down the icy pathways.

"Due west," Toivo said while pointing north, but Jönsson simply followed the fresh tracks in the muddy ground. The Finns and the Swedes had much in common, but language was not one of them, and so Jönsson communicated in broken English with the young Finlander who had a better mastery of the language. Jönsson liked having Toivo around because he reminded him of Tomas, his *lillebror*, even if Tomas had keener wit than empty-headed Toivo.

At the edge of the camp, acrid smoke poured out the chimney of the smithy's shop above the clang of steel on steel, of hammer and tong, forge and bellows. A few miles into the forest, the trail intercepted the Little Kettle River, and Jönsson watched with wide eyes as river-rats--the special breed of jacks who floated logs down the river--danced across the raft of logs bobbing in the current, leaping from one log to the next, using their hooked peaveys and twenty-foot pike poles for balance and to steer the logs into the current. The danger and delicacy enticed him, and Jönsson watched with envy. He would have been good at it, he thought, but, of course, that was closed to him now with a bum leg.

Jönsson built a fire of fresh-cut pine boughs that crackled and spit sparks before turning to embers. The slash was everywhere. After the jacks felled a tree, swampers lopped off the branches, sawed the logs into manageable lengths, and stamped the ends with McGregor's brand. Only the thick trunks were of value, and the swampers discarded the bushy crowns of pine needles, twigs, and branches, and the crew would trample onward to pillage the next stand of straight-grained pines that would become the skeleton and skin of the architecture for the burgeoning American empire.

Jönsson knew lumbermen from Sweden who left the farm in autumn and returned in the spring, spending winters in the north country, and they boasted of their prudent logging practices where the forestland was harvested selectively and replanted after cutting, but the promiscuous laying of waste of vast swaths of America's virgin forests struck him as immature, brash, selfish, and obviously short-sighted. The almighty dollar was lord, and the lumber barons its disciples.

But the remaining slash made handy kindling for a quick fire, and Jönsson boiled coffee while Toivo lined up the canisters and utensils on a rock outcropping.

"Toot your whistle," Toivo said to Jönsson when all was ready.

Jönsson self-consciously blew, but only a barely audible squeak came out.

"Blow it like you mean it," Toivo encouraged.

The loud blast that came out of the whistle in his mouth surprised Jönsson, and he immediately felt uncomfortable as the center of attention, but that changed when Pete made a grand entrance. Driving a team of four oxen, the diminutive Frenchie stood tall atop a wagonload of logs piled high, delicately balancing with flexed knees as the wagon lurched forward. After reining in the oxen, he jumped down, a span of three times his own height. Spouting a blue streak in mixed French-English, Pete claimed his place at the head of the line, but he crossed himself and fingered his rosary before thrusting his tin plate forward.

The river-rats dived in behind him and, despite their obscene criticism of the pork and potato stew, they insisted on portions that spilled over the sides of the tin plates, which they quickly wolfed down while standing in place or leaning against a deadfall, sopping up the sauce with chunks of bread. After a quick smoke, the river-rats returned to their raft of logs that had already jammed up, leaving Jönsson and Toivo to load the mess onto the wagon for the return journey to the camp.

"Dis is just the beginning," Toivo explained.

"The river-rats will float the logs down the Little Kettle—past the Wilson camp—and into the Kettle River, but when the Kettle spills into the St. Croix, our boy's job is done."

Toivo had been around lumbermen his whole life, and he seemed to have a handle on how things worked.

"The main river crew steers t'ousands of logs all the way to the booms of Stillwater. Dat's why McGregor's stamp is branded into the end of each log. Somehow, the lumbermen figure out how to split up the money when the mills rip the logs into lumber. More'n enuff to go 'round, I spect."

The raft of logs had already disappeared around a bend in the river by the time the wagon was loaded with empty containers and dirty utensils. Life seemed fast in America. Time was money.

"Floating past the Wilson camp is the trickiest part," Toivo continued. "Never knows what Wilson's jackasses will do, but come Saturday night, our boys will show 'em what fer. By the looks of you, I spect you kin handle yerself."

Standing over six foot and with square shoulders and big mitts on muscular arms, Jönsson knew he could manage, but for an anonymous man who hid in the shadows, a Saturday night skirmish would be stupid.

With the wagon loaded, it was time to return to camp.

*"Skutt!"*

Jönsson urged Mimir to speed up.

*"Skutt!"* he said again, slapping the reins on the gelding's haunches. He was showing off for Toivo much like he showed off for Tomas, his little brother.

Toivo grabbed the bench with both hands and looked at Jönsson with puzzled delight as Mimir broke into a trot. When the empty canisters bounced about in the back of the wagon, Jönsson laughed out loud.

BANG!

Suddenly, the crack of a rifle shot silenced the chirps and chittering of the forest critters, and a white-tail buck staggered onto the cart way and collapsed.

"Whoa! Whoa, Mimir!"

Toivo jumped down, and as he gaped at the dying deer, an Indian brave stepped from the bushes with a Springfield musket slung over his shoulder. The brave stood tall and erect with long black braids twisting beneath a tall bowler hat. The hat, denim jeans, broadcloth shirt, and boots typified the European-style clothing of the braves who frequented the camp. The white man and the red man eyed each other with suspicion as they approached the hunter's fallen quarry. Toivo stepped back as the brave ripped a bone knife from a sheath at his waist. The hunter kneeled and slit the animal's throat. Blood spurted from the beast's neck as the brave sliced open the belly to gut his kill.

"Didja see dat," Toivo said as he clambered aboard the wagon. "Dat was Chief Hole-in-the-Lake."

Jönsson's eyes were squeezed tight, and his chest heaved

with short, gasping breaths. Sweat beads from his brow dribbled down his nose and over his blanched cheeks. Something about the sudden rifle shot or the knife-play sparked his anxiety.

Like the fickle, ever-changing Minnesota weather, Jönsson's moods swung wildly in those first months after arriving in the lumber camp. The fresh air and sunshine of the north country buoyed his spirits, but then like storm clouds gathering on the horizon, his mood would darken at a shout, a stranger's lingering glance, or questions about his identity or his past.

And so, the brash youth--who challenged the village priest and his own father and who crossed the sea and half the continent chasing the dream of America--morphed into a solitary man, a man who would be invisible, a cautious, nervous man watching from the shadows.

# CHAPTER FIVE

O n the fourth Saturday of July, Jönsson received his first pay. After he settled his account at the Brennan Mill company store in Hinckley, Jönsson returned to the bunkhouse with a roll of crisp bills which he stashed in a sock tucked in the bottom of a footlocker, nearly twenty dollars.

Just then, the high-spirited teamsters burst in, led by Pete the tiny French-Canadian. Usually, the crew would work long hours into the late evenings of summer in the north country hauling logs from where they had been felled and dumping them into the Little Kettle, but this was Saturday and payday, and they knocked off early.

"Whiskey first, then we fight the Wilson boys!" Pete crouched and circled with fists raised like a banty boxer as he teased Jönsson. "Come to town and drink whiskey with us."

Perhaps a small celebration was in order. As a farm boy in Sweden, he knew home-brewed barley beer and the neighbor's Brännvin distilled from potatoes but never real whiskey and never in a saloon.

"Yah, I go vit' you."

Jönsson twirled the combination on the padlock that secured his meager possessions in a footlocker and removed a single dollar bill from his sock while Pete preened in front of his mirror.

After a quick supper in the cook house, Pete drove two of his four oxen pulling a wagonload of river-rats and teamsters eager to descend upon Hinckley. Jönsson sat silently but listened attentively to the bold boasts that ranged from fighting to whoring. Many of the jacks would wind up at Emma Hammond's with her bevy of rouge-cheeked prostitutes. Tales beyond his virgin imagination echoed in Jönsson's innocent ears.

"Viskey," Jönsson said when he squeezed up to the bar alongside the others.

The teamsters lined up along a dark wooden bar with a brass foot rail running along the front with spittoons strategically located at each end of the rail. Behind the bar, whiskey bottles and glasses were stacked in front of a large mirror with the head of an antlered white-tail buck presiding over all. The proprietor peered over his wire-rimmed glasses at the lineup of jacks as his hands manipulated the spigot to his barrel of freshly brewed beer. He sported a bloused shirt with sleeve garters and a skull cap over dirty-blond hair. His handle-bar moustache twitched as he exchanged banter with the lumbermen. He worked quickly and efficiently to keep the glasses full, but a saloon girl seemed unsure of herself.

Under pinned-up brown hair, an innocent face unaccustomed to rouge-dabbed cheeks and cherry-red lipstick struggled to smile. Dressed in a long skirt billowed with petticoats and a low-cut top that revealed plenty, she avoided eye contact, and her wrinkled chin suggested clenched teeth.

"Don't pay her no never mind," the saloon keeper said. "She's new, but she'll learn soon enough."

Pete threw back his head and downed two fingers of whiskey and slammed the glass on the bar.

"Another," he bellowed.

Jönsson attempted to emulate the Frenchie, but he gagged as the whiskey burned his tongue and throat, and he spit most of it back on the bar. American whiskey was apparently much stronger than Swedish Brännvin.

"Sarsaparilla for the boy," Pete said in a loud voice. "Better yet, milk. Do you have some warm milk?"

The saloon girl happened to step near just then, and Pete grabbed her breast through the dress and wrenched it.

"Mother's milk is what he needs. Suck on one of these—or maybe I will myself!"

The teamsters hooted, Jönsson felt his face scalding red, and the girl broke away and fought against tears.

The saloon keeper wiped up Jönsson's spittle with a bar rag, and Jönsson asked for a glass of beer. He took his glass and retreated to a table. He would like to smash the Frenchie's face, and he could do it alright. Over and over, he clenched his large hands into fists. He was as tall as any and stronger than most, but he thought the better of it. He was no coward, but he had his reasons for self-restraint. He must remain a watcher from the shadows.

As Jönsson nursed the beer over the next half hour, Pete continued to harass the saloon girl. He grabbed at her skirt and forced a sloppy kiss on her. She would break away, but no one defended her, not even the proprietor. Jönsson squirmed in his seat and looked around for someone to stand up to the little bully. He would do it, but …

When jacks from the Wilson camp arrived with shouts and insults, he slipped out. He retreated to the wagon with six bits remaining in his pocket. He felt more comfortable mingling with the oxen than the jacks, and he would stay out of trouble. An occasional gray cloud whisked across the wash of stars, and an owl hooted from a nearby perch. The waning moon slice dipped low in the western sky. He spent the first hour whittling "Jonas" on the bench of the wagon, but then he carved it out leaving nothing but a gash in the seat.

Sometime later, hoots of the returning teamsters roused

him from sleep, and as the only one sober enough to drive the oxen, he took the reins for the return trip. The wagon-load of drunken teamsters sported bruised knuckles and facial scrapes. Long red scratches marked each side of Pete's face.

Long before they reached the camp, shouts had dissipated into snores, except for Pete who sang unintelligible French ditties all the way with occasional interruptions to criticize Jönsson's timid manliness.

"Stop, I'm gonna piss," Pete said about a mile from camp.

Jönsson stepped down with him, and they stood side by side pissing into the bushes.

"Fuck!" Pete said, "That fucking bitch was a virgin and now there's blood all over my prick."

*God dammit, he should have done something. He should have slugged that bastard and knocked him cold when he got grabby with the poor saloon girl. But then, he would likely be out of a job and on the run again. At worst, the law might have a look-see.* His rationalization made sense enough but justifying his inaction increased his disgust with himself.

"I'm surprised you stand and piss," Pete said as he released a ripe fart. "With such a teeny pecker, I thought you'd squat like a girl."

Pete stumbled around in the bushes as Jönsson climbed back onto the pine slab bench. Jönsson reached deep into his pocket and pulled out his pocketknife. He opened the folding blade, but quickly snapped it back, and returned the knife to his pocket as Archambault returned to the wagon. *One day, though. One day the sonofabitch would get what he had coming.*

The slamming bunkhouse door awakened him, and Jönsson raised his head and shoulders while leaning on his elbows.

Discordant snores rumbled and wheezed from otherwise life-less lumps, but Pete's bunk was empty. Jönsson sat at the edge of his own bunk and began to pull on his socks when he remembered that today, like all Sundays, would be a day of rest and washday for soiled clothes and foul-smelling men. He would switch to fresh socks and underwear after his swim in a nearby lake. The risen sun splashed through the doorway when Pete returned from his morning piss, again allowing the door to slam behind him.

"*Bonjour,* my virgin friend. I hope your dreams satisfied you. Was she a dark-haired beauty? A redhead? Or was she as pale as the palm of your hand?"

Jönsson clenched his jaw and sucked in an angry, deep breath, but he said nothing.

When Jönsson returned from his own visit to the four-holed privy, he quietly closed the bunkhouse door behind him. Even before his eyes readjusted to the dim-lit bunkhouse he saw it. The padlock on his footlocker hung ajar. As he fell to his knees to check inside, he knew the sock full of bills would not be there.

# CHAPTER SIX: 1893

W hen winter snows blanketed the forest floor, wooden runners replaced wheels, and the teamster's wagons became sleds. The bunkhouse swelled with new arrivals, the pace of the lumberjack camp picked up, and the French papist remained insufferable. Jönsson was sure Pete had been the thief who raided his locker, and the Catholic display of rosary ritual was merely false piety that magnified his guilt. Jönsson sometimes considered challenging the thief with his pen knife, but then unsettling darkness would sweep over him, and he never confronted the Frenchman, but he took strange comfort in the notion that Louis Archambault wouldn't be so God dammit cocksure if he knew that he slept next to a killer.

The first time Jönsson encountered his employer was the spring morning Angus McGregor delivered four grey Percherons, massive draft horses imported from France. Built like a squat barrel, Mr. McGregor, the New England Yankee lumber baron now headquartered in Stillwater, sported a beaver-fur coat that extended to his ankles and a silk top hat that lied about his short stature. The rich man's air of superiority was exceeded only by his pride in the Percheron team that stood calmly with heads held high as McGregor moved around each one with reassuring pats as he inspected fetlocks and hooves with grunts of approval.

When he finished, he faced the teamsters with a broad smile, but the high-pitched squeaky voice seemed at odds with the stout figure.

"Now, who shall have the honor—and the responsibility,

LOST IN THE LAND OF MILK AND HONEY

mind you—of tending to these splendid creatures," McGregor asked, but he had already made his choice.

Jönsson was not in the running compared to the veteran teamsters around him, and no one was surprised when McGregor reached out and clasped the shoulder of tiny Pete who was as short as the boss but carried half the weight. Much as Jönsson despised the Frenchie, Pete was the unquestioned leader of the teamsters by dint of personality and horse sense. Jönsson turned away to tend to Mimir, cleaning his hooves, currying his coat, and keeping his unpretentious friend fat and sassy with oats and hay.


"Pig slop again, I see."

"Then it's too good for the fucking likes of you," Berta replied, and she doled out a smaller than normal portion, and the jack moved along.

In the lumber camp pecking order, the cook ranked high because of the importance of keeping the men well-fed, healthy, and happy. In the keen competition for labor where jacks were free to move from employment in one camp to another, the reputation of the camp cook was an important consideration, and Berta, the queen of the mess hall, was known to serve the best camp fare.

With thick hair wrapped in bun, the fiery redhead dished it out as good as the foul-mouthed lumberjacks she cooked for. Better than six-foot tall with broad shoulders, Berta could be strong and mean if necessary. Once, when an unsuspecting jack played grab-ass, she whacked him across the face with a cast iron frying pan, breaking his nose and knocking him cold. It never happened again. Berta's husband had belonged to the "First Minnesota," but he died at Gettysburg, leaving his fifteen-year-old bride to fend for herself. Later, she birthed two daughters by different fathers, and the girls served as her cook

51

shanty assistants along with Toivo and half a dozen Ojibwe women.

After stabling Mimir, Jönsson arrived in the mess hall before the gang of rowdy lumberjacks poured in following their workday. As winter wound down and the days lengthened, the foreman drove the jacks hard before the spring thaw set in. Twelve-hour workdays stretched to fourteen or sixteen, and Jönsson spent idle time waiting in the cookhouse.

In a daily ritual, Jönsson scoured the newspaper he picked up in town while enjoying a cup of hot coffee. Jönsson spent two cents for a copy of the local newspaper that helped hone his command of proper English, which was different than the lingo of the lumber camp where he worked with swampers, jacks, river-rats (also known as beaver bait), road and water monkeys, gut robbers (bad cooks-not including Berta), jill-pokes (lazy workers), buckwheaters (greenhorns), and the main say (foreman). Americans spoke strange languages.

The first daughter slowly but methodically arranged the serving table with tin plates, soup bowls, and cups. The oafish older girl named Hulda was sullen and silent, and by her manner slow-witted. The younger daughter named Ayasha also remained silent around him, but the sparkle in her brown eyes and her wry smile hinted at a lively spirit and keen wit. Her braided black hair, acorn-brown skin, and Ojibwe name suggested she had been sired by a native father. Ojibwe braves supplied the camp with venison, deer hides, and fresh fish. Jönsson assumed that one of these had fathered Ayasha.

The door on the cook house slammed behind him, and a voice boomed out.

"Lookin' fer a man. Recent arrival."

Jönsson slouched as a tall man under a Stetson hat and a duster extending to his ankles stepped past him to speak to Berta. He couldn't hear what they said, and then the man wheeled and departed but with a fierce glance in his direction.

"Ya could use a glass of water by the looks of ya," Berta said to Jönsson, "or mebbe somethin' stronger. That bill collector scare ya?"

After the winter snows melted, and the yellow petals of cowslips heralded spring's arrival, the pace of the camp slowed down. Farmers who wintered as sawyers and axe-men departed to get their crops in, and the piles of logs stacked during the winter dwindled as the teamsters dumped the logs into the fast-flowing, ice-free river, and the rats took over. Rafting replaced chopping and sawing, and the crowded cookhouse thinned out.

By the time of Jönsson's first anniversary in the lumber camp, he became increasingly aware that the younger daughter, with the fresh blush of a young woman, had blossomed into a beauty. By their glances and obscene whispers, it was obvious that the men noticed that she was no longer thin as a twig, but Berta kept a close eye for any man who tried to get fresh with her daughter. Jönsson dared not pay too close attention under Berta's threatening glare, but furtive glances from Ayasha's brown-saucer eyes encouraged him, and it became his habit to spend idle time in the company of Berta and her daughters each day before supper.

"Ma wants to know if yer going to the Independence Day Fair."

Mimir raised his head from his pail of oats, unaccustomed to a soft female voice in the stable. Jönsson stood awkwardly silent; he had seldom heard Ayasha speak.

"Well, are ya?"

Jönsson turned back to his currycomb and repeatedly

stroked the back of the gelding that was already smooth and shiny.

"Yer gonna wear a hole in that horse's hide."

Jönsson moved to Mimir's neck whose perked ears followed the human conversation.

"Well, yah." He cleared his throat. "Well, yah, I go to da fair."

"Ma wants to know if sister and me and her can ride into town with ya?"

And so, it was arranged.

The fair celebrated Independence Day, 1893, and many in McGregor's camp would participate in the competitions. Berta's pies would likely win blue ribbons again, and Ayasha would run foot races with the girls, which he heard she easily won. The older sister would simply be there.

Pete Archambault and his team of Percherons would participate in a skid-pulling competition, and Jönsson now understood why McGregor had invested in the muscular French breed. A team of four bulls from the hated Wilson's camp had been champions for years, and the competition would be vicarious warfare between the lumber baron rivals.

On the morning of July 4th, Jönsson filled the back of his buckboard with straw for seating. Berta gingerly placed two linen-covered baskets filled with pies made with blueberries picked fresh in the woods and strawberries from the camp garden. The two sisters rode in back, and Berta plopped down on the plank seat next to Jönsson for the hour-long trip down the forest road to Hinckley.

For the first few miles, they all sat in awkward silence, but then the girls began to jabber in the back.

"Mind those pies, girls," Berta said, and then the interview began.

"Does ya come from a strong family?"

Jönsson looked at Berta with surprise.

"Well, yah," he said, but a dark shadow passed through his mind, and he quickly looked back to the road. Her question reminded him that he had lost touch with the folks back home.

"Ever been married?"

It was clear that Berta had more in mind than merely transportation, and Jönsson was horrified that she was considering him as a suitor for herself. *God dammit, woman, you're old enough to be my mother!* He answered her questions but stared straight ahead and flicked the reins to encourage Mimir to hurry along.

"*Skutt!*"

"Are ya a drinker?"

"Nah," he answered truthfully, "but I like a glass of beer."

"Does ya gamble?"

"Nah," he answered, but there was that one time he tried five-card stud poker, and he quickly lost a whole dollar.

"Does ya carouse with whores?"

"Course not," he said, but he cringed inside at his virginity. Maybe he should exaggerate a bit.

After a few minutes of silence, Berta reached the point of her interrogation.

"Ya may call on Ayasha if ya like," Berta said.

Jönsson exhaled a deep breath, relieved that the camp cook wasn't after him for herself. After a few seconds, the import of what she said dawned on him, and he exhaled another deep breath as the tall smokestack that towered over the Brennan Lumber Mill came into view.

Two or three times a week, Jönsson passed by the mill on his trips to town. Tucked into the northwest corner of Hinckley alongside a millpond of the dammed-up Grindstone River and the tracks of the St. Paul and Duluth Railroad, the mill was usually a hive of worker bees. On workdays, a furnace pumped out soot and smoke through the tall chimney, steam from boilers billowed out the sides of the main building, and the whine of steam-driven circular saws reached all corners of the village. The saws bit into log after log, some with diameters of five feet, and spit out milled planks, but on July 4th, the boilers were cool, and the saws remained still and silent. The forty-acre site of the mill would serve as fairground. Mounds of sawdust and stacks of hewn boards awaiting transport aboard a rail car came into view as Jönsson and his passengers joined the swelling crowd of fairgoers.

Over two hundred Brennan men that ripped, stacked, and sorted millions of board feet of lumber joined with the villagers, lumber camp denizens, and the whole country to enjoy a holiday. Berta's pies won, of course, but the skid competition was the main event. A deputy sheriff standing near the grandstand entrance casually tipped his hat or nodded as the audience filtered past and clambered onto the fresh-sawed planks that would serve as seats. Jönsson did his best to appear at ease and mix with the crowd, and he took a seat at the far end away from the watchful eyes of the deputy. Youngsters watched from atop stacks of lumber. A dozen teams from lumber camps as far away as Wisconsin competed, but only three teams made the finals: four mixed-breed steers from a Willow River camp, Archambault's Percherons, and the defending champions from Wilson's camp—four brown-and-white-spotted Ayrshire bulls in harness.

After the finalists were announced, and the skids loaded with heavy rocks, the swelling crowd murmured in anticipation. The beer stand emptied for the moment. Jönsson had been sitting down low, but he climbed to the top row of the grandstand.

The Wilson bulls went first and easily dragged the skid weighted with rocks the set distance. The Willow River steers tried next and moved the skid off the starting line but stalled halfway to the finish despite the lash of the whip under their teamster's hand. The Percherons leaped from the line and nearly trotted as they crossed the end line. More rocks were added and again the bulls made the mark as did the Percherons. Finally, the load became too much for the bulls, and when one of them bellowed and collapsed to his knees, their teamster threw up his hands in mock surrender. Still, the Percherons must drag this load, or the contest would be a draw. With a collective snort, the proud French draft animals stepped out, and the smug-ass Frenchie hopped onto the skid to add his own weight as they crossed the end line.

When Pete ascended the bandstand to accept twenty-five silver dollars as his prize, he did a pushup with one hand before jigging his way to the man with the megaphone, but it was McGregor the lumber baron who most appreciated the victory. He, too, ascended the bandstand and grabbed the megaphone, and droned on as if the victory of his Percheron team was about God and country. In a way it was—the Percherons did the heavy work, guided by the able hands of the French-Canadian, but the man who worshiped the wads of bills stuffed in his pockets took the credit.

As the grandstand crowd dispersed, Jönsson went the opposite direction from the rest of the men who found their way to the beer tent, saloons, or to Emma Hammond's painted women; instead, he watched the children's games, and Ayasha easily outsprinted the younger girls who did not yet share Ayasha's womanly curves. As she crossed the finish line, she glanced in Jönsson's direction, and a thin smile creased her face when their eyes met.

Not a word had been spoken to Ayasha, and not a word from her, but on the return journey to the camp, she took the place on the plank seat next to Jönsson. From the back, Berta sang camp songs. Soon, Ayasha joined in, and Hulda traced the melodies with a finger in the air. Jönsson's head subtly swayed side to side in rhythm with the music.

By the time, the wagon creaked into camp beneath the setting sun, Berta and Hulda snored in the back, and Ayasha rested her head on Jönsson's shoulder.

# CHAPTER SEVEN

S ummer in the north country was splendid. Hot days and cool nights. Fresh rains that encouraged ferns sprouting in beds of pine needles. Spires of white pines tickling wispy clouds lazing across azure skies. Spotted fawns flashing white tails as they leaped behind their doe into the thicket. And the lakes! Blue as the heavens and filled with fish to sizzle in Berta's fry pan.

Jönsson no longer concealed his glances at Ayasha in the cookhouse, Hulda scolded with a clucking sound of tongue against cheeks as she methodically set the table, and Berta sent her youngest daughter to deliver the first cut of fresh pie to the lunch wagon driver. When Ayasha set the pie on the table in front of him, her fingers deftly raked over his hand.

"Shall I warm yer cup?" she asked, and her coffee-colored eyes sparkled.

"Yah, please."

As she turned and walked away, his gaze traced her single-black braid down her back to her behind. When she returned with a steaming cup of coffee, she asked, "Will ya have time tomorrow to take me and sister berry pickin'? There's a blueberry bog 'bout a mile sout' o' here."

Jönsson carried a bucket full of blueberries in each hand and set them in the back of the wagon. Mimir seemed anxious to return to camp, but there were still a few empty buckets to fill. As he returned to the girls, he became alarmed and dropped the pails and moved quickly through the tangle of brush. Three Indian braves were speaking to Ayasha, and the conversation appeared animated, but as he approached, the braves melted into the tall trees.

"Are ya ok?"

Her eyes shot arrows toward the tree line, and her high cheekbones jutted out prominently.

"My brother ain't the boss o' me. He thinks I should take up with the *Ojibwe,* but I told 'im I'd choose my own man, and he might not have red skin."

Hulda sat in the back of the wagon humming to herself on the short journey back to camp, oblivious to the anger seething in her half-sister. Ayasha sat silently on the pine bench next to Jönsson with pursed lips and a clenched jaw.

That night after supper, Jönsson strolled along the edge of camp, puffing on a pipe full of tobacco. In the twilight, he spied Ayasha sitting on the stoop off the cook's quarters at the rear of the cookhouse, and he joined her.

For a moment they sat in silence, and then she blurted a question without facing him.

"Do my dark skin bother ya?"

It was as if the encounter with her half-brother triggered a realization that she and Ole Wobble were not just any man and woman, as if she realized for the first time that her eyes, hair, and skin were different from her sister, as if she feared her mixed blood was the overweening, defining characteristic of her being, and a disqualifying one at that.

For Swedes in the home country, marrying a Norsky or a Dane was scandalous enough, and any person other than a white-as-flour Scandinavian was unthinkable, but then, there really weren't any dark-skinned persons around in homogenous Småland. Walking the streets of New York before railroading to Minnesota had been a real eye-opener, and then the biggest surprise upon arriving in Minnesota was that Swedes weren't alone in seeking the promised land. In St. Paul, he had been offended by the abundant papists and unnerved by unfamiliar tongues. Now, the hard work and harsh conditions of being thrown together in the north country produced a leveling, a mixing, a commonality. In this American lumber camp where a babel of languages bubbled up in the bunkhouse and shades of skin blurred into sameness--burnished by sun and soot--it didn't seem odd that he looked at Ayasha through color-blind eyes. Although he had expected peasants and nobles to drink from the same trough in America, he hadn't considered race or blood or skin color. Now the question was upon him, and he didn't flinch.

Her braid had fallen apart, and her mussed hair hung loosely down her back and over her shoulders with strands dangling over doe eyes. With the back of his thick hand, he brushed away her hair and wiped away a tear. He started to lean in but hesitated when she turned to face him, and he tumbled into the deep pools of her eyes before their lips met.

Ayasha sometimes rode along on Jönsson's forays into Hinckley to haul supplies to the camp, with the dim-witted sister usually seated between them, but on this day, Hulda remained in camp with Berta and Toivo to peel potatoes. On the return journey, Jönsson rested his gelding under a familiar stand of lakeshore birches.

"Whoa, Mimir."

Mimir willingly halted under the quaking leaves, knowing that buckets of cool lake water and a lunch of fresh grass was in the offing. Mimir pulled a wagonload of fresh-butchered beef, a barrel of pork, four forty-pound sacks of flour, half a sack of sugar, a tub of lard, and a cage of squawking chickens, together with replacement saw blades and axe handles.

With a giggle, Ayasha disappeared into the bushes; usually, the sisters would follow a familiar path to a hidden cove where they would raise their skirts and cool their legs, but today Ayasha disappeared alone.

After Mimir drained a full bucket of water, Jönsson plopped down on the bank where winter's ice had pushed up a sod wall along the lakeshore. A solitary loon, black and white and missing the red throat of the loons that frequented the lakes and ponds near the farm back in Sweden, dove under the water, only to reappear with minnow tails flopping out the side of his beak. The loon seemed pleased with himself. As Jönsson listened, the loon sounded his full repertoire. First was the contented low hoot between dives. Then the wail to locate his mate, followed by a threatening yodel to warn other males to stay away, and then the concluding crazy laugh as if to say that life as a loon was good, and Jönsson should be so lucky.

"Bear!"

Ayasha's shrieks awakened Jönsson who had dozed off. He jumped to his feet as Ayasha burst through the bushes and rushed to his arms.

"Black bear," she stammered and pointed toward the cove.

Although there was a double-barreled shotgun loaded with buckshot under the plank seat of the wagon, Jönsson was distracted. The woman in his arms was completely unclothed. Many times, he had gone swimming with his naked sisters, but they were merely girls and here was a woman with breasts and a patch of dark hair between her legs.

He awkwardly removed his hands from her bare back, but there seemed to be no place for them, and they simply remained suspended in the air. He turned his head, but his body wouldn't follow because she wouldn't let go.

"Please, hold me," she said.

He cautiously returned his hands to the back of her shoulders. He looked past her toward the cove as if he expected her clothing to appear within easy reach. Mimir snorted, and Jönsson's body stiffened.

"The bear," he said. "I'll git the shotgun."

She slowly released her grip, her hands moved to the stubble on his chin, and she cupped his face in her palms, holding his gaze. Ayasha's brown-saucer eyes bore deeply into his, and she stifled a laugh.

"My shy boy, there is no bear."

His face flushed as it dawned on him what was happening, and he dared a quick glance at her glorious nakedness before his eyes returned to meet her gaze. She grabbed a handful of hair at the back of his head and kissed him hard. For a moment, they held each other tightly and swayed, but then she stepped back slightly to grasp his oversized paws and moved them to her breasts. She seemed too soft for his rough hands. Her own hands moved to the buttons on his fly, and then she laid back onto the grass, and he followed. He had barely entered her before he knew what he had only known in fleeting dreams that left him embarrassed and his bed clothes sticky.

Breathing heavily, he flopped onto his back on the grass, listening to the loon warbling in the nearby still waters. When the loon hooted to call his mate, Ayasha pulled her man back on top of her.

The second time passed more slowly.

"She's yours now; swear you'll have no other," Berta said. "Wat's yer true name? 'Ole Wobble' ain't the name yer mother giv' ya, is it? What surname will ya have your wife carry?"

He hesitated, started to speak, then hesitated again.

"Jönsson," he said as he kissed Ayasha on her forehead. "You'll be Mrs. Jönsson."

Was there a warrant for *Jonas* Jönsson? A wanted poster? Hopefully, the Minneapolis sheriff had given up on finding the robber who murdered the saloonkeeper, but just to be safe, he remained Ole, short for Olaf. Olaf Jönsson. Along with the Irishman who bled out on the plank floor of a Minneapolis saloon, Jonas Jönsson died better than a year ago. It would be Olaf Jönsson who would stand before a justice of the peace and speak his vows of marriage.

But first, Berta insisted that he seek the blessing of Chief Hole-in-the-Lake, Ayasha's father, the hunter-fisherman who speared large pike through a hole chopped in the crust of winter's ice. Although the chief barely acknowledged the daughter born of a white woman, Berta insisted that Jönsson offer gifts to secure the father's blessing. Berta arranged the interview with the chief in the nearby native village on the shores of a blue-water lake. Jönsson hoped it would go better than his first encounter with the chief when he was struck with a panic attack.

Jönsson approached the *wiigiwaam* of Chief Hole-in-the-Lake cautiously. Surrounded by a dozen or more *wiigiwaams*, Jönsson stood at the door flap of the one surrounded by drying nets made of bark-fiber cord and nettle-stalk twine. The lone woman who washed the nets in a liquid from the leaves of sumac looked upon Jönsson with curious contempt, before stepping forward to open the deer-skin flap and urge him inside.

In the dim light before Jönsson's eyes adjusted, the chief was barely visible, but Jönsson recognized the iconic bowler hat and a pair of black braids draped around the chief's neck and forward onto his chest. For the occasion, the chief wore beaded necklaces of varying lengths that laddered over his buckskin tunic, and a single eagle feather protruded from his hat band. Jönsson awkwardly squatted cross-legged on the dirt floor covered with animal skin rugs, and waited for the chief to speak, but he said nothing.

The surreal moment was not lost on the Swedish farm boy who had heard wild stories about bloodthirsty American savages, and now he sat in a *wiigiwaam* awaiting dialogue with a chief over marriage. The realities of America often smashed his naïve expectations, but nothing seemed as incongruous as this scene. In the low visibility, Jönsson's wit was keen, and he was alive in the moment.

Finally, Jönsson reached inside his sack and pulled out a small cloth bag of Virginia tobacco and set it before the inscrutable chief. Hole-in-the-Lake grunted and barely nodded. Next, Jönsson pulled out a jug of Kentucky whiskey, and again the chief nodded slightly. Lastly, Jönsson pulled out a varnished wooden case twice the size of a cigar box and etched in gold lettering with the name *Samuel Colt and Company*. He opened the hinged top and lifted out a .45 caliber six-shooter revolver and set it down gently. For the first time, the chief showed interest. He picked up the revolver and inspected it from every angle. He spun the empty cylinder in place then flipped it open and spun it again. He cocked the hammer back and then gently released it with his thumb as he pulled the trigger.

He replaced the revolver in its ornate case then rose to his feet and rummaged in the corner. He returned holding a civil war vintage Springfield musket. With a broad grin, he displayed the single-shot rifle and said, "Deer gun." He set it down and picked up the revolver. "Skunk gun." He again flipped open the empty cylinder and looked quizzically at Jönsson. "Bullets?" he asked.

Jönsson rummaged in his sack and pulled out a box of

cartridges.

"Come. We shoot," the chief said and gestured for Jönsson to follow him outside. The chief's woman and others from the small settlement gathered to watch.

"Tree. You shoot tree," he pointed at the trunk of a willow leaning over the lakeshore.

Jönsson fumbled with the revolver but managed to load six cartridges. He held the pistol with both hands, pulled the hammer back and pulled the trigger.

BANG!

The pistol jerked back, and the bullet splashed in the water beyond the willow.

"Ha ha," the chief faked a laugh. "I shoot."

Jönsson handed him the pistol. The chief took careful aim holding the weapon in one hand and squeezed the trigger.

BANG!

No splash, and a fresh gash ripped the willow trunk. The chief nodded and smiled.

"Skunk gun shoot good. I shoot good. I shoot many skunks with skunk gun. Maybe weasels."

The chief flipped open the cylinder and replaced the two spent cartridges with live rounds.

"Come. We smoke."

He pulled back the flap on his *wiigiwaam*, and the men entered to parley with tobacco and whiskey.

Jönsson squatted down and crossed his legs as the chief filled his pipe with the fresh Virginia tobacco gifted by Jönsson. The chief puffed and pulled flame into the tobacco then handed the pipe to Jönsson once it was well lit.

"My people from the morning sun," he said, "but we followed the evening sun."

Jönsson didn't catch his meaning.

"Rising sun," he said, pointing east.

"Setting sun," he said, pointing west.

"My people come from the Great Salt Water near the morning sun, but we journeyed here, following the evening sun. Many, many grandfathers travel many, many, moons. Now I here."

Jönsson handed the pipe back to his host. He jabbed his finger into his own chest.

"Rising sun," he said. "I too come from the morning sun. My home was far, far across the Great Salt Water, but my grandfathers remain under the rising sun. I come alone to start a new family and a new life with Ayasha."

The chief probably knew that, knew about the arrival of the white man, knew about the false gifts and lies of the land-stealing Europeans from across the Great Salt Water, but he smiled appreciatively, nonetheless. He seemed pleased with the tobacco, and the whiskey, and especially the skunk gun, and it appeared he would trust this white man to care for his half-white daughter.

He grunted loudly as a signal to his woman, and she entered the wiigiwaam.

"*My* woman," he pointed at her.

"For *your* woman," he said, and the woman handed Jönsson a tanned doeskin garment. An embroidered string of red and green beads curled around the collar in a stitched floral vine theme. The same motif appeared around the sash. Fringes completed the sleeve ends and skirt bottom. Ayasha normally wore European style broadcloth clothing, as did the other women who worked in the mess hall, and the doeskin garment would be for a special occasion. Ayasha would be pleased with the gift from her father. Jönsson was pleased.

The chief again rummaged in the corner, and with a beaming smile, he presented Jönsson with a skinning knife in a dyed and fringed buckskin sheath. Jönsson reverently pulled out the knife for inspection. "*Tack*. Thanks." The oak handle was wrapped in strips of tanned buckskin, and the blade was honed from the bone of a large animal. "Bone of deer?" Jönsson asked.

The chief shook his head.

"Bear?"

This time, the chief shook his head with a sly smile cracking the corners of his mouth.

"Moose," he said. "Killed by my grandfather."

Jönsson was overwhelmed, and his meager gifts paled in comparison to the gifts from the chief, much less the gift of Ayasha herself.

"You take many scalps," the chief said with his fingers touching his forehead.

Jönsson smiled a wan smile, unsure whether the chief was joking. When the chief broke into a belly laugh, Jönsson realized he was being teased, and he grinned sheepishly.

The men smoked bowls of the tobacco together and consumed a large portion of the whiskey. Hours later, Jönsson staggered through the woods to return to the lumber camp, carrying gifts and a father-in-law's blessing.

Ayasha donned the doeskin tunic for the justice-of-the-peace wedding ceremony the next day before a local barber who served as the officiant. He was dubious, but Berta could be persuasive and offered double his normal fee for a mixed-race ceremony. After the wedding, Berta cleared out the pantry behind the women's quarters off the cook shack and filled flour sacks with sawdust for a passable mattress. Late summer and autumn passed with hot nights filled with the sounds of conjugal ecstasy. Each morning the couple was greeted with Hulda's teasing but affirming clucking sounds generated by her tongue against the roof of her mouth.

These were Jönsson's best days since he stepped onto the three-master in Karlshamn on the far side of the sea. Ayasha's fetching smile lingered in his mind's eye and cheered his working hours until he could return to the cook shack for coffee and pie. Yes, there was passion in his life but also hope. He would sire a son, then more sons and daughters; they would become farmers with a red barn and spotted cattle, tall cornstalk fields, and a strawberry patch. He no longer kept his stash of dollar bills in a sock but regularly deposited his wages into the bank in Hinckley; his account was growing, and one day soon he would buy a homestead, and his American dreams would come true.

Jönsson's good fortune put him in a writing mood. In his idle hours in the mess hall, he worked purposely on a Christmas letter to Sweden. No, the streets were not paved with gold, he wrote, and he hadn't become a rich man, much less a farmer. But he had taken a bride and soon the sons would come, he was sure. He dared mention that he worked as a lumberman, and he assured the family back home that he had good prospects. He didn't identify his location or write of his maimed leg. In fact, in case of prying eyes of the law, he merely signed the letter, "your son."

He delivered the letter to the postmaster himself, unaware that the letter would be stamped with a Hinckley postmark.

# CHAPTER EIGHT: 1894

On Thanksgiving eve 1893, Jönsson and Ayasha conceived a child, but they didn't know it until January 1894, and the mother-to-be didn't show until spring.

Toivo figured he would be an uncle. His mother and Berta were long-time friends, which is how he got his job as *cookee* in the lumber camp when his sawyer father was killed by a thick pine trunk that kicked back. Toivo and Ayasha grew up together as dirty-faced urchins; under the grime, one was white as a bite of an apple, and the other brown as a raisin. Toivo attended grammar school in town, but it was unschooled Ayasha who helped him scribe his letters on his slate and learn his arithmetic ciphers. If it was her brains that helped him get along, he thought of himself as her protector when the bullies threatened the "Injun brat." Not that he was brawny, but his intervention protected her from her feisty self when she might be inclined to kick someone in the balls.

If Toivo reminded Jönsson of Tomas, his *lillebror,* the feeling was mutual now that Jönsson married Ayasha, and Toivo was eager to tag along on Sunday sleigh rides during the winter months and walks in the woods when spring arrived. On a sunny April Sunday, they built a campfire near the lakeshore that had become a favorite spot of Jönsson and his bride—for reasons known only to them.

"If the baby is a boy, name him 'Toivo,'" the Finlander said as he skittered a stick across the sheet of ice that receded from the shoreline during the spring melt.

"Doncha think he should carry his papa's name?" Ayasha

replied with a wink at her husband.

Jönsson remained silent. "Ole" or "Olaf" didn't seem right, but neither did "Jonas"—at least not without an explanation he didn't care to share. Maybe "Toivo" was the best choice.

Toivo underhanded a stone the size of a melon high in the air toward the ice, but it fell short and landed in the open water.

*Paloosh!*

A beaver fresh from winter's hibernation answered with a tail slap.

*Whap!*


Soon, the Little Kettle was free of ice. As spawning walleyes and suckers moved upstream, the river-rats rode the swift currents downstream and floated McGregor's logs to the Kettle and then the St. Croix. As usual, the lumber camp thinned out as logging operations slowed following the winter's harvest. April became May, and May became June.

"Ain't it hot? Hotter'n usual?" Ayasha said.

She didn't ask a question so much as make a point, and she was right. The dog days of summer, with high heat and humidity, arrived early. Jönsson removed his felt hat, wiped his brow with his sleeve, and peered through the haze at the reddish sun before casting a worried glance toward his wife. Ayasha placed her hands on her hips and pushed forward with her thumbs while urging her shoulders rearward to ease a sore back. Riding on the plank seat of the buckboard didn't help, but her mother insisted she ride into town to visit Doc Holtan for a checkup.

She had been spotting.

Ayasha climbed the steps to the stoop of Doc's house, but Jönsson had barely hitched Mimir to the rail for that purpose before Ayasha returned with pursed lips and eyes shooting black sparks.

"What the hell?" Jönsson said.

"Let's go," she said, jutting her chin.

Doc Holtan shrugged his shoulders when Jönsson burst through the door.

"If it was up to me, I'd gladly exam her, but people talk. If word got out that I was treating Injuns, and, well, you can understand ..."

Jönsson breathed hard, clenching his fists. He felt helpless to support his wife. For all America was cracked up to be, "decent" didn't seem to apply. Slugging the Doc would do no good except to placate his rage, and he couldn't muster the words to express his frustration.

Finally, he spit out the words. "Where, then? Where kin I take her?"

Again, the doctor shrugged his shoulders. "I s'pose the Indian Mission office in Milaca."

"That's forty fuckin' miles!"

"Well, I don't imagine Biddy Wilson the midwife would be willing, either. I don't know what to tell you."

Jönsson spun on his heels, but before he reached the door, the doctor had a suggestion.

"There's that gypsy woman. Don't know her name or much about her, but I hear tell that she does for Emma Hammond's whores. She might see your wife."


The Independence Day fair on the grounds of the Brennan Mill came and went. Berta's pies won again; McGregor's Percherons won again; but the girls' races had a new winner as Ayasha sat demurely and matronly in the shade. After regularly drinking the herbal concoction suggested by Fawni Durriken, known by respectable folks as *that gypsy woman,* she felt better. Judging by the ferocious kicking from inside her womb, it appeared her pregnancy was back on course. The crowds at the fair were smaller than the previous summer, probably owing to the hard times of depression that spread outward from the cities to every hamlet in America.

Men looking for work often passed through McGregor's camp, but seldom latched on.

"Oliver is the name, but you can call me 'Big Ollie,'" one such disappointed jobseeker said.

"If'n you don't mind, I'd like a square meal before I move on," he said to Berta. "I ain't got no coin to spare, but I'll share my story, and it's sumpthin every workin' man should hear. And woman, too, gosh dammit," he added.

She nodded toward the pine bench next to Jönsson who enjoyed his customary cup of coffee and newspaper in the quiet cookhouse before the rats burst in for supper. Big Ollie was tall as Jönsson, but skinny as a rail. His threadbare jacket over a loose-fitting vest and flat-top straw hat were out of place in the north country, nor did he have the look of a lumbering man, but his calloused hands said he knew physical labor.

By the time the crew of teamsters and river-rats poured in, Big Ollie was downing his third plate of pork chops and beans. He belched with obvious satisfaction before wiping his mouth on his sleeve, and then he climbed atop the bench to hold court.

"Organize," he said, and then repeated himself. "Organize."

The man could have been a preacher with his cadence and sense of timing, and even Pete remained silent and listened reverently.

"Working men and women must organize or George Pullman and his ilk will eat us alive. I know. Pullman already took a bite out'a my ass."

He patted his rump for effect for his appreciative audience.

"Less'n five year ago I fell for his false promises when I happened across one of his flyers advertising employment in his railroad car factory with a place to live in his company town just outside Chicago."

He drew himself up with a deep breath and scanned the eyes of his listeners before he continued.

"Our children are born in a Pullman house, fed from the Pullman shops, taught in the Pullman school, catechized in the Pullman Church, and when they die, they shall go to the Pullman hell. Shit, it turns out that the Pullman hell is here and now."

He shook his head and made a *tsking* sound with his tongue.

"You all know about the bank panic, and Pullman used the depression as excuse to slash our wages. But did he lower the rents on the company houses? Or lower the prices on milk and eggs in the company store? Hell no."

Berta handed him a glass of water, which he drank down with Adam's apple bobbing.

"Aaaah. Thank you, missus." He handed the glass back to her.

"That's when I met Debs. Eugene Debs. 'Organize,' Debs said, and 'organize' I say to you, and strike if you must."

That's when Muley Peck, a skilled river rat with a wife and kids, piped in.

"What did that get you? I heared about the strikebreakers

who busted your heads. Then soldiers started shooting. How many Pullman workers died in the Debs rebellion? Ten? Twenty? I heared it was more'n thirty."

Restless murmurs rose to the log rafters of the cookhouse, but Peck wasn't through.

"Did you get yer wages restored? What the hell are you doing here? It's 'cause you and the rest lost your jobs, ain't it so?"

"You're a wise man and well-informed," Big Ollie said. "But this war ain't over. Capital might 'a won this battle, but tis no time to cry in our beer. Organize, I say. Lumber men with railroad men. Miners and dockworkers. Farmers, too. And women." He looked straight at Berta with a nod. "Well, I best take my leave. Thanks, missus, for the hospitality. Luck to all of youse."

Jönsson slipped out while the men continued to grouse. He didn't know what to think. Things were good right now with a wife plump with pregnancy and a bank account that swelled by the month. Near as he could see, it was best not to upset the apple cart.

In mid-August, Ayasha accompanied Jönsson on a trip to town. While Ayasha shopped for baby clothes in the Brennan Company Store, Jönsson read the latest edition of the Hinckley Enterprise:

*Hinckley is a city that is rich in good schools and churches, its people are bold in enterprise, firm in purpose, liberal in supporting public measures, moral in their lives, warm in their hospitality, and ever glad to help you climb the ladder of success.*

So long as you're white as wheat flour, Jönsson thought to himself. From here, they would visit Fawni Durriken and not Doc Holden. The gypsy woman and not the good doctor would deliver their baby, due any day now. He folded up the newspaper and tucked it under the buckboard seat when Ayasha appeared on the boardwalk outside the Brennan store amidst other mothers coming and going, shopping for back-to-school clothes for their children.

"See what a smart shopper I am," she beamed, and her cheeks glistened with sweat and the blush of impending motherhood. "Six cloth diapers and a baby gown,' she said, "and I still have change on the dollar!"

Jönsson remembered his own mother pregnant with his younger sisters; *Mor* seemed fat and ugly to him then, but Ayasha's beauty awed him.

# CHAPTER NINE

A month and a half after McGregor's Percherons again embarrassed Wilson's bulls during the Independence Day fair, the competition with the Wilson camp took an explosive turn.

Jönsson's lunch wagon headed east from camp following a string of searing August days. Drought winds swirled the scent of wood smoke from fires scattered along the railroad tracks. The previous winter, McGregor's jacks had cut a half-mile swath of pine, and Pete Archambault's teamsters were busy piling the logs high along the bank of the Little Kettle northeast of camp, but Jönsson delivered lunch to the river rats a few miles downriver who floated the logs toward the mouth of the Little Kettle.

"They ain't moved since yesterday," Toivo reported the obvious.

A few rats aimlessly moved across the stalled raft, but most of the crew milled about on the riverbank, filled with pent-up energy. Wilson boys watched from across the river, and insults flew back and forth. Wilson logs had jammed up in a bend in the Little Kettle where she necked down. The Wilson log jam prevented the McGregor logs from moving.

"They ain't doing a damn thing." Again, Toivo stated what was plain to see.

The Wilson rats across the river simply watched and chided the McGregor crew. They made no attempt to break up their logjam.

When lunch was ready, Jönsson didn't bother blowing

his whistle since the foul-tempered rats were already milling about. They didn't scarf their food down like they normally did, and their slower pace allowed greater pissing and moaning than usual. After Jönsson and Toivo cleaned up, several rats rode Jönsson's wagon back to camp. Nothing else to do.

When Jönsson arrived early for supper like usual, a cloud of blue tobacco smoke hung over a pine slab table where the scaled-down summertime crew had gathered, and Pete held court.

"Break those fucking logs loose yourselves," he chided the river rats.

At first, no one stirred. Messing with the log raft of another camp was not something that was done. About that time, McGregor himself burst into the mess hall.

"If you sonofabitches don't get my logs to the St. Croix, I'll close this damned camp down," he said.

He didn't say much more; he didn't need to because the lumberjacks believed him. McGregor had other camps, and he didn't need to pour bad money into an unproductive camp. Or, if the national panic over failed banks continued, maybe he'd just take his money and run. Even in the remote forests of northern Minnesota, the unwashed rabble of lumberjacks knew about the bank failures that panicked the entire nation and spiraled into economic depression. Should the nation trust silver or gold? Or lumber? Bankers? Jew bankers, they said. Greedy Jew bastards.

Was Jönsson foolish to deposit his earnings in the Hinckley bank? Couldn't be worse than a sock in his footlocker. Is the banker in the village a Jew? Had Jönsson ever seen a Jew? What does a Jew look like? Different, that's for sure, with big-hooked noses, heavy eyelids, thick lips, pot bellies, thick hands, crooked legs, and flat feet. Jönsson had seen such drawings way back in Sweden, and more than once he had heard *Fader* say, *"jäkla jude,"* words that stayed with him because *Fader* rarely swore. "Damn Jews" seemed like a single word in his father's mouth.

There was more to it than just Jew bastards and bank failures. When depression strikes the land, the workers who mine the mines, the railroad men who build the cars and lay the tracks, and the jacks who strip the forests for the lumber barons, know that they would be first in line to feel the pinch of poverty. A job was a sacred thing when scarcity threatened.

Just a few weeks earlier, Big Ollie, the fired worker for George Pullman, passed through camp, and he reported that the workers who built railroad cars for Pullman had been crushed when they protested drastic wage cuts. When their protest grew into a nationwide railroad strike, strikebreakers busted heads and federal troops intervened, and the strike was broken. Pullman punished his own workers by laying off nearly six thousand, pushing families into poverty.

The cause of the working man was set back in the bloody labor dispute, and there was no telling when conditions might improve. The rich men of means had won, and labor had lost, no doubt about it. No, the jacks of McGregor's camp knew on which side their bread was buttered, and they believed the boss man when he threatened to shut down the camp.

After McGregor departed, Pete repeated himself. "Break those fucking logs loose yourselves."

First thing the next morning, Jönsson hauled a wagon load of rats downstream, and he waited around to watch them break up the Wilson log jam. With hooked peaveys, two men set out, but Muley Peck soon moved to the front, which wasn't surprising since he was the most agile of the river dancers. Loose-limbed and willowy, he floated across the raft of logs, caressing and guiding his twenty-foot peavey like a feather-light dance partner.

*Skip, skip, skip to my Lou. Skip to my Lou, my darlin'.*

CRACK!

Everyone heard the rifle shot, and Jönsson saw a puff of smoke from the bushes on the far side. Muley was stunned. The bullet splintered his peavey just beneath his fingers. For a moment, he froze in place while the half-loose band of his hat flapped in the breeze, oblivious to the sudden danger. When Muley dropped the stump in his hands and turned to scramble back without his magic wand, his dancing feet became clumsy, and he slipped off a spinning log and disappeared under water. He was lucky because the river was shallow at that point, and he stood on the gravel bottom with his neck and shoulders above the water with logs bobbing around him in the roiling current. Jonesy Jones, the second rat on the log raft, extended his peavey toward Muley.

CRACK!

The second shot smashed the second peavey, and Jonesy retreated. He made it to shore and joined the other rats hiding behind trees and stumps. Jönsson peeked from behind the trunk of a basswood that leaned over the water, watching Muley stranded in the river, waiting for the rifle shot that would blow the top of his head off.

Jönsson didn't know Muley well. The rats hung together, much as the teamsters did, but Muley was a family man—that much Jönsson knew. Two or three kids from some town to the south. Come Saturdays, Muley headed home, but he was always back in time for Berta's Monday morning flapjacks and salt pork. He was a good man, so far as Jönsson knew.

Jönsson tried to look away, but his eyes kept returning. Muley lost his hat when he hit the water, and his bald, wet head glistened in the morning sun, like a floating ball but oddly moving upstream against the current. Sometimes the head disappeared as Muley ducked under a log, reappearing closer to the shore. As the minutes passed, Jönsson wondered what was going through the mind of the crack shot on the far shore. Was the shooter waiting for a clear shot? Drawing out the tension to enhance the terror by shooting just as safety appeared near?

"Run, dammit!" Jonesy yelled as Muley splashed through the shallows and slogged up the riverbank with water streaming out his sopped shirt and wool pants.

The pack of river rats peeled away from their hiding spots and clambered aboard the wagon; Jönsson was already there.

"Hurry up," Jönsson shouted from the seat. "*Skutt*, Mimir," he said when the last one climbed on board, and he slapped the reins across his gelding's haunches.

At first, the men in the wagon remained silent during the ride back to camp, but jabber picked up as they moved away from the river and spilled into the mess hall. When the teamsters returned from dumping logs into the river miles north of the jammed up-river bend and heard about Muley's close call, the yapping swelled to the log rafters. As the crowd grew, a stone jug of whiskey appeared, and belligerency spiked.

Pete pranced around on top of a pine-slab table. "Who's with me? I say we fight fire with fire."

In the safety of camp and following a few snorts of whiskey, false bravado soared until Jonesy pounded on a table to gain attention.

"Let's hear what Muley says, he was the one in the gun sights."

The murmuring quieted and all eyes turned to the man whose clothes dripped with river water but not with blood. Muley cleared his throat and spoke softly.

"I ain't hired on for no gunplay."

The serious but matter-of-fact tone of his voice chilled the bellicose talk.

"I got a life ahead a me and a wife and kids who need me."

The experience of being shot at informed the voice of reason, and although blood ran hot, and the loggers feared for their jobs, a shooting war was not what they signed up for. This was more than a barroom brawl with the Wilson boys to let off steam, way more.

Jönsson listened from the rear. Muley was right, as far as he was concerned, but Jönsson was not one to speak up and call attention to himself. He also had a wife, and soon a kid, and a future. The north woods had proven to be a safe sanctuary away from the prying eyes of the law, and he didn't need them poking around now with their questions.

Something had to be done, but no one offered a plan other than further investigation, and a pair of volunteers were enlisted to sneak down after dark to see what could be seen. Hours later, Jönsson was asleep on his bunk when he heard the ruckus caused by the returning scouts, and he joined the parley in the mess hall.

"There's pilings there, I tell you," the scout reported with wild gesticulations of his arms. "It's no accident, dammit. Three sets of pilings have been driven into the riverbed to hold the logs in a jam. Those logs will stay there until kingdom comes unless the Wilson boys remove the pilings."

"Or we blow them the fuck out of the water," Pete said, and the loggers hushed.

Jönsson wasn't part of the plan, and he was against it, but he said nothing. Not that he objected to the right or wrong of it, but he knew the law would come with their questions. Questions that he didn't want to answer. If he didn't have a pregnant wife with a baby due soon, he might have disappeared right then and there. In one more year, maybe two at the most, he would pull his savings out of the Hinckley Bank—if a Jew banker didn't steal it—and buy a farm.

The conspiracy went underground and Jönsson heard no more except for whispered snatches. Dynamite. Blasting caps. Detonation cords. The blistering winds, drought, and flash fires that heated the August landscape seemed to be ominous signs of a coming rage.

Two weeks later, on another scorching day in a string of suffocating August days, Ayasha went into labor. As she settled restlessly onto the seat of the buckboard for the trip into Hinckley and Fawni Durriken's shack, Pete handed Jönsson a note with instructions to pick up a special load that arrived by rail. Jönsson feared that hell was about to break loose, even if the townspeople went willy-nilly with their daily lives.

Jönsson drove Mimir to a shack on the backside of the village that was shaded by a single, tall burr oak. He lifted Ayasha's elbow gently as she stepped down from the wagon. He handed her bag to Fawni Durriken who greeted them at the door.

"When next you see me, you shall have a son," Ayasha whispered through a brave smile, betrayed by the tears streaming down her cheek.

Jönsson kissed her and mumbled, "I love you," before spinning on his heels with clenched teeth to fight his own emotions. Already, he missed her, but he dared not show his free-floating foreboding. Was it the danger of childbirth, the mayhem that the Frenchie and his cohorts were about to unleash, or the ominous weather and smoky air?

A steam engine snorted and hissed as Jönsson pulled up to the bustling depot of the St. Paul and Duluth railroad.

"Your parcels are piled there," a young, raw-boned depot

attendant said, removing his undersized billed cap and mopping his forehead with a stained sleeve below bicep garters.

"Ten a.m. and already the temperature is ninety fucking degrees," the depot man said, tapping the mercury thermometer hanging in the shade of the roof over the open platform.

A farmer in coveralls and straw hat walked past carrying a cage of squawking chickens, mumbling to no one in particular,

"Too late. Too late. No rain in months. Too late."

Jönsson loaded the parcels quickly. Just as he flicked the reins to depart, the steam whistle on the locomotive shrieked, and Mimir lurched forward.

"Easy boy," Jönsson said to calm his gelding if not his own nerves. No need to shake up his potent cargo.

# CHAPTER TEN

H owling wolves kept Jönsson from sleep, and when three distant explosions split the night, the bunkhouse erupted in cheers. An hour later when Pete and his crew of sappers returned from their clandestine mission, Jönsson departed to tend to Mimir in the stable. His eyes watered from acrid wood smoke suspended in the still air, and the stars died quickly as dawn approached. Soon, a blood-red sun peeked over the eastern horizon.

The high-spirited river rats jabbered as he drove them to the river. Sure enough, the jam was blown, and a few stray logs floated through the river bend. With a little maneuvering with their pikes and peaveys, the rats should get the whole mass moving. He departed to the hoots of river rats at work.

But when he returned hours later, the mood had darkened and so had the daylight. After he blew his lunch whistle, the crew of river-rats numbly stood in line, and an eerie silence hung over the shoreline—no squawking blue jays or scolding red squirrels. Even though logs surged through the chute where the Wilson pilings had been dynamited, apprehension replaced exhilaration. Whether the saboteur's provocations were cause or merely coincidence, the suffocating stillness that descended upon the forest signaled that great evil was afoot, and nature waited with dread.

The muted blue sky had appeared milky with smoke from scattered brush fires for weeks, but as Mimir pulled the swinging dingle lunch wagon back to camp, a dull metallic sheen loomed overhead, like unpolished copper. The accumulation of slash—piles of pine limbs and needles scorched brown under the summer's drought sun—lined the sides of the trail back to camp. The wagon lurched along as the trail descended into a tamarack swamp where sapling logs had been laid in a corduroy fashion to allow passage through the bog, but the roadway was certainly not soggy now, and the tamarack needles had browned prematurely before the arrival of autumn.

"I smell Lucifer," Toivo whispered as the wagon lurched over the St. Paul and Duluth railway tracks.

Jonas glanced sideways at the boy whose watery eyes bulged in apprehension. True enough, the stinging scent of sulfur hung in the air.

As Jönsson and Toivo arrived in camp, the breeze freshened from the southwest chasing the still air--at least for the moment. When Jönsson unloaded the lunch canisters into the mess hall, he caught Berta's worried eye, but they said nothing. Jönsson stepped into the bunkhouse, and he heard the snores of the Frenchie who had done his sapper's work in the middle of the night and now rested from a job well done.

Jönsson led Mimir by the bridle toward the stable, but he decided against unhitching the wagon. He curry-combed his gelding with nervous glances toward the southwest.

He sensed it—not just with his stinging eyes and nose but deep in his gut. Something was there. Something was coming. Something wicked.

Ash like black snowflakes floated in the air and settled on Mimir's back, and Jönsson quickly brushed the flecks away. The milky-yellow sunlight grew darker.

The wind picked up now, and gusts swirled around him, whisking his broad-brimmed felt hat over the stable's roof. The rush of wind carried a muffled grumbling sound, much different than the normal whoosh of air through the treetops. Windborne cinders landed here and there. When he looked again to the southwest, he dropped his curry comb and flew to the mess hall. An immense tower of smoke, billowing and roiling like a thundercloud, but bigger and blacker, tumbled and rolled toward the camp.

Jönsson shouted one word into the mess hall and one word only:

"FIRE!"

He only said it once, and the mess hall emptied.

"Climb on, climb on!"

Berta and Hulda clambered onto his wagon alongside Toivo, but the native women ran into the woods toward their *wiigiwaams*. Pete appeared from the bunkhouse wiping the sleep from his eyes, but when he saw the roiling dark clouds, he jumped onto the plank seat next to Jönsson.

"Give me the reins," Pete demanded.

"Like hell," Jönsson replied and shoved Pete onto the ground, standing up to the Frenchie for the first time. Pete jumped onto the back of the wagon.

Other scattered souls piled on as Jönsson slapped the reins across Mimir's haunches. Red and yellow flashes of flame erupted from the pillar of smoke and scalded the heavens.

"*Skutt.* God dammit! *Skutt!*"

Jönsson expected the lurching wagon to break apart as he urged his gelding to a full gallop. They followed no trail, plowing their way through the tangle of brush and slash. Jagged branches tore at Mimir and thorns scratched Jönsson's face and ripped the threads of the homespun cotton dresses of Berta and Hulda. Smoke closed in, and Jönsson steered blindly. A doe and two fawns, no longer spotted, bounded past.

He was unsure whether they raced toward the fire and not

away from it, but then a wall of flame appeared at their back, swirling and rising a hundred feet or more into the air, crackling through the tree tops, roaring and devouring everything in its path like a red serpent with eyes of burning coals, writhing and snaking its way after them, crawling on the ground but with a tongue of flame licking at the tree tops, setting crowns of pine on fire, growing as it devoured every living thing in its path—tall birches and short junipers, rabbits and racoons-- bulging like a garter snake that swallowed a frog, spawning foul offspring at her sides: a growing, squirming nest of evil.

Fiery demons whirled around them setting the slash on fire, and the crowns of standing jack pines exploded into balls of fire. Flames rippled through the clouds above without any connection to the ground, as if the sky itself burned, tossing firebrands here and there. Jönsson's passengers beat at smoldering patches of clothing.

When the wagon wheel bounced over a small boulder, a solitary figure flew into the air and landed with a thud, dragging behind, tangled in a rope.

"Whoa, Mimir. Whoa!"

"Leave him! He is lost, save the rest of us!"

It was Pete who lay unconscious, the God dammit Frenchie who stole his sock full of cash, who teased his limp and questioned his masculinity, the self-righteous rapist who ought to burn in hellfire.

For a single moment in eternity, time stopped. The flames stood frozen in place, and the souls in the wagon sat mute as Jönsson purposefully descended from the plank seat of the buckboard and walked slowly to the fallen Frenchman. Jönsson momentarily stood over the still body before he unsheathed the bone skinning knife gifted to him by his father-in-law.

*"You will take many scalps,"* the words of the chief rang in his ears.

*"Focka,"* Jönsson swore.

Jönsson raised the bone knife high over his head before whipping his arm down violently. He flung the blade, and it stuck in the soft middle of a pine stump, the handle quivering.

He reached into his pocket and pulled out his pen knife and flicked open the blade.

*The tall beech reached for the sky, and the cluster of leaves near the top rippled in the rising morning breeze. The sun-dappled shoreline of the pond remained wet with dew as the five-year old knelt to cut into the bark. His "J" was squiggly at the bottom, but Fader encouraged him.*

*Moist snowflakes sifted through cracks in the shanty wall in winter's last gasp. The flakes melted as soon as they lit on the floor. He sat at the edge of his bunk and sliced away the willow bark, one deliberate stroke at a time. Soon, a pile of shavings lay at his feet, and he turned to the knots in the gnarly branch, using the small blade of his pen knife.*

*He should say something to the wide-eyed Mick as hot blood gurgled over the mother-of-pearl handle of the pen knife. "I mean you no harm, and I'll help you mop this blood off the floor before you open for business. Let's share a tall glass of beer together, and all will be well."*

Jönsson knelt over the still body with his open pen knife in his right hand. With his left, he lifted Pete's head. He thrust the pen knife forward and cut the rope. He lifted and carried the limp body to the wagon.

*"Skutt!"* he said, and the fire roared again.

The tracks of the St. Paul and Duluth Railroad loomed ahead, straddling a marsh. Mimir smelled water and lunged forward as the wagon bounced over the tracks, skidded down the bank, mashed down cattails, and splashed into the shallow slough. With the wagon wheels mired in mud, Jönsson unhitched Mimir and they followed the passengers who waded in knee-deep water toward the center of the shallow pool. Jönsson and his horse found deeper water nearly to his armpits and Mimir's withers. His passengers from the lumber camp sat or squatted with heads above water, awaiting the passover of God's death angel. The Frenchie joined them, revived when the wagon splashed into the cool water.

Over the grumble that rolled from the approaching tower of smoke, a sound like a snorting steam locomotive reached Jönsson's ears.

By God, it was a train! A steam engine chugged along, pushing burning railroad cars in reverse! Flames leapt from the roofs of the passenger cars and licked their undersides.

A solitary man with a bucket emerged from the train engine. He stumbled into the shallows, filled his bucket, and splashed muddy water onto the burning steps of the forward passenger cars. Confused passengers began to emerge and slipped down the bank into the water, some on the east side of the tracks and some on the west.

A black man wearing the uniform of a porter emerged from the rear car with a fire extinguisher and sprayed the exiting passengers and encouraged them toward the slough. When his extinguisher ran dry, he led passengers by the hand to the marsh, kicking down a barbed wire fence. Jönsson was there on the far side, urging the passengers through the gap in the fence and tugging on the shirts of those who hesitated.

The first man returned to the train engine, and he escorted the wounded, burned, and blinded engineer toward the water.

All now seemed safely off the train, but when a child screamed from inside, someone clambered up the bank, kicked away burning splinters on the ground, and entered a fiery car with his arm covering his face. He reappeared a moment later with his hair singed, shirt and trousers smoldering, clutching a young girl wrapped in his coat.

It was Pete Archambault.

Some made it to waist-deep water, others lay prone in knee-deep shallows, and a few could only writhe in the mud. By now, the blaze engulfed the railroad cars, and the towering firestorm bore down on the hapless souls, with flames shooting hundreds of feet into the sky.

For nearly an hour, the fire raged overhead. Along with the resident muskrats, human heads poked above the waterline, awestruck and watching mute, except for occasional shrieks as waves of gaseous flames dipped low. There were no rational thoughts, only confusion. The human mind cannot comprehend the incomprehensible. All other emotions were overwhelmed by fear, but after the firestorm passed, and the survivors realized they lived, agony crept in.

"We shoulda stayed in Duluth!"

A young man standing near Jönsson tried to comfort his wailing woman, but she seemed to blame him.

"I knowed we shoulda stayed in Duluth!" she repeated, pushing her man away.

"It was God awful," the man said to Jönsson, "and she's still afeared, but she'll come around." He tried to convince himself.

"We was riding the train to Minneapolis for our honeymoon. As we reached the outskirts of Hinckley, we saw people running toward the train, and the engineer slammed on the brakes. Some were running with their clothes afire. Some fell and didn't get up."

"We shoulda stayed in Duluth," the woman moaned again.

"Yes, honey, but how was I to know?"

Then he tried to deflect blame onto a scapegoat.

"We shoulda backed up right away, but that God dammit n---r stepped off the train to help folks climb aboard, and the engineer didn't ram the throttle down to pick up steam and accelerate backwards away from the fire until it was damn near too late."

The woman shrieked, and she began to pummel her husband.

"You bastard! You coward! There was women and babies that coulda used a strong man, but you just stood there. The last I saw, they was still running after the train."

Her shoulders shivered and sagged as she clenched her eyes against the image. She had lost her hat, and her pinned-up hair was coming undone. She wore a fine jacket over a ruffled blouse. Unlike many, she did not appear to be burned, but who could tell about her scorched soul.

Jönsson attempted to speak but barely stammered, "Did, didja see a native woman?"

His words were swallowed by the wind, and the squabbling couple moved away. The devastation that surrounded him faded away with the horrible realization that the fire had reached the north end of Hinckley. What of the southside where the tall oak leaned over Fawni Durriken's shack?

Jönsson survived the holocaust. So did Toivo and Berta and Hulda and Pete Archambault and many of the three hundred or so who arrived at the marsh by train, but what of the citizens of Hinckley? What of his pregnant wife?

As evening approached, Jönsson kept a worried eye toward the south, waiting for the flames to die down. All around him survivors shivered and wailed in the marsh or moaned on the banks. Some slept peacefully. Some slept eternally. Jönsson and the Frenchie assisted the black porter tend to the living, and that helped to keep Jönsson's mind occupied. Berta comforted the mothers and children. Hulda nestled a child in her arms as the mother lay dead alongside them.

Nothing remained of the passenger cars except twisted metal. The coal in the locomotive tender burned like a beacon, shooting flames fifty feet into the air. Sometime after dark as stars struggled to shine through pockets in the smoke, Berta came to him.

"You must go now."

Jönsson climbed onto Mimir's back, and his knees pressed his gelding forward. The horse who knew Jönsson's heart splashed through the shallows and onto the bank, turning south to follow the twisted tracks toward the village. Although the horse was already exhausted, he broke into a gallop, slowing here and there when the smoke became too heavy to see more than a few lengths ahead, which was often, but the gelding trusted the hands of his master. Jönsson dared not leave the tracks or he would lose his way. Burning stumps glowed like fireflies in the dark.

They finally reached the banks of the Grindstone. The railroad bridge was gone, and there were charred bodies in the sawdust in the dry creek bed. The lumber and sawdust of the Brennan Mill still burned, popping, cracking, and shooting flames and sparks. When Jönsson urged Mimir up the far bank, his loyal gelding collapsed, done in by the race through miles of noxious smoke. No time for regret, but Jönsson was alone now.

Not a building remained standing as far as Jönsson could see in the darkness. He followed the twisted tracks to the smoking pile of rubble that had been the St. Paul and Duluth train depot, but from there, he had no further bearings. What had once been a town of streets and buildings had become random piles of ash, drifting and swirling in the benign breeze that followed the tornado winds of fire. Lumps of melted glass had been windows, twisted iron straps had been the trunks holding a family's treasures, porcelain shards had been pottery or a baby's doll.

What had been a bustling community full of life had become *helvete*, the inferno of the dead. Animal carcasses with legs pointing skyward were either horse or cow, but he couldn't tell which. Intense heat had incinerated the hides leaving red and cracked flesh. He tried to ignore the human corpses—black and withered, crisp, and faceless with lips and noses burned away--but when he smelled the aroma of burnt meat, he retched. Some died alone and others clustered with family, their arms entwined.

Not everyone perished, and that gave him hope. Ghouls wailed and wandered aimlessly amidst the smoke and ash and carcasses of the dead, crying out for children, or a wife, or a husband. Singed survivors reported they endured in the shallow, slimy water of the gravel pit on the east edge of town, others in the metal railroad roundhouse that deflected the heat and flames even though it was like an oven inside, still others in the few wet patches that remained of the Grindstone, still others in wells or root cellars—if they didn't suffocate--still others face down in the furrows of potato fields. He heard reports of a whole trainload escaping on the Great Northern Line that led to the northeast with a locomotive pulling and another pushing a string of Pullman passenger cars and box cars loaded with human cargo. Pray God that Ayasha waited for him in Duluth!

As he wandered, Jönsson recited what he remembered of the catechism taught by the parish priest across the sea. He was willing to believe that the whale swallowed Jonah if that would save Ayasha. This is most certainly true. He even repeated the Frenchie's Hail Mary that he had heard for endless days.

*Je vous salue, Marie pleine de grâce.*

He confessed his sin of murder and every other transgression that only God could know, and he begged forgiveness and pleaded for mercy. Had he not earned redemption when he saved the Frenchie's life that very day?

In the pale light of breaking dawn, he spied the skeleton of a scorched tree. As he came close, it appeared to be the charred trunk and main branches of the tall oak that stood sentinel over the gypsy woman's shack. He approached with urgent dread. Each footfall kicked up a cloud of ash.

Crows silently circled overhead. When one landed on a blackened branch, Jönsson feared that it was Korp the village priest, come to watch with beady red eyes, come to witness his hellfire threats come true, come to claim damnation for the apostate farm boy.

There Jönsson found them. Fawni clutched an amulet that failed to protect her. The beaded embroidery was all that remained of Ayasha's bridal dress. The scorched remains of his love clutched his son who lived and died all in a day.

He now understood the absurd laugh of the loon. His burned-out, empty soul produced no tears so Jönsson sat on the bank of the lake alongside the ashes of the *wiigiwaams,* contemplating the wisdom of the crazy bird. There was no trace of the chief and his small band. Only the wolves and the crows knew where they lay.

He sifted through the ashes of Hole-in-the-Lake's *wiigiwaam* and found what he was looking for: a charred case holding a fully loaded Colt 45 revolver, the skunk gun. The metal clasp had melted, but he twisted the case open with his pen knife. The wooden pistol grip had turned to charcoal, which he stripped away from the metal frame. He held the pistol close to his ear and listened to the clicking as he spun the cylinder. The skunk gun seemed to be operational. He cocked the hammer with his thumb then eased it forward as he pulled the trigger.

The wind blows snow, and the wind blows flame, but who is to blame?

Did God in heaven punish the murderer of a saloon keeper? Jönsson was not vain enough to believe this devastation was about him, but maybe just a little. Maybe he owned the death of his beloved and his unnamed son--*the sins of the father--* but other deaths must be blamed on other sinners. Of course, the cut and slash lumber barons bore responsibility, but what of the summer-long drought that had parched the land, which was certainly God sent? Was this monstrous evil the fault of human or divine hands? Perhaps Toivo was right, Lucifer came near. What was worse, a god who caused catastrophe, a god who allowed it, a powerless god, or no god at all? If God truly existed, he ought to be ashamed. Maybe nature herself spit fire and fanned the flames to purge the despoilers and purify her beloved forest.

Then he knew. It was the loon. The fucking loon. He blamed the fucking, fickle, laughing, mocking, absurd loon.

BANG!

When the bullet splashed near, the bird took flight, wings slapping the flat water, until it disappeared into the haze. The creature sought his mate; gradually his wail receded into the far shoreline.

*********

*"I need a stiff drink," Pastor Don said. "How 'bout you?"*

*I hadn't felt the bite of whiskey on my tongue in quite some time, but "Hell, yes," I replied. We both could use an elixir to boost our spirits. LaDonna be damned if she objects.*

*Pastor Don checked his smartphone for a liquor store nearby.*

*"Still partial to Scotch?" he asked as he paused at the door.*

*"Chivas," I replied.*

*The wan December sun lingered until he returned, and the red birds arrived about the same time as he reappeared in my doorway with his glove curled around a brown bag.*

*A single finger of Scotch in a glass from the cafeteria was my limit, and I sipped judiciously, but I coughed as the warmth tickled my throat.*

*Don splashed an ample measure into his own glass, which he quickly downed, but after pouring a second draught, his glass sat on the side table as he watched the cardinals flit about.*

*"I had no idea," he said in a barely audible voice after a long silence. "No idea of Grandpa's burdens."*

*A gray female cardinal lit on my windowsill and lingered briefly before hopping to the ground and the sunflower seeds scattered beneath the feeder.*

*"I once led the senior's group from my church on an outing to Hinckley," Don said, remembering out loud. "We toured the fire museum and after lunch at Tobie's Restaurant, we briefly walked around the mass grave where hundreds of the dead from the Hinckley fire now rest."*

*He shook his head.*

*"I wish I had known." There was anguish in his whispers. "Perhaps Ayasha and her babe, my own uncle, lie there!"*

*He looked at me with the sudden awe of realization. "Why,*

*that would be your own brother!"*

*He took a large sip and his lips contorted with the whiskey burn. I sensed a bit of self-reproach in his murmuring. Perhaps nostalgia is the normal response to the tale of a long-dead relative, but Don's hearing of his grandfather's story cut deeply, and I heard remorse in his breathy voice for not having known, not having understood, not having appreciated the complexities in the life of the immigrant whose legacy is our own. The twists in the trail followed by the one who came before us and the burdens he carried humbled our own comfortable existences. I could see that Don sensed this acutely. More than a century later, the calamity that befell Jonas Jönsson retained power to pinch his grandson.*

*Suddenly, Don looked straight into my face; his eyes sparkled with curiosity.*

*"How did Grandpa struggle through this unspeakable tragedy? How did he come to marry Grandma and raise a family? How were you born, and my mother? How am I even here?"*

*Then, he canted his head with a puzzled expression.*

*"And, how do you know all this?"*

*I drained the last of my whiskey. My telling of the Hinckley chapter in Papa's saga confirmed for me that I was right to pass on the intimate stories that Papa shared with me so long ago. This was a process to be worked through. We would search for the light in the darkness.*

*"All in due time, dear nephew," I said. "I'll see you in the morning."*

# CHAPTER ELEVEN: 1895

Burned out and hollow, Jönsson survived the winter of 1895 with a cauterized soul. It could only be so following the holocaust of the Hinckley forest fire and the loss of life and love, for a man with feelings would certainly perish or suffer perpetual torment, and so he sought emptiness.

He might have tried heavy drinking, but he couldn't afford even a nickel glass of beer. Perhaps the whores of St. Croix Street near the ship canal could have provided passing comfort, but he had no heart for it, much less the coin, and the painted women weren't allowed to take charity cases, even if the honorable citizens of Duluth had otherwise thrown open the doors of hospitality to Hinckley refugees. Hospitals were filled with burn victims, applying generous doses of all manner of salves, but there was little to offer a lonely soul.

Fear of capture and arrest receded under crashing waves of guilt and grief. What did it matter if the sheriff came knocking on his door? He had already been punished beyond what the law could do to him.

Visions of his brown-eyed woman, of lakeshore walks under budding birches, of sweaty lovemaking on a sawdust mattress—all the joys of love now lost--only taunted him and spiked his grief, and so he fought against remembering, but that left him alone. If he shooed the memories, what else was there? If the past was too painful to confront, how he could he face a forlorn future? In the empty hole left after the fire consumed his love, his hopes, and his happiness, loneliness seeped in.

Destitution didn't help.

When the entire town of Hinckley went up in flames, the bank and his savings burned with it. Turns out the bank was no safer than a sock. He found himself destitute in Duluth, the Zenith City, at the mouth of the St. Louis River that deposited sandbar buffers for the great harbor at the head of the Great Lakes, and the daddy of them all, Lake Superior.

Jobs were scarce as depression choked the entire nation, and more so for a cripple with a bum leg. He knew horses, but horseflesh was giving way to steel, and the Duluth docks and the railways that spidered outward into the forests, mining towns, and western prairies looked to steam locomotives that harnessed horsepower by the hundreds. So Jönsson the horse-man slept on a church pew, and accepted handouts when he wasn't hired as a day laborer, often arranged through the good offices of Pastor Emil Bergquist.

At first, he felt obligated to sit through Sunday church services in the building that had become his refuge. Perhaps he also sought meaning and comfort. Pastor Bergquist, a fellow Swede and immigrant, was a squat man, and his clerical collar pinched his throat. When he sermonized, his squeaky voice bounced off the low ceiling and filled the small sanctuary, and when his sermon reached a rhetorical flourish, his Adam's apple would often burst his white, clerical collar open. But the pastor was a kind man and generous host, and his wife also, who was even rounder than her husband. She always offered a slice of buttered bread or bowl of soup if Jönsson the homeless man was hungry.

But Jönsson stopped attending services after Easter even as he continued to sleep in a pew because he couldn't deal with the melancholy triggered by a song that had become the anthem of Swedish immigrants.

*Hälsa dem därhemma, hälsa far och mor,*

*Hälsa gröna hagen, hälsa lille bror,*

*Om jag hade vingar, flöge jag med dig,*

*Svala, flyg mot hemmet, hälsa ifrån mig.*


Greet my family at home;

Greet my father there, And my dear old
mother, My love with golden hair.

If I had wings of a swallow, I'd fly across the sea;

Go home, little swallow, Greet them all for me.


Had *Fader* and Alfrid plowed the rocky field? Had *Mor* cut up potato eyes for planting? Had Tomas and his sisters stretched string to mark garden rows straight and true? Had the ewes birthed any lambs and the cow a calf?

# CHAPTER TWELVE

J önsson's circumstances improved the day he mingled with the wealthy men of Duluth who came together to honor John D. Rockefeller, the richest man in America.

On a June evening in 1895, Pastor Bergquist arranged for Jönsson to work as a waiter for a major social event. Jönsson was outfitted in a white jacket and white gloves and told how to serve champagne and keep his mouth shut. The affair took place at a rich man's social enclave called the Kitchi Gammi Club. Lumber barons, steel men, shipbuilders, railroad men, lawyers, and bankers gathered that day—big shots and others who wanted to be--to toast the richest God dammit men in the whole country, or at least that's what the stewards and waiters whispered. Among those who arrived by steamer from Buffalo New York at the opposite end of the Great Lakes, John D. Rockefeller was the biggest name.

As Jönsson donned his white jacket and gloves, a fellow waiter whispered, "Have you heard the sad story of the 'Seven Iron Men?'"

The wait staff filled in the gossipy details as they readied themselves for the party. Jönsson learned that seven members of the enterprising and risk-taking Merritt family of Duluth had discovered rich iron ore on the Mesabi range--near the surface and easy to mine--just a couple of years earlier, but when they borrowed money to build a railroad to Duluth to transport their ore to port, the depression smashed their dreams.

"Rockefeller is here to pick up the pieces," the gossip concluded.

Jönsson wondered at dog-eat-dog American capitalism. In feudal Sweden, the lords and masters were born to their station—as were the peasants and servants beneath them—but America encouraged dreams, aspirations, and achievements only to see the hopes of some gobbled up by others. Capitalism could be ruthless. Only the wealthiest had capital to spend during the depression, and they cannibalized the entrepreneurs who did not. Rockefeller and his deep pockets came to Duluth to buy up the stocks of more adventurous men than himself, and the rich men of Duluth came to celebrate the victors and forget the losers.

Off in a corner by himself, one of the least of the great men in the room stood alone, and Jönsson offered him a glass of bubbly from his silver tray. The spectacled man was plain-looking with slicked-down dark hair parted in the middle. He looked to be about a dozen years older than Jönsson.

*"Kan jag få en öl, tack,"* the man offered a sarcastic smile, spoke Swedish, and said he preferred a beer, even as he accepted the champagne. He awkwardly grasped the glass with a hand missing the tip of his thumb.

Jönsson smiled at hearing his native tongue, and the men had forged a bond that came to fruition hours later when the man discovered that his own horseman, who had driven his buggy to the affair, was dead drunk, and he was fired on the spot.

Jönsson appeared out of the shadows.

"I'll drive ya, mister," Jönsson said with a slight bow.

The man stroked his chin and quickly nodded even as he boasted, "I could drive myself, you know, but that wouldn't appear proper to this crowd."

And then he blurted out a question. "Are you a cripple?"

Jönsson was flummoxed, but before he could answer, the man held up his right hand that was missing the end of his thumb. "So am I," he said.

For the first five minutes of the twenty-minute drive east along Superior Street, only the clop-clop of the horse was audible, but finally the man spoke.

"I'm not like those other men," he said. "My wealth is meager by the standards of the evening, and I have no ambition to build a fortune on the backs of the working class. I'm content running a newspaper that speaks the truth."

Another silent mile passed under the carriage wheels.

"Well, maybe I am like the others," the man mumbled under his breath, "for my newspaper was purchased with tainted funds."

Not another word was spoken until they arrived at the man's splendid house at the east end of Superior Street. A white picket fence glowed in the moonlight. The house stood tall with pitched gables, an expansive porch in front with ivy creeping up over latticed sides and winding around white pillars that defined the porch edges, and a smaller pillared porch at the back door, facing the carriage house. A widow's walk looked down the hill toward the great lake below. Stained glass transoms adorned many windows. A sugar maple and lilac bushes defined the front yard.

"There it is. Turn in here. Please put the horse in the carriage house, and you may sleep in the quarters above the stable. Tomorrow, I must ride the train north as that gilt-edged entourage journeys to the Vermilion Iron Range to inspect their holdings there, but my wife needs a driver for the day while I'm gone."

He climbed down from the buggy and headed toward the back porch, but then he turned and said, "They say you lost everything in the Hinckley fire. Is that true?"

Jönsson nodded without looking him in the eye. *Everything* was accurate enough, but the word seemed too small to speak the truth of it.

"My name is Teo, by the way, Teodor Swensson."

He extended his maimed hand, and Jönsson awkwardly shook the palm with a short stump for a thumb.

"And you are?"

"Jönsson, Ole Jönsson. Pleased to make yer acquaintance, sir."

A bright morning sun shimmered on the great lake, and a chilly breeze lifted from the deep water that never warmed. Jönsson donned an oilskin duster he found in the carriage house, but the newspaperman wore only a light jacket for the trip to the Union Depot and the train ride north. Swensson remained silent the entire journey; perhaps he had already confessed too much the evening before, and the unburdening had not dispelled his discomfort.

Swensson finally broke the silence as he stepped down from the carriage onto the platform in front of the Union Depot.

"I slept on it, and I decided. The job is yours. Stock your larder," he said, and he placed a twenty-dollar, double-eagle gold piece in Jönsson's hand.

After Swensson climbed aboard the passenger train along with the steel and railroad titans, Jönsson headed for a market and purchased a pound of coffee, two loaves of wheat bread, half a pound of butter, a dozen eggs, a pound of salt pork, a smoked pork sausage, five pounds of potatoes, a small truckle of cheddar cheese, filets of lake trout caught the day before, and a block of ice for his icebox. His grumbling belly had been mostly empty for a long while, and he splurged with his new-found good fortune.

He made a slight detour before returning to his new abode in the Swensson carriage house. Jönsson retrieved his kit from Emil Bergquist's church that included a six-shooter wrapped in a tattered coat. He spun the cylinder with one spent cartridge that had been fired at the crazy loon but five loaded with live cartridges.

Before leaving, he poked his head in the parsonage next door. "Is the good pastor to home?" he asked.

"No," replied Mrs. Bergquist. "He'll be back soon."

"Well, missus, I must t'ank him, and you, too, of course, for I have been offered a yob, and now I must take leave of yer yenerous hospitality."

"Why Mr. Jönsson, I am pleased," she said with eyes sparkling, "and Emil will be so happy to hear, as well. Do visit us."

"For the offering plate," Jönsson said, and he left a silver dollar with Mrs. Bergquist.

"My, my, your circumstances have improved," she said.

Indeed, they had, and Jönsson regretted that he couldn't thank the good man personally, who bore little resemblance to the puffed-up priest back in the home parish. He wondered whether all Lutheran clergy in America were so kind and whether all clergy in Sweden so harsh.

After saying his goodbye, he descended steep steps toward the street where Swensson's horse and buggy awaited him. The lumber camp swing-dingle lunch wagon, with a long and loose tongue, was built of rough-sawn lumber with a plank seat, but the fancy black buggy owned by Swensson featured a passenger compartment with leather seats and backs with a roof sweeping up from the back but not so far as to cover the driver. The passenger seats remained open to the front and the driver's seat which also had a back. The shorter tongue to the harness kept the driver close enough to reach forward and scratch the horse's hindquarters.

"*Skutt*, Jenny."

The mixed-breed mare trotted east along the Lake Superior shoreline as the late-departing steam locomotive pulling a dozen passenger cars chugged past the carriage; half the wealth of America rode in those cars.

After depositing his foodstuff upstairs—first clearing the icebox of rancid milk and moldy cheese and pouring out half a pail of stale beer--Jönsson unhitched the bay mare named Jenny from the buggy. She turned and took his measure, and when he scooped oats into a pail, she nuzzled his back and followed him to her stall. Fluttering breaths signaled that she appreciated the curry comb in the hand of her new master. He assumed that she was named for Jenny Lind, *The Swedish Nightingale,* the famous soprano of the generation just passed who made all Swedes proud, not just for her artistry but for her charity, using her substantial wealth earned in the concert halls of Europe and America to fund free schools back in Sweden.

As he pitched hay, Jönsson hummed the only Jenny Lind aria he knew. Although he never heard Lind himself, *Mor* often spoke of hearing the great singer when *Mor* was just a girl, and *Mor* sang what she remembered and hummed the rest with her own sweet but untrained voice, even if she couldn't reach the high notes. Jönsson couldn't tell you the name of the opera—something about a huntsman--but he recalled the hope tinged with melancholy expressed in the aria's first line:

*Even though a cloud may hide it,*

*The sun abides always in heaven's tabernacle.*

The splendid carriage house offered comfortable living quarters above and an ample stable below, and both he and the horse were fortunate. In addition to a bin for hay and another for straw, the stable housed the carriage, a small general-purpose wagon for hauling what the household required, a tack room—where he had discovered the duster hanging on a hook on the wall--and a wide stall for the mare. Just outside, a coal bin, wood bin, and a cast iron well pump with a long handle offered handy access to what he needed.

After feeding Jenny a dessert of oats and combing her down, he went upstairs. The stall needed mucking, but there was more to do before meeting Mrs. Swensson and transporting her as required.

His new abode was impressive. Two rooms and a pantry: a kitchen with a wood burning cook stove and a separate coal burner for heat in the bedroom. The apartment was arranged for a husband-and-wife team, which most employers preferred: a man for tending the stable and outside chores and a woman to cook and clean inside the house. Jönsson would soon learn that a married immigrant Italian woman rode the trolley each day from the west end of Duluth. Her husband worked on the ore docks, while she tended Swensson's house.

His first task was to clean up the mess left by his predecessor and to gather the man's belongings, in case he showed up to claim them. Empty whiskey bottles littered the kitchen, and dried beer spilled on the kitchen floor needed mopping. He boiled coffee and wolfed down slices of cheese and sausage and a chunk of bread. Seated at the kitchen table of the carriage house, he could glimpse the great lake through the trees, but that wouldn't last because another tall house was under construction across the street. He would soon learn that as lumber, steel, and shipbuilding money poured into Duluth, much of it would be spent constructing great houses on the east end of Superior Street and a few city blocks in each direction.

It was time to meet the mistress.

Elmira Swensson appeared on the back porch wearing a blue taffeta dress that reached her ankles. Her broad-brimmed straw hat with a chiffon ribbon tilted forward over her coifed blonde hair. She appeared much younger than her husband, and she proved to be much chattier.

"Please drive to the West End Social Club for the NAWSA meeting."

Jönsson refused the bait and didn't ask, but Mrs. Swensson quickly added,

"NAWSA. You know, the National American Women's Suffrage Association."

Jönsson didn't have a clue what she was talking about, but he did wonder at an "East Ender" daring to mingle with the women from the poorer neighborhoods of the west end of the city.

During the cross-town journey, Jönsson listened and learned. Elmira Swensson carried on a breathless monologue during the entire trip.

"My husband was born on the west side, you know."

Jönsson didn't know that, but he knew that west Duluth was home to the working poor, the immigrants and unskilled laborers who toiled long hours at the docks and the rail yards, and the women who rode the trolleys to the East End to work as domestics.

"Teo and his mother lived in a one room apartment in the tenements. He lost his thumb as a switchman in the railroad yard, ducking under moving cars to couple and uncouple them."

Mrs. Swensson hesitated briefly awaiting Jönsson's re-action. When he remained silent, she continued.

"Teodor Swensson Sr. was a scoundrel who was rarely around, running off for the false allure of gold during the Lake Vermilion gold rush before entering into a slippery arrange-ment to homestead land in name-only on behalf of the money men who opened the Vermilion Iron Range in the 1880s."

Jönsson's inscrutable disinterest remained fixed on his face, but he had wondered how it was that the wealthy ac-quired forest land for their lumber camps or mineral rights for their mines or rights of way for their railroads. That's where the proxy poor came in.

"Two Harbors. Have you heard of the town of Two Har-bors?"

Much as he didn't want to become involved in a discussion, Jönsson nodded. It would be impertinent not to. He knew that the money train which carried Teo Swensson and the aristoc-racy of America would travel twenty-odd miles up the shore-line to Two Harbors before turning inland toward the ore mines of the Vermilion Range.

"When the town of Two Harbors grew up around the bay where the steamships would dock and load the ore from the Vermilion Range, Teo's father ran a shanty-town 'business,'" Mrs. Swenson wrinkled her nose and spit out the word. "A 'business' that catered to the workmen who built the ore docks. There were painted women involved, if you know what I mean." She spoke with an affected air of disgust.

For the first time, Mrs. Swensson remained silent for a few minutes, allowing her revelations to sink in for full effect. Then she continued,

"When Teo's father was caught cheating in a poker game, he was shot dead in 1884, and that was the last poor Teo heard of him until a lawyer came knocking on his mother's door a few years later. It turns out that his untimely death meant that he never transferred ownership of the land to the money men as he had secretly agreed to do, and his homestead claim now boasted the richest iron ore mine on the Vermilion Range."

She searched Jönsson's face looking for a sign that he was impressed. He wasn't.

"Two hundred thousand dollars. Can you believe it? Teo accepted only two hundred thousand dollars to sell that land. Why, we would be rich as Rockefeller if he hadn't felt guilty about his father. Of course, that was before I knew him, and we courted after he bought the newspaper and moved to the East End with his mother, but wealth was too rich for her blood, and she soon passed away. I come from a good family; you know."

If she expected Jönsson to feel sorry at the bad deal Teo had made, his face gave no hint that her words resonated with him at all—because they had not. She spoke of things he didn't understand or care about. For the hollow man with dark memories, empathy for the trivial misfortunes of the rich was beyond unlikely.

When they arrived at the West End Social Club, other carriages milled about but many women stepped off trolley cars, wearing homespun dresses. Mrs. Swensson went straight toward a hatless, black-haired, nut-brown woman in a plain brown dress and kissed her on the cheek before they headed off, arm-in-arm. Just before they entered the shadow of the doorway, the dark woman tossed her head back, smoothed her free-flowing hair with her hand, and glanced at Jönsson.

# CHAPTER THIRTEEN

Jönsson punched the drunk in the gut and threw his belongings in the street, chasing the sonofabitch out the gate.

"Don't come roun' this way agin, unless ya want what fer." Jönsson warned, shaking a fist.

The hunched-over drunk rubbed his belly and eyed the imposing figure. Jönsson wasn't a fighter but standing over six feet with broad shoulders and mitts like fry pans, he looked the part. The former chauffeur had arrived with a snoot full to reclaim his possessions, if not his position, and refused to leave until he could speak his mind to his former employer.

"Betcha he'd like to know who the missus shakes her ass fer."

That was enough, and Jönsson gave him the bum's rush. The stringy drunk looked mean as a weasel, but there was no bite to him, and he gathered his things and turned tail. Jönsson didn't mention the skirmish to Mr. Swensson.

Jönsson quickly settled into his new life. He drove Mr. Swensson to his newspaper office downtown first thing each morning and picked him up in the evening. Some days, there would be news to track down, and Jönsson appreciated being near the action. When he wasn't out sleuthing a scoop with his editor employer, he ran errands for Mrs. Swensson and kept the lawn trimmed and the flowers in fine shape. He thought about suggesting a vegetable garden next summer, which he would be happy to tend. Jenny the mare likely received better care than she had seen in some time; Jönsson mucked her stall regularly, and she enjoyed fresh straw daily.

Jönsson had to learn to cook for himself, and he ate plenty of bread, cheese, sausage, and smoked lake trout. He scrambled eggs with fried onions and enjoyed oat porridge with fresh cream and sugar. He learned to fry pancakes that he slathered in butter and maple syrup. He passed the Fitger's brewery coming and going along Superior Street, so he usually enjoyed a bottle of beer with his supper, alone at his table on the second floor of the carriage house.

At first, the inquisitive newspaper man questioned Jönsson about his past life, but he caught on quickly that Jönsson had no interest in talking of such things, and they came to an accommodation. Swensson would do the talking, and Jönsson would do the listening, but it was an easy and comfortable relationship unlike the pinched and proper master-servant duality of Sweden.

Following an August blue moon near the first anniversary of the Hinckley holocaust, Swensson invited his carriage driver on a journey.

"My newspaper will do a story," Swensson explained, "a personal story about one of the emerging leaders of the city who hasn't forgotten his origins or the little people who helped him on his way. We shall spend a day with Frank Hibbing."

With the horse and buggy safely checked into in a stable, Swensson and Jönsson met the story's subject at the Union Depot; the man in the high-top derby hat led the way past a snorting steam locomotive and climbed into an ornate passenger car, followed by Teo Swensson and Jönsson bringing up the rear.

"Good morning, Frank," said the black-skinned porter.

"Good morning, Charles," Hibbing replied. "Please bring us coffee."

Soon, the Duluth, Missabi, and Iron Range Railway train

chugged up the incline to the west before reaching the ridge overlooking the lake and the city. Then, it was straight north along the rails that led to Mountain Iron, seventy rollicking miles through pines and rocky ledges and lakes as blue as sky.

Jönsson was in the company of a pair of earnest men; the newspaper man earnestly sought the truth, which he earnestly believed would reveal humankind's innate benevolence. The entrepreneur earnestly pursued the common good; what was good for his associates and his employees was good for him. And the earnest men were complementary; Swensson earnestly listened while Hibbing earnestly carried the conversation. The newspaper man peered over his wire-rimmed spectacles as he listened and pushed them back on his nose when he scribbled his notes. Jönsson felt odd sitting with Swensson and Hibbing, earnest men of accomplishment, but their affable manner eased his discomfort.

"Rockefeller stole this railway," Hibbing said, rolling his eyes. "Have you heard how he bought out the Merritt boys when the depression forced them to abandon their dreams?"

Hibbing and Swensson shared similar haircuts--slicked down and parted in the middle, neatly trimmed at the edges—but the clean-shaven face of Swensson the introvert contrasted sharply with the immense, bushy, handle-bar moustache of Hibbing the extrovert. There was more hair under his nose than on the top of his head.

Each of the three men wore suit jackets over white shirts with stiff, high collars. Jönsson and Swensson each wore wide ties with four-in-hand knots, but Hibbing sported a bow tie. Hibbing placed his derby hat on the seat next to him; Swensson did the same with his flat-topped boater-style straw hat with a red, white, and blue band; but Jönsson's floppy newsboy hat with a short bill in front remained atop his head.

Jönsson couldn't help himself, and a thin smile betrayed

the somber expression that was normally frozen on his face. Although he was deliberately disinterested in affairs of business, riding in a Rockefeller-owned railway car, sipping Rockefeller's coffee from Rockefeller's china cup, sitting on Rockefeller's plush leather seats, and smelling the smoke of Rockefeller's coal burning in Rockefeller's locomotive pleased him.

As they neared journey's end, the train passed a yawning hole that disappeared into the earth.

"That's the first iron mine on the Mesabi," Hibbing said. "Rockefeller stole that from the Merritt brothers, too."

After reaching the end of the line, their host arranged for a two-horse team and a buckboard with a pair of plank seats for the last leg of their journey, a twenty-mile jaunt to the west. Jönsson sat alone on the front bench with the reins in his hands, and his passengers sat on the second pine bench. With the mid-morning sun at their backs, they set out on a bumpy ride down a roadway, if it could be called that, twisting through the rocks, following a fresh slash through the thick forest.

"I built this road," Hibbing said, and added with a chuckle, "well, me and a crew of thirty."

Hibbing dominated the conversation coming from the rear seat, but the wind whispering through pine boughs distracted Jönsson, and the pine-scent laden breeze encouraged deep breaths. It was good to be outside the city for the first time in months. Deer flashed their white tails before bounding away while eagles circled overhead.

The road was well-traveled with wagons and riders on horseback headed east.

"Hello, Frank," many called out.

"Hello, John" or "Hello, Will" or any of a dozen names that Hibbing tied to faces. He greeted each one with the same refrain, "It's a great day for the race!"

Jönsson mostly sat mute, intent on steering the horses through the crags and stumps, but Swensson finally asked, "What race?"

"Why, the human race, of course." Hibbing sucked in a deep breath of the fresh forest air and said it again. "It's a great day for the race."

Hibbing told his story with pride but without boasting.

"I'm just a German immigrant who got some lucky breaks. When I come to America, I worked in a Wisconsin shingle factory, but I weren't much good at it. When I damn near cut my hand off, I tried to study the law, but I couldn't master the damn English language."

His bushy handle-bar moustache twitched with a self-effacing smile.

"I hired on as a 'timber cruiser,' tromping the wilderness seeking stands of white pine for others to harvest. Soon you'll see it, the spot where my fortunes changed. I stood on a rocky ledge surrounded by pine forest beyond what the eye could see, and I said, 'I believe there is iron ore under me, my bones feel rusty and chilly.'"

Hibbing slapped his knee and expected Swensson to laugh. Swensson obliged half-heartedly, but he was not a man disposed to humor.

"I burn my furnace low because I like to remember that feeling of being cold."

Swensson again forced a laugh.

When the bustling town of spanking new buildings came into sight, the sun burned high in the western sky. Jönsson again gulped a deep breath of the northern air, now mixed with the fumes from many chimneys. Civilization had come to the north country.

"Hurry along," Hibbing said to Jönsson, "Mr. Swensson and I have people to see. There's the livery where you can tend to the horses, and there's the hotel. Get us three rooms; tell Alonzo at the front desk that they're for Frank. We'll meet you there in a couple of hours."

Jönsson took his time currying the horses and wondering at this "Frank" that everyone seemed to know and like. He was an amiable fellow, that was easy to see. Jönsson had already figured out that he was the town founder and wealthy because of it, but the respect accorded Frank Hibbing seemed genuine and not borne of envy like the fawning over John D. Rockefeller.

Jönsson arranged for three rooms at the hotel, but it didn't seem right to go upstairs until the others arrived, so Jönsson waited in the lobby. It was nearly dark when Frank burst in with Teo in tow and bellowed toward the hotel's dining room, "Burn us three venison steaks and make sure the beer is iced!"

The next day, Swensson and Jönsson returned to Duluth alone; Hibbing had more business to attend to in his town, and Teo Swensson the newspaperman had his story. During the return journey, Swensson's straw hat remained atop his head.

"I'm no socialist," Swensson said, rolling his fingers on the armrest of the plush seat of the Pullman railway car, as if such action propelled his thoughts. "The entrepreneurial spirit needs encouragement, which the profit motive provides."

When Jönsson did not respond, Swensson continued his musing.

"But what of the spirit of benevolence? How are the Frank Hibbings of the world to be encouraged? How shall the toil of the workers be properly rewarded? Do you know how little the workers on the coal docks earn in a day? On the dangerous ore docks where injuries occur frequently? On the wheat trains that bring the fruits of farm labor to the ships that carry food to a nation?"

He hesitated as he turned to face Jönsson, waiting for an answer. When it didn't come, he answered his own question.

"A dollar and seventy-five cents a day," he said with a sigh. "Such a paltry sum barely provides a proper meal for a family. Give us this day our daily bread, Lord."

Jönsson listened silently. He was well-paid at $20 a week plus lodging.

The speed of the train lessened as they rounded a curve and began to climb over a ridge. Only the drumming of Swensson's fingers split the silence. After the locomotive reached the crest, the train accelerated on the downslope, and Swensson again gave voice to his stream of thought.

"Perhaps the socialists have it right. Perhaps collective rather than private or corporate ownership of the means of production would improve the lot of the workingman. And woman. You know that women will get the vote one day, and that will be better for them and the rest of us, too."

More drumming. Clouds churned in the western sky.

Swensson removed his glasses and leaned into Jönsson. "What do you think, Ole?"

Jönsson worried whether Jenny back in the Union Depot stable received a proper ration of hay, whether the axle on the carriage needed grease, whether he had brought his slicker in case of rain. Bigger questions than these led the mind into dangerous territory. *What if he had remained in Sweden? What if he had understood the commands of the Mick saloonkeeper? What if the Hinckley summer of '94 had been cool and rainy rather than hot and dry?*

"I don't know, Mr. Swensson," Jönsson replied.

"Please, call me Teo."

Jönsson wasn't sure whether his boss truly meant that gesture of equality. Perhaps it was merely Swensson's lack of self-esteem. Teo was an earnest man. Too earnest. He tried too hard to do right, to be good. To be himself wasn't enough. He must be better. Fate smiled on him, but he was from the west end, and he feared he deserved a frown. He was not a true capitalist like the other men at Kitchi Gammi club. They didn't fret over their good fortune. They claimed it as matter of worth, just desserts, entitled grandeur. Teo's problem was that he was a good man, and he didn't know it.

"I don't know, Teo," Jönsson said. "Looks like rain."

# CHAPTER FOURTEEN: 1895-1896

E lmira Swensson was short; her friend was tall. Mrs. Swensson spent an hour daily putting up her blonde hair just so, her ever-changing wardrobe cost plenty, and her mouth spilled most everything that flowed between her ears, but the coal-black hair of Miss Natalia "Natty" Einstein draped loosely over her shoulders and down the back of her bland, homespun dresses. Mrs. Swensson's jabbering carried the conversation from the back of the buggy as Jönsson transported the women here or there. Miss Einstein spoke sparingly, but when she did, Jönsson sensed depth, passion, and an agile intellect, and her friendship with his employer's wife made little sense.

There was also the matter of economic status. The stylish Swensson house in the East End compared to Einstein's ram-shackle dwelling, a shanty really--built on the marshes of Rice Point, a sandbar peninsula on Duluth's west end that jutted into Duluth's inner harbor--only added to the incongruity. Rice Point, or Rice's Point as the old timers knew it--named for the man who once ran a ferry across the harbor and across state lines to Superior, Wisconsin--was lined with wharfs along water's edge and tenement houses and tar paper shacks on the interior.

Jönsson often travelled alone to gather Miss Einstein from her dwelling and deliver her to the Swensson home where she would spend the evening in the company of both Mr. and Mrs. Swensson before Jönsson returned her to the west end. The labor-friendly stories that appeared in Swensson's newspaper following her visits suggested Teo's interest in the mysterious woman. Her connections to the west end working class apparently provided inspiration for Swensson's newspaper articles. *WILDCAT STRIKE BY STREET WORKERS OVER UNFAIR WAGES. EXUBERANT CROWD GREETS EUGENE DEBS. UNSAFE CONDITIONS ON ORE DOCKS THREATEN WORKERS. NORTHERN PACIFIC 'DETECTIVES' ROUGH UP STRIKING RAILWAY WORKERS.*

Jönsson couldn't help but notice Duluth's labor unrest in the face of burgeoning and unfettered capitalism in shipping, rails, lumber, and a steel-hungry nation that increasingly looked to Duluth to feed its insatiable appetite. Jönsson continued his habit of poring through newspapers, especially because Teo always supplied "fresh off the press" copies of his own publication.

James J. "Slippery" Hill and his "lick-spittel hirelings," "Judas Iscariot" Rockefeller and his "band of gilt-edged highwaymen," and the "monster of depravity," railroad man George M. Pullman, made frequent appearances in Swensson's newspaper. Together with other unnamed "monopolists, gold-bugs, and slimy capitalistic robbers," the industry barons contributed copious sums of capital to the economy and demanded cheap labor in return. Women schoolteachers earned half the meager $1.75 a day that municipal workers, dock hands, and trolley drivers earned. Miners included boys who had not yet grown whiskers on their chins. Injuries to dock workers kept hospitals busy and meant the likely loss of a job. Trade unions struggled to organize in the face of fierce capitalist resistance and often fought amongst themselves with crosscurrents of socialism, temperance, feminism, and suffrage. Cultural differences among the immigrant or first-generation labor force abetted the capitalist's efforts to prevent the workers from organizing and presenting a united front.

Whether it was the influence of his newspaperman boss and his articles, his own experiences of American capitalism, or his own natural inclination, Jönsson agreed with the labor-friendly thrust of the newspaper articles—not that he would ever say anything or do anything about it.

Late in the depression year of 1895, the frequency of Einstein's visits increased dramatically, and Jönsson guessed it had to do with the newly-formed retrenchment committee established by Duluth's city council to slash the salaries of municipal workers—schoolteachers, firemen, policemen, and day laborers who maintained the streets--to lower taxes.

On one of the few times Miss Einstein spoke from the back of the buggy, she spit out "austerity" like it was a swear word. "Why must we respond to economic hard times by piling the burden on the workingman and woman?" she asked, but Jönsson didn't know.

The upcoming year of 1896 would prove to be a pivotal point for labor in Duluth spurred by the threat of reduced wages, and Jönsson increasingly believed that Natty Einstein was a power behind the scenes. When her portfolio of papers spilled in the buggy one day, he realized she was the actual author of the labor-friendly stories that appeared in Swensson's newspaper. With greater respect for her intellect and influence came greater awe and distance. When he carted her around, she sat silent as the sphinx in the back of the buggy; of course, he never dared speak to her.

After a stretch of balmy days that suggested the winter of '96 would soon end, a sudden March snowstorm was the occasion for Jönsson's first real conversation with Natalia Einstein. Caught in whipping winds and blinding snowfall when he exited the sheltered streets of downtown Duluth for the exposed marshes of Rice Point, Jönsson delivered her to her shanty after a cross-town journey that took hours. She sat in the covered back of the buggy, but Jönsson drove from the exposed front seat. Instead of allowing the shivering and wet driver to return to the Swensson carriage house at the far end of east Superior Street, she invited him inside.

"Put your horse up in that empty shed," she said, pointing. "And come inside. You'll freeze to death if you try to return tonight."

"I'm sure we can manage, and Mr. Swensson will need me first thing in the morning."

"Don't be a fool," she said, and he felt stupid.

The cozy interior belied the sorry outside appearance; the dimly lit single room was neat and clean but Spartan. Piles of books and magazines overflowed every available shelf and stand. Miss Einstein emptied the last of the coal pail into her stove and placed a tea pot on the flat top.

"Get out of those wet clothes," she said. "Wrap yourself in this blanket."

Jönsson couldn't place her accent, foreign to be sure, but not northern European. He surveyed the single room without any private areas.

"I'm good," he said and backed up against the stove.

"You'll die of pneumonia," she said, and she removed his fur coat and began to unbutton his shirt.

"I'll do it," he said, and soon he stood near the stove in his union suit, sipping hot tea. If he felt the fool in her presence before, now he seemed to be no more than the village idiot.

After she spread his wet clothes over the back of her single chair and across her small table, first clearing away her inks and papers, she sat down on the edge of her bed, the only remaining seat in the room. If she had previously avoided eye contact, now she fixed her gaze, and her brown oval-eyes held his own. Her hands brushed across the sides of her face to her hair, which she smoothed and tossed behind her head. Her fingers moved to the buttons at the front of her dress. Without taking her eyes off him, she slowly removed her dress and then her undergarments.

He had not been intimate with any woman other than Ayasha, and many months had passed since then. The whores of St. Clair Street were of no interest to him. Nor had he ever thought of the mysterious Natty Einstein in that way, but as she sat naked in front of him, his virile instincts swelled. Along with her garments, she removed the aura of unapproachability, of aloofness, of intellectualism, of being all about her business. In revealing herself, *she revealed herself*, and he was captivated. His awe of the influential labor-sympathizer was instantly replaced by his desire for the *woman* who invited him in.

As the oil lamp flickered and flared, she moved to him. Long fingers threaded his hair and rubbed his day-old whiskers; when she slipped his union suit from his shoulders, she kissed his chest.

As the storm raged through the night, Jönsson learned the artistry of lovemaking under the tutelage of a master teacher. When the morning sun spilled through the hut's only window, he awoke. His breath clouded in the frigid air. They had fallen asleep just an hour or two earlier. He caught his foot in the blanket and stumbled as he moved toward his clothing, and her gentle laugh followed him.

"You may fill the pail from the coal bin around the back."

When he returned after checking on Jenny who spent the night safely if not comfortably in a dilapidated shed, she was dressed. She started a fire and offered to share half a biscuit.

"I must leave, the Swenssons will worry, or at least wonder, at my fate in the storm."

As he stood at the door in the bright sunlight but biting wind, she kissed him, then held a finger to his lips. Jönsson added a secret to his collection of memories, but this one would not be so nightmare-inducing as others.

Or so he thought.

# CHAPTER FIFTEEN

"Y ou shall not press down upon the brow of labor this crown of thorns; you shall not crucify mankind upon a cross of gold."

When the newspapers of Duluth published news of the July 1896 surprise selection of William Jennings Bryan to be the Democratic nominee for President, the first reaction of many in Duluth was, "Who?" but when they read his "cross of gold" speech, he was instantly proclaimed to be the savior of Duluth's working class.

Swensson rubbed his spectacles with his hanky then replaced them on his nose.

"Listen to this," he said from the back of the buggy, and he read excerpts of the speech printed in his own newspaper.

"'The miners who go down a thousand feet into the earth, or climb two thousand feet upon the cliffs, and bring forth from their hiding places the precious metals to be poured into the channels of trade are as much businessmen as the few financial magnates who, in a back room, corner the money of the world.'"

"By God, that's good stuff," Swensson said, and he continued reading. "'Upon which side will the Democratic Party fight; upon the side of the idle holders of idle capital or upon the side of the struggling masses?'"

Jönsson leaned back and cocked his head to listen, even as he steered the carriage down the street. Swensson continued to read aloud:

"'There are two ideas of government. There are those who believe that, if you will only legislate to make the well-to-do prosperous, their prosperity will leak through on those below. The Democratic idea, however, has been that if you legislate to make the masses prosperous, their prosperity will find its way up through every class which rests upon them.'"

Just then a clanging trolley passed by and Jönsson turned all the way around and asked, "Teo, could you read that last part again?"

Jönsson worked most evenings. It seemed Teo Swensson seldom spent time at home with his wife, and he often summoned his carriage driver to take him to this meeting or that; on such evenings, Jönsson would wolf down his supper, and then they were off. On other evenings, Teo stayed home, and Jönsson transported Elmira here or there.

When he did have time to himself, Jönsson wandered the streets of the east end to check on the flurry of construction activity as the next rich man sought to build a mansion grander than the rest. His path led to a favorite vantage point under a tall red pine on a knoll that overlooked the great lake at the bottom of the hill, and here he would await the dusk while whittling with his pocketknife.

When purple smears of sunset surrendered to the moon and the stars, he would toss the wood chunk and return to his carriage house, but one day he started to trim a pine knot that reminded him of a horse, and he tucked his project into his pocket when he returned home. For more than a week, Jönsson and his pen knife worked to tame a wild horse into a domesticated Dala pony. Then came two coats of red paint, and finally the meticulous task of drawing a white mane, bridle, and saddle. When he finished, he set the pony on the table where it would catch the glint of the sun sparkling on the sea below.

In the early summer of '96, Jönsson attended his first meeting at the Knights of Labor Hall. Perhaps it was curiosity at the excitement spreading from immigrant worker to immigrant worker, from Swede to Norwegian to Finn and even to the Mick and Wop and Bohunk. Perhaps it was the spark of hope that had begun to glow inside. Justice would come to those willing to stand and fight. Or perhaps it was because he expected Natty Einstein to be there.

She attracted the attention of the press. *SUFFRAGIST NATTY EINSTEIN SAYS WOMEN DESERVE THE VOTE. RADICAL FEMINIST NATTY EINSTEIN DEMANDS EQUAL PAY FOR WOMEN. UKRAINIAN NATALIA EINSTEIN SPEAKS TO IMMIGRANT GARMENT WORKERS.*

The capitalist newspapers contained sharper headlines: *IS NATTY EINSTEIN A COMMUNIST? JEWISH SOCIALIST NATALIA EINSTEIN ORGANIZES RESTAURANT WORKERS.*

Hmm. A Jew? He was making love to a Jew? He had never seen a Jew, or had he? He had heard Jews were different. Hook noses. Jesus killers. Shylocks. Jews were barely human—it was said--but he had mingled with her flesh and tasted her taste. He could attest—in spades—that she was not a lesser being.

On a sweltering July night, Natty slept in Jönsson's bed on the second floor of the carriage house as Jenny nickered in her stall below. After he dropped Teo and Elmira Swensson at the Union Depot for a train trip to Minneapolis, Jönsson headed to Rice Point to pick up Natty for a planned tryst in the carriage house. Natty continued to insist on secrecy for their encounters.

The following morning, Jönsson fixed breakfast dressed in trousers only. Natty sat at the table wearing his shirt.

"Did you make this?" she asked as she turned the Dala pony in her fingers.

Jonas glanced over his shoulder as he forked curled strips

of sizzling salt pork from the fry pan.

"Yah, dat crude trinket. I should yust t'row it avay."

"Don't you dare," she said. "It's darling."

"Do you t'ink so?" he said, as he set a plate of eggs and bacon next to her mug of coffee. It hadn't occurred to him that a Jewess might not eat pork, but she picked up a strip with her fingers and bit off the end.

"Den, it's yers. Ve call 'em 'Dala ponies.'"

She reached up and placed a hand behind his neck, pulling him in close for a kiss.

"I will treasure my little Swedish horse from my Swede," she promised.

After that, Jönsson didn't see much of Natty through August because of a lack of opportunity. On the first Saturday of September, he went to the labor temple, hoping to see the woman who was the movement's darling--and his as well--and he was not disappointed. He watched from the rear, glad of his height that allowed him to see over the raucous crowd.

"Who can stop a thousand? Who can stop two thousand? Three or even four? That's how many oppressed workers in Duluth have thrown off their shackles to say, 'Enough!' Almost four thousand workers have joined the union movement this year alone: men and women, those born here and those born across the sea, dock workers and domestics. Who can stand in the way of justice when thousands join in unity and demand it? Not the monopolist, not the gold-bug, not the capitalist robber!"

She could tell it. God dammit, she could tell it. She was a revivalist preacher, and many answered her altar call by stepping forward to sign up for the cause. The crowd pressed around her, and Jönsson couldn't get close. Once, he thought she spied him, but she quickly turned away to continue hearing the testimonies of the converts and bestowing her blessing, but then she disappeared before the crowd dispersed. He was hurt, but he rationalized that she had important work to do and people to see with the election just around the corner, and he ignored his jealousy toward the campaign workers who claimed her time.

The next opportunity to see Natty came the following Monday at the Labor Day parade. After the brutal railway strikes of 1894 when the cause of labor had been crushed, President Cleveland offered up a peace offering to the labor movement by creating a national holiday to celebrate labor on the first Monday of September. He refused the suggestion that it be on May Day--May 1--the international day of the worker. Much too socialist.

Jönsson expected she would be a marcher or float-rider, and he found himself a spot with a good vantage. A band marched by, then this union followed by that union, then another band and more unions with a few floats mixed in. The parade stretched two and a half miles, according to the reports. Four bands. Thirty-seven different unions. A hundred floats. But no Natty Einstein. Hours after he departed the Swensson house, he returned, and there she was. Natty Einstein and Elmira Swensson stepped down from the front porch as he arrived.

"Oh, Jönsson," Mrs. Swensson said. "Did you watch the parade? We're just leaving for dinner. Don't worry, we'll take the trolley. It's Labor Day, enjoy your day off!"

Natty fussed with her handbag and didn't make eye contact until they were about to disappear down the sidewalk when she stole a furtive glance back.

After Jönsson heard Swensson read from the "cross of gold" speech of Democratic candidate William Jennings Bryan, Jönsson followed the upcoming election with keen interest. Late in the day on a balmy September afternoon, he read yesterday's newspaper while he waited to transport Swensson home; he didn't see the publisher bound down the steps from his office, and he was startled when Swensson leaped into the buggy, causing it to shake.

"Look at this!" Teo said, holding up the front page of the paper just off the press.

*PRESIDENTIAL HOPEFUL BRYAN TO CAMPAIGN IN DULUTH!*

Teo jabbered incessantly all the way home, and even Jönsson managed a few comments. He was as excited as the editor of the labor-friendly newspaper, and he couldn't wait to share the excitement with Natty, but he wasn't able to see her until mid-October when Bryan made his appearances in Duluth.

Because of the expected crush of exuberant supporters, two speeches were scheduled—in addition to brief comments at the Union Depot and a private reception at the home of Republican Congressman Charles Towne, who had flipped and now ran for reelection as a Democrat. First, Bryan spoke to twenty-five thousand men, including Jönsson, at the streetcar barn in the West End, but Jönsson had to leave early to pick up Elmira Swensson for Bryan's second appearance before women at the Lyceum Theater downtown.

Jönsson waited outside with other livery men while Bryan spoke to the boisterous assembly of women. When it was over, Mrs. Swensson had Natty in tow.

"I'll find my own way home, Jönsson," Mrs. Swensson said, "but Natty is one of the honored few to be invited to a private reception for Mr. Bryan at the home of Congressman Towne. Aren't you impressed? She should have her own carriage for such an auspicious event."

Elmira kissed Natty on the cheek and waved as Jönsson moved the carriage into the street traffic. Never a gabber, Jönsson nevertheless was the first to speak, but mindless small talk was all he could manage.

"Was it a good speech?"

"Have you been busy with campaigning?"

"Hear the click of the hooves on the street? I just reshod Jenny."

Natty mostly nodded, or shrugged, or offered one-word answers, and soon they arrived at the party. Jönsson helped her down, and she said, "Thank you," but nothing more. He waited outside, of course, listening anxiously to the exuberant sounds of partying seeping from inside. With each passing minute, his envy of the insiders swelled.

Finally, she appeared on the porch in the company of two men, and his jealousy flared.

In contrast to her stand-offish demeanor on the ride to the party, Natty was quite chatty during the ride to her shanty. "The candidate is quite the charmer," she said, "and more than ever I'm convinced that he'll be a great president."

Jönsson was even jealous of old man Bryan.

"Oh, I'm a little giddy,' Natty said. "Even though Mr. Bryan supports temperance, a few flasks appeared in the anterooms."

Before long, they reached her shanty. He stepped down to assist her from the back of the carriage and waited as she unlocked her door.

"Aren't you coming in?" she said.

Jönsson the neophyte electioneered in his own small way. He carried placards in the buggy and placed them where he could. "Bryan for President." "Truelson for Mayor." "Towne for Congress." Following Natty's encouragement, he took out "first papers" which would allow him to vote in the fall election. Along with many immigrants, Jönsson waited in line to speak with the city clerk.

"Do you have a dollar? It costs a dollar to get your 'first papers.'"

Jönsson plunked a silver dollar down on the desk. The dollar was his own, but Natty supplied many of the immigrants with the necessary coin.

"Where were you born?"

"*Sverige.*"

"Don't you mean Sweden? If you're going to be a citizen, you need to learn the language." The clerk seemed offended by the entire process.

"Yah, Sweden."

"When did you come to this country?"

"18 and 93."

He lied. He had arrived in 1891, but if he arrived in 1893, he wasn't here when a certain saloonkeeper was murdered in 1892.

"Where did you land?"

"New York City."

The clerk spoke offhandedly without looking up. "Ellis Island opened in 1893. You must have been among the first arrivals."

"Yah."

God dammit! He was caught in his lie. He landed on the south tip of Manhattan before Ellis Island became the immigration center. What if they question him further? What if they check the records? Fortunately, the disinterested clerk just wanted to move the process along.

"Raise your right hand, please. Do you swear that it is your *bona fide* intention to become a good American citizen?"

"Yah."

The clerk slid his "first papers" to him with a smile and a whisper.

"I don't mind helping good white immigrants like you," she said under her breath with a quick glance around, "but I have a problem with the dark-skinned Jews and Catholics from eastern and southern Europe. Poor stock, I say, who dilute true American bloodlines."

"Thank you," Jönsson said, trying his best to smooth his rough accent. After a quick glance at the document, he carefully folded it and put in his shirt pocket with a pat for assurance. When he returned to the carriage house, he smoothed it out and admired it before tucking it safely into a drawer.

Optimism swelled as election day approached. There was talk, and the immigrant workers believed it, that times were changing, that industrialism in America would mature into a classless utopia, that this would be the day when the dream of America came true. A bright line existed between the parties and the candidates. Democratic President Cleveland had not been the workingman's hero, but William Jennings Bryan would change all that. For the first time, a major party was on the side of labor. True enough, the Republican nominee, William McKinley, had moved away from labor and embraced the capitalists, but the watershed realignment of 1896 would inaugurate the day of the worker. Born a generation earlier and spurred on by the deep depression that began in 1893, the maturing labor movement in Duluth, as a microcosm of America, was ready to take its place at the forefront of industrial American society.

Democracy was a grand idea. Americans picked their own leaders through voting booths and ballot boxes. No king by dint of birth, but a president elected by the people. No royal appointments of sheriffs and bishops. One vote for the horse-and-buggy driver and one for Rockefeller.

On election eve, Natty asked Jönsson to serve as runner to gather voting results from the precincts and deliver them to Democratic party headquarters. The jubilant party workers cheered with each new tally Natty posted on a blackboard, and Jönsson beamed at his small part in the process. He appreciated the back slaps when he delivered positive news, as if he was more than mere messenger. Except for the East End precincts, Bryan was sweeping Duluth. A German immigrant, Henry Truelson, would be elected mayor and put a stop to the retrenchment in the wages of municipal workers. Well, it wasn't all good news as Democratic convert, Congressman Towne, was defeated.

Natty, Jönsson, and a few others remained to clean up after most had departed the festivities when the telegraph machines clicked out the dispiriting news. Bryan had gone down to defeat, and McKinley and his anti-labor crowd would soon be in the White House. Disappointment to be sure, but disbelief was the stronger sentiment. With such a clear-cut choice between the people and the monied interests, how could the voters of America be so wrong? Maybe democracy wasn't such a grand idea after all.

There was no lovemaking that night. Natty Einstein's sobs at midnight became defiant rage by sunrise. Jönsson was merely disillusioned.

# CHAPTER SIXTEEN: 1897

In the summer of 1897, Swensson and Jönsson returned to the city that now bore Frank Hibbing's name. Frank wanted to show off the water plant and electrical plant he had built, at his own expense, for the benefit of the city. By the time of their return visit, the rugged trail west from Mountain Iron to Hibbing had been replaced by a spur of the railroad.

Soon after departing Duluth, Hibbing's bouncy demeanor changed, quiet replaced his jabber, and the color drained from his face.

"A spot of indigestion," Frank said.

When they finally reached the terminal in Mountain Iron, Hibbing walked gingerly across the platform to a bench to await the arrival of the train that circled the twenty-mile loop between Mountain Iron and Hibbing several times each day.

"Sure is God dammit hot," Frank said, fanning himself with his felt hat. Truth be told, the late July day was overcast and cool.

When the doors opened to the passenger car, Hibbing staggered briefly as he stepped onboard, but he pushed Swensson's helping hand away.

"God dammit, I ain't a feeble old man."

Hibbing collapsed into the Pullman leather seat, panting heavily as sweat poured down his pasty-white cheeks. After an interminable wait, the train lurched forward, and Hibbing winced and grabbed at his belly. He grit his teeth, and his glassy eyes showed fear.

"Tell the engineer to pour on the coal, and bring the man some ice," Swensson said to the porter, who soon returned with ice chips wrapped in a bandana, but the pain was in the gut not the head.

"Open the God dammit window, I can't breathe!"

The porter opened the window, but the smoke and cinders seeping in from the locomotive's smokestack didn't help. The short trip along the spur passed quickly, even if it didn't seem so. Hibbing sucked and chewed up all the ice chips.

When the engineer blasted the steam whistle signaling the approach into the railway station, Swensson said, "Run and fetch a carriage," and Jönsson jumped from the train before it pulled to a stop.

"Hey, boy, I need this wagon. It's for Frank Hibbing."

At first the lad slowly driving the buckboard down Hibbing's main street didn't respond, and Jönsson jumped onto the plank seat and pushed him to the edge, grabbed the reins, and jerked the horse and wagon around. White-faced and sagging, Hibbing descended the platform with the porter under one arm and Swensson under the other. The two hoisted Hibbing onto the back of the wagon, and the gasping man lay prone.

"Vere's a doctor, boy?" Jönsson demanded, but the bug-eyed boy with the slack jaw didn't answer.

Just then, a clerk appeared alongside the wagon, and gestured with his arm. "Follow me," he said, and he jogged down the rutted cart way with the wagon lurching along behind him. When they reached the tiny white building at the end of the street, Jönsson grabbed Hibbing's legs, and Swensson cradled him under the armpits, and they carried him over the porch and into a doctor's office with a very pregnant young woman waiting in the anteroom.

A bespectacled, clean-shaven man with pork-chop side-burns appeared from a back room, stepped to the side, and gestured that Hibbing should be carried straightaway into the room from where he had emerged. The man's appearance suggested he was too young to be a doctor, but he exhibited a confident manner and quickly took charge. They laid Hibbing on a table, and Hibbing squeezed Jönsson's hand and mouthed, "thank you." Through a window, Jönsson could see that a crowd was gathering as word of Hibbing's condition spread from shop to saloon and to every corner of the young city.

"Leave the bottle, please," Swensson said, and he poured three fingers of rye whiskey into his glass. Jönsson did the same. They sat in the barroom of Frank Hibbing's hotel.

Swensson took a big swig, wiped his lips with the back of his hand, and said, "Forty."

Jönsson gave him a quizzical look as he took a small sip of whiskey.

"Forty fucking years old. That's all."

The doctor's diagnosis was a burst appendix, usually a death warrant. Some are doing surgery for it, the doctor said, but he had never seen it done, much less attempted it himself. By then, Hibbing had lost consciousness.

"Do it," Swensson said, but it was already too late. Just as the doctor was about to slice the abdomen open, Hibbing sat straight up with eyes wide. "My bones feel rusty and chilly," he said and exhaled a deep breath before sagging back, dead.

"It's all fucked up," Swensson said, pouring another three fingers.

Jönsson looked askance at his boss. He had never heard him swear. Jönsson took another sip of his whiskey.

"Greedy bastards with deep pockets always win," Swensson said. "They bought and paid for McKinley, they hire thugs to smash the heads of the workingman who dares ask for a livable wage, and somehow when a lone capitalist stands up and pays a decent wage and starts up a town where a man can make a go of it, God strikes him dead. How the hell did Rockefeller manage that?"

Jönsson drank down the rest of his whiskey in one gulp and filled his glass again. He had no answers, but he figured Swensson was right. God in heaven seemed to be on the wrong side.

"Where is the justice, much less any mercy? Tell me Jönsson, why do the people despise the Rockefellers yet envy and emulate them? Standing on the necks of the broken-down and humble, men of privilege--often in cahoots with the government—live lives of rampant self-interest devoid of empathy or altruism."

Jönsson didn't understand all the big words of the newspaperman, but he agreed, and added his own two cents. "Vot is more," Jönsson said, "the rich and powerful believe all the while dat dey earned and deserved dere station."

By the time the whiskey bottle was half empty, Swensson's despondency had moved from the universal to the personal.

"You know, that prissy little bride of mine despises me," he said, wrinkling his nose and attempting to emulate her voice. "'Oh Teo,' she said on our wedding night, 'I'm just not ready.'"

"Well, I tell you what," Swensson said, pushing his face up close to Jönsson's, "It's been four fucking years, and she still ain't ready—I should say, four NON-fucking years." He leaned back quickly and heavily and nearly tipped over his chair. Then, he became pensive; perhaps he was embarrassed at having said too much.

If Jönsson was surprised at Teo's brutal candor, the revela-

139

tions regarding Mrs. Swensson matched his own impression of her. She was prissy. And scatterbrained. And self-indulgent. She was a social-climbing opportunist who married for money and then disrespected her husband because he didn't care much about his wealth. Jönsson assumed the profound Natty Einstein tolerated the shallow Elmira Swensson only because of access to the pages of Teo's newspaper.

Jönsson respected his boss. More than that, he liked him. Today, he felt sorry for him. He had always considered Teo to be a good man whose major fault was his own self-effacing earnestness. And naivete—not only regarding his wife but regarding the way America worked. The plight of the working-man? Of course, big men beat up on little men. Of course, the world was unfair. Always has been, always will be. Poor Teo could use a dose of the disillusionment Jönsson felt following the '96 election, then disappointment wouldn't be so disappointing.

After a minute or two of silence, Swensson leaned in and resumed the conversation, but he changed course and moved away from his own concerns. He poured his glass full and Jönsson's also. "What about you, Jönsson, are you a lover or a fighter?"

For the first time that evening, a broad smile spread across Teo's face, and he poked Jönsson in the ribs.

"Been sleeping over at Einstein's lately?"

Jönsson drank down half his glass, hesitated, then drank down the rest. Even though Teo apparently knew about Natty, there was a hell of a lot more he didn't know, and Jönsson wasn't about to spill the beans.

*A lover or a fighter? He knew the touch of a woman well enough, but his youthful lovemaking with his native wife had ended in tragic emptiness, and who knew where he stood with Natty Einstein? He was hardly a fighter even though he had killed a man, but that was only because he had bungled a simple act of robbery.*

Jönsson had swallowed more than enough whiskey to loosen the tongue of most men, but his secrets were too dear and too deep.

"'Tis time to call it a night," he said without answering Teo's question. "Ve need ta transport poor Frank's body back ta Duluth in the morning."

When they returned to Duluth, Swensson had been scooped. A rival newspaper told the story:

*The news of the death of no man in Duluth would be received with greater sorrow than that of Frank Hibbing. His friends are found in every walk of life. His hand has always been ready to extend assistance to others in their distress and the worthy person never asked his aid in vain. The poor who have received coal and provisions from him when cold and hunger were knocking at their doors are without number, and they have reason to appreciate fully the sincerity of his charity, for he gave without ostentation, satisfied with having done a good deed without advertising his virtue to the world.*

When the wind blew from the east, Duluth was a summertime icebox, but it was a hot September day under a west wind when Jönsson's life was again to take a turn. Labor Day speeches had riled up the workingman and woman. Jönsson idled in the street when he spied Swensson burst from the offices of his newspaper.

"To the docks!" Swensson blurted. "Paid ruffians are challenging the strikers."

A wildcat strike had broken out earlier that week, a not uncommon occurrence, and neither was the news that the industrialists responded with violence. Swensson hopped into the back of the carriage while Jönsson slowly climbed to his seat and draped his oil skin duster over his shoulders after first checking the pocket.

His revolver was there.

Although Teo would have disagreed, Jönsson considered his duties to have expanded to include the role of bodyguard for his earnest, idealistic employer. After the death of Frank Hibbing, it seemed Swensson was willing to be more than a reporter on the scene, and he already had a nasty gash on his arm because he intervened in a shoving match between a union man and a hoodlum hired by the bosses. The capitalists held sway in Washington, and labor bashing had become acceptable. Strikebreakers swinging clubs incited violence that invited chaos, and Jönsson packed his pistol, just in case.

Following a fast trot toward the grain elevators of Rice Point, Jönsson reined Jenny in along a high point in the street, and Swensson stepped down from the buggy to survey the situation. Long, tall, but narrow wooden elevators served as holding depots--intermediaries between trainloads of grain from the western prairies and the ships that would carry the grain to cities in the east. Elevators neutralized time and allowed the trains to offload the grain on their schedule and the ships to come and go according to theirs.

Wildcatters had pulled up the railway track to prevent a waiting train from offloading. The locomotive snorted and hissed belligerently, but the dockworkers understood the railroads' greatest vulnerability—without track, even the massive steam beasts were helpless.

Not so the line of strikebreaking goons that stood opposite the wildcatters. With clubs in hand, they rhythmically slapped their wooden cudgels into their opposite palm; with each beat, they took a step forward despite the taunts from the workers.

A few policemen stood in the space between the antagonists, but as the gap narrowed, they retreated to the sides.

A shrill whistle blast signaled the start of battle; the lines broke and men on both sides surged forward with shouts. The police danced helplessly along the sidelines, arresting those on the periphery who were easy prey and not the prime combatants, and you never knew about their allegiance, anyway.

Swensson and Jönsson watched in silence as the fighting spilled their way. Swensson twisted his body this way and that. A single dockworker became isolated and ran toward the buggy with two thugs chasing behind. They caught him and pummeled him with clubs as he fell to the ground, attempting to ward off the blows with bent and broken fingers.

"No, sir. Please don't!" Jönsson shouted as Teo Swensson joined the fray, pushing one of the goons away from the helpless dockworker, but when several strikebreakers rushed toward Swensson, Jönsson couldn't help himself.

BANG!

As Jönsson's bullet hurtled skyward, the hooligans stopped in their tracks and backed off, and Jönsson returned the pistol to his pocket. Swensson helped the beaten man to his feet, and a pair of policemen approached. When the police clasped handcuffs onto Swensson's wrists, it was time to go. Jönsson didn't care to be questioned by the authorities. Swensson would be safe in the paddy wagon, and he would soon be released from jail, once his wife appeared to claim him.

"*Skutt*, Jenny. God dammit, *skutt!*"

At first Jenny trotted, but traffic downtown slowed them before the buggy again picked up speed and bounced along East Superior Street. Night had fallen by the time Jönsson bounded up the back porch of the Swensson residence and bolted through the doorway, without knocking, something he had never done. He entered the kitchen, where he was met by Elmira Swensson wearing only silk drawers that covered her hips to her knees but nothing above.

"Why, Mr. Jönsson, I declare." She casually crossed her arms over her bare breasts.

"I ... I'm sorry ma'am," and he fumbled with the doorknob.

"Don't go," she said, "you've caught me in a dalliance, but don't run off to poor Mr. Swensson without knowing the truth of it all."

Jönsson turned back toward her with his eyes on the floor. Mrs. Swensson dropped her arms and placed her hands on her hips and swayed a few steps closer. He couldn't help but see her boyish figure with small breasts and pointy pink nipples.

"Why Mr. Jönsson, I do believe you're blushing."

Without taking her eyes off him, she canted her head and called over her shoulder.

"Sweetie, come and say hello to Mr. Jönsson. It seems he's caught us in the act, so we may as well make a clean breast of it." She giggled at her joke and wriggled her shoulders.

"Come, come my love, don't be shy," she said, and this time she turned her whole head toward the sitting room. "Come out and say hello to Mr. Jönsson."

Jönsson had enough and again turned to leave when Natty Einstein appeared, wrapped in a blanket.

The gun remained in his pocket, and he could have used it on any of the three sorry beings in the room.

Suicide might have been the most likely. Once he had been knocked off his feet by the sudden and unexpected kick of a milk cow that struck the side of his head, and once he fell from a tree and lost his breath, but Natty's appearance hit him harder and more suddenly. He was confused, to be sure, but lack of understanding of what transpired around him was of small consequence. He was breathless, the room was spinning, and his knees threatened to give way beneath him.

If darkness wouldn't claim his own life, perhaps blood-curdling anger welling up from the black crevices of his being would kill his betrayer: the Jew with the crooked soul, the shylock who stole his love, the Jesus-killer who hung him on a cross. What had their passionate lovemaking meant? What did anything mean? In a speck of time, love became hate: searing, raging, and vengeful.

That left the blonde with tiny tits and perky nipples. She married a good man for his money but wouldn't share his bed. Now, she cheated with the one who made Jönsson's day worth waiting for the next, who graced his sweet dreams and chased his nightmares, and who put a smile on his face as he greeted the sunrise. Could this tawdry little tart love? Make love? *The two women curled together, writhing about; Natty cooed, and moaned, and gasped, and panted ...*

Jönsson yanked the pistol from his pocket, pulled back the hammer, and jerked the trigger. His aim was true, and the bullet shattered the glass of the gas light hanging on the wall and extinguished the flame. He had nothing against the light; it was just there; it was something. The screaming women ran into the sitting room as Jönsson fled into the darkness.

Three live cartridges remained in his revolver.

# CHAPTER SEVENTEEN: 1898

W hen the great unsalted sea wasn't screaming, she laid down and whispered. The rhythmic waves lapping the island at city's edge beat a slow and steady pace where a troubled soul could seek solace. Cool mist licked the faces of asylum seekers, and the familiar scent of pine needles grounded the wanderer. The dialogue between the foghorns and the steam whistles of the great ships that sought safe harbor promised redemption.

Here is where Jönsson retreated after firing his pistol in the Swensson kitchen and disappearing into the night, never to return. He didn't run far, but it seemed he landed on a distant shore. The seven-mile-long sand spit that sheltered the inner harbor of Duluth from the rages of Superior had been severed from the mainland to become an island apart, connected by ferry or skiff, and here he began a new life, on the narrow edge between wrath and serenity. Jönsson had been twice wounded in love, and he first lost trust in God and now in womanhood, two gaping holes in his soul that only time and space could heal.

Mother earth in Minnesota birthed four great rivers: the state's own namesake, the Minnesota, that began on her western borders and traveled south and east to join the Mississippi under the bluffs of Fort Snelling; the Mississippi that was the greatest of them all, pouring out of a small northern lake to begin a journey all the way to the Gulf of Mexico; the Red River of the North that began near the headwaters of the Minnesota River but flowed in the opposite direction north to Winnipeg in Canada where she joined other waters on the way to Hudson's Bay; and the St. Louis River which created and defined the island on which Jönsson now found himself.

The St. Louis River was the most confused of the four with uncertain intentions and a split personality. With headwaters near the Vermilion Iron Range, she slowly twisted west for a hundred miles along the Mesabi Range before she abandoned her attempt to join the Mississippi and instead lurched south toward the western end of Lake Superior. Along her journey, she initially flowed gently through lakes where the Ojibwe harvested wild rice before rushing through miles of cascading rapids and waterfalls and then slowing again to become an estuary emptying into Lake Superior.

First came the Dakota Indians, then the Ojibwe, then the French fur trappers and traders known as Voyageurs. One of these Frenchmen undoubtedly named the river that spilled through the rocky crags in the region north of Duluth in honor of his king, Louis XIV of France. The city itself was named after a different Frenchman tramping these woods and plying these waters about the same time, Daniel Greysolon, *Sieur du Lhut*.

Before the arrival of the French and the other white tribes, the estuary had been a sacred stopping point for the Ojibwe wanderers after crossing Gitchi-Gami, following their mythic and mystic migration westward from the Canadian shores of the Atlantic to Minnesota and Wisconsin, a journey spread over five hundred years. Now, this estuary served as the expansive inland harbor shared by the twin ports of Duluth and Superior, sheltered by the sand spit island called Minnesota Point.

During the eons of her bewildered journey, the St. Louis River picked up grains of sand and deposited them where the river mouth met the great unsalted sea, creating sand dune peninsulas that became key locations in Duluth's harbor and city. Rice Point, home to Natty Einstein was one of these, and Park Point, also known as Minnesota Point, was another, and this became Jönsson's new home.

Jönsson rented a single-room hut sheltered in the red pines overlooking a sandy beach of Park Point with an endless vista across the great inland sea. He received meager pay as a mule-driving-trolley-car operator for the Park Point Traction Company. He worked sixteen-hour-shifts six days a week, but the busyness kept his melancholy at bay, and the rhythm of waves pounding the beach drowned out his nightmares. The trolleys of Duluth had been electrified for years, but mules still pulled the Pine Point dinkies that carried passengers back and forth three miles down the island sliver.

Mules were stupid beasts, he heard. True. Mules were stubborn, they said. True again. He soon discovered that driving two mules created double the stupid and four times the stubborn, so, he preferred to hitch one at a time to his outdated, hand-me-down trolley called a "dinky." When the mule strayed off course, which was often, the dinky jumped the tracks, and the passengers would unload and lift the tiny trolley car back onto the rails.

The dinky featured five rows of double wooden seats with backs separated by an aisle to the side entrance at the rear. Twenty passenger capacity. The passenger compartment had a roof and walls with windows, but Jönsson drove the mule while standing on a perch that was completely exposed to sun, wind, rain, and snow. Just inside the perch but closed off to Jönsson, a coal-burning stove kept the chill off the passengers during the harsh winter months. At each end of the three-mile line when Jönsson reversed course, he would also stoke the stove and add coal, his few moments of respite from the elements. He wished he still had his lumberjack wardrobe, and he soon acquired a heavy buffalo robe covered by a knee-length oilskin slicker. He covered his head with a wool cap with floppy earflaps, and an oilskin hat in wet conditions. When he fled from Swensson's kitchen, he had retrieved his belongings from the carriage house, including his tall boots with room for layers of wool socks.

The Park Point Trolley company owned a second trolley car, which was outfitted with rudimentary fire-fighting equipment and ladders strapped to each side. Jönsson's back-up driver was a former fireman, but it was the duty of the Park Point male citizens to jump on board and serve as the fire fighters.

The passengers on his trolley tended to be either regulars who lived on the island or summertime beachgoers who played and camped in the pines and sand dunes and swam off the warmer harbor side beaches while occasionally dipping feet into the chilly waters of the great lake itself.

One of the regulars was Harry Holcomb, first mate on a tugboat that plied the harbor and assisted the great ships in and out of their berths. Harry also lived alone on Park Point, and the two bachelors struck up a friendship, but Harry didn't intend to remain a bachelor for long. He boasted constantly about his sweetheart back home in Cleveland. Harry was a hulking giant of a man who occupied a full double seat on the dinky. He was no prince charming with a swollen, pockmarked nose under a receding hairline, but he spoke of his intended with reverence due a princess.

"It won't be long now, and I'll have a missus. Betsy sent me a sweet letter today, and she pines for my return."

Harry had been dispatched with the tugboat a year earlier to assist a Cleveland steel mill's ships coming and going in and out of the port of Duluth. The captain of the tug was soon retiring, and Harry's prospects improved with expectation of a promotion to captain. He could soon afford a wife, and all he needed to do was persuade dear Betsy that Duluth was the place for them.

"I haven't heard from Betsy for a while now, and I expect

that's due to lonesomeness. She just can't bear to think of me here at the end of the world so far away from good old Cleveland."

After a wooden seatback in the trolley cracked when exuberant beach partygoers got a little rambunctious, Jönsson replaced it with a seat from the fire-fighting trolley, and he dragged the broken seat to the beach in front of his cabin, where it became his perch for watching the comings and goings of the whaleback steamers and double-and-triple-masted schooners.

Whaleback steamers--with black rounded hulls and the look of a cigar with bent-up ends, boasting lengths up to 350 feet—had recently ruled the Great Lakes' fleet, plying the thousand miles to the eastern cities of Chicago, Detroit, Cleveland and Buffalo with cargo holds filled with grain or iron ore and with coal on the return. Duluth, and especially West Superior, hosted the shipbuilding yards that produced the whaleback fleet for the Great Lakes, but now a new breed of ore-hauling steamer appeared: the Bessemer, longer and faster with much greater capacity with an ever-stretching center section of holds separating bow cabin from stern engine room. In 1895, the first Bessemer-style ship appeared, and Duluth saw her first 400-foot vessel. To feed the nation's unquenchable thirst for steel, Rockefeller once again rocked the steel-producing world, ordering a dozen Bessemer-style ships up to 475 feet in length. Even the red-painted hulls that matched the tint of the iron ore cargo suggested that Bessemers were the ore boats now.

There is an allure to ships at sea. In the warm summer months of 1898, Jönsson often ate his evening meal of a sausage and cheese sandwich chased with a bottle of beer while seated on his broken beach chair, watching a ship's lights fade away on the darkening eastern horizon. On many nights, a wash of stars splashed across the heavens. On other nights, moonbeams shimmered on the waves. Green and yellow northern lights occasionally flared in the sky beyond the city and northern shoreline. Some nights he fell asleep on the chair only to awaken under a freshening morning breeze with a crick in his neck. Or a ship's horn would jar him awake, and he would trudge into his cabin and collapse on his bunk.

One night, the mist turned to a drizzle and then a steady rain, but he remained on his bench. His soul needed a good washing, and there was therapy in the warm rain shower. He stripped and sat naked, and the drenching was a holy ablution. It was good for him to be here, tired and sore from long days standing with reins in his hands, basking in the starlight or moonbeams or rain showers, with sand between his toes.

"Come with me to Cleveland," Harry said one November day at the close of the shipping season. "We shall ride the train, and you can help persuade my dear Betsy to join me in Duluth."

"Nah," Jönsson replied. "Mebbe next spring when the trolley vill be shut down for expansion down the island and electrifying the lines."

Jonas would stick around for a last winter as a mule-driver for the Park Point Traction Company. When spring permitted expansion of the rail line, the dinky would be replaced with an electrified trolley. Harry rode the train alone to spend his winter in Cleveland in the company of dear Betsy.

Jönsson's beach hut faced the sea, but sometimes he was drawn to walk the beaches that fronted on the harbor on the other side of the sand-spit island. Across the inner bay, the lights of Rice Point seemed near. Natty's shanty was there, and that knowledge both drew him to walk on the inner beaches but also repelled him. She was close. Perhaps too close.

He returned to his own beach fronting the sea, walking

miles in the sand as the first snowflakes of the season floated aimlessly in the breezeless evening, and the splash at water's edge formed an icy crust on the sand. He was interested in travelling east but for different reasons than Harry imagined; Cleveland waited beyond the eastern horizon and Chicago and Buffalo as well. New York City beyond that, connected by rail lines. And then the Great Salted Sea, the Atlantic. The Swedish port of Karlshamn was hidden in the evening mist with a road to his village just a day's ride inland.

Jonas should write a Christmas letter home, but what would he say? He had no news he cared to share. Wild thoughts sometimes intruded into his evening solitude. What if he journeyed home? A surprise visit to the family. A prodigal's return?

He flipped shells and stones into the surf and expected the waves to return an answer.

# CHAPTER EIGHTEEN: 1899

Jönsson passed the winter of 1898-99 perched on Park Point's mule-driven dinky for one last season, outfitted in buffalo robes and a scarf covering everything except eye slits to protect against frostbite. There were days when spit would freeze into a chunk before landing in the snowbank alongside the rails. Shifting snow drifts curled around his cabin, and he passed the evenings devouring newspapers in the yellow glow of a kerosene lantern.

*December 18, 1898: Automobile sets amazing speed record of thirty-nine miles per hour!*

He was especially interested in reports from the Duluth Life Saving Station.

*December 20, 1898: In the shipping year just ended, the Duluth Life Saving Station performed eighteen rescues. Most were sailboats, sloops, or yachts, but the sixty-ton steamer "Record" sank in the Duluth Harbor early in the summer and three lives were lost.*

The Life Saving Station was tucked into the harbor side of Jönsson's island under a tall flagpole; each morning a crewman hoisted a large American flag and each evening the flag was lowered. Immense sliding doors on the backside opened to a matching pair of thirty-foot rescue boats on wagons ready for a speedy launch. Jönsson frequently spotted the crew drilling in the calm water of the inner harbor. Six burly oarsmen sat three on a side with the captain at the tiller. The yawls featured an upturned prow and a stern to match with high freeboard in between.

Sonny Boy Huivonin lived on Pine Point and rode Jönsson's trolley to and from his daily duties as a crew member. Sonny's wife often baked cookies for the men of the station, which Sonny shared with Jonas. The Finlander's given name was Soini, but the captain jokingly called him Sonny Boy, and the nickname stuck because Soini was no boy. He was thick as a tree trunk with flaming red hair like autumn's sugar maple. His tangled orange beard fit his ruddy face. The oars seemed like matchsticks in his gnarly mitts with hairy knuckles. But he was a gentle giant and a friend to Jonas. After Christmas, Sonny's wife sent leftover ham slices with mustard and pastries with plum jam inside and a coating of powdered sugar for her husband's solitary friend who lived alone in the cabin in the pines.

Teo Swensson's paper remained Jönsson's favorite, and the articles often stirred thoughts of Natty Einstein although it was highly unlikely Teo and Natty were on speaking terms, much less that she still was the source of his labor-friendly articles. He regretted abandoning his friend, or at least commiserating with him over their shared experience of Elmira's cheating. Jönsson heard that Teo moved out of his east-end mansion and Natty moved in with Elmira. Teo should rightly have kicked Elmira out, but Jönsson wasn't surprised that Teo, always bending backward to be fair, was the one to leave. Perhaps lack of self-esteem also interfered with fighting for what was rightly his.

*January 7, 1899: Organized labor in Duluth growing. Duluth boasts fifty-six labor unions. The organizing spirit seems to be taking hold of the boys and they are just hustling.*

*February 18, 1899: Rabbi to leave Duluth after three years. The rabbi has been known as one of the most learned men in Duluth with influence even outside Jewish circles, and he has done much for the Hebrews of this city, including starting the construction of a synagogue that is now nearing completion.*

Natty wasn't a whit religious, but the intellectual rabbi was one of her supporters.

On a March day in 1899, a cool breeze lifted the aroma of Jönsson's pipe tobacco over an icy path across the frozen inner harbor. He leaned over the concrete wall of the ship canal as he enjoyed a smoke before returning down island with his dinky. The canal waters flowed under a veneer of treacherous ice due to the current below; meanwhile, the ice over the inner harbor remained solid and trustworthy, and a well-worn path connected the island with the mainland of Duluth. A sheet of ice extended a mile or so into the great lake with mist rising over open water on the eastern horizon. A solitary figure trudging along the icy path over the inner harbor caught a whiff of Jönsson's pipe smoke, waved, and quickened his pace. Jönsson waved back, and a broad smile split his face.

"Wait just a minute," Jönsson said to the three passengers on board the dinky. "I see another passenger coming this way." He stuffed coal into the stove and poured coffee grounds into a fresh pot of water to boil and brew.

Harry Holcomb had arrived at the Union Depot after spending the winter in Cleveland, and now he returned to the island. Jönsson dropped Harry at his shack near the offices of his tugboat employer.

With a worried wink, Harry said, "Come to my hut after your shift is through. I'll have beer."

There were no passengers on the last run, and Jönsson stabled the mule half an hour early before heading to Harry's place.

When Jönsson appeared at his door, Harry blurted out his bad news, "Betsy threw me out. 'Come back when you're made captain of your own boat,' she said."

Bowed under the flickering light of the kerosene lantern, Harry's hulking figure seemed small. Dark snuff rills highlighted the creases in his ashen chin. If his job as tugboat mate wasn't good enough for Betsy, he certainly wouldn't hold her favor with his looks.

"Now that I'm here, the company says to take it up with the home office. God dammit to hell! I just come from the home office."

He downed his bottle of beer and flipped open the bottle stop on another.

"Dear friend, come with me to Cleveland. Betsy will listen to you."

Jönsson figured Harry was grasping at straws. There was no reason Betsy would pay any attention to a trolley car driver. But, after thinking on it during the winter months, Jönsson was ready for a test run. He still wasn't sure whether he should remain in Duluth, and the ambiguous beckoning and repelling of the lights from Rice Point left him uncertain. He decided he would take advantage of the hiatus while the Traction Company constructed electric trolley lines.

On a June day in 1899, Harry and Jonas departed on an ill-fated journey—at least, for Harry--aboard a whaleback steamer bound for Cleveland. As an employee, Harry booked cheap passage in a double-berth crew cabin aboard a company whaleback. The cramped crew quarters featured a pair of bunks and a coal-burning stove and room for a steamer trunk. Compared to Jönsson's steerage compartment on the New York bound steamer eight years earlier, this was the lap of luxury. Harry was a decent bunkmate, but he sure could chatter. Jönsson realized how much of a loner he had become, and he preferred the quietude of living alone in his beach hut.

Compared to the high freeboard of the Atlantic steamer,

the fully loaded ore boat seemed damn low in the water, but no one seemed concerned, and to Jönsson's untrained eye, the heavy vessel handled the waves well enough. With regular hot meals cooked in the ship's galley and plenty of time under sun and blue skies above decks, the voyage passed quickly. Jönsson even indulged himself with a hot shower on the day before they pulled into the port of Cleveland, but he was surprised when a mirror revealed a few gray hairs on his chest and a bit of flab around his belly. His next birthday would be his thirtieth.

Why did he join Harry on this Cleveland journey? Jönsson had the time while the Pine Point Trolley was shut down for expansion and electrification, but he harbored no illusions that he could help Harry. No, he was testing the waters, so to speak. Cleveland was only days from New York by railway. Ships departed the New York harbor for Europe practically every day. And he would test himself—his feelings—as he stepped away from the Minnesota shores. Would the allure of the rocky pastures of Sweden increase or decrease?

Smokestacks of the great Cleveland steel mills dominated the skyline as Harry and Jonas stepped onto the docks and headed toward a streetcar. Would the new electric trolleys of Pine Point be so fine as this specimen? He watched the actions of the motorman and imagined himself doing the same. Harry jabbered away, but Jönsson paid little attention.

*What's this?* The trolley slowed in the middle of the street as a crowd gathered outside. An angry crowd. A threatening crowd. A rock crashed through a window, spilling glass onto Jonas' lap. The agitators began pounding then pushing the sides of the car until it lurched back and forth.

"We must get out!" Harry said, surprisingly calm under the circumstances, but the aisle was jammed with passengers jostling and falling over each other.

"Johnny, Johnny!" a mother shrieked when the passengers surged toward the rear exit, and she was separated from her boy.

Jönsson opened his jacket and pulled the boy inside and shepherded him off the trolley and reunited him with his wailing mother. As the last passenger stepped down to the street, the crowd tipped the trolley car onto its side with a crash of splintered wood and flying glass. The motorman Jönsson had been admiring lay on the ground with hands and arms protecting his head as ruffians pummeled and kicked him, cursing and shouting,

"Scab bastard!"

Jönsson knew the violence of labor strife, but mostly from the side of strikebreaking thugs hired by the bosses. He had heard the word "scab" shouted in derision, but he had never actually come close to someone who took a union man's job. He and Harry had no idea the trolley was driven by a by such a man who seemed to be a regular type of fellow, and Jönsson watched him operate the trolley with admiration.

Neither Jönsson nor anyone else was brave enough to intervene, but then a shot rang out and policemen on horseback appeared with nightsticks and pistols held high. The bullies who beat the poor man melted into the crowd and disappeared. Jonas and Harry slipped away as flames flickered from the toppled streetcar.

The railway strike in Cleveland during the summer of 1899 was not the first nor the last violent labor protest to ignite across America in the tumultuous years before and after the turn of the century. Jönsson's sympathies lay with the workers but being a near victim of labor mob violence confused his sensibilities.

Big picture: the capitalists increased their wealth on the

backs of the workers who toiled long hours for meager pay, often in dangerous conditions. When laborers demanded their due, the capitalists quashed their protests with club-wielding strike breakers. Small picture: strikes often became violent and innocent victims were caught up in the mayhem. Even the scab motorman probably had a family to feed and was only doing what he could to get by. And what of the public whose goods were delayed or services curtailed when labor strife interrupted the flow of commerce?

Then again, the capitalists would turn public alarm to their own advantage and demonize the worker. Fear was the name of the game. Fear--manipulated by the industrialists, and their newspapers, and their politicians--became the greatest weapon of the entrenched rich man, and the worker on strike became his own worst enemy when prodded into violence.

The following morning while Harry had his sit down with the company man, Jönsson filled his belly with hash and eggs at the counter of a small café near the docks. The diminutive, balding proprietor in a soiled apron worked as fry cook and waiter.

"More coffee, mister?"

Jönsson nodded.

"Nasty business, yesterday, with the trolley car," the man said, noticing that Jönsson was reading the story in the newspaper.

Jönsson nodded again.

"I vas dere," he said.

The proprietor's forehead knit in wary creases.

"Is you a union man?"

"Nah, I'm yust an out-of-towner vot rode on the trolley car."

The proprietor seemed satisfied.

"Well, I suppose Hanna's boys will take care of it."

Jönsson lifted his gaze from the paper to the waiter.

"Senator Mark Hanna, if'n you don't know. He's got the ear of McKinley, and they'll give those anarchist unionists what fer."

It dawned on Jönsson that Cleveland was the home of Republican Senator Mark Hanna, friendly to the industrialist and antagonistic to the working man, who managed McKinley's presidential campaign. Listening to Teo Swensson and reading his newspaper had educated him as to who was who in national politics, and Hanna was a name he remembered.

"I s'pose yer right," Jönsson said as he tamped fresh tobacco into his pipe.

If labor chose to beard the lion in his den, Cleveland was the place, but then the chances of being eaten alive were plenty high.

Just then the bell over the door jangled, and a crestfallen Harry slid onto the red vinyl upholstery of the stool next to Jönsson.

"They fired me," Harry said through clenched teeth and over a jutting chin. "The whalebacks are done and so are their tugboats. It's the day of the Bessemer now."

Harry lost his job by stating his claim, and the striking railway workers lost theirs. Jönsson's sympathies for the labor movement didn't change, but he wondered about tactics. Did smashing and burning a trolley car help or hinder the cause of the railway unions? Did such violence play into the fearmonger's hands?

# CHAPTER NINETEEN

J önsson had an epiphany in Cleveland. Duluth called to him, not the far away port of Karlshamn.

For eight years--his entire adult life--he had lived on this side of the Atlantic. America was not at all that he expected, much less hoped for. The labor mess in Cleveland was only the latest example of societal dysfunction. And yet, it was clear to him that he was no longer a Swede but an American. For good or ill, he had decided long ago that America would be his home, and the trip to Cleveland convinced him there was no going back. Somehow, he accepted the reality of the world he lived in, and he saw that the idyllic pull of the pastures of Sweden was just as illusory as the naïve dreams that brought him to America in the first place. There is no wishing away of the circumstances that fate imposes on you, and he would return to the cabin in the pines that was now his home.

He was who he was, and his life would be what it would be, and he accepted that without joy or sadness.

Without a job and rejected by his dear Betsy, Harry had nowhere else to go, so he followed Jonas back to Pine Point. Jonas put in a good word, and Harry found employment with the Life Saving Crew. A strong, broad-shouldered man who knew the harbor meshed well with the crews of the oar-powered life-saving yawls.

Even if it was a second-hand import from across the ship canal, the electrified trolley car was new to Jönsson, and he marveled at the improvements: longer with a capacity of thirty passengers. No more balky mules to struggle with. Jönsson's own perch offered the biggest improvement. Enclosed behind glass panes and open to the warm passenger compartment. Jönsson packed his buffalo robe and oilskin slicker away.

Jönsson sat on a stool in the front—no more standing for hours at a time--with the controller handle at arm's length. He got the hang of the controller easy enough. The controller handle was a steel bar with a wooden knob at the end. By cranking the handle through various points, the controller connected motors and resistors to allow the car to accelerate or decelerate. A second handle operated the discs that would clamp against the steel wheels to brake the trolley.

On New Year's Eve, 1899, Jönsson gathered with others at the home of Sonny Huivonin and Juuli, his wife. Jönsson and Harry Holcomb arrived together. As they walked up a snowy path to the front door, Sonny greeted them outside to share a swig of aquavit to get the evening started--maybe two swigs. When the door swung open, bright light, the boisterous sounds of children, and the energy of women preparing a meal spilled out.

The women inside were Juuli's sisters: Anna-Leena and Helvi. Jönsson could see they were sisters by their looks: tall, thin, high cheeks, hazel eyes, and golden-brown hair the color of crowns of wheat. Anna-Leena's hair was bound tight and pinched atop her head, Juuli's was thick but cropped short and parted in the middle, and Helvi's flowed freely over her shoulders to mid-back.

Harry greeted Juuli with a kiss on the cheek and eagerly awaited an introduction to her sisters. Jönsson trailed behind and stayed close to the door, removing his boots.

"This is Anna-Leena who travelled by train from Mountain Iron for the holidays," Juuli said. "The two boys roughhousing in the corner are her sons."

Anna-Leena barely looked up from the stove where she stirred a pot and mumbled an inaudible greeting. Sonny had previously explained that Anna-Leena was the oldest sister and a widow, having lost her husband in a mine accident a year earlier. Both Jönsson and Harry had met Sonny and Juuli's three daughters many times. The girls were younger than their boy cousins, but that didn't slow them down, and the cousins were obviously having a good time.

"And this is Helvi," Juuli said. "She's the youngest, and she tends house for a snooty family on the east end."

"Oh, they're not so bad," Helvi protested.

Harry grabbed her right hand and shook it vigorously. Helvi beamed and offered a slight curtsy. Harry was eager to participate in Juuli's matchmaking. Under a fresh haircut and shave, he wore a crisp starched shirt buttoned tight around his neck, and he had washed away the snuff runnels that usually darkened the creases defining his chin.

The three sisters parted ways with their personalities. Anna-Leena was hard and cold, but Helvi was quick to blush and giggle. Juuli herself was the housewife in control; her children minded, and her kitchen sparkled.

Right after introductions, the evening started on the ice for the menfolk and the children while Juuli and her older sister stayed inside to finish the meal preparations. Juuli's two-year-old remained inside also. Using flat shovels, the men scraped the snow away from a patch on the inner harbor near Sonny's home to form a small skating rink. The boy cousins from Mountain Iron and the oldest girl cousin had found skate blades in their Christmas stockings. While Sonny strapped the steel blades onto the children's boots, Jönsson gathered wood and started a bonfire. By the time the children dared their first slippery steps with an adult at their elbow, Jönsson had the bonfire roaring. Flaming pine branches shot sparks into the sky. Ann-Leena's oldest had skated previously, and he had the hang of it; he glided proudly, if not gracefully, from the bonfire to the far side of the rink and back again. The chink and the grind of steel etching the ice mixed with laughter and pine pitch crackling into flame.

Helvi had borrowed a pair of blades, and Harry assisted her with the leather straps around her boots, and then he remained at her elbow as she attempted the first, halting steps, squealing as she moved awkwardly. When she lost her balance and Harry tried to stop her fall, he ended up on top of her on the ice.

"Pardon me," he said, "I guess I'm a clumsy oaf."

Helvi giggled. Helvi was too quick to blush and giggle, Jönsson thought, but Harry ate it up. Sonny had previously warned Jönsson that Anna-Leena was still too bitter to consider remarriage, and that was just fine with Jönsson. In fact, if it had been otherwise, he would have found an excuse not to come.

As a boy, Jonas skated on wooden skates on the pond back home on the farm, and he excelled at it. There were no steel blades for him to try now, but he ran a few paces and then slid on the ice, ran again, and slid again. His lame leg didn't object.

Sonny's four-year-old didn't have skate blades, but she made it to the center of the rink on her boots; Jonas took her by the hand, and pulled her, sliding to the far snowbank. Jonas spun her around and she fell into his lap when he plopped down in the snowbank. She tossed a mittful of fluffy snow in his face and giggled.

"Again," she squealed. "Pull me again!"

He did, but soon he sat on a log near the fire with the girl on his knee.

"Uncle Ole, why don't you have any kids?"

164

He was caught unawares without his guard up, and the question immediately drew him into uncomfortable thoughts. If his son had lived longer than a day, he would be around her age. Darker skin than her alabaster. Brown eyes not blue. Maybe a year older.

He gulped a breath of the night air and said, "If'n I could have a child as sweet as you, I vould." The magic of the high-spirited play on the ice was gone for Jönsson, and the child returned to the ice alone as the bonfire died down.

While the others were skating, Juuli and Anna-Leena—with the two-year-old underfoot--set out a fine feast of smoked lake trout, ham slices with mustard left over from Christmas, potato sausage, liver and rice sausage, a truckle of yellow cheese and a smaller one of white cheese, yogurt, and several round loaves of dense rye bread. Bottles of dark beer cooled on the porch. After porridge with cranberries, milk, and sugar, the children were put to bed (the two youngest girls already slept), and the aquavit came out.

When church bells pealed in the still night, Sonny raised his glass.

"To the new year," he said. "Nah, to the new God dammit century."

"Hear, hear," Harry said, smacking his lips as he took a big swig of the caraway-scented clear liqueur.

"May the new year be better than the last," Anna-Leena said, but the grit in her voice sounded more a complaint about the past than a hope for the future.

"May young women find good men for husbands," Juuli said, staring at Helvi who blushed.

"May God protect the brave men of the Life Saving Crew," Helvi said, lifting her glass toward her brother-in-law but glancing sideways at Harry.

"Thanks," said Harry, "and I toast the wives, and mothers to be of children not yet born." Helvi looked away when Harry winked at her, but then her eyes returned to his with a look that said, *please dear Lord, let it be so. Let him be the one.*

The room fell silent as the church bells ceased ringing.

"Come on, Ole, offer a toast," Sonny said after a moment. "What do you wish for in the new year and the twentieth century?"

"I can't t'ink of nothin,'" Jönsson said. Just as the pause was about to become uncomfortable, he raised his glass and said, "To yer health and happiness."


Fat snowflakes gently sifted through the yellow glow of the gaslights as he walked home, face flushed and belly warm with aquavit. Jönsson curled his collar around his neck and pulled his hat over his ears. He had a mile to walk before he would arrive at his hut in the pines.

Harry had found his bride-to-be, all right, and good for him. Jonas had no interest in the other sister--or in marriage itself, for that matter. True enough, he got the horn like any man but that was a poor reason for taking a wife. He had visited St. Croix Street more than once after too many beers or shots of whiskey, but afterwards he always felt he had wasted his money. He didn't expect to find the exuberance of Ayasha or the passion of Natty again in his life, and so the bachelor's life of solitude would be his lot, and the cabin in the pines overlooking the shoreline of Superior suited his needs.

As he remembered the toasts offered by his friends still ringing in his ear, he chided himself at own his meager effort, but what could he have said?

*Here's to hopin' that the new century doesn't make ya a cripple, or a killer, or a vidower with a burnt-up baby, or a lover but yer girlfriend takes up vit another voman.*

He merely hoped there would still be embers burning in his coal stove and that the coal pail would be full.

# CHAPTER TWENTY: 1900-04

"Four More Years of the Full Dinner Pail."

Much as he disagreed with the policies of President McKinley, Jönsson had to admit there was truth to his campaign slogan during the 1900 campaign. Elected four years earlier during severe depression, the nation's economy had rebounded and now thrived in the cycle of boom and bust. Of course, McKinley touted the soaring economy as he sought a second term, but Jönsson suspected there was more to economic ups and downs than mere presidential policy, especially when that policy was anti-worker and pro-industrialist.

Four years earlier, Jönsson had dipped his toes into politics, but this year he merely followed the campaigns of McKinley and William Jennings Bryan in the newspapers and conversations with friends. He doubted he would even bother to vote.

"Eugene Debs, he's the man," Sonny the Finlander said, echoing the thoughts of many of his radical countrymen. "There's not a dime's worth of difference between the Democrats and the Republicans."

Early on a muggy Sunday morning in August, Sonny sat on Jönsson's bench seat overlooking the great lake. The orange orb of the sun had barely cleared the horizon. Under a slight off-shore breeze, gentle residual waves lapped the shore. Harry sat next to Sonny on the bench, and Jonas sat on the ground, his barefoot toes digging into the soft sand.

"Waste yer vote if'n ya please," Harry replied to his new brother-in-law as he dipped into his tin of tobacco and placed a pinch inside his lower lip. "Debs ain't got no chance."

"He's on the ballot, ain't he?" Sonny argued. "First time for a socialist, and there won't be a next time if'n he don't get no votes."

Sonny checked the rise of the sun and confirmed the time with his pocket watch.

"The church bells will ring soon, and I best get my ass there before they do," Sonny said as he departed.

Harry and Jonas sat silently for a few minutes, soaking in the serenity as the orange sun climbed and yellowed. Eventually, Jonas stood up, brushing the sand off his rear and headed to the water's edge. The always frigid lake water washed around his ankles, sucking away the sand from under his feet. Harry removed his boots and joined Jonas, and they slowly walked the shoreline, flipping stones into the water. Squawking gulls circled overhead. Beach birds—plovers, they called them--scurried about, pecking in the sand and devouring critters too small for the men to see.

"Teddy Roosevelt, he's better'n McKinley, and I'll vote Republican 'cause of him," Harry said, returning to the conversation about the upcoming election.

Of all the personalities on the ballot, Teddy Roosevelt was certainly the most intriguing. Because McKinley's vice-president had died in office during the first term, the Republicans chose the popular war hero to be McKinley's running mate this time around. Everyone knew the image of Colonel Roosevelt on horseback leading the charge of his Rough Riders up the slopes of San Juan Hill in Cuba during the short-lived Spanish-American War two years earlier. The quick and easy victory over the European Spaniards was a source of national pride, and Roosevelt turned politician was the beneficiary of the jingoism.

"I ain't sure a warring man is best for America," Jönsson

said.

"Yah, but ain't nobody goin' to mess with him or America if he's in Washington. Besides, we give Cuba back to the Cubans once we kicked out the Spaniards," Harry said. "We ain't colonialists. We're America, the beacon of freedom and liberty for the world."

As he spoke excitedly, brown snoose juice dribbled down his chin.

"How 'bout the Filipinos," Jonas replied. "We ain't give the Filipinos the islands back."

"Don't mean McKinley's an imperialist, only that America has a friend in the Pacific. Anyways, Roosevelt is a reformer," Harry said, switching gears. "Just look at his record as governor of New York. He broke away from the Republican machine and supported the worker, regulated election law, banking, and corporations."

"I'll grant ya that, but vot power does a vice-president have ven the president is for the businessman and against the vorker?" Jönsson asked. "Doncha know that the New York Republicans tired of him as governor and kicked him upstairs to be vice-president vere he vould be toothless?"

Harry shrugged.

Jonas knocked the ashes out of his pipe and tamped in fresh tobacco. The forecastle of an ore boat appeared on the horizon under the eastern sun, heading toward the ship canal up the beach. As he sucked in the match flame and puffs of gray smoke rippled in the slight breeze, he finished the conversation with one last comment.

"Republicans may like Roosevelt's popularity, but I'll be damned if'n dey like his politics."

The regular Sunday morning sit-down on Jönsson's beach

was over. These were the best hours of the week. Much as Jönsson spoke of politics with disdain, he followed newspaper articles religiously, and after Harry and Sonny departed for church, Jönsson's papers came out.

Harry returned to the bench to tie his boots before departing.

"Helvi will be home from church soon, and I best not be late. She's ornery enough with the morning sickness, and she don't need no more agitation."

On October 1, 1900, Jönsson's trolley chugged along with an oversized load, bursting with folks anxious to get to the mainland for a speech from William Jennings Bryan, the favorite of the laborer and again the Democratic candidate for the presidency. Bryan campaigned in Duluth four years earlier, and Jönsson remembered carting Natty to the after party before spending the late night in her arms. Some of the fervor for Bryan had worn off from his earlier candidacy—he had lost, after all—but thousands still jammed the Third Regiment Armory to hear the silver-throated orator. Jönsson assumed Natty was there, and he wondered if she had been invited to the after-speech party as before. She certainly hadn't accompanied the Bryan entourage that morning for Sunday worship at a local church. Bryan's conservative Christianity was coming to the fore.

A month later, the ticket of McKinley and Roosevelt easily defeated the Democrats. Jönsson voted for Bryan but not with great gusto. He almost didn't vote at all.

As the routine of Jönsson's bachelor life slowed down, the days sped up. One foot after another soon became a far distance. After lake gales chased the orange, red, and yellow foliage on the shore across the bay, snow drifted in, but soon

April showers awakened the purple crocuses and yellow daffo-dils springing up in the gardens along Jönsson's trolley tracks. Together with the friendship of Sonny and Harry, the flow of jibber-jabbering passengers provided all the human compan-ionship Jönsson required.

By the summer of 1901, the word "trust" came to dominate the chit chat on the trolley and the Sunday morning parleys on the beach bench in front of Jönsson's cabin. Ironically, no one trusted the trust. There were no industrialists who rode Jöns-son's rails but plenty of workingmen and women who toiled on the docks, or mines, or the railways that dumped tons of burnt-red ore into the bellies of the Bessemer steamers bound for the steel mills in the east.

It wouldn't be long before Rockefeller, Carnegie, and J. Pierpont Morgan the banker—and lesser industrialists--would have it all. Their holdings in rail, steamers, mills, and mines came together as a massive trust under the name of United States Steel. How could the workingman stand up against such monstrous, monopolistic, consolidation of power?

Leon Frank Czolgosz had an idea. Tear down the in-stitutionalized instruments of oppression. Anarchy was the answer. Destruction of the prevailing order. Destroy the old to make way for the new. About the same age as Jönsson, Czol-gosz was born soon after his parents and older siblings immi-grated from Poland. He toiled in steel mills around Cleveland and was a veteran of violent labor strikes in and around Ohio—perhaps he had been among the crowd pounding on the side of the Cleveland trolley car before tipping it over. Czolgosz drifted into moderate then radical socialist circles, but he soon found himself among those promoting anarchy.

Others preached; Czolgosz acted.

On September 6, 1901, Czolgosz tucked his .32 caliber re-volver into the folds of his jacket and headed to the Pan-

American Exposition in Buffalo, New York. He waited patiently in line with the pistol at the ready under a handkerchief, and when President McKinley extended his hand in greeting, Czolgosz fired two shots at point-blank range. The president died eight days later, the third presidential assassination by pistol shot in thirty-six years in this supposedly civilized nation, and now a rough-riding cowboy would ascend to the presidency.

Jönsson listened intently to the back-and-forth conversations in his trolley, and at the end of his shift, he gathered all the newspapers that had been left behind, and he devoured them—along with his sausage, bread, and beer—in the light of the kerosene lantern in his hut in the pines. For two months that fall, the papers competed for the latest news of the trial or insights into the character of the assassin. The defendant refused to communicate with his appointed attorneys or to raise any defense. He attempted to plead guilty, but the judge wouldn't accept his plea. It seemed to Jönsson, and probably Czolgosz, that a trial on the merits was a waste of time; the man was guilty, and he was ready to accept his just rewards. The jury, press, and public agreed with one voice, and seven weeks after the death of the president, his assassin died from three jolts in the electric chair.

Few would argue that the crime didn't merit the punishment, but Jönsson wondered. The assassin had killed and willingly died for a cause he deemed righteous. The newspapers reported his last words: "I killed the President because he was the enemy of the good people – the good working people. I am not sorry for my crime."

The whole affair left Jönsson uneasy; when he couldn't sleep, he walked the beach. When the wind was in the east, the waves crashed the shore, but when the night air was calm and the sky clear, he sat on the bench and hoped for a shooting star. Often during those weeks, the north shore was visited by green and yellow ghosts dancing across the sky.

One man killed for a cause, yet the nation applauded when jolts of electricity boiled his blood and melted his eyeballs, but another had killed merely for self-preservation, and he escaped to a humble but decent life under the pines. Whose sin was greater and whose was lesser? Guilt wasn't quite the right word for Jönsson's feelings. Disquiet. Restlessness. Doubt. There was no sense to it, and that left Jönsson anxious.

The executed man was a zealot, to be sure, who acted in good conscience--if not in good sense--who saw his extreme resistance to an oppressive system to be just. Shall the zealot decide what is just? If the cause is just, are there no limits to action? Not for the zealot; not for Czolgosz. Although Jönsson agreed with the cause of labor against the capitalist, his self-doubt negated the unrestrained self-assurance of the zealot. No, the assassin was a fool whose rash act only played into the narrative of those who would scapegoat the immigrant, the labor organizer, the radical. True enough, Theodore Roosevelt would bring his progressive reforms to the presidency and bust some trusts, but the capitalist tilt would not change, and the plight of the workingmen and women—especially those with darker skin or thick accents—would continue.

After the tumultuous autumn of 1901, Jönsson's life returned to the routine. Days turned into weeks and months into years. Seasons turned as the gales blew and the snow drifted. The fickle lake alternately raged and soothed. Fortunes were made on the great ore boats and lives were lost.

Late season newspaper accounts reported the toll of lost ships lost, mostly small and mostly old and seldom the great Bessemer steamers.

*December 15, 1901: Twenty-Five Great Lakes' vessels were lost during the season just ended.*

*December 18, 1902: The latest shipping season witnessed the loss of twenty-two vessels.*

*December 12, 1903: Worst losses in history: thirty-four vessels went down this past shipping season.*

*December 30, 1904: Duluth eclipses London as the $2^{nd}$ busiest port in the world! Owing to the late shipping season that saw over one hundred vessels clear the Duluth harbor as late as December, final statistics for the year just ended smashed all records, and Duluth now trails only New York City as the busiest port in the world: Passenger arrivals—32,862, departures—34,304; ship arrivals—3,618, departures--3,674.*

If the weather and waves of 1904 allowed late-season shipping, 1905 would not, and Jönsson would be in the thick of the greatest November storm in Duluth's history, which would lead directly to a knock on his door six weeks later during a January blizzard.

# CHAPTER TWENTY-ONE: 1905

"Morning, Sonny. Morning, Harry."

Jönsson touched his short-billed newsboy cap in a salute to his friends who stepped on to his trolley.

"Morning, Ole. Happy Thanksgiving," Sonny said. "Here's a batch of sugar cookies from the missus." The 1905 autumnal holiday was three days away, and the sailors headed for Monday morning duty at the Life Saving Station near the ship canal.

"Your four-year-old godson sent this yellow maple leaf," Sonny said. "Best remember to thank him when you come for Thanksgiving dinner."

After dropping off his friends, Jönsson's trolley reached the end of the line next to the gondola of the new-fangled aerial ferry bridge over the canal. The gondola of the aerial bridge replaced the boat ferries earlier that year and greatly increased passenger traffic on Jönsson's trolley. Massive steel cables from above supported a gondola that traversed the 300-foot canal, and kept the passengers high and dry, even in bad weather. Every five or ten minutes the gondola would move back and forth, sometimes empty but sometimes carrying as many as thirty or forty passengers.

The trolley reversed course and headed down island with a load of passengers from the gondola. An hour later, Jönsson reached the end of the line, and he took a five-minute break for coffee and a sugar cookie before setting out on the return journey along the causeway back toward the ship canal.

When the trolley reached the concrete and stone pier that lined the southern edge of the ship channel, jutting nearly half a mile out into the lake and paralleled by a similar pier on the north edge of the passageway, Jönsson noticed red storm flags fluttering in a light easterly, which seemed a bit odd under a benign sky. When a 250-footer departed port at noon, followed by a 400-footer pulling a barge nearly as long a few hours later, and then a fully loaded 500-foot ore boat a half hour after that, he was not surprised. The ship captains barely trusted the science of weather-forecasting, and often followed their gut, and the ship's crews hoped to settle in for winter in their home ports far to the east in the company of family. That, and the pressure of the stockholders for one more run to maximize profits. If they didn't leave now, the ships and their cargo would spend the winter in the Duluth harbor. The ill-fated ships headed for open water despite the red storm flags posted on the pier.

After the sunset, Jönsson took a fifteen-minute break to scarf down his sandwich and smoked lake trout with coffee warmed on the trolley's coal stove as huge orange snowflakes glowed in the gaslights lining the street. Soon the wind picked up. When his shift ended at 10:00 pm, he trudged the short distance to his hut with the wind and snow whipping his face, and he nearly dropped the jar of beer he carried under his arm. His leg ached, as it often did with the onset of bad weather. Once inside, he chomped down the last of his smoked trout, chased with the beer. After relishing a couple of sugar cookies, he fell asleep in his chair.

Wet socks and a throbbing leg awakened him. Three inches of water covered the floor. After he pulled on thick, dry wool socks, he donned boots that reached his knees, a buffalo robe covered by a slicker, a thick wool cap that covered his ears, and he limped into the roaring night with the aid of a cane that he used only when necessary. Huge rollers crashed on the beach and water streamed across the sand all the way up to and around his hut.

Blackness had settled on Pine Point. The gas lamps were out, and he nearly tripped over a downed telegraph wire. Like the ships at sea, he followed the foghorn that blew from the end of the south pier. After fighting the wind for a mile, he approached a dim glow on the far side of the channel. When he came closer, he realized that hundreds had gathered, with gas lanterns swinging in their grasp and bonfires blazing in the wind. They had come to see who would live and who would die, some with deep anxiety, others with morbid curiosity.

When the first ship appeared out of the storm, one last, great peril became apparent. The half-mile chute of the ship canal funneled the storm surge, and the waters lifted and fell, rushing in then out, then in again. A relatively small vessel, not even 200 feet in length, was the first to shoot through the chute after first spinning three times at the channel mouth. When the outrushing water reversed course, the ship was sucked in with the surge, and miraculously lined up bow-first and surfed into the inner harbor safely.

The blizzard raged through the darkness, and first light only brought more swirling snow. The churning lake was chaos without rhythm. On any other day, the waves, sometimes large and sometimes small, would reach the shore with regularity and order, but now the monstrous swells that pounded the coast were met with fierce resistance, and the land repelled the sea with a reverse undertow that riled the onrushing waves and created a confused whorl of chop and foam. Valleys nearly reached the rock and mud of the lake bottom while rising volcanos of water with frothy peaks erupted in the gale.

It was nearly noon the next day when the sailors of the Life Saving Station were called away to rescue the men on a beached ship a few miles down the coast on Jönsson's island.

Jönsson tagged along with Sonny and Harry and the others and helped drag the rescue equipment over branches and downed trolley wires, but he was shocked to discover a 400-footer beached on the sand south of his cabin. They had done the drill before, and the rescue crew fired their short-barreled cannon to carry breach buoys and a rope line on board. Soon a few crew members rode the rescue chair down a rope line, but most of the crew stayed on board, as the ship was firmly beached in the sand and in no further danger.

While the Live Saving crew packed up and recoiled their lines, Jönsson returned to the pier; he had barely arrived when the same 500-foot ore boat that had departed late the prior afternoon appeared out of the whirling snow, coursing through the hills and valleys of confused chop. Like an elongated hobby horse, the Bessemer rocked from fore to aft. The bow alternately plowed under the waves before shooting skyward. Crowds on the shore and on rooftops and hotel rooms first cheered at the sight, but then all hushed as the ship approached the final test by challenging the finicky surge of the channel. Just as she entered the chute, her bow was slammed against the north pier, and she was turned nearly broadside, but under full throttle with black smoke pouring from the smokestack, she nosed in and through the canal to the cheers of the onlookers.

Next to arrive was the *Mataafa*, the 430-foot Bessemer that had departed nearly 24 hours earlier. Somewhere on her journey back to port, the barge she pulled had been lost or cut adrift. From his Pine Point perch, Jönsson had watched the comings and goings of the Bessemers for years, and he could see that she was loaded with ore by the way she sat low in the water. A dozen wooden hatches covered the holds, an expanse of a couple of hundred feet that separated the ships' captain, mates, wheelmen, and watches in the forecastle from the oilers, firemen, cooks, and stewards below decks in the stern. Jönsson expected that the chief engineer would also be aft to answer the call for full steam ahead.

The captain piloted the ship straightaway toward the chute, and all was well until the storm surge rushed out and merged with an incoming swell to create a mountain of water that lifted the stern of the *Mataafa* high, but the bow sank low, like a seesaw, scraping the mud and rocks at the bottom of the lake, just outside the channel. Slammed off course, but at full speed and surfing the storm surge, the fully loaded steamer smashed head-on into the solid concrete of the north pier. The wind swallowed up the screams of the onlookers. The ship shuddered and fell back, but each wave slammed her forward again. Water burst in the stern compartment, dousing the coal-fire in the boilers, shutting down the steam engine. Her steering was lost, and so was the power. The 430-foot ship sprawled dead in the water and broadsides to the 300-foot channel. The wind and the waves pounded the helpless vessel amidships against the north pier.

"My God," Jönsson heard himself say, "She's going to break in half!"

Soon after the waves smashed and splintered the ship's lifeboats, a solitary figure appeared from the stern decks and leaped toward the pier that seemed tantalizingly close, but his timing was wrong, and he jumped as the ship rocked back. He came up short and disappeared in the froth.

Gradually, the current drifted the great ship north and away from the pier where she ran aground, a mere 700 feet from shore and safety and 100 feet off the tip of the north pier. The ship's captain was visible through sheets of mist as he shouted through a megaphone toward the hordes watching from the shore; although the storm stole his cries, all knew what he pleaded: "Save us!"

"Only God could do that," Jönsson mumbled under his breath.

But mortal men would try.

Broadsides to the wind and waves, the *Mataafa* soon cracked at hatch number eight, and ore oozed into the water, and a blood-red sheen washed toward shore. Each crashing wave drenched the men in the stern, forced topside by the flooding below. The poor bastards sought cover behind the smokestack and waited for intervention or inspiration. Eventually, the crowd hushed as one brave soul attempted to traverse the 250 feet, hatch by hatch, to reach the high and dry front cabin. He crabbed his way forward and disappeared as each ten-foot wave crashed over him, but when he reappeared each time, the crowd cheered, only to gasp at the next wave. Twelve hatches. He made two, then four, then eight. Jönsson could sense that the chilling waves were beating the man down and sapping his energy and his resolve. He stopped moving as a wave and a second and a third crashed over him, but then he regrouped and moved again. As he reached the twelfth and final hatch, someone rushed out from the forecastle and hugged the man forward. Just as the man disappeared into the cabin, he raised his arm to signal the others at the rear that it could be done, that survival was possible.

A second followed the same course and reached safety, but the third was swept overboard. But wait! He reappeared to cheers, as he pulled himself up with the strength he had earned as a coal-shoveling fireman. A second and a third time he was washed overboard, and each time, his grasp of the wire railing allowed him to climb back, but he made little progress forward. As the crowd chanted, "Nooo!" he retreated and returned to the others at the stern of the ship; he passed another already heading forward, who also made his way safely to the men watching from the cabin high above the ship's bow. Fifteen men now benefited from the cover of the forecastle, but nine remained in the rear, exposed to sea and wind and temperatures well below freezing. No more would tempt fate by moving forward.

"Send lifesavers," read the message scrawled on a board that washed ashore, but the sailors of the Life Saving Station hadn't yet returned from their mission to rescue the ship beached in the sand a few miles to the south.

The hordes on the beach now numbered in the thousands, maybe ten. As darkness settled over the scene, twenty-four hours after the storm picked up, dancing flames from the bonfires lit up anxious faces. The *Mataafa* was now a dark silhouette against the eastern sky except for a light from the forecastle. Cheers lifted as the Life Saving crew appeared with their Lyle gun, the cannon that would shoot a lifeline to the ship. The first shot missed and so did the second. The third seemed successful but also failed when the pair of ropes became tangled and frozen. The fourth and final attempt also missed. Seven hundred feet was too great a distance for a rope line under freezing conditions.

The despairing crowd slowly dissipated, but Jönsson stayed, standing alongside Harry and Sonny and the rest of the Life Saving Crew, but at midnight the crew was ordered to stand down to rest for the morning.

"I'll stand watch for ya," Jönsson said, slapping the backs of his friends as they departed. "Give yer kids a squeeze fer me."

Two hours later, the light in the forecastle flickered and died. Daybreak revealed the ghastly sight of the body of the oiler who had jumped for the pier rolling in the waves on the beach. First light also disclosed a ghost ship encased in ice all the way to the tips of the masts fore and aft. As soon as there was light enough to see, a man with a spyglass stepped to the front of the crowd.

"They're all dead men standing," he said. "The men in the rear are frozen statues."

His words sparked gasps and moans, but by the time the bad news spread to the far reaches of the crowd, the man with the spyglass shrieked, "There's still life in the forecastle," and cheers replaced the gloom.

Jönsson shifted uneasily on tired legs as the Life Saving crew returned from their short sleep. He knew these good men, with families of their own, must soon launch their boat into the froth, but the waves showed no sign of relenting. He wondered at the farewell conversations between Sonny and Juuli, between Harry and Helvi. Had the men been honest with their wives about the task before them?

The crew watched from the front edge of the crowd as their leader paced at the edge of the beach, hoping to detect a lessening in the waves that crashed at his feet, forming a crust of ice where sea met shore. A thirty-foot yawl, his rescue boat, had been carried to the beach and awaited his command. Shaped like a banana, the specially designed vessel featured a high, pointy prow and stern with plenty of freeboard in between. It was his sworn duty to attempt a rescue, but his worried gaze alternated between the shipwreck and the men of his crew. The grumbling in the crowd didn't help. When the ship's captain reappeared on deck with more pleas from his megaphone, the pressure increased.

By midmorning, the seas had calmed only slightly, but the order came to shove off. With a sailor in the bow ready to handle lines, and the captain at the tiller, all the rescue vessel needed was a full crew of husky oarsmen, but they were a man short.

The Life Saving captain shouted to the crowd, "Can I have a volunteer?"

Jönsson stepped forward and touched his mitt to his wool cap in his familiar salute to his friends of the Live Saving crew.

"Morning, Sonny. Morning, Harry."

# CHAPTER TWENTY-TWO: 1905-06

A long with the others who rescued fifteen survivors, Ole Jönsson was interviewed and photographed by every God dammit newspaperman in Duluth and even some who had ridden the train up from St. Paul as word spread of the unfolding tragedy.

What had it been? Six years? No, eight.

Whatever it was, it was a God dammit long time, but here was Teo Swensson with graying hair and thick spectacles, his former employer and newsman, and Jönsson was God dammit happy to see him again as adrenalin coursed through his veins. When it was Swensson's turn, the newspaperman and his former livery driver shared some good times, laughed a little, but neither mentioned Elmira or Natty or the thing the cuckolded men held most in common.

On the eve of Christmas, Jönsson paused on his stoop, gulped a breath of crisp air, and peered over the calm sea at the vast sky of sparkling stars that melded together in a soothing oneness. He departed his cabin and climbed aboard the trolley as a passenger, not pilot. As the trolley pulled away in the direction of the aerial gondola, his mind returned to the questions that had rolled over and over since that day when he spontaneously stepped forward to help the Life Savers.

Why had he been so impulsive? His memory was sharp, and every detail pressed firmly into his consciousness: ice water splashing over his slicker and wool cap, muscles taut as he leaned into his oar as the yawl climbed straight up one side of a swell before diving down the backside, the fear in the voice of the crew leader as he shouted commands, the wooden hull of the yawl grinding against the ship's steel plates as a rope was tossed up to frozen hands, survivors huddled on deck awaiting their turn to be lowered down--first seven men who would live to tell the tale then eight more, including the ship's captain, on a second trip. He remembered every detail of *what* happened, but he could not fathom *why* he had volunteered and climbed aboard the rescue boat so calmly and with matter-of-fact assurance.

Perhaps it was an act of friendship, of solidarity, with Sonny and Harry whose lives were on the line. The prospect of his own death was no deterrence. Was potential death an incentive? Was his spontaneity recompense for his earlier act of impulsiveness in a saloon?

He stepped off the trolley and climbed aboard the gondola and soon he was walking up the Duluth hills toward the small Swedish church that had sheltered him a decade earlier.

Does life have a purpose? Was his lifesaving heroism his purpose? Were those hours bobbing in the churning slush his fulfillment? If so, was there more to come?

Jönsson encountered fellow Swedes often enough, but now he listened to Pastor Emil Bergquist's sermon, the hymns, and the prayers all delivered in the mother tongue. When the electric lights dimmed, and the candles glowed, he was fully alive in the moment as the first notes of the sending song lifted to the rafters. Tears flowed freely down his cheeks.

*Stilla natt, heliga natt.*


The January 1906 wind whistled off Lake Superior six weeks after the *Mataafa* storm, as it came to be known. When the east wind blew like tonight, there would be snow, piles of snow. The walls creaked, the windows rattled, and someone pounded on his door.

Who would be stubborn enough to seek him on such a night?

"Jonas. Jonas Jönsson. Open the door!"

The warnings were true.

"Someone has been asking about you—where you come from, where you live, things like that," his supervisor at the Park Point Trolley Company informed him.

Who remembered his name, his real name, the name that *Fader* and *Mor* gave him, the name he chose to forget in a Minneapolis saloon? For a decade and a half, he had been hiding from the law under a false identity as Ole Jönsson, but now, the storm called his name. Along with drifts of snow, the easterly was the bringer of truth.

"Jonas. Jonas Jönsson. Open the door!"

He slowly chewed on the last soft morsel of his cookie--he always had cookies from his regular passengers on the trolley—and drank the last of his milk. *I will sleep one more night in my own bed. If the caller returns in the morning, then I will open the door.* His windowless, single-room hut grew dark when he blew out the lone candle.

"Jonas. Jonas Jönsson. Open the door!"

He had slept well enough, but now the fateful morning had arrived, and the knock on his door again interrupted his solitude. Jönsson surveyed his abode--for the last time, he assumed—before unlocking the door. Drifted snow tumbled in when the door burst open, and Jönsson staggered back. He was prepared for the law. He was prepared to be taken away in handcuffs. He was prepared to answer for the saloonkeeper.

He was not prepared for the man standing in the doorway, his face haloed by the morning sun. It seemed to be his father, but as his father appeared to him when Jönsson was merely a tyke, a father who existed only in his childhood memories: strong, tall, and young, younger than Jönsson himself.

Jönsson rubbed his eyes and shielded them from the sun. The man stepped into the room.

"Jonas, is that really you?"

Jönsson numbly nodded his head.

The man burst out laughing. "You don't recognize me, do you! I'm Tomas, your brother."

"Tomas? Tomas! My brother? *Lillebror!* Tomas, you're a man!"

When Jönsson last saw his brother, he was merely a lad of ten, but now he was a strapping image of their father as a twenty-five-year-old.

"We thought you were long dead!" Tomas said. "From the postmark on your letter home, we traced you to Hinckley, and I looked for you there when I arrived in America two years ago, but I assumed you had been burned up in the fire. No one in Hinckley knew anything about Jonas Jönsson."

He pulled out a newspaper clipping.

"That's Jonas I said to myself when I saw your picture. Quite a hero you turned out to be. But why is your name listed as Ole?"

# CHAPTER TWENTY-THREE

T welve years. A dozen. A decade plus two. It seemed a blink of his eye since Jonas had been in touch with the family back home, but he knew that time was shaded by dark and light, with comings and goings, and although he wanted to hear the good of it, he dreaded the bad. Thus, he hesitated to the ask the question that ached to be heard. *How are the folks back home?*

Without waiting for the question, Tomas answered.

First the good.

"*Mor* is well, and she thrives in the role of doting grand-mother. Alfrid lives in the big house with his wife and two daughters, and Anna's two sons are nearby. Anna married Olaf Olafsson—do you remember the Olafssons from the farm two miles east? Olaf was the pimply-faced youngest son, and he teaches at the kinder school in town. The boys catch frogs around the pond and chase their girl cousins."

Jonas smiled, imagining and remembering.

Then the bad.

"*Fader* passed on months before I left for America. He had been ailing following a stroke suffered four years ago—no, five —and that's when Alfrid became the head of household."

Jonas didn't despise his father, but neither were they close, and that is also how he responded to news of his death—with sadness but not grief. He was a good man who provided for his family as he knew how, but he was also limited and un-even with his children. Alfrid was the clear favorite, the girls were just girls, and Tomas was an afterthought. And where did Jonas fit in? He was *Mor's* boy, and *Fader* left it at that.

Tomas drew a deep breath before explaining that Alfrid's wife forced their parents out of the big house and into the broken-down cottage out back. Alfrid and Tomas replaced the roof, repaired the broken windows, and everything else that needed fixing.

"Elsa moved in with them, and she sees it as her calling to stay there with *Mor* until …, until, well, you know."

The brothers sat quietly, each contemplating the tyranny of time. Jonas was thankful for sister Elsa for doing what he could not. His anger flashed at Alfrid, which made him realize how much he despised his older brother, but the anger was also self-directed, and a shock of guilt rattled his bones as he realized the selfishness in his decision to leave Sweden and his family, a selfishness compounded by a dozen years of silence. We owe each other ourselves. It was certainly not a plan, not a wish, not even a conscious thought, but somehow, he expected a homecoming at the last when all would be happily reunited.

Jonas barely noticed Tomas slip out to the biffy in back. The somber mood was broken when he returned.

"Say, what do you have to eat?" Tomas asked.

Over buttered bread and coffee, Tomas' interrogation of Jonas began. "And what of you? Update me."

Jonas answered with half-truths that left out the full story of his limp, of his sudden departure from Swede Hollow, of his burned-up son, of Natty Einstein, but his fake name of "Ole" hinted at more. There was doubt in the eyes of his brother; twelve years of silence said more than Jonas' hollow words, but Tomas didn't question his older brother further.

The day passed comfortably and joyously. A bright sun followed the storm, and they crunched through the snow on the beach and looked out through the fog of their breaths over the shoreline sheet of ice to the rising steam over open water far from shore. The locals called it sea smoke. The deep waters never fully warmed in summer nor fully cooled in winter. They walked to the end of the pier. The icy remains of the *Mataafa* had not yet been salvaged, and Jonas told the story one more time, and *Lillebror's* eyes shone with familiar admiration. They remembered and smiled, sometimes laughed. They teased and laughed some more.

That evening, Jonas boiled lake trout fillets and fried potatoes in a skillet. He didn't often eat such a feast.

"I bought forty acres," Tomas said. "There's work enough for two to build something and make a life. I've been clearing the land, but I could use your help."

"I have a life, and I'm comfortable enough," Jonas replied.

Tomas hesitated before continuing. Jonas could tell he was contemplating whether to continue, to encourage like he had done when Jonas was hesitant to call on that freckle-faced girl back in their small village.

"A trolley car driver? The brother I looked up to aspired to something. He was an ambitious man, and now you settle for this?" Tomas' eyes scanned the scant, windowless hut: a bed with a ragged quilt but no sheets; a single coal-burning stove that doubled as heater and cookstove; an icebox with a broken door hanging from one hinge.

"You're a beaten-down-old man by the age of thirty-five. What has become of you?"

Jonas keenly felt his brother's disappointment, but he responded defensively.

"Who are you to judge? You don't know the half of it!" Jonas replied, but he wasn't about to reveal the rest.

The fugitive murderer, the widower, the cuckold, the recluse who retreated to a solitary life on the shores of the great lake was not yet ready to resurrect the man his brother remembered, the man of hopes and dreams who died on the beer-swollen planks of a saloon. "Go to your farm," Jonas said. "That is your dream, not mine. I have chosen a different path—or maybe God has chosen it for me—but here I will stay."

Jonas looked away. The coal fire had died down, and Tomas' disappointment chilled the room. Jonas would remain in Duluth, and his sibling would leave alone. With promises to remain in touch, Tomas and Jonas separated. Tomas would board a railway car to return alone to central Minnesota.

The morning after Tomas' departure, Jonas held his razor before his throat as the mirror revealed the gray beard stubble and the tufts of gray hair that lay behind his ears. There were wrinkles etched into his cheeks that he hadn't noticed and crow's feet around his eyes. The luster of his emerald eyes had faded to the color of dull moss. He saw himself as his brother must have seen him.

He mouthed the name he had long ago abandoned, then said it aloud: "Jonas," the sound seemed a mere grumble caught in his throat. The name lodged in his gut, and he passed a few days without appetite. The nightmares returned, and the ice sheet prevented the comforting waves from reaching the shore.

He wrote a letter home that was neither triumphal nor morose. He didn't tell all but neither did he attempt to rationalize his silence for which he expressed remorse. He offered a superficial summary of twelve years of no real news. But he again established a link with his family, and he signed the letter, *Jonas*.

A small step.

As the winter months passed into spring, events conspired against him, or perhaps for him.

First, he was fined by his employer when a stooge, an anti-union spy from management, reported him for accepting cookies from a passenger. Fines for silly infractions proved the worth of the informers to their masters. Trolley drivers were at the bottom of the labor ladder, working interminable hours for absurd pay, but the job and a solitary life on the island had suited Jönsson for years. The episode soured Jönsson's attitude toward his unseen bosses and the job he had devoted himself to.

But, it was a funeral that would allow closure and end his Duluth sojourn.

Jönsson remained in the shadows as the eulogies remembered the much-too-young socialite who died soon after a diagnosis of cancer, and he quickly spotted the person he came to see. Dressed in a trim black dress, Natty Einstein was one of the few who had not covered her head, and her draping dark hair had streaks of gray. She sat alone, and not with the siblings of the deceased or the mother or the estranged husband who did the respectful thing by attending, but she was the only one who shed tears.

Jönsson slipped out before the pall bearers carried the casket down the aisle, and he watched from the shade of an old oak. Natty did not follow the procession behind the casket, and Jönsson feared he had missed her, but suddenly she was at his elbow, clutching his arm.

"Did you come to shoot the place up?"

Many years had passed since that day, but it seemed just a snap of the fingers since he made passionate love to her. Despite the gray hair and a few facial creases, she was the same woman who stirred his blood. As the funeral cortege departed in one direction, Einstein and Jönsson walked arm-in-arm toward their familiar haunts of the canal district.

"I was proud of your heroics on the water," she said.

"I see you're still organizing," he said.

"Yes, I'm working with the Wobblies now. The trusts are winning, and labor must become more confrontational."

When the shadows of smokestacks stretched tall on the lake, small talk turned serious.

"I am so, so sorry, it ended the way it did," she said, "and I am so, so glad that I can offer my apology and explanation, if you will listen. If you choose to forgive me, so much the better."

Jönsson had long ago forgiven her, but he would gladly hear an explanation, perhaps to put his confusion to rest.

"You were a good man, and I did love you," she said. "No, it's true, I did, but I loved her also, and I stayed with her only because she could accept that I had slept with you, but I expected that you wouldn't accept that I slept with her. Don't ask me to explain, because I don't fully comprehend myself, but it is who I am, and Elmira, for all her faults, didn't judge me, and I expected that you would."

They continued in silence until they reached the north pier of the ship canal. Jönsson's thoughts rattled around like billiard balls caroming every which way after a break. He could smear her face with kisses right now and carry her off to his cabin just down the way, but he also sensed that she was right, that it could never be the same after Elmira Swensson had wagged her pointy little tits in his face, as if to say, these are for Natty, and the rest of me, too. That image, and the truth that Natty's body and soul were shared would never leave him. He might have dared to compete against another man, but the very thought of competing for her affection against women befuddled him. The natural order of things was askew, it seemed, and she was certainly right; he would be unable to rise above his predispositions.

A trolley car from the Duluth side rattled down the tracks toward them, and Natty moved in that direction. As the trolley brakes screeched on the iron rails, Natty reached into her handbag and pulled out the red Dala pony painted by Jönsson.

"This is yours," she said, "and you may take it back if you wish. I have always carried it with me, and I'd like to keep it, but only if it's alright with you."

Jönsson attempted to speak, but the words caught in his throat. She touched his tear with her thumb, her fingers raking the hair over his ears and returned the pony to her bag.

She climbed up the first step before turning and kissing his forehead, and then she was gone.

He rode the gondola and returned alone to his beach. He sat for a moment on his broken trolley seat before removing his boots. It was like and not like. When he had walked the sandy beaches of the Baltic Sea, the breeze carried the scent of salt air and the promise of adventure on far shores. Now, the great unsalted sea reminded him of family left behind, his failures and dashed hopes. Still, there was solace in the sand that squeezed between his toes, and the sharp edge of a clamshell against his heel seemed less an irritant than a reminder that he still lived, that he remained flesh and blood, and that life was for the living.

He flipped stones into the water, and the waves returned an answer.

**********

*With each passing day, I tired more easily, and Pastor Don often departed when I fell asleep in the afternoon, but as I wound down the story of Papa's Duluth sojourn, I talked through the arrival of the red birds and into the dinner hour.*

*"Shall I bring each of you a dinner tray?" LaDonna asked from the doorway. I looked at Don, and he nodded.*

*Usually, Don merely listened, asking a question here or there, as my telling of Papa's story unfolded, but now it was his turn to speak:*

*"I have been to Duluth many times for church conventions or just passing through on my way to a north shore vacation. I have gazed from the top of Spirit Mountain, with skis on my feet, at the bird's eye view of Duluth, her inner harbor, and the great lake beyond. I once attended a cocktail party at the Kitchi Gammi Club where Grandfather Jonas served champagne to Rockefeller, Swensson, and the rest. I have walked the concrete pier that lines the canal into the inner harbor, and I have marveled at the great ore ships that ply those waters—I understand they are up to one-thousand-feet long these days! I have dined at the restaurant called 'Grandma's Saloon and Grill,' just across the ship canal from Grandfather's trolley line. I have hummed along as Gordon Lightfoot remembered the Edmund Fitzgerald and the gales of November."*

*LaDonna paused at the door, sensing that the moment was not right to enter.*

*"Now, I am anxious to return," Don said, "for it will be a pilgrimage. I have never crossed over the aerial lift bridge, but I will do that now, and I will walk the sandy beaches of Park Point."*

# CHAPTER TWENTY-FOUR: 1906-07

J önsson chose the longer, southern train route because it would take him through Hinckley, but that was a poor decision. New growth of poplars couldn't hide all the black-scarred spires of pines that remained after a decade. After arriving at the Hinckley railroad junction and awaiting a departure to St. Cloud, his anxiety grew with each passing minute. There were ghosts afoot, and when the conductor blew his whistle, Jönsson was the first to board, carrying two burlap bags stuffed with the whole of his possessions. The bags were bulky and awkward to handle. Jönsson's leg ached, and he wished he hadn't left his cane on the broken trolley seat overlooking the lake. It seemed a good idea at the time, to start afresh, but his leg reminded him that wishing to leave things behind doesn't make it so.

Upon reaching St. Cloud, he again switched trains for the thirty-mile trip following the Mississippi north to Little Falls. One of Minnesota's oldest cities, Little Falls was not his destination but merely a waypoint, as it had been for the Dakota and the Ojibwe; the French and the English; the explorer, the missionary, the fur trader, the lumberman, and now the railroad man. The Mississippi was the great watery highway that sluiced through the heart of the territory that became a state, and the waterfall called the Little Falls located here forced a portage and offered a convenient overnight camp that grew into a small city.

Jönsson spent that night on the west bank of the great river near a lumber mill, and the roar of the falls aided his sleep. He awoke with an empty belly, and his irritation grew as Tomas was late. Finally, his brother arrived driving a borrowed wagon and mule, and they traveled west through rocky hills thick with oak and maple and swampland with stands of tamarack. Jönsson had seen newspaper pictures of vast wheat fields in the farmlands of Minnesota, but this countryside seemed more like the poor farms of his Swedish homeland.

"That's a nasty limp," Tomas said when they stopped for a piss break.

"I can manage," Jonas said and did his best to smooth his gait without the diamond willow cane he left behind.

The sun was still high in the western sky when the sod hut, cut into the side of a hill, came into view. Compared to this dirty, mean dwelling, the Duluth cabin was a mansion on the East End. Tomas walked him to a promontory that overlooked the forty acres. God dammit, there would be much work to do before you could call this wilderness a farm.

Time to get started.

Jonas would tend to the animals—as soon as they had livestock—and Tomas would labor in the fields—as soon as the land was cleared and ground broken. Jonas brought one significant asset to their enterprise. His reclusive and frugal life in Duluth had allowed him to accumulate a sock full of bills and coins, nearly $200. Their first purchase would be a horse. And then a plow. Then a scythe to cut meadow hay to store up for the horse over the winter. Then a fork to pitch the hay. Then a hammer and nails to construct a lean-to shelter for the hay and the horse when the winter winds would blow. And then the money was gone.

It had been fifteen years and a tangled journey to reach this humble beginning, but the meager farmstead rekindled Jönsson's dream despite all the detours and setbacks. On July 4, 1906, Jönsson became a farmer in the land of the free and the home of the brave.

"*Framåt, flicka.*"

His money was well-spent on a painted filly in her third year. She was a sturdy young girl, and Jönsson was confident she would be a loyal friend. Sure, he could have spent more on a larger and stronger gelding, but the filly had an air of dependability that the horseman spotted, and she would thrive as a saddle horse when she wasn't under harness pulling a plow or a wagon. And, it was his money, so the filly it would be despite Tomas' disagreement. But Jönsson acceded to his brother on the matter of naming the filly, sort of.

"Ve're Americans, now, and *framåt, flicka*, should be 'Giddap, girl.'"

"Giddap, *Gurli*," Jönsson said, choosing a Swedish feminine name, and each brother figured they won the argument.

Breaking the sod with a shiny new double-handled, single-blade plow pulled behind Gurli would fill Jonas' first day in the field.

Nomads had roamed this land before him: the Dakota, the Ojibwe, the French and the English. Perhaps there were arrow heads buried here, or a musket ball, where a bison had been felled and roasted over an open fire. But none had broken the sod. For untold eons, this hillside meadow awaited this day. Did the land anticipate him with the same dreams he wished upon the land? He was the one—and Tomas, of course—to awaken this sleeping ground, to loosen the topsoil from its wait, to sprinkle seed and urge new life, not wild and untamed but domesticated and civilized. Here he would build a farm and a life. He, too, had been a wanderer, but now he would sink his roots, and deep. The pine and the oak had come and gone and come again, but now it would be corn and wheat; instead of the deer and the bear, it would be horses and spotted cattle. The land was his, and he was of the land.

He arose before dawn and chased a breakfast of beans with boiled coffee. Except for a short lunch break of sausage and hard bread, washed down with a jar of water from the creek that edged against their forty, he didn't quit until the sun was low in the west. He curried his girl and made sure she had plenty of water as she grazed on a grassy hillside. He finally returned to the sod-hut with a sunburn that turned his skin bright pink, blisters on his hands, a throbbing leg, mosquito bites up and down his arms, and a general state of exhaustion.

It was all good, so very good.

After ten acres had been readied for spring planting, Jonas hooked a chain to the oak logs that Tomas felled and stripped of bark and Gurli pulled each log to the site of their new cabin, to be tucked into standing maples on high ground overlooking the creek. Tomas planned and supervised the construction, and he chopped out the saddle notches at the ends of each twenty-foot log, and he arranged a rope and pulley apparatus to hoist each log into place. Jonas chinked the one-inch gap between each log with clay and woodchips and daubed the cracks with a clay-dung mixture bound together with sawdust. While Tomas placed low-sloped rafters in place, Jonas cut strips of water-repellent birch bark to be placed atop the roof planks, inside up and held in place with chunks of sod that would provide a warm layer of green for a generation.

Before a stone fireplace and chimney could be constructed, the autumn harvest was in full swing, and the brothers hired out for six weeks of field work before they returned to their cabin and fireplace construction. Next year, it would be their own fields. In addition to replenishing Jonas' coin sock, the brothers were rewarded with the wagon that Jonas drove behind Gurli, which Jonas soon loaded with melon-sized fieldstones. While Tomas fashioned a fireplace inside, Jonas split and piled oak firewood. By the time of the first snowfall on Thanksgiving eve, smoke curled up from the fireplace inside the toasty, single room cabin.

Beginning in January, the brothers rode the wagon to Little Falls each morning and returned after dark. They worked through the winter at the Pine Tree Lumber Company sawmill owned by Charles Weyerhaeuser, who lived in a posh mansion just downstream on the river's east side. The sawmill ripped the pine logs that floated down the Mississippi during the summer months into slabs then into boards for shipment by rail during the winter months.

Tomas did the heavy lifting as an "off-bearer," carrying everything that went through the whining circular saws. If it was a slab, it went to the slab pile; if it was a board, it was stacked with the other boards of the same size. Jonas worked as a "lumber-trucker" pushing a two-wheel cart loaded with boards to a waiting train. The walking made his leg plenty sore, but the cart handles provided balance instead of a cane.

More coins for the sock.

In mid-April, the brothers returned to farming. They joined the farmer's cooperative in the nearby village of Kalmar, where they would buy their seed and sell their harvest, if they should be so God dammit lucky. Yellow Cowslips sprouted before the last patches of snow disappeared. Little bluebills searched for open water, followed by flocks of greenhead mallards that darkened the sky, soon outdone by honking geese, often heard before they were seen.

Plowing was much easier in the spring after breaking the sod the summer before. Every time Jönsson reached the end of a furrow, he would follow a little ritual. After turning Gurli around, he would kneel and sift the dark, loamy soil through his fingers. After plowing, Gurli and Jonas would pull a harrow borrowed from a neighbor to break up the clods of soil and smooth the ground for planting. Tomas followed behind with a hoe, digging a small hole for potato eyes and after a few rows, he switched to kernels of seed corn.

"You left no ground for wheat," Jonas complained when he saw that Tomas covered the whole field with potatoes or corn.

"In America, wheat is planted in the fall," Tomas replied.

"What foolishness is that," Jonas scoffed, "the green shoots will come up and freeze in winter's cold."

Tomas would win that argument, and Jonas wasn't pleased. Back in Sweden, Tomas the young tyke idolized his older brother, but now it seemed that Tomas had an uppity attitude and showed his older brother no deference.


Gurli would flutter her nostrils when she heard the cabin door creak open, and nicker as Jonas approached the lean-to, but on this May morning, the lean-to was ominously silent.

"Wake up, Gurli. Are you asleep?"

She wasn't there. The lean-to was empty. Had he forgotten to tie her? She wouldn't wander far. He whistled. He whistled again.

"Gurli. Come Gurli, where are you?"

Dawn's first rays peeked over the eastern ridge through aspen leaves that rustled in a freshening breeze.

"Gurli," he yelled. "Gurli, Gurli, come Gurli." He yelled louder.

By noon, he was resigned to the truth. Thieves. God dammit to hell. Fucking horse thieves. Do they still hang horse thieves? They fucking should.

"I'll let you know if we hear anything," the sheriff's deputy said as he stuffed his note pad in his pocket. "Willy Peterson always has ponies for sale, if you need to get your crops in."

Jonas listened from the lean-to while Tomas did the talking. Jonas remained skittish around the law, and he had urged his brother to refer to him as "Ole."

"Well, that's the name I been using. For no good reason, mind you, but that's how I been known."

As the deputy rode off with the sun at his back, Tomas muttered, "That's the last we'll hear from him."

Fucking horse thieves. They ought to be hung, if you could only catch them.

# CHAPTER TWENTY-FIVE: 1908-1912

"Hail the cabin!"

Jonas Jönsson rose from the supper table where he ate alone; Tomas was off to Little Falls on an errand. Outside, a drummer sat on a mule leading a donkey laden with saddlebags bristling with tin pots and pans.

"Good evening, kind sir. Might you spare a dipper of water?"

Jönsson obliged.

"Aaaah, that soothes the throat. Might I have another?"

Instead of slurping it down like he did the first, he sipped the second portion.

"Fine farmstead, yours is, and I've seen plenty."

Jönsson waited for the pitch, which he would reject since he and Tomas had decided to spend nearly all their cash on a new horse, but the pitch never came.

"Word is, you're missing a horse, a spotted filly, I hear."

He handed the dipper back to Jonas.

"May I get down? My rump gets a little raw this time of day."

Jönsson said nothing but gestured with his hand. The peddler gingerly dismounted and patted his mule's hindquarter.

"This old sonofabitch has seen better days, and I could use

a filly myself, but I won't take yours, even if I know where she could be bought for a song."

Jönsson suddenly paid close attention and found a reason to be hospitable.

"Would you like some beans and bread?' Jonas offered.

"Yes, I'll take a meal, and I'll tell you what. I'll inform you where you can find your filly, and if I'm right, well maybe you'd like to look at my wares the next time I pass through."


With the information provided by the drummer, Jonas made plans to rescue his horse, but he said nothing to Tomas when his brother returned. After Tomas went to the field the next morning, Jonas found the Colt revolver in the bottom of his burlap bag. The skunk gun. He spun the cylinder and checked. Three spent cartridges and three live. He should buy a box of cartridges, he reminded himself, but three ought to be sufficient for now. Tomas was busy hoeing the corn planted earlier, and Jonas slipped out the cabin and ducked behind the lean-to before setting out toward New Warsaw, a village populated with Polish immigrants, eight miles to the southeast. He would reclaim his horse from the fucking thief, alright, and maybe exact a little justice. Do they still hang horse thieves?

The sun was high in the sky by the time Jonas reached New Warsaw. His directions said there was a horse trader next to a swamp a mile east before you reached the Mississippi. As he walked down the cart path leading to a ramshackle shed that apparently served as stable, he spotted a pen of horses milling about on the far side. Before he saw her, she whinnied, and his pace quickened as he figured on how he ought to play this. He stashed his walking cane in the bushes and checked his gun again, tucked in his pants beneath a billowing shirt.

As he neared the stable, a lanky, square-shouldered fellow

emerged from the shed. A dirty-yellow, straw Stetson with rolled up sides and a sloping bill shaded the man's eye slits, and Jönsson couldn't read him. Salt and pepper stubble bristled over a square jaw. He chewed on a cheroot butt. A buttonless vest fit snugly over a blue work shirt with muscles bulging under tight sleeves. A polished brass buckle covered the pinch of the leather strap that held up faded jeans.

"Looks like you need a horse, Hayseed," he said, removing the cigar butt from his mouth and spitting out tobacco shreds. "Well, I got some." He pawed the dust with a pointy-toed boot.

The man was probably not the one who snuck onto the farm in the dead of night and stole away with Gurli, but the thief knew where to sell a stolen horse, and the fence was as guilty as the thief. Jönsson put one foot on a rail and leaned into the pen as if to check out the herd. After a moment, he said, "I like the looks of that painted filly."

"A fine piece of horseflesh, I raised her myself."

Jönsson nodded. After a brief hesitation, he whistled, and Gurli trotted to him. The big man set his jaw, and he hunkered down.

"Well," Jönsson said. "She's already my horse, stolen from me not a week ago."

"Humph. The law says possession, and I got possession right now, old timer." The goliath rocked back and forth on his heels and clenched and unclenched his fists.

Jönsson played his ace. He pulled the pistol from his belt, pointed it aloft, and squeezed off a round. That alone may or may not have frightened the oaf, but in one of those fateful moments that you can't explain, the bullet blew the head off a solitary black crow that happened to be flying by and minding his own business at the time. With nary a squawk, the dead carcass landed at the feet of the horse trader, who jumped back, knocking off his Stetson and sending his cigar flying.

"What the fuck!"

The burly man retrieved his hat, slapping it once across his knee to knock off the dust, while keeping a wary eye on the man who could shoot crows out of the sky as if it was nothing.

"If the horse is yours, mister, then the horse is yours. Take her."

"I'll take a bridle, too, if you please," Jönsson said, and he flipped four bits into the dust at the man's feet. The fifty-cent piece nearly landed on the crow, and the trader retrieved the coin while cautiously avoiding the dead bird.

It was a fine day for a ride. White clouds strolled across a blue sky. Yellow-breasted meadowlarks chased bugs in the grasslands along the road. A male on a fencepost serenaded him with a flutelike song as he passed.

When the farm came into view and Tomas still hoeing, Jonas and Gurli broke into a gallop.

"Yippee! Yippee!" Jonas screeched as Gurli circled the field.

"But, but, how ..."

Jonas slipped the six-shooter into his sack before Tomas returned. Two live cartridges remained.

Fencing in four acres for pastureland occupied the brothers the summer of 1907, and now their task was completed. Jonas put his hands on his hips and pushed as if to straighten his stiff back. It was a familiar gesture that signified the end of the workday. He knew that a peppery stew in a new tin pot to be served in new tin plates—recent purchases from a certain drummer--awaited their return to the cabin after the brothers spent the day stringing barbed wire. He tossed his tools in a bag and headed toward the cabin.

"Wait," Tomas said. "We've one more chore to complete."

Jonas looked back and saw nothing. Tomas headed down toward the creek and a stand of tall cottonwoods as a bemused Jonas trailed behind. The trees had long since released their cotton-like tufts into the summer winds, creating the illusion of snow on the ground, and now the leaves fluttered in the slight breeze, producing a rustling chorus. Tomas waded into the creek, stopping in the middle and filling his hat before pouring it over his head. A baptism of sorts. On the bank, a root flair bulged the soil around the base of a large tree. Tomas walked past the tall specimen to a younger cottonwood with smooth bark.

By the time Jonas joined him, Tomas had etched a "T" in the bark with his pocketknife. Time collapsed, and Jonas was suddenly back in Sweden as he remembered the fifth-year birthday ritual of *Fader* and his sons. The bark was soft, and Tomas was quick with his task.

"Here is where the names of our sons will be recorded," Tomas said. "Your turn. Where's your pocketknife?"

Jonas reached into his pocket and pulled out the knife gifted to him by his father so long ago and far away. He fingered the mother-of-pearl handle, remembering the smears of the saloon keeper's blood, the limp body of Louis Archambault as flames crackled overhead, and the Dala pony carved for Natty. It seemed much of his life was tied to that pocketknife, and now he would use it to memorialize a new beginning.

He etched his name in the bark of the cottonwood tree. When he finished, he pulled out his hanky and blew his nose.

By Labor Day, a pair of black-and-white spotted heifers

explored their new domain. The bred cows would calve come the next spring. Tomas returned to work for Pine Tree Lumber that winter, but Jonas tended to the farm and expanded the lean-to. In 1908, the brothers dug a well, covered by a pump with a long handle for drawing water. They weaned a pair of calves by the first snowfall, and Jonas began the twice-a-day ritual of milking the cows. Tomas returned to winter work at the sawmill, and Jonas tended to their small but growing herd through the winter of '09. That summer, the brothers doubled the size of the farm by purchasing an adjacent forty. They expanded the pasture and tilled ten additional acres.

On a lazy August day in 1910, Jonas walked to the promontory that looked down on the pasture. Crops were in. Hay laid up. Fall harvest not yet due. He sat in the grass and surveyed the small herd of two cows, two yearlings, two calves, and two horses. Gurli had gained a partner, a gelding who stood two hands taller, but Gurli remained the boss. Jonas plucked a blade of grass and chewed and ruminated. He had an idea, but he must first run it by Tomas, who just happened to be on his way from the corn patch. Tomas plopped down next to his older brother and joined him in gnawing on a blade of grass.

"It's time," Jonas started the conversation.

"If I know what you're getting at, you're right. It's time. You first."

"Nah, we should draw straws, we'll let fate decide."

"God dammit, Jonas, you'll be forty years old next year. Time's a wasting."

Jonas slapped a mosquito. The sun was dipping low. Time for milking. And then Tomas began to sing.

*Ah hoo. Wee hodee do. Ah hoo. We hoo. Wo wee!*

Jonas broke out laughing. Tomas called the cows the way Jonas taught him twenty years earlier. *Kulning.* The traditional way. The old way. The Swedish way. High-pitched, singsong, wordless.

"You do it," Tomas said.

Jonas laughed, then tried to be sober. *Hoo ha …*

His voice cracked and both brothers laughed and laughed harder. Jonas wadded up a clump of grass and tossed it at *Lillebror* who jumped Jonas, and the brothers wrestled in the grass and laughed some more. Breathing heavily, the brothers each laid back to follow the terns circle high in the sky. Fall would be here soon enough.

"I mean it, you first," Tomas said, breaking the idyllic silence.

It was decided. Jonas would be the first to take a wife, and arrangements began to fall in place, through contacts with the folks back home, for a bride to be sent to America. Money was saved for the cost of transit. After six months, a sock bulged with rolled bills. When a second sock was filled, Jonas sent a letter to *Mor* to complete the arrangements. A photographer in Little Falls prepared a portrait of Jonas, in one of the photographer's suits used for that purpose. Jonas primped in front of a full-length mirror. Did the silver streaks in his hair suggest maturity or merely that he was getting old? He stood up straight and tall against his natural slouch, but he remained unconvinced. What woman would want such a man?

Hilma Andersdotter, that's who, the daughter of a distant cousin, but when Jönsson saw her picture, he nearly cancelled the arrangements.

"She's so God dammit young, she could be my own daughter!"

When the Titanic sank in April 1912, drowning dozens of Swedish emigrants along with thousands of others, the world was shocked, and so was Hilma's mother, who nearly pulled her daughter out of the arrangement, but the headstrong young woman was adamant, and she would sail to the new world and a new life. Much like Jonas over two decades earlier, she dreamed of an America filled with opportunity, especially for younger daughters with poor prospects in the home country. This was her chance, and she would not be deterred. Thus, she boarded the Titanic's older sister, the Olympic, and departed Europe in the fall of 1912. While the great ship plowed the waters westward, the Jönsson brothers doubled the size of the farm cabin by adding a bedroom for the wedded couple and a storeroom/pantry.

Jonas purchased his own suit and boarded a train in Little Falls, bound for the Union Depot in St. Paul as the demure Hilma sat impatiently on the leather seat of a Pullman car rumbling west from Chicago and New York City before that.

# CHAPTER TWENTY-SIX: 1912-1913

Following a silent three-hour train ride from St. Paul's Union Depot and another hour's journey by horse and wagon from Little Falls to Kalmar, Jonas and his bride-to-be waited on the steps of the Swedish Lutheran Church while Tomas summoned the preacher who had promised to conduct the wedding ceremony. Pastor Charles F. Halstrom, a recent graduate of Augustana Seminary in Illinois, and Agnes, his wife, each carried a kerosene lantern as they made their way from the parsonage next door under a moonless but starry sky. The clergyman and his wife were born in America of Swedish immigrants, and they were both bilingual.

"Come, come, dear girl," Agnes said in Swedish. The bride's doe eyes moistened. Agnes removed Hilma's hat, smoothed her crinkly red hair, and used a kerchief to wipe the dust from her freckled face.

Jonas shifted uneasily from one foot to the other, waiting for the young woman to object, to say she had changed her mind. Or maybe the pastor or his missus would intervene, to say this isn't right, that he was too old, and she was too young, that this arrangement hadn't been properly considered, that the young girl needed more time to reflect on her decision.

"Are we ready?" the pastor asked, looking to his wife for assurance, who in turn peered into Hilma's glistening eyes.

When an owl in a nearby tree hooted, Hilma gasped, and Jonas sensed they were about to make a huge mistake. Standing here on the stoop of Kalmar's modest country church that seemed a mockery of the magnificent Kalmar cathedral on the shores of the Baltic epitomized the grandiose immigrant dreams. Once again, he had played the fool and expected more than his circumstances permitted. If she regretted her decision, he regretted his the more. Oh, she was fetching and seemed sweet-tempered, and he could grow to love her quite naturally, but only an old fool would expect her to reciprocate. That he had sought her out, that he had asked her to come to America, that he had encouraged her by paying her way, now embarrassed him—no, more than that—he felt guilty at his deception for the fickle promise of America had repeatedly tripped him up yet he preyed on her naïve attraction to the same thin hopes.

"I'll put you back on the train and pay for your passage home, if that is your wish," Jonas said.

Hilma jerked her head toward him and slapped his face.

"Bite your tongue, husband."

Tomas laughed out loud.

Hilma clenched her jaw in resolute determination and nodded. "I'm ready," she said.

Clutching Hilma by the arm, Agnes escorted her up the aisle through the empty pews to the rail that formed a half circle around the altar. Under the dim-yellow glow of the kerosene lanterns that barely shooed the dark, subdued voices spoke the vows that formalized the marriage of the couple who met mere hours before. Tomas stood up for his brother and Agnes for Hilma. Jonas wore his new suit and Hilma the same dress she wore on the train.

"Giddap, Gurli."

Jonas lightly flicked the reins across Gurli's haunches, and the newlyweds headed toward the humble cabin where she would become the mistress of the house. Tomas sat at the back of the wagon with feet dangling, leaning against the immense "America chest" that had accompanied Hilma across the sea, carefully packed with everything a young bride might need on the American prairie.

The ancestral clothes trunk had been pulled from the cobwebs by her mother who scoured the inside and polished the rusty iron bands that held the oak slats together before she supervised the packing: underwear and outerwear; aprons and house dresses; boots, shoes, and slippers; a pair of Sunday blouses and skirts; knitting needles, scissors, and thread; sheets and pillows—who knew what her bachelor fiancé slept on; soaps, salves, and tiny medicine bottles; and a gift for her husband-to-be—a shaving mug filled with a lavender-scented bar of soap, a marble-handled shaving brush, and a straight razor. The bulkiest contents were for the frigid cold of Minnesota winters—a full length wool coat, a wool jacket, wool hats, wool sweaters, wool socks—even wool underwear.

Jonas made no assumptions, much less demands, regarding their wedding night. Tomas delicately offered to sleep in the hay mow, and Jonas was prepared to spend the night in the main room, especially when the door to the bedroom remained closed, but then it opened. Nevertheless, it was all too much, too soon, and their clumsy attempt at intimacy proved disastrous. The experienced husband attempted to be gentle, and she did what was expected of a bride, but when he finished, she wept. She also wept the next morning and for many days after that. They would not attempt lovemaking again for many months. Hilma wanted to be brave, but the reality of a child bride in a strange land, living with strange men, far from the counsel of a mother, was more than her twenty-year-old soul was prepared for.

Tomas never returned to his bed in the cabin's main room.

"Seems like you need it for now," Tomas said to Jonas. "I'll take a room in Little Falls until it's my turn for a wife, and we'll build a second cabin."

Jonas didn't argue, but he heard a tinge of resentment in his brother's voice. The cabin seemed just right for two brothers, but woefully inadequate with the addition of a woman.

Hilma coped through her busyness. She cooked, she cleaned, she darned the holes in his socks, and she even mucked out the lean-to. She spent evenings seated at the wedding gift from her husband, a splendid Singer sewing machine atop a wrought iron pedestal with curly cues on the sides. The rapid clickity clack of the foot-powered Singer filled the cabin until the sound slowed, signaling that the day was done.

For his part, Jonas was patient even as he felt old and foolish for expecting that this contrived marriage could work. They barely spoke, but he appreciated her efforts at being a helpmate. He knew she was frightened and overwhelmed, but she didn't sulk or complain.

As autumn gave way to winter, a routine developed for the last hour of each waking day. Under the light of a candle, Jonas pored over the latest newspaper delivered by Tomas while Agnes let her hair down and slowly brushed it while humming softly, almost imperceptibly. Jonas stole glances. Her thick, crinkly hair seemed even redder backlit by the glow of the fireplace, and her freckles danced in the flickering candlelight. Even in the low light, her green eyes glistened. When she sensed his gaze, the tips of her lips curled up, and dimples appeared. After one hundred strokes with her brush, she rose to her feet, standing nearly as tall as her husband, and she moved with head held high and purpose as she threw another log on the fire before disappearing into the side room that was her bedroom. Jonas slept in Tomas' bed in the main cabin.

As the winter months passed, Jonas warmed to his good fortune. An arranged marriage could go bad, but his fondness grew for the young woman who became his bride by chance rather than choice. Although she had neither Ayasha's exuberance over the discovery of her sexuality nor the mature passion of Natty Einstein, she would become affectionate in time, he hoped. If he just remained tolerant, their relationship would be tolerable, and in time it would become more, he hoped. In time, she would bear him many sons, he hoped.

Jonas had promised to be a church-going man, and Hilma held him to it. Each Sunday he donned his new suit and hitched Gurli to the wagon, or a sleigh once snow covered the ground, for the twenty-minute journey to Kalmar and the Swedish Lutheran Church. The white-boarded church was the second-largest building in the village, next to Ingemar Jorgenson's General Store, and thanks to the cross atop the steeple, she was taller than all else, including the pair of white pines that stood as sentinels over the graveyard behind the church that was the resting place for the first generation of Swedish immigrants that founded this community. Originally built with a shallow foundation, there was talk of lifting the whole structure and digging a basement underneath. The women of the congregation had recently purchased a cast bronze bell-- shipped all the way from Philadelphia--paying more than the preacher's annual salary for the timeless tolling of the bell that called to worship, to community, and to Sabbath. Nearly everyone in Kalmar was a Swede, with a small enclave of "Happy Danes" nearby, and the pastor tended a large flock.

Many of the Kalmar Swedes were older than the young village, which was an odd juxtaposition since the village's namesake was one of Sweden's oldest cities. Similarly, the inland Minnesota village with a plain-white church and humble young pastor contrasted with the Swedish seacoast city that boasted a cathedral that had been home to bishops. The part-time, volunteer mayor's log cabin on the banks of the creek that trickled through the village was hardly the castle of kings overlooking the Baltic. Kalmar Minnesota ironically exposed the grandiose dreams of the immigrant.

Pastor Charlie was the first full-time pastor called by the church. Before him, circuit-riding preachers sent by the Synod served the congregation. Pastor Charlie was also unique in having been born in America and receiving seminary training on this side of the Atlantic, but he conducted services in the traditional Swedish tongue.

As usual, Jonas had a hard time staying awake during Pastor Halstrom's long-winded sermon, delivered, of course, in Swedish, but Hilma's sharp elbow saved him from the embarrassment of snoring. Coffee and pastries always followed the services, and Jonas waited impatiently, as usual, while Hilma socialized. The older women doted over her, but Hilma usually ended up hanging with Agnes Halstrom, the pastor's wife, who was only a few years her senior.

After the Easter service of 1913, Hilma requested to spend a couple nights in town at the residence of Pastor and Mrs. Halstrom.

"She shouldn't be alone in that big parsonage when Pastor Charlie is gone to conferences," Hilma said. "She's pregnant, you know."

Jönsson suspected there was more to it than that, but he consented, and he delivered her to the Halstrom parsonage for two April nights.

When he returned to town to pick her up, he first stopped at Jorgenson's General Store to replenish his supply of Prince Albert pipe tobacco and to purchase a sack of fresh ground coffee. Jönsson never cared much for the snoose preferred by many of his countrymen, but morning coffee and an evening smoke were pleasures that suited this simple farmer. Each time he opened the door and crossed the threshold into the store, the tinkling bell that announced his arrival triggered a hazy unease. Part of it was the cloud of condescension that hung in the air, but Jönsson also coveted the many shiny things that tempted his wants beyond his needs, and so he disciplined himself not to linger but to do his business straightaway and then move on.

Proprietor Ingemar Jorgenson stood tall and broad under a shock of white hair and an equally white handle-bar moustache with waxed tips. His standard uniform consisted of a cotton duck apron hugging his barrel chest and reaching his ankles. Jorgenson would have you know that he was Kalmar's most successful entrepreneur, except perhaps for Henry Alekson, the banker.

As Jorgenson ground the coffee, his wife appeared from the living quarters in the back, and the cloud of condescension thickened. Few knew her name was Evangeline, much less Evie. Mrs. Jorgenson seldom spoke, but her squinty eyes behind thick spectacles expressed disdain. Even in their customary pew at the church—God forbid anyone else should sit there —her frost chilled. The childless couple never participated in the ritual of Holy Communion, and they disappeared without socializing following Sunday services. After a brief glance at Jönsson, she sorted through her ledgers. Certainly, a critical clucking under her breath would follow her review of Jönsson's balance on account—make no never mind that he was current--but just then a mother and her three urchins came through the bell-ringing door, and Mrs. Jorgenson's attention was diverted to ensure no grimy fingers found their way into a jar of hard candy. No samples allowed.

"Are you a bachelor these days, Jönsson?" proprietor Jorgenson teased. "Your missus was here yesterday in the company of Agnes Hallstrom."

"I'm on my way to pick her up right now. She kept Agnes

company while Pastor Charlie was at conferences."

"She purchased two yards of fine linen on your account. Hardly enough to keep out winter's cold if she makes a garment of that sheer material. Not sure that the black lace will help much either," he said with a smirk. "Well, the vegetable seeds she bought will keep her busy."

Later, on the journey to the cabin after Jonas gathered Hilma from the Hallstrom parsonage, she clutched a package, which was more obvious because she tried to conceal it. She also carried a bag filled with seed packets for a vegetable garden. A hint of a smile tugged at the corners of her lips, and she hummed softly.

"I think I would like to sing with the choir," she said. "Would that be alright?"

When they arrived at the cabin, Hilma disappeared inside as Jonas unhitched the wagon, but Tomas soon appeared and said he was headed to Little Falls for unstated business and would spend the night. He departed with a wink that piqued his older brother. While Jonas milked the cows, he heard a chicken squawk as Hilma chopped off its head.

Her humming continued as she fried chicken and potatoes, unusual extravagances for a weeknight without entertaining. She was chatty as they ate, sharing news of townsfolk and parishioners from church, often bordering on gossip, and laughing frequently. After supper, Jonas sat outside and puffed on his pipe while Hilma cleared the table and cleaned the dishes. Just as the sun disappeared over the oak ridgeline to the west, Hilma appeared at the door.

"I've drawn you a bath," she said. "Come inside before the water chills."

It wasn't Saturday, and Jönsson wondered why he needed a bath, but he stripped and stepped into the half-barrel that served as their multi-purpose wash tub. Hilma disappeared into the side room and soon returned in a frilly garment that must have been in her secret package. Her strawberry hair was unbound and curled around her neck, draping forward over a lace-lined linen camisole that barely veiled her nipples. She was tall and athletic, and Jönsson pursed his lips and slowly exhaled as she approached. She took a cloth and began scrubbing Jönsson's back, neck, chest, and ... *Oh my God!* She stroked him as she began to kiss his chest, down to his belly, and ... *Oh my God!*

If Hilma didn't become pregnant that night, it was the night after that, or the next, or it could have been any of the following spring nights after Jonas moved into their bedroom and her bed.

After services the next Sunday, Jonas caught Hilma winking at Agnes. Jönsson had new appreciation for Pastor Charlie's sermons but even more for the lessons taught by Agnes.

J onas sat straight up in bed. Had he been dreaming? Had he heard a scream? In his sleepy muddle, he realized Hilma was not lying next to him. He jumped out of bed, but what had awakened him? Where was his wife? What should he do?

"Jonas, come!"

There was blood in her shrill cry, and he bolted through the already open doors of the bedroom and the cabin. He heard her sobbing in the biffy behind the cabin, and he found her on her knees, wiping a gory mess off the floor with pages torn from the Montgomery Ward catalogue that usually served a more utilitarian purpose.

"Where is my baby? Where is my baby?"

The next morning, Tomas fetched Agnes Halstrom while Jonas comforted his wife.

"Oh, Jonas, I'm so sorry. I have failed you."

Jonas certainly didn't feel that way. He understood that miscarriages happen for no good reason, they just do. When Agnes arrived, she confirmed that sentiment.

"Dear, dear, dear. Don't fret. Hush, hush."

It was good that she came for she could provide the empathy that Jonas could not. Although his mind could understand Hilma's sense of loss, of failure, even of guilt, his heart could not feel those feelings like another woman could. There was also greater authority in Agnes' words of comfort.

"It happens, my dear, more than you realize, but you will get pregnant again, and next time you will likely see a bouncing baby boy!"

Jonas' sadness was for her and not for himself. For his part, Jonas sensed hope. He was optimistic. Although he had imagined children, and he and Hilma had often talked about their future family, this was real. The bloody mess on the floor of the biffy was actual, and in the apparent tragedy of the moment, there was also future promise. They had conceived once; they could do it again, but when a second miscarriage occurred during the winter of 1914, the buoyant encouragement from Agnes and Jonas rang hollow.

On a lazy summer day after the crops were in, Jonas repaired the roof of the lean-to while Hilma pulled weeds in her vegetable garden. He watched with curiosity as a horse-drawn buggy entered their driveway. When he recognized Evangeline Jorgenson at the reins, he called down to Hilma, "I told Jorgenson I would pay our bill by month's end. She has no call to come and pester us for money."

Mrs. Jorgenson didn't notice Jonas atop the lean-to and addressed Hilma when she pulled up, "That's as big a garden as I've seen in these parts."

Hilma jerked to her feet and quickly brushed the mud from her knees with her work gloves. She seemed surprised to hear that her garden was larger than most, and she surveyed the green sprouts as if for the first time: long straight rows of peas, beans, potatoes, carrots, onions, rutabagas, squash, pumpkins, beets and cucumbers that would be pickled, and sweet corn already higher than the rest along the north side where the stalks would not shade the shorter plants. Empty seed packets capped the stakes at each row's end, identifying the vegetables planted in that row, but the strings used to hoe straight rows had been removed. A carpet of green leaves and white blossoms adorned the strawberry patch at the south edge.

"I've baked a pie," Mrs. Jorgenson said. "Shall we have a piece with coffee?"

Rubbing her hands on her garden apron, Hilma hurried out of the garden, hesitating briefly as she reached Mrs. Jorgenson and her buggy, "Yes, of course, please come in."

Mrs. Jorgenson stepped down and followed Hilma inside. Jönsson wished he was a mouse in the corner of the cabin. *Why was biddy Jorgenson making friendly? What will she think of our meager cabin? Did I draw water from the well? Did we use the last of the coffee this morning? Should I intrude and remind her that our bill would be paid as I promised?*

For more than half an hour, he puttered about, more concerned with what was going on inside the cabin than the job at hand. Across the way, Tomas walked behind their unmatched team of horses pulling a cultivator to root out the early weeds competing with six-inch corn stalks.

"I'll do it," Tomas said earlier when Jonas began to hitch the team to the implement. "Managing the fields is still my responsibility, you know."

Tomas frequently arrived for farm work late in the morning and sometimes not at all, but he chafed when Jonas did his work. Jonas figured the plan for a second cabin and a wife for Tomas couldn't come soon enough.

Finally, the cabin door creaked open, and Mrs. Jorgenson stepped outside, followed by Hilma. After Jorgenson climbed into the buggy, Hilma extended a hand, and Jorgenson clasped it in both of hers and held it. The women spoke softly, and Jönsson strained to hear Jorgenson's parting words.

"Dearie, don't follow my path. If children are in your future, accept them as the blessing that they are, but if not, seek and find acceptance. Don't allow fate to dictate your life. Don't become an old crone like me, uglier on the inside than the outside."

Jönsson climbed down as Mrs. Jorgenson drove away.

"What was that about?"

"Just girl talk. She's really a very nice lady inside, but childlessness has created a thick crust. Come inside, her pie is delicious."

Jonas watched as the buggy disappeared over a hill. It hadn't occurred to him that they might not have children. As the cabin door slammed behind Hilma, he sensed for the first time the emotional burden his dear wife carried following her two miscarriages. He felt helpless.

# CHAPTER TWENTY-EIGHT: 1914-1915

E xcept for a brief flirtation with the candidacy of William Jennings Bryan in 1896--inspired more by the love of a woman than affection for the candidate--that ended in disappointment and disillusionment, Jönsson never involved himself in politics even though he followed the newspapers with keen interest, and he voted when elections rolled around. During the 1914 congressional campaign, local Congressman Charles Augustus Lindbergh—a Little Falls attorney—offered his campaign stump speech from the porch of Ingemar Jorgenson's general store. By the time he was finished, Jönsson was a convert.

When Lindberg stepped to the front of the boardwalk, he stood tall and blond and looked every bit the Swedish immigrant that he was. True, he was a Republican, but he was an insurgent, not in the pocket of the money interests, and he spoke for the little man.

With the sun overhead, Lindbergh began: "A radical is one who speaks the truth."

He had fought long and hard against a banking bill recently passed by Congress, and he continued to rail against it, even though it was now the law of the land.

*This plan is the Wall Street Plan. It means another panic, if necessary, to intimidate the people. This is the strangest, most dangerous advantage ever placed in the hands of a special privilege class by any government that ever existed. The system is private, conducted for the sole purpose of obtaining the greatest*

*possible profits from the use of other people's money. They know
in advance when to create panics to their advantage. They also
know when to stop panic. Inflation and deflation work equally
well for them when they control finance.*

Jonas didn't understand all that Lindbergh said, but he
knew he agreed, and so too the other Swedes who listened
from the street. Lindbergh wasn't particularly eloquent, but he
was earnest. He was overly academic, and his big words often
soared over the heads of his listeners, but they believed him
because he believed himself. Even though he was an educated
man and lawyer, he remained one of them, rooted in the fron-
tier farmland of central Minnesota, and he knew in his bones
that the sweat of the farmer and the workingman was the true
wellspring of the American economy. But there was a problem
—a problem that only collective action and the government
could solve—for a "money trust" siphoned off far more than
their fair share, and government had the role and responsibility of muting the self-interest of the big banks and investment
houses of Wall Street.

From that day forward, Jönsson followed Lindbergh
closely and vocally supported him in Kalmar conversations,
but that was hardly necessary as the Swedes of Kalmar
counted themselves among Lindbergh's strongest supporters.

On a day late in July, Tomas didn't arrive until suppertime.
Jonas had finished his day's work, and Tomas' field work as
well when Tomas burst in.

"The God dammit Germans invaded Belgium and threaten
France," Tomas reported after returning from Little Falls.
"There'll be no bride for me."

It was Tomas' turn to seek a wife from the home country, but the muddled affairs of Europe intervened. A political
assassination, tangled alliances, and nationalistic bellicosity

exploded into warfare on the continent, and passenger travel from Scandinavia ceased.

Jonas had no love for the French or the eastern European Serbs aligned on one side of the expanding conflict. He wasn't too sure about the Germans on the other side, either, but Germany and Sweden shared the Baltic Sea; fair-skin, blond hair, and blue eyes; and rough similarities in language.

"Don't see that it's any of our damn business," Jonas replied.

"My God, you don't excuse the German aggression?"

"No, I favor no side, but I find the whole affair to be absurd. We know many Germans—immigrants like ourselves—shall we go to war with them? Shall we sneak down to Stearns County—it's only a few miles down the road—and start shooting the German farmers there?"

Tomas did not reply but merely stalked around the room as Jonas continued,

"Why, they say the Kaiser is the cousin of King George of England. If that doesn't sum up the stupidity ..." Jonas' voice trailed off before continuing. "Let Kaiser Wilhelm have a fencing dual with King George; let the Krupps of Germany who manufacture the guns and the warships pick a champion to arm wrestle Rockefeller. Monarch against monarch. Industry baron against industry baron. Then we can be done, and we don't need to spill the blood of farmers."

The war in Europe became the latest source of bickering between the brothers. Lindbergh was reelected with over 60% of the vote in the fall 1914 election. Nationally, anti-war sentiment persisted, but that was changing.

In May of 2015, Tomas slammed the newspaper on the table, almost as an accusation. The headline blared at his brother. *German U-boat sinks Lusitania: American lives lost and*

*American neutrality threatened.*

"What does Wilson wait for? Advice from Bryan the panty-waist pacifist?" Tomas spit out the names of the president and chief cabinet secretary like they tasted sour. William Jennings Bryan, the political hero of an earlier era, was the pacifistic Secretary of State.

"Says here that the liner carried munitions to the Brits," Jonas replied. "When you paint a bulls-eye big as a ship, can't blame the Germans for taking aim."

Tomas rose to his feet and kicked over his chair. He stared at Jonas with a look that asked, *who are you?*

Jonas couldn't understand why his younger brother couldn't see the folly of it all. If the United States joined the war, who would benefit? The big-money munitions makers, that's who. The trusts who could use war to manipulate the economy. Certainly, not the workingman who would be nothing more than cannon fodder. It would be red blood spilled on the battlefield, not the blue blood of big money. If only his hot-headed brother could see the truth.

"You know, our congressman speaks in Little Falls on Sunday," Jonas said to Tomas. "Maybe you and I should have a listen."

Tomas merely grunted. The anti-war sentiments of Congressman Charles August Lindberg were well known.

After services on a fine Sunday in May, Jonas and Pastor Hallstrom departed for Little Falls where they joined up with Tomas. A bandstand had been erected on the courthouse lawn, and the trio found seats together in the white-wooden-folding chairs set up for day. The congressman appeared at ease as he sat on the bandstand during his introduction, pointing and smiling at people he recognized in the crowd. He had been a successful attorney in Morrison County, located here in the county seat, before he was sent to Congress four elections ago, and his farm home overlooked the Mississippi just south and west of town.

Lindbergh received polite applause as he approached the podium. The audience knew he had been critical of American entry into the European war, and most people were still sorting out their own thoughts on that, and they were curious to hear the congressman's views, but they weren't necessarily prepared to agree.

After first repeating his well-known animosity for the money trust of big banks, he turned to the question that was foremost in Jönsson's mind.

*It is true that Europe is ablaze, and the destruction of life and property is tremendous; but nothing should be destroyed here in our homeland as a result of the war, so why should we allow the European war to destroy our reason?*

After introducing his theme with this relatively innocuous question, he then launched into a full-throated condemnation of American entry into the European conflict. Not surprisingly, he blamed an inner circle of war profiteers who led the jingoistic charge toward war.

*At no period in the world's history has deceit been so bold and aggressive as now in attempting to engulf all humanity in the maelstrom of hell. The whole world is sizzling. Sober men and women who measure the conditions with unselfish judgment and suggest sane action are pounced upon by the devils in command of the "hell-storm" in an attempt to have them labelled cowards and to force us into war over a standard of false national honor. Many of the highest officers of Government fail to sustain their moral courage for common sense and add to the confusion of the excited by trying to support the demands of speculators.*

*Amid all this confusion, the lords of special privilege stand serene in their selfish glee, coining billions of profit from the rage of war. They coldly register every volley of artillery, every act of violent aggression, as a profit on their war stock and war contracts. They commercialize every excitement, scalp in and out of the market alternately, taking profit both ways on a fluctuating market.*

Applause was polite but weak when he ended. Jonas' head bobbed in an assertive nod as he turned to gauge his brother's face, but Tomas stared straight ahead with a set jaw. Jonas feared his brother's mind was set, but so was his own, and this was not a matter that would soon be resolved between the brothers.

Jonas and Pastor Charlie departed for Kalmar alone. Tomas retreated to his nearby apartment.

"Giddap, Gurli."

As Jönsson's wagon moved west from Courthouse Square and passed through Little Falls' main intersection, he glanced up at the inscription chiseled in stone atop a corner building. "German-American National Bank," and he wondered how long peace would hold in the nation, the state, the county, and his own family.

# CHAPTER TWENTY-NINE

She hadn't said a peep, and she didn't until midwinter 1915 when her husband caught sight of her silhouetted figure.

"Hilma, my dear wife, are you alright?"

She blushed.

"Yes, but I think I should tell you. There is a baby growing inside me!"

After that, Jonas outdid himself. He cooked and cleaned and mucked out the lean-to, hoping to avoid another miscarriage.

"Will it be like this after the baby comes?" she teased.

"Just take it easy," he said. "What can I get for you?"

Agnes visited regularly. The women were all secrets and nodding silences. Most of the time, Hilma seemed pleased, but sometimes she whined about the damnedest things. Jonas muttered to himself but responded with a smile to some of her crazy requests.

The midwife said late May, and on May 20th, Agnes Halstrom moved in. Jonas slept in the hay with the horses and the cattle.

"Rest easy, Gurli," Jonas grunted to his spotted mare, who had been his favorite female years before he took his wife.

The lanky Swede leaned against the sweat-stained oak handles of a single-blade plow and wiped his brow with a red hanky he pulled from the rear pocket of his bib overalls.

"God dammit,' he muttered as he glanced skyward. The piercing sun was much too intense for May in Minnesota.

A quarter mile away, their tiny log cabin shimmered in the noon-day heat. The mid-wife was there with Hilma and Agnes. Jönsson, already forty-five, cursed the sun even as he prayed for a son. He picked up a clod of sandy loam and filtered it through his fingers.

He would normally return to the cabin for a lunch of beans, old-country rye bread, and coffee, but today he limped to the shade of a nearby burr oak where he had stashed a lunch pail and a jar of water. The womenfolk in the cabin didn't want him around as they tended to the matter of childbirth. After munching on hard cheese, he dozed off, but the high-pitched cries of his firstborn carried over the upturned humus of his plowed field and roused him.

He leaped with a start, imagining crackling fire in the trees around him. A newly turned furrow of black loam seemed a burned body, and he fell to his knees clutching at handfuls of dirt. But then he came fully awake, and he leaned back, breathing heavily with sweat pouring down his face. *Ayasha came to him, dressed in her fringed deerskin bridal gown and held out a crying babe. "Husband, behold your son."*

Again, the wail of a newborn carried over the plowed field. With a mixture of joy tinged with regret, he rose to his feet, brushed off his overalls, and slowly began the walk to the cabin to meet the son who lived. Halfway across the field, he unconsciously turned to see if Ayasha followed; he saw nothing, but he felt she was there, watching, but he couldn't tell if she wore a smile or a frown.

Agnes Hallstrom met him at the door with a washtub and soft soap.

"Make yourself fit to meet your son. He won't be impressed with an old farmer with mud on his face."

A wave of self-reproach swept over him, and the awesome fatherly responsibilities that suddenly fell upon him weighed him down. Agnes hadn't meant to sound critical, but she was right; he was merely a poor farmer with dubious prospects and an old man with a dark past. He had been full of anticipation of what a son could bring to him, but now he worried about what he could bring to the son. Of course, the son would be bright and bold, strong and just, someone to be respected and followed, but if he was such a one, would he not be disappointed in his miserable father?

He washed quickly and rushed into the bedroom, straight to kiss Hilma whose red face beamed as happy tears rolled down her cheeks.

"I have borne you a man-child," she said and handed the boy to his father. Jonas handled the child gingerly and awkwardly.

"Keep his head up," Agnes encouraged, "and cuddle him close."

When the babe's eyes fixed on his own, he melted.

Jonas retired to the front porch with his pipe and tobacco while Hilma fed their child. For now, his doubts and misgivings were dispelled. The journey to his American dream had been arduous and filled with traps and snares, but that didn't matter now. Despite his tribulations, despite the many delays and detours on the road that brought him to this place and this time, despite the soul-searing memories that triggered his nightmares, life would now be all that he hoped. With his son, and more to come, he would build a grand farm with a tall barn and herds of spotted cows and sturdy horses. The rains would come in due course, the sun would warm the fertile soil, and

God in heaven would smile upon all he had wrought.

Tomas reveled in his new role as uncle, but Jonas wondered. Tomas made one suggestion, borne of his attitude toward the European war, that Jonas accepted. No more Swedish words would be spoken in the cabin. English only. Hilma agreed, and husband and wife worked at smoothing the rough edges of their accents. The American immigrants were no longer Swedish emigrants.

Soon after the child was born, there was the matter of a christening. Agnes Hallstrom seemed a logical choice for godmother and Tomas as godfather, but Hilma had another idea.

Because the General Store was especially busy on a Saturday morning in June, no one noticed the ringing bell when the Jönssons entered with their newborn, but when baby Anders put up a fuss and began to wail, all eyes turned to the new family. Hilma marched straight ahead and handed her crying babe to the startled woman behind the counter who seemed unsure of what to do.

"Just whisper in his ear and pat him on the back."

Evangeline Jorgenson did as Hilma instructed, and the baby began to coo.

"Evie, we would like you and Ingemar to serve as godparents."

Now, it was Evangeline Jorgenson's turn to cry.


Before the August sunrise, thick mists filled the low spots.

"Jonas, look at the dwarfs asleep in the meadow," Hilma said with a smile.

Jonas nodded and grunted approvingly at his wife's vivid imagination. She was right, the wheat shocks seemed like hairy beasts dozing in the field, waiting for the sunrise to warm them awake. Even Gurli stopped to survey the bundles of bound wheat stalks awaiting the thresher. Baby Anders cooed, sensing the tranquil spirit that hung in the morning fog.

"Giddap, Gurli."

Jonas clucked with his tongue against the roof of his mouth and lightly flicked the reins on Gurli's haunches. Hilma adjusted the wrap around her babe and snuggled close to Jonas on the buckboard bench. They were off to team up with the threshing crew at the Willy Peterson farm, two miles to the west. Hilma would join the womenfolk--who would fawn over Anders--as they prepared a lunch of fried chicken, mashed potatoes, bread and biscuits with homemade butter and jam, green beans, lettuce, peas, onions, tomatoes, ham or roast beef, iced tea, lemonade, and apple or cherry pie for dessert.

Jonas had already been up a couple of hours—the cows needed milking—before they headed out.

Jonas and Gurli, teamed with Tomas' gelding, hauled shocks of wheat from the field to the immense threshing machine where Tomas and others pitchforked the stalks into the feeder. A steam engine tractor provided the power, transferred to the thresher by a huge belt that whirred and dipped and spun the blades that separated the kernels from the husks, spitting the grain into a hopper that poured into sacks while shooting the straw onto a hay wagon. A "water monkey," a small wagon with a fifty-gallon tank of water, kept the steam engine from over-thirsting. The whistle on the steam engine announced shift changes, lunch, lemonade breaks, and quitting time.

The hard work was done by the locals, but the threshing machine, steam engine, and other equipment was owned and operated by Mose Allen who followed a Midwest circuit each summer. The squat man wore the same dirty overalls and sweat-stained shirt day after day, sleeping under the stars and never bathing. His nose bent sharply to the left, and dust crusted over his thick eyebrows.

"Glory be, that man stinks," Aggie Peterson, the mistress of the house, said. "Take care and watch his roaming hands," she added, "and shut yer ears to his filthy mouth."

Gram Peterson, Aggie's mother-in-law, sat in a rocker in the corner, talking baby talk to Willy Jr., born a year before Anders.

Jonas and his family had been following this routine for the better part of a week, moving from one farm to the next. Tomorrow, the crew would arrive at their own humble farm. Purchasing the extra land and expanding the field had been prudent, especially since reports from the great mills of Minneapolis promised record prices in a war economy. While the family subsisted on the vegetable garden, chickens, pigs, and cow's milk, the wheat was a cash crop, and the profits would buy that which could not be grown, sewn, or hewn, with any excess poured back into the farm or saved for construction of a real house and a proper barn.

Wife and child had long since fallen asleep when Jonas finished with the evening milking, but he sat for a while on the front stoop, filled his pipe with Prince Albert tobacco, and watched the fireflies in the meadow.

When bursts of the northern lights flashed across the night sky interrupting his serenity, Jonas shuddered as if artillery shells exploded around him. For the moment, as a proud, new father, Jönsson had an understandably limited and narrow view, and rather self-centered at that, for if God truly watched the affairs of man, he would not be smiling as other father's sons perished in the blood-soaked trenches of Europe, mowed down by machine guns or choking on poison gas or dying by any of the countless means humans had devised to kill one another. The essence of the suicidal assaults "over the top" served as metaphor for the war itself. The war was so far away and irrelevant to his existence and that of his family, but the exploding northern lights portended that the conflict could somehow ensnare America, Minnesota, and even the Kalmar community.

Why the hell didn't Tomas see the dangerous insanity of war?

*********

*"I wondered when you were going to show up!" Pastor Don said, and he teasingly looked at me over the top of his glasses.*

*"Well, I mean to tell Papa's story, but I guess you'll be seeing more of me now that I made my debut appearance."*

*We remained silent for a few moments.*

*"That was a damned long time ago," I said, finally breaking the silence," nearly a century, but I won't last until my $100^{th}$ birthday next May."*

*Pastor Don didn't reply.*

*"In fact," I continued, "I doubt I'll see the new year."*

*Again, Don didn't disagree. I'm sure he could see I had declined since we began our conversations.*

*After another period of silence, Don spoke.*

*"He saw you as his golden boy, right from the start, didn't he?"*

*"Yes," I replied. "I was blessed and cursed with high expectations, I suppose, and I know I disappointed him."*

*"Really?" There was skepticism in his voice and in the wrinkles of his forehead. "Disappointment in the son who was aide and confidant to Senator Hubert Humphrey before becoming Chief Justice of the Minnesota Supreme Court? You are one of the most distin-*

*guished jurists in the history of Minnesota."*

*"He was sorely disappointed when I chose the university over the farm. He plowed virgin ground, not merely for seeds of corn, and rye, and wheat, but to plant deep family roots that would prosper and grow into his legacy."*

*By now, my choking voice was barely a whisper. "In that, I failed to meet his expectations."*

*I surprised myself when those words slipped out with un-expected emotion choking my windpipe. Don rubbed his clean-shaved chin as he considered my statement. His squinty eyes said he remained dubious.*

*Although it was still early in the afternoon. I was tired, and I needed a nap. Outside the window, snow swirled in a gusty wind.*

*"Storm's coming Don. We need to break for the day."*

*"Of course, Uncle, but I'll be back in the morning. Now that we've started to meet Hilma's babies, I'm expecting to learn more of my own mother. You know, she was always reluctant to reveal much about her life. Will we meet her soon?"*

*"Of course, we will. Patience, nephew. All in due course."*

*Don hesitated at the door, turned to say something but then ducked out.*

# CHAPTER THIRTY: 1916-1917

The sniper scoured the wood line through the v-notched rear sights of his rifle as dusk settled over the mossy topsoil of the swamp. The i-shaped front sight at the tip of the gun barrel ranged back and forth, waiting to fix on the slightest movement. All was silent as the hunted peered from the bushes, sniffed the air, and surveyed the field. Ambush awaited his first step into the clearing.

BANG.

A branch shattered above the spike buck who immediately bolted back into the bushes and disappeared.

"Missed high," Tomas said.

Jonas handed the rifle back to his brother.

"Best leave the shooting to you," Jonas said.

Through the late summer months and into the fall, the brothers observed the small herd of white-tail deer that appeared at the edge of the woods each evening to munch on the meadow grass. Tomas eagerly anticipated the hunt. He killed a doe the evening before with the Winchester lever-action rifle he recently purchased, but Jonas failed at his turn. Never mind, Tomas would return and fill Jonas' tag soon enough. Fresh venison steaks and chops, stews, and dried jerky would be welcome protein for the farm table.

After another harvest, crops fetched premium prices again, and socks bulging with rolled bills would carry the growing family comfortably through the winter of 1916-17 with plenty left over to save for a proper house. The herd was growing, and the animal's lean-to shelter had been walled in and expanded, but it still didn't seem right to call the second-rate structure a barn, but one day …

Anders tottered around the cabin on the new plank floor that covered the bare ground. Newborn sister Olga waved her arms, kicked her legs, and squealed with glee each time he peered into her crib. Hilma flipped venison steaks that sizzled in a cast iron fry pan atop the new wood-burning range and oven.

"He kept us out of war," argued the headline over the opinion page in the newspaper.

"And that's the problem," Tomas said. "Wilson has no balls."

Tomas spoke without looking up from the newspaper. Next week on election day, he would vote for the Republican challenger, Supreme Court Justice Charles Evans Hughes, who urged military preparedness. Once again, Jonas would vote for Woodrow Wilson the Democrat but without enthusiasm. He harbored no illusions that Wilson would keep the country out of war, no matter the slogans, and the only politician who caught his eye, Lindbergh of Little Falls, had surrendered his congressional seat in a failed attempt at securing the Republican nomination for Senator from Minnesota earlier that summer. Peace candidate Lindbergh finished well behind Frank B. Kellogg, the war-readiness candidate. Casualties of the European conflict included progressive Republicans, especially insurgents like Lindbergh, and their call for economic justice.

When the Sarajevo assassination sounded the downbeat for war two and a half years earlier, American sentiment clearly preferred neutrality, but by election day 1916, there appeared to be no chance of silencing the crescendo of the drums for war.

"Hush your warmongering," Hilma said as she placed a plate with a juicy venison steak atop Tomas' newspaper.

Although Tomas might argue war politics with his brother, he never crossed his sister-in-law. He seemed to appreciate that she was the queen of the cabin, as she should be. He nodded and smiled and sliced off a big chunk of venison, which he chewed with lips smacking.

On April 6th, 1917, the inexorable came to pass; President Wilson requested a declaration of war, and Congress duly complied. The Germans made his task easier by loosening their rules of engagement for their lethal U-boats, and all commercial vessels, including those flying the American flag, were in danger of a surprise attack, but it was the telegram from Zimmerman, the German foreign minister, to the Mexican government that rendered American intervention inevitable and immediate. British intelligence intercepted the Zimmerman note that invited the Mexicans to make war against their neighbors to the north, and the Brits gleefully shared the intelligence with their American friends.

Tomas assisted with the plowing and spring planting, but by the time the first crop of hay was ready for stacking, his mind drifted elsewhere.

"I've made an appointment with Lindbergh," Tomas said. "You need to join me."

Jonas smelled a rat. Something was afoot.

Lindbergh the politician was out of a job, and he had returned to his Little Falls law practice, but the meeting was to take place at Lindbergh's residence south of town. On a Sunday afternoon, the three Swedish immigrants strolled along the riverbank and soon reached the mouth of Pike Creek where it emptied into the Mississippi. Lindbergh's fifteen-year-old son, Charles Jr., briefly joined them before persuading his father to allow him to drive their spanking new Saxon touring car on the country roads.

"He's a good boy, but he sure likes the new-fangled contraptions," Lindbergh noted as his son sped out of the yard, "especially if they go fast."

"Zebulon Pike the explorer wintered here, you know," Lindbergh said as they reached a creek that emptied into the big river. When he saw the blank look on the faces of the Jönsson brothers, he explained.

"Pike has a Colorado mountain peak named after him, but before he became famous for his mountain explorations, he sought the source of the Mississippi, and his party camped right here during the winter of 1805-06."

With his back to the others, Tomas tossed small branches into the flow of the creek and watched as they swirled into the main current of the big river. The small into the large. The lesser into the greater. The destiny of one man subsumed in the fate of humankind.

"Tell me Congressman," he said over his shoulder, leading to the setup question for which he had come and which he wanted his brother to hear. "Now that America has entered the war; shall we resist, or shall we support?"

"You know I considered American participation in the war to be the height of folly," Lindbergh answered, "and I resisted with every bone and sinew."

"Yes, yes," Tomas said, "but that was before the decision was made. What say you now?"

Now it was Lindbergh's turn to pause and reflect on the eddies of the great river. He drew a deep breath and slowly exhaled.

"It is best not to do anything now to discourage, for the

thing has been done, and however foolish it has been, we must all be foolish and unwise together and fight for our country."

Jonas wondered what his brother had heard that alerted him to Lindbergh's willingness to be carried along with the flow of history. Whatever it was, he knew that Tomas had bested him in this argument, a trivial thing, but what came next would not be.

Jonas picked up a pine branch with a huge knot and flung it with all his might far into the river. It bobbed and circled before the current swept it quickly downstream. Jonas watched with his back to the others. He suspected what Tomas was about to say.

"I have joined the army," Tomas said, "and I think it best if I sign over my share of the farm to my brother. Counselor, could you draw up the papers?"

Nils Lagerquist wasn't much of a farmer, but the whole length of his forty acres ran along the low shoreline of Little Dipper Lake, and he rented his rowboat for two bits a day. The Jönsson brothers departed straightaway after Sunday services. As if he knew the brothers were anxious to escape, Pastor Halstrom droned on and on, but finally the fishermen were off. Hilma packed sandwiches and bottles of beer, and Tomas secreted a flask of whiskey into his bag. Sporting store-bought bamboo cane poles from Jorgenson's General Store, the fishermen had high expectations.

First came the frogs for bait. The marsh around the lakeshore was hopping with green leopard frogs. The laughter started early when Tomas slipped and planted his face in the mud.

"Did you get it?" Jonas teased. "That's a curious technique."

Truth be told, there was a method to it, and Jonas remembered chasing frogs around the pond back home. The trick was to move slowly and attack from the front. Spread your hand wide and slowly move to within a foot then strike! If the frog leaped, it would be straight into your swooping hand. Soon, their damp burlap sack wriggled as if alive.

Next came the decision as to who should man the oars. Jonas, as the senior, made the first attempt, but he seemed to only row in circles.

"Too much beer," Tomas teased. "Take a drink of whiskey," he said and laughed as he passed the flask to his brother and took his place at the oars.

Next, how to bait the hook? Jonas jabbed the barbed hook into the fleshy white chin of the frog and up through the nose, exiting between the nostrils. The poor creature clutched at the hook with all four legs.

"Doesn't that hurt?" Tomas asked.

"Nah, I've been doing it this way for years, and the frogs are used to it."

Tomas nearly slipped off his plank seat, laughing and holding his gut.

Next, how to cast? Tomas tried the overhand method, thrusting the tip of the cane pole forward from behind his head in a broad arc, whipping the line with the frog at the end toward his target. Too violent, and the frog went flying.

"Underhand and gently," Jonas said, demonstrating. Finesse proved better than power, and soon the brothers had the hang of it.

Next, where to fish? For the first half hour, they tried the lily pads without success, except to snag their lines, and the lily pads stems proved to be ornery adversaries. Same with the bulrushes.

"We need to get the frogs down where the fish are," Tomas said, and he dug into the bag from the General Store. "Here, clip this lead sinker to your line."

The sinker did the trick and so did deep water, and the brothers managed to catch plenty of black bass over the next couple of hours.

"Old Lagerquist says there's whitefish in this lake," Tomas said.

"I hear they're good if you smoke 'em," Jonas added.

"Really, which end do you light?"

The afternoon passed too quickly, and soon the red sun squatted on the pine ridge to the west.

"This one swallowed the God dammit frog, and I can't remove the hook," Jonas said.

Tomas watched with amusement and finally set his own pole down and stepped over the seat in the boat's middle to show his brother how to do it, but he also had trouble pulling the hook out from deep in the stomach of the bass. Finally, he shrugged his shoulders.

"There goes your pole," Jonas laughed and pointed.

Tomas turned around just as the butt end of his pole slid over the side of the boat, pulled in by a fish on the end of his line. As the fish swam away, the cane pole followed, floating on the water's surface. Tomas quickly shed his shirt, pants, and boots.

"You're not, you're not going in?"

"Dammit to hell, if I ain't."

He dove in and soon caught up to the floating bamboo. He held the pole at the butt end and lifted the other end high out of the water, but the fish dove deep and pulled the pole tip down. Tomas lifted it up again, and down went the fish. Tomas was having great fun, but for the fish, it was a struggle for life or death.

Jonas managed to row the boat near the ruckus in the water.

"Hand the pole to me," Jonas said.

Tomas passed the pole to his brother and grabbed onto the gunwale, but he was too tired to easily climb aboard.

"Give me a hand," he said, but Jonas was busy fighting the sea monster.

Tomas could do nothing but hang on and watch as his brother eventually hoisted leviathan into the boat. As the whale flopped in the boat's bottom, Jonas finally pulled his brother aboard. Jonas grabbed the great bass and stuck his whole fist into the bucket mouth.

"That's quite a fish I caught," Jonas said.

"You caught! That's my fish! My pole, my hook, my frog, my God dammit pants soaking in the bottom of the boat!"

The brothers each slumped backwards, shaking with laughter.

After a fine day of fishing, the brothers rode east with the purple hues of the setting sun at their back. Only then did reality stifle the laughter.

"*Lillebror*, must you go?"

"*Erst schaff dein Sach, Dann trink and lach*," Tomas repeated a phrase learned in the Little Falls lumber mill. "First do your duty, then drink and laugh."

Perhaps Tomas intended the irony, but Jonas failed to see the humor in Tomas' recitation of a German proverb.

# CHAPTER THIRTY-ONE: 1918

J önsson figured that no news was good news. Late each afternoon, he limped out to the township road that skirted the edge of the farm to wait for the rural free delivery mail carrier, but his anxiety at waiting for the mail was paradoxically a hope that no letter from the war department would come. Tomas' rare letters from the front never spoke of war or of himself, but by saying little, they said much.

Few words had been spoken on that Monday following the Sunday fishing trip, but the brothers' handshake was especially firm and said what needed to be said before Tomas climbed aboard the train at the Little Falls depot. His immediate destination would be Fort Snelling on the bluffs overlooking the confluence of the Mississippi and Minnesota Rivers where he would join the 151$^{st}$ Field Artillery.

While awaiting the mailman, Jonas sat with his back against a tall burr oak, whittling a cane out of a willow branch. There was something cosmic—good and evil--in that inert pen knife. His story was hidden in the cloudy mother-of-pearl grip. *Fader* and the big beech tree were there. Swede Hollow was there. A gold-lettered safe was there. Louis Archambault was there. Unfolding the blade revealed his secrets. If he pricked his thumb, the blood of others dripped.

He wondered if Tomas carried his own pocketknife with him. He hoped so.

Whittling helped to clear his thoughts. On this overcast and cool day in May 1918, he considered a request from Congressman Lindbergh who was running in the Republican primary for Governor of Minnesota against the incumbent, J.A.A.

Burnquist.

"I need a driver for a week," Lindbergh said. "My son, Charles Jr., is with his mother in Detroit, and my regular driver must travel out of state to bury his father. Can you spare a few days away from your farm to drive my Saxon touring car as I campaign?"

"I've never ridden in a motor car, much less sat behind the steering wheel," Jönsson replied.

"For a man whose hands have held the reins of a balky horse, you'll get the hang of it easy enough. Wait till you feel the power of fifty horses at your fingertips awaiting your command!"

Lindbergh's assurance wasn't assuring, but there was something noble and adventurous in the request, and there was no apparent downside. Lindbergh was the only politician Jönsson respected.

As always, Lindbergh had great concern for economic justice, and he was swept up in the populist wind that blew in from North Dakota. They called it the "Nonpartisan League" or "NPL" for short, and the NPL proposed elimination of the middlemen through state ownership of terminal elevators, flour mills, packing houses, and cold storage plants. The League also proposed tax exemptions for farm improvements, state-offered hail insurance, and state-run rural banks with credit offered at cost. Like Lindbergh, the League doubted the wisdom of joining the European war but voiced support for the war effort once the doughboys crouched alongside the Frenchies and the Brits in the trenches.

The newspapers said the war effort was hugely successful, but who could tell in the fog of war? It was not going well for the mothers who received the dreaded letter, that's for sure. And who could make sense of the goings on in Russia with the strange names and places? Czar Nicholas. Lenin. Trotsky. Kerensky. Petrograd. Brest-Litovsk. Bolsheviks. Soviets. Reds and Whites. Was the worker's revolution a good thing or bad? The triumph or failure of socialism?

After the mail carrier passed by with a wave but no mail, Jönsson limped toward the setting sun and the cabin in the woods just beyond the promontory. His latest diamond-willow cane fit his hand well and was just the right length. When he reached the grassy hillside, he placed both hands on the cane and leaned into the view. Soon, he spied his wife. With Anders in tow clutching her left hand and Olga on the right, Hilma walked toward the lean-to and the pasture beyond. Baby Signe rode along in a wrap on her back, much like Jönsson remembered the native women of Hinckley carrying their papooses. A tinge of regret shivered through his body as he thought of Ayasha and his own papoose, but it passed as soon as he heard his wife calling the cows:

*Ah hoo. Wee hodee do. Ah hoo. We hoo. Wo wee!*

Kulning. The traditional way. The old way. The Swedish way. High-pitched, singsong, wordless. Her voice was the most beautiful he had ever heard. Strong and pure. Song and singer conveyed emotion, and he heard joy, which gladdened his own heart. He was proud of his little farm and family. He pulled his hanky from his rear pocket and blew his nose. As the mooing cows eagerly hurried toward the ramshackle barn, Jonas whistled, and his two urchins ran to greet him.

"No mail today," he said and kissed his wife.

"Have you decided to help Lindbergh?" she asked. "You have my blessing. G-ma Evie will stay with me and help with the baby."

With actual grandparents far across the sea in the mother country, the godmother to Anders had become a surrogate grandmother.

"The crops are in, and it is not yet time for haying," she continued. "Per Larsson will sleep in the hay mow and tend to daily chores."

The raw-boned Larsson boy was thin as a stick and just as dumb, but he didn't know it, and he did just fine as a farm laborer filling in when Jonas needed him. Farm work is hard, but there is an ebb and flow to it, and the son of the village smithy answered Jönsson's call during peak times. Sitting pridefully atop his two-wheel bicycle, he'd come whistling with his straw hat dangling behind from a cord around his neck. Thick rubber bands held the eight-inch cuffs of stiff blue jeans tight around his calves to prevent the jaws of the bicycle chain from biting and chewing.

While Tomas hunkered down in a trench somewhere across the sea, Jonas' farm prospered, and the extra help provided by Per Larsson contributed. Continued war-time inflation in the price of farm produce more than offset the expense of hired help.

Then too, there was the contribution of Jonas' farm wife who mothered his children, managed his household, and her keen eye for ciphers added prudence to the family finances. As she cleared the table and washed the dishes, Jonas took charge of the children. Anders clung to his right leg and Olga to the left as he rocked baby Signe in his arms and pretended to be a horse and carriage.

*Rida, rida ranka,*

*hästen heter Blanka.*

*Liten riddare så rar*

*ännu inga sporrar har.*

*När han dem har vunnit,*

*barndomsro försvunnit.*

Ride, ride a rocking horse

The horse's name is Blanka.

Cute little knight

You have no spurs yet.

When you have won them

Your childhood will disappear.

By the end, only Anders held on to his leg. Olga had climbed into his lap and Signe slept. He placed Signe in her crib and Anders and Olga in the bed they shared before joining his wife at the table. He tamped out burnt tobacco and refilled his pipe.

"I shouldn't go. I worry about you and the children alone for the better part of a week."

"Don't worry about us," she replied. "You're the one stepping onto unknown ground. You and that big Saxon car. I should like to see that! Worry about yourself."

# CHAPTER THIRTY-TWO

Jönsson said yes, and he became Lindbergh's driver. He couldn't know that the simple request from the congressman would expose him to the ugliest side of American politics and culture, a phenomenon borne of hyper-nationalism, often provoked by war or its aftermath, when the American melting pot melts down, when the beckoning flame of Lady Liberty goes dark, when the land of the free and the brave becomes the home of the bully and the bullied, when the freedoms of the press and of speech become license to smear and exaggerate and lie, when dissenters are demonized as disloyal and debate becomes sedition, when bigotry and nativism masquerade as patriotism, and the flag becomes a golden calf, when self-evident truths become false hopes, when life, liberty, and the pursuit of happiness are for some but not all, and when the promise of America becomes a bitter lie.

Fear. Fear triggers the hysteria. Ignoble fear. Fear chases angels and beckons demons. Fear makes enemies of friends and monsters of men. Fear blunts altruism, blots out hope, and forgets decency. Fear confuses the good with evil and evil with good. Fear seeks the like-minded and shuns the other and unleashes insular tribal instincts.

Such a period of tribal darkness descended upon America at this point in Jonas' story, and the cloud was especially black over the Republican primary for governor of Minnesota in the year of our Lord, 1918.

Lindbergh's first scheduled appearance would be in Duluth, and Jonas hoped to see Natty Einstein in the crowd. Maybe share a few laughs and memories. He would boast of his growing family and farm and dreams coming true. Over two decades earlier, she opened his eyes to the oppression of the worker. What would she think when he accompanied Lindbergh to the podium! Lindbergh and the NPL melded the interests of the farmer and the laborer; just a week earlier, Lindbergh and the Minneapolis mayor, a darling of the labor unions, appeared together at a Minneapolis campaign rally.

Jonas expected that Lindbergh would be Natty's man in this election, and he would be pleased to bump into her in Duluth, but it was not to be. Despite pre-paying rent for venues, the halls refused access, and the capitalist press of Duluth fanned the flames with editorials condemning Lindbergh as "TRAITOR OR ASS?" and labeling the NPL as "seditious elements." The labor press—Jönsson wondered whether Natty Einstein was behind the articles—countered by condemning the foul methods and threats of violence against Lindbergh's party and claimed the money trust was the puppet master pulling the strings against Lindbergh.

Lindbergh's party detoured to Osakis in Central Minnesota, not far from Lindbergh's birthplace near Melrose. Jönsson steered the oversized Saxon touring car through well-wishers gathered in a farm pasture, and it seemed the mass would never end. When the motor car finally reached a hastily constructed platform and podium and Jönsson stood among Lindbergh's entourage, the crowd stretched as far as Jönsson could see. Later someone said ten thousand enthusiastic farmers gathered that day to cheer the prairie populist.

Lindbergh recited the speech that had been intended for Duluth. Recognizing the effect of the charges of disloyalty—due to his well-known opposition to American entry into the war—he attempted to defuse the issue.

"We are at war ... and every true American should insist that we fight this through to victory with the least possible delay."

The crowd cheered. They cheered again and again as Lindbergh assailed the big money interests who were bleeding the farmer dry.

"The war profiteers are the real disloyalists who stab our boys in the back to serve their own greed!"

Things would change if the people elected him to be governor of the great state of Minnesota, that's for sure.

"Only the Nonpartisan League will support legislation favorable to the farmer and the laborer and offer a progressive government like the Scandinavian countries."

Jönsson was as convinced and enthusiastic as any of the farmers—most of them immigrants or the sons of immigrants: Swedes or Norwegians or Danes. This was his tribe.

Jönsson slept in a private hotel room that night, the first time since Frank Hibbing hosted him in the city that bore the good man's name. Earlier, he devoured a well-done beefsteak chased with glass after glass of red wine. He sat in and listened, even offered a comment or two, as Lindbergh and his campaign staff plotted strategy. With such an auspicious start, what would the morrow bring?

Burnquist, the incumbent Republican, settled on a campaign of fearmongering. Lindbergh was in cahoots with the Germans and the Bolsheviks. Against the backdrop of war in Europe and Revolution in Russia, it mattered little that the charges were logically inconsistent. War hysteria. Tribalism. Conspiracy. Fear and uncertainty in a chaotic world. Just as in Duluth, some county officials—supporters of the Republican governor--prohibited appearances by the seditious Nonpartisan League and its candidate.

After the high spirits of the Osakis groundswell, the next

day got off to an ominous start. A hastily arranged appearance was interrupted by Burnquist patriots with shouts of "traitor," "Bolsheviki," and "coward." Jönsson had got the hang of driving the Saxon, but he nearly stalled the engine when birdshot rained down upon Lindbergh's Saxon as they departed.

"Don't drive so fast, Mr. Jönsson," Lindbergh said, "they will think we are scared."

The main appearance was scheduled for a farm in rural Martin County in southern Minnesota along the Iowa border, but as Lindbergh opened the car door, a deputy sheriff wrestled Lindbergh to the ground and placed him in handcuffs upon orders from the county attorney. The double-barreled charge was unlawful assembly and conspiracy to interfere with military enlistments.

"Follow along," Lindbergh said to Jönsson as the deputy bullied the candidate into the back seat of the sheriff's vehicle. "We'll get this straightened out, and I'll be released straightaway."

Organizers jumped into the Saxon and others joined the short motor car parade into Fairmont--not quite the police escort they might have hoped for. The small crowd followed Lindbergh into the courthouse, but Jönsson parked the Saxon in the shade of a cottonwood to wait alone outside. He could not know that war hysteria sickness would soon afflict him in this bucolic setting in a sleepy small town.

Under a high sky, the cottonweed leaves rustled in a gentle breeze. Snow-like fluff danced and fluttered before blanketing the green courtyard lawn in a layer of white. The clock in the courthouse tower said 2:15.

Jönsson wiped the mid-afternoon sweat from his brow and tried to spot the pair of Cardinals singing somewhere in the branches of the cottonwood. He found the red male soon enough, but it took a while to locate the subdued gray of the female. He remembered waxwings in Sweden with similar sharp crests, but the male cardinal boasted an unmatched coat of red. Even the female carried red accents and such a sweet song the pair could make at dawn and dusk at the farm! Only two days on the road, but he was already homesick.

The minute hand on the big clock face moved slowly. It seemed he had waited much longer than forty-five minutes, and he was surprised when the clock struck 3:00. What could they be doing inside the courthouse?

The street was mostly quiet. Perhaps the townsfolk napped. Jönsson grabbed his willow cane and crossed the street to pass the time, but soon returned to leaning against the Saxon. He glanced again at the clock. Jönsson walked around to the opposite side of the Saxon and leaned against the passenger door.

The only sign of life came from down the street where muted sounds of male voices seeped through closed doors. He could barely make out the sign over the door. "Something or something Tavern."

Two hours had passed since they arrived. *Hilma will be calling the cows about now. Clover will need mowing soon.* He checked the sky from east to west. Nary a cloud. *We could use a spot of rain.*

A patchy-haired mutt sniffed about under a nearby arborvitae hedge, and a cotton tail rabbit scurried out the other side. The clueless hound continued to scratch and sniff, and finally lifted his leg and pissed on the bush, as if that settled the matter.

At long last, a single man emerged from the courthouse. He glanced at the Saxon before pulling his cap low over his eyes. He hurried down the street, disappearing into the tavern.

A pair of disinterested geldings clop-clopped down the

street pulling a wagon loaded with a farm family. Four kids in tattered clothing argued in the back, the missus nagged at her slope-shouldered husband, who blankly drove on while muttering under his breath at the team, but they were ... disinterested.

5:13. Funny. The songbirds had departed, and the silence closed in on him. He hadn't heard the clock strike 5:00. He spied half a dozen men spill out of the tavern and head his way; they appeared animated, but he couldn't hear them. He shifted the weight from his bum leg and leaned heavily on his cane as he watched the men approach. By their swagger and stagger, it appeared they had a snoot full.

"Oof!"

The silence dissipated in an instant as someone came from behind him and kicked out his cane, and he fell heavily into the dust. As he clambered to his feet, his attacker was joined by the men from the bar, who formed a circle around Jönsson. The ringleader moved to the front of the car and fingered the ornament on the hood.

"Saxon. Anybody heard of a Saxon? Sounds German."

He twisted and broke the ornament and flipped it into the dust near Jönsson's feet. Jönsson shook his cane at the man and said,

"Watch yourself!"

"Are you threatening me, you fucking cripple?"

He came close and looked up into Jönsson's face. He was half a foot shorter, but he acted the banty rooster--easy enough when half a dozen brutes backed you up.

"Give me that fucking stick," he said, and he attempted to grab Jönsson's cane, but Jönsson resisted, pushed the man back, and swung the cane, striking the short man on the side of the head. As the man touched the bloody smear alongside his ear, his eyes narrowed in surprise.

"Fuck you, you God damned kraut."

The others took their cue and wrestled Jönsson to the street, kicking and pummeling him.

"Fucking kraut! America for Americans!"

His cane was gone, and Jönsson heard the tinkling of glass as the cane smashed the headlights and windshield. Jönsson lay helpless, restrained by the Americans for America, as they stripped his clothes off. Soon, someone poured a sticky liquid from head to toe, molasses by the smell of it, followed by chicken feathers. When his front was covered, they flopped him over and his backside received the same treatment.

The short man leaned against the Saxon, holding a hanky to the bloody side of his head.

"Stick it up his ass," he said. "Stick his fucking cane up his fucking ass. Show the fucking kraut how America will butt-fuck the Kaiser and the rest of the Krauts!"

A red mist settled on the street. Bright shades of crimson. Redder than the setting sun. Redder than the ever-present hanky in his hip pocket. Redder than the ripe strawberries in Hilma's garden. Redder than the cardinal that fled from the cottonwood. Red as the mess that Hilma scrubbed on the biffy floor, the unborn child whose sole existence was as blood and gore, membrane and placenta. Was life just so much jelly and water? Was live birth better? Was being--full of tribulation and humiliation--better than non-being? Jönsson was the one who lay on the outhouse floor. He was the bloody muck. His was the life that was stillborn. *A flaming red torch rose from the mist in a hand held high. From the deck of an arriving steamer, an immigrant Swede listened for the voice of Lady Liberty, whose lips moved but her words were swept away in a swirling wind.*

Jönsson didn't expect to survive the moment, nor did he want to. He wished he had brought his pistol with two bullets —one for the sonofabitch patriot and one for himself. Death and quickly would be better than this manner of dying.

Suddenly, the bullies fled as shouts erupted from the court-house steps. Only when Lindbergh gently extracted the cane from Jönsson's rectum did the Saxon driver feel the pain.

# CHAPTER THIRTY-THREE

Jönsson's stomach growled, and he slammed the axe blade into a stump and tossed the split oak chunks onto a pile before beginning the slow trek toward the cabin for lunch. A few wispy white clouds floated across the high blue sky on a warm November day. Mottled orange and brown leaves carpeted the ground of the woodlot where Jönsson laid up firewood for the winter.

*What was that sound?* Jönsson stopped in his tracks and turned to face the warm southerly breeze, but he heard nothing more. He wiped his sleeve across his forehead and slung his jacket over his shoulder. He refused to use a cane, and he ambled slowly toward the cabin. *There! There it was again.* He halted and canted his head to better catch the snatches carried on the wind.

He spied Hilma watching his approach from the porch with Signe in her arms and Anders and Olga clutching her skirts. There had been no recent baby-making. When he neared, he saw her face wondering at the faint pealing they heard in the distance. Jonas tossed his work gloves onto the porch and grunted as he cocked his head toward the stable. He would saddle Gurli and follow the bell.

"Jonas," Hilma said sternly, and he turned and kissed her on the forehead, but their eyes did not meet. Anders hugged his father's leg before Jonas pulled away.

By the time the spires of the white pines standing sentinel over the Lutheran church came into view, the tolling of the church bell had settled into a steady, rhythmic monologue that

alerted the townsfolk to the news of armistice. Per Larsson and other boys took turns yanking the rope hanging from the bell-gable that tipped the bronze bell back and forth against the clapper. The streets bustled, and joyous shouts accompanied the rhythmic ringing of the news. Jönsson wrapped Gurli's reins around a pole in front of the General Store and climbed the stoop where he joined Ingemar Jorgenson, the proprietor, enjoying the hubbub in the street.

"By yiminy, the boys will be home soon!" Jorgenson said as he slapped Jönsson on the back. Jönsson didn't return Jorgenson's sideways glance as if the proprietor realized he had misspoken; everyone knew that the letters from Tomas had stopped months ago. He offered Jönsson a snort of whiskey from a flask, but Jonas declined.

As he rode home toward the setting sun, Jönsson envied, even resented, the high spirits of the townsfolk. When he crested the promontory and the cabin came into view, he saw Anders disappear into the cabin from the front porch, probably to report his father's return. The boy soon joined Papa in the stable, announcing that Mama had supper ready. The young man was bundled in a hand-me-down coat inherited from a church family with a wool scarf wrapped twice around his neck then tucked in front behind the jacket buttons. A short-billed cap covered his blonde hair and flared his ears out sideways as he followed Papa into the cabin.

"Pass the potatoes," Jönsson kept his view low, but then stole a quick glance into Hilma's eyes. "Please," he added.

In that brief look, he saw a plea shine through her concern. Yes, husband. Eat hearty. Fill your belly and the rest of you, too.

He was once again a hollow man. Decades earlier when he lost his first wife and son, he forced emptiness upon himself as a protection against the pain. Now, the emptiness came naturally. On that June day while minding the Saxon, his existence had become a hollow void. His rage had long since dried up, and he gave up trying to make sense of it because it made no sense. He was no German or German sympathizer; he was American just like those God dammit Americans for America. His wondering and his anger always led nowhere except to remembering his humiliation, and so he shut down and became empty inside—no feeling heart, no thinking brain, no animating soul. In the red fog of his assault, he had been rendered stillborn: alive but lifeless. And silent. Especially silent. He refused to speak of the atrocity, of Lindbergh, or of the election—which Lindbergh soundly lost and Burnquist and his bullies won. Now, America claimed victory in Europe and so too would the warmongers, but farm mothers whose sons lay buried in France or the farm fathers whose maimed sons could only watch the fieldwork would have no solace, save "a world safe for democracy" but look what democracy gets you—Americans for America.

"Tomas will return soon now that the war is over," she said.

Jonas again made brief eye contact. *Did she believe what she said?* They had not received a letter since the summer, and the lack of news from the front contributed to his emptiness, and they had not talked of the war for months. In his glance, he sought reassurance. The pealing of the bells that afternoon interrupted his despondency but agitated his anxiety.

After supper, he retreated to the porch and looked over the wheat stubble in the field toward Kalmar; the distant bell continued to sound even as dusk descended, and his ears strained to catch the snatches. Despite his lethargy during the summer of 1918, his neighbors assisted with the harvest of his bumper crops, and his farm continued to prosper. They knew something tetched him early that summer, and they pitched in without questions, even as he suspected they gossiped out of his earshot. To the west, smears of purple outlined the tops of the cottonwoods that grew along the creek, and he wondered if the bark had closed in over the names of the brothers etched there.

"Papa." Anders tugged on his father's overalls. "Papa."

His three-and-a-half-year-old son brought his pipe and tobacco pouch. Jonas sat down in his rocker with Anders on his left knee. The son watched closely as Papa tamped the tobacco and struck a match. He sucked to draw the flame down into the bowl; with each breath, a larger puff of smoke rose. When the pipe was well-lit, Jonas blew smoke rings, and Anders poked a finger into each one, looking at Papa for approval each time.

After Hilma and the children fell asleep, Jönsson sat alone in the light of a kerosene lantern and reread the letters he had accumulated.

August 14, 1917: "We remain in Fort Snelling. I grow restless waiting, waiting, waiting for orders to ship out. Today we learned that the 151$^{st}$ Field Artillery has been assigned to the Rainbow Division, and there is great excitement that our time will soon come. We'll put the Boche to the run!"

October 31, 1917: "Fourteen difficult days at sea are now behind us, and we have arrived on French shores. Yesterday, the men forgot about seasickness when word came that German U-boats torpedoed a nearby merchant ship, but when we safely disembarked, enthusiasm replaced fear. I am exhilarated! Our destiny awaits us!"

November 15, 1917: "On the road today, we encountered our first Huns, but they were less frightful than pitiable. German prisoners of war shoveled in the ditches as we marched past. Gaunt faces seemed disinterested in our presence, unless someone tossed a morsel of bread, but such humanity drew rebukes from our officers, and so we shuffled along."

December 25, 1917: "Christmas has never been so solemn. Today, we have a grim appreciation of time and space. Home is a far-off fantasy. We opened packages in silence—thanks to Hilma for the wool socks. We have yet to experience real action; perhaps our first taste of combat will get the juices flowing again.

February 21, 1918: "Trains delivered us near the front, and we marched in the rain to our positions. Our mood is lighthearted, and the gallows humor teases reality without full appreciation: 'A month from now, you'll be thirty days dead!'"

March 22, 1918: "Mud and blood. Is this the essence of existence? Buried deep in our dugouts while German shells explode around us, we pop up like gophers and fire our own cannons for a moment, and then duck down again when the Boche take their turn. I think I shall climb out of our bunker tomorrow and sow wheat in the ground the shelling has plowed around us."

July 4, 1918: "Enjoy independence. Light firecrackers. Wave the flag."

Jönsson carefully folded the letter, the last one received just weeks after the Americans for America humiliated him and returned it to its envelope. He turned off the lamp and sat in the dark.


The blizzard wind whistled outside and rattled the windows. Jönsson shoved a log into the woodstove, then another; as the cabin warded off a January snowstorm, Jönsson's children struggled with raspy coughs and fevers, and Hilma fretted about the Spanish flu that raged in the land, claiming the lives of the strong and able-bodied, Per Larsson their hired hand among them. As if the angel of death was dissatisfied with the quick end to the war, healthy young men like Larsson, and young women—especially those bearing a child in their womb—perished soon after nose bleeds, throbbing headaches, and a bluish skin sheen appeared. Hilma prayed and consoled herself that her children merely experienced normal seasonal afflictions.

The cold and snow had arrived well before Christmas and refused to leave. Jonas tried to play solitaire with a deck of cards— "old man"—he called his game, but he could not settle his restlessness. Anders' cold seemed to be lessening, and he was out of bed for the first time in three days. He tried to follow his father's moves with the cards, but Jonas made no attempt at using his son's interest as a moment to teach numbers. Hilma and the two girls remained in the bedroom.

Jonas bundled himself in his winter coat and boots and pulled his wool cap over his ears to step outside to empty the piss pot. In weather like this, the biffy was off limits, and he emptied the pot every time it was used—at least, it was something to do. After emptying the pot and placing it inside the door of the warm cabin, he bowed his head to the blowing snow that blotted out the sun and followed the rope line connected to the lean-to that passed for a barn. His tracks from hours earlier had filled in, and a four-foot drift curled around the corner of the barn. Gurli nickered as he entered, but Tomas' gelding seemed disinterested. Snow sifted through the cracks in the wall and settled in small piles here and there. The back end of the lean-to was open to the elements, and the small herd of cattle pressed together and as far into the shelter as possible. He spread hay with a pitchfork just as he had done a few hours earlier, and then he sat on the milking stool for a smoke, but as he struck a match on a stone, Hilma's screech pierced the wind.

"JOOONAS!"

He rushed outside, plowing through the snowbank, and he nearly tripped over the limp body on the far side. Wearing one boot and a jacket but no cap or mittens, Anders lay whimpering in the snow.

# CHAPTER THIRTY-
# FOUR: 1918-1919

J önsson ran his finger under his stiff collar that seemed too tight. Hilma insisted he buy a new white shirt for the funeral. Once again, the wooden church under the tall steeple hosted a funeral for one of her own. War dead and flu dead. Once again, Pastor Hallstrom attempted to make sense of death in his sermon to the living. You would think he would get the hang of it, for he had rehearsed plenty in recent months, but the fresh mounds of earth dotting the grassy graveyard tested the preacher's faith. Dust to dust.

Just a week after Per Larsson, the smithy's son, led the ringing of the church bell on the day of the armistice, the flu from Spain tracked him down—just as it found millions of others around the globe--and he died before the season's first snowfall. At least, the gravediggers didn't have to contend with frozen ground.

With the forefinger of his right hand, Jönsson poked under his tight collar as if he couldn't swallow, and his sweaty left hand grasped the handle of the pine casket that carried his hired hand. After the pall bearers deposited the coffin atop the ropes that would lower the boy to his eternal resting place, Jönsson stepped back with the others while Pastor Hallstrom prayed. Agnes, the pastor's wife stood behind him and the grieving family, but Hilma remained home with their own children, and Jönsson's thoughts flittered back and forth between here and there.

A solid bank of slate clouds obscured any view of the heavens. A single crow watched the proceedings from the top of one of the twin pines that swayed over the cemetery. Was it Korp, the village priest from long ago and far away? What else could the beady-eyed bird see from his lofty perch? A soldier limping home? Which farmhouse in the bird's view would be the next to mourn?

Across the fresh-dug hole in the earth, the smithy removed his wool cap, and the November breeze ruffled his disheveled hair. The ashen-faced father sunk in on himself with chin quivering but dry eyes. Not so his wife, whose face was wet and red from weeping, and her body heaved under a gray winter coat. Today was their day for pity, but in a way, Jönsson envied Larsson the smithy and his wife. They knew, and the tolling of their season of grief had begun. Jönsson didn't know the fate of Tomas, and his anxiety told him that unknowing was worse than knowing.


Two months after the funeral, Anders Jönsson survived the snow drift as he followed his father to the barn. He didn't lay in the snow long enough for frostbite, and after a frightful night and following day, he returned bouncing around like a normal three-year-old, and the important piece of the story is the effect the incident had upon Jonas, the father, who carelessly left the door unlatched and allowed his doting son to follow him into the storm.

That tale begins with the scolding inflicted by Hilma. She said nothing that night or the next day as she tended to her feverish firstborn, relying upon lukewarm baths, damp cloths on his forehead, and icicles to suck on. On the morning of the second day, the storm broke and so did the fever. When a bright morning sun pierced the bedroom window and awakened her, she discovered Anders in the main room playing with his father's deck of cards. Jonas methodically pulled on his boots to tend the morning milking.

As Hilma slathered her children's hot porridge in thick cream, adding an extravagant spoonful of sugar, Jönsson could sense her seething anger, and he sensed there would soon be an explosion.

When the door to the lean-to creaked open, Jonas looked up from tugging on the teats of Old Bessie, their cow who was always the best milk producer. He quickly rose to his feet, kicking over the milk stool in the process.

"Is ... is Anders ok?"

"He's fine, and I **closed the door** tightly behind me."

Jonas left hand raked down his nose and over his mouth and chin as he sucked in a deep breath. *Yes, go ahead. Accuse me. Indict me. Prosecute me. Convict me. I am guilty.*

Her sarcastic remark was all she said about his carelessness, and she moved on to her real point.

"When will you stop feeling sorry for yourself? You mope about like a spanked child."

Jonas squinted as if he didn't understand. *Not all casualties of war bear visible scars, you know,* he wanted to say, but he didn't speak. *I bleed inside.*

"I know those evil men hurt you and humiliated you, but don't you think it's time to get over it?"

*If only it was that easy. How do you will away sadness? How do you forget when the nightmares haunt?*

"Since that day, you have been a stranger in our house. Isn't it time again to be a man, a husband to me, and a father to your children?"

Jonas steadied himself with a hand on the haunches of Old Bessie.

"Your son idolizes you, he wants to be like you, and he nearly died because he followed you into the night even though you barely pay attention to him. God dammit, husband, you're a lucky man. Act like it!"

Jonas took a step back and leaned against Bessie for support. He had never heard Hilma curse, much less at him.

"Huh," she said. "What do you have to say for yourself?"

He had nothing. He breathed hard as if building himself up for a response, but still nothing.

Hilma whirled to leave and pushed the door open, but then she turned and looked back. Jonas felt faint. She returned and grasped his stubbly, unshaven chin between her thumb and forefinger with her freckled face pressed close to his. Her moist eyes darted and poked, digging deep for signs of life, and then she kissed him, hard.

His deep breathing turned to gasps.

"I … I'm sorry," he stammered.

"The bedroom door remains open," she said. "You better return soon, or I'll dry up like an old crone."

# CHAPTER THIRTY-FIVE

I n the spring of 1919, Jonas returned from plowing to find a Montgomery Ward catalogue open on the table, but Hilma slammed it shut and returned it to a shelf before he could see what items were displayed on the page she had been studying. He started to inquire, but she placed a finger on his lips.

"Never mind," she said. "It's something for myself."

He knew that the coffee can on the shelf was heavy with coin. What he didn't know was that she was conspiring with Agnes Hallstrom, and Evie Jorgenson was their accomplice. The women and their purchases would soon become the talk of Kalmar.

The season of Lent curtailed the normal Sunday socializing after services—not merely for proper piety but to allow the choir to rehearse for the musical pageantry of Easter morning. Each Sunday, Jonas returned to the farm with the children while Hilma lingered behind with the choir—to be delivered later by Agnes or Evie.

On Palm Sunday 1919, a week before Easter, Jonas stood alone in a pew with Signe in his arms as Hilma and the choir led the procession into the sanctuary, followed by the children. The choir took their place at the front while Anders and Olga and the other children peeled off and circled around the pews waving spruce branches while the congregation sang. Jonas merely mumbled because he didn't follow along in the hymnal; instead, his clouded eyes followed his children. It didn't help that Signe's spruce branch kept hitting his face.

Despite a few mutterings of "we've never done that before,"

Pastor Hallstrom was an innovator, and the congregation repeated the hymn in English as the children continued to circle and wave their spruce branches. The Great War hastened the Americanization of the immigrant Swedes.

All glory, laud, and honour

To Thee, Redeemer, King,

To whom the lips of children

Made sweet hosannas ring.

After services, Hilma once again remained behind with the rest of the choir; back at the farm, Jonas led Gurli in circles with his children taking turns riding on the mare's bare back when he noticed what appeared to be a pair of giant daddy-long-legged spiders moving slowly along the roadway where it crested the nearby promontory. Jonas shielded his eyes against the mid-day sun as the creatures slowly began descending, picking up speed as they neared.

"Mama!"

Anders was the first to recognize his mother. Agnes Hallstrom was the second creature. The women perched high on bicycles, scarves streaming behind, hats ajar, with smiles like watermelon slices.

Jonas better understood the scrapes on Hilma's elbows he had noticed a few weeks earlier, which she merely pooh-poohed at the time. He wasn't sure what to think, and his feelings were mixed. He was offended at the riskiness of it all and perhaps the audacity. He was envious, even jealous of Hilma's affection for her dear friend, Agnes, and of the secrets they shared. It would have bothered him to learn that they stole puffs on a cigarette, and so that remained their secret. He said nothing about the two of them appearing hatless in church, even if they drew askance glances. He felt old and worn out compared to his full-of-life wife who still enjoyed the decade of her twenties. Hah! You wouldn't catch him on such a contraption! But he later defended her when he overheard a snide remark, and it dawned on him that he was proud to have such a modern woman as his wife. Truth be told, he was a lucky man, and he knew it; when she lined up to vote in the 1920 presidential election—following the enshrinement of women's suffrage in the 19$^{th}$ amendment to the constitution--he was pleased to stand with her, even if she wasn't wearing a bonnet.

Easter Sunday 1919 dawned bright and clear. The boys of the town began to yank on the rope ringing the bronze bell a full fifteen minutes before the scheduled start to the service. Women in their best finery escorted children in bonnets and bow ties up the steps as the menfolk tended to their horse drawn carriages. Older kids scooted this way and that. Those who lived in the village emptied the back streets and poured down main street toward the white church. Soon, the sanctuary brimmed with folks standing at the rear and sides and clustered around the double-door entrance. Latecomers crowded into the small foyer called the narthex. Sunbeams streamed through the spanking-new stained-glass windows featuring scriptural motifs. Jonas' favorite was the one depicting Jesus leaning on his staff while tending his sheep—a farmer like himself.

Pastor Hallstrom offered his sermon in English based on an English translation of Mark's gospel, and Jönsson was struck by the ambiguity of the reading:

*And he saith unto them, Be not affrighted: Ye seek Jesus of Nazareth, which was crucified: he is risen; he is not here: behold the place where they laid him. But go your way, tell his disciples and Peter that he goeth before you into Galilee: there shall ye see him, as he said unto you. And they went out quickly, and fled from the sepulchre; for they trembled and were amazed: neither said they anything to any man; for they were afraid.*

After the sermon came the Holy Supper, but Jönsson nearly forgot to step forward, enthralled by Hilma's soprano solo, and he was the last to kneel at the communion rail. He was mystified when the choir suddenly halted mid-verse and Pastor Hallstrom froze with a morsel of bread half-extended in his hand. When murmurs rose behind him, Jönsson finally turned to see the miracle that appeared in the double doorway. Haloed in the sunlight stood a man in a drab brown uniform buttoned to the neck with hat in hand.

At that moment, Jonas believed in the resurrection.

Tomas' face bore the scars of searing, blistering mustard gas, but the real pain was inside. In fact, the facial scarring was most prominent to Tomas himself, who avoided mirrors, but only noticeable to others upon close inspection. Jonas heard the footfalls on the wood floor of the cabin at all hours of the night. Sometimes, Tomas would be missing in the morning, to be found sleeping in the barn or returning late in the day after carousing in Little Falls. Once, he didn't return for three days. Pine Tree Lumber in Little Falls, his former employer, had no jobs and was about to close with the depletion of area pine forests. Tomas dutifully tried farm work, but his mind was elsewhere, and his heart wasn't in it. He was sharp with the children and with Hilma, but then he would apologize profusely and sob.

He found salvation in the American Legion.

About the time of Tomas' return, a fraternal organization of veterans was a mere concept, but the sudden end of the war dumped thousands and thousands of doughboys on American soil, and the Legion became a movement. Although Tomas shared nothing, Jonas imagined what only his brother and his comrades could know: their eyes witnessed limbs ripped from the bodies of comrades; their tongues licked the salt of their own blood; their ears listened to bullets whistling overhead; their bodies shook when a Krupp artillery shell exploded nearby; and their noses sniffed the sweet and spicy scent of mustard gas. They smelled it still. Jonas could imagine but he couldn't understand. Hilma didn't understand. Only those-- like Tomas—whose souls had been seared by hellfire truly understood.

And there was more. The warm welcome the returning vets received was not matched by employment. Jobs left behind had been filled by others. The sudden wrenching of a war economy to one of peace created massive unemployment and spiraling inflation, and the vet was the one without work.

And there was still more. The war ended suddenly, and war fever still burned hot. Oh, the vets were happy enough to be out of harm's way, but the Great War was a moral crusade— Uncle Sam needs you to fight the war to end all wars and make the world safe for democracy —and the pent-up patriotism of the crusaders needed an outlet, expressed in the Legion's founding statement:

*For God and Country, we associate ourselves together for the following purposes:*

*To uphold and defend the Constitution of the United States of America; to maintain law and order; to foster and perpetuate a 100 Percent Americanism; to preserve the memories and incidents of our association in the Great War; to inculcate a sense of individual obligation to the community, state, and nation; to combat the autocracy of both the classes and the masses; to make right the master of might; to promote peace and good will on earth; to safeguard and transmit to posterity the principles of justice, freedom, and democracy; to consecrate and sanctify our comradeship by devotion to mutual helpful-*

*ness.*

It was all well and good that Tomas had found a supportive fraternity, Jonas mused, but Tomas' zeal worried him. Just as the brothers never shared their experiences or their feelings, Jonas wouldn't confront his brother's radicalization. Jonas didn't know all that happened to Tomas, and he never told Tomas about his humiliation at the hands of Americans for America. Jonas could see the worry in Hilma's face when Tomas would go off on a rant.

Common purpose, heroism, and moral idealism fermented a heady brew, but under the froth lay darker, aggressive impulses. Although the shooting had ended, the 100 per center still hunted the adversary—the German-American and other hyphenated ethnicities, labor radicals, and dissenters from strict orthodoxy—especially those perceived to have been draft dodgers or otherwise soft on the war effort. The drills, the propaganda, and the fervor of combat fostered a dualistic black and white worldview. Good versus evil. Friend versus foe. America versus the Hun. 100 per cent Americanism versus anything less.

One evening, Jonas and Tomas sat silently at the table reading newspapers while Hilma finished cleaning the supper dishes.

"Hah, that'll show 'em," Tomas nearly shouted. He held up a picture of strikebreakers attacking union organizers with sticks. "Poke it up their ass!"

Jonas felt the color draining from his face. His humiliation remained fresh and painful but unknown to his brother. Challenging his brother's demons would merely loose his own, he feared, but he didn't expect his wife to be his defender. With a clatter, Hilma's soup ladle hit the floor. She picked it up and shook it in Tomas' face.

"Mind yourself, brother, or you'll not be welcome here. There are children listening with big ears who don't need to learn your foul language and hateful ways. Not everyone thinks as you, you know, in your world without colors."

She was wrong. In his world of black and white, there was one color.

Red.

# CHAPTER THIRTY-SIX

"Ole Hanson is coming to town," Tomas said.

"Who?" Jonas replied.

"Why, Mayor Hanson of Seattle, of course."

The name still didn't register with Jonas, but Mayor Hanson had become the darling of the 100 per centers. Early in 1919, labor unions in the northwest called for a general strike, which remained peaceful but alarmed those who saw a Russian style revolution quelled by the strong-armed tactics of the Seattle mayor, Ole Hanson. Jonas reluctantly acceded to his brother's request to listen to the red-headed son of Norwegian immigrants whose speaking tour was making him a wealthy man. The capitalist was capitalizing, reflecting public opinion while also inflaming it. He gave his 100 per cent audience what they wanted to hear.

> The Seattle strike was an attempted revolution. That there was no violence does not alter the fact. The intent, openly and covertly announced, was for the overthrow of the industrial system; here first, then everywhere. True, there were no flashing guns, no bombs, no killings. Revolution, I repeat, doesn't need violence.

Jonas was one of the few who didn't respond with robust cheers and applause. Tomas slapped him on the back and encouraged him to his feet along with the rest of the throng, but Jonas remained seated and stone-faced.

Mayor Hanson's passion was rising as he fed off the emotions of the audience, and a lock of his carefully coifed red hair fell across his forehead.

*I am tired of reading rhetorical, finely spun, hypocritical, far-fetched excuses for bolshevism, communism, and syndicalism. Nauseated by the sickly sentimentality of those who would conciliate, pander, and encourage all who would destroy our Government, I have tried to learn the truth and tell it in United States English of one or two syllables.*

*With syndicalism — and its youngest child, bolshevism — thrive murder, rape, pillage, arson, free love, poverty, want, starvation, filth, slavery, autocracy, suppression, sorrow and Hell on earth. It is a class government of the unable, the unfit, the untrained, of the scum, of the dregs, of the cruel, and of the failures. Freedom disappears, liberty emigrates, universal suffrage is abolished, progress ceases, and a militant minority, great only in their self-conceit, reincarnate under the Dictatorship of the Proletariat a greater tyranny than ever existed under czar, emperor, or potentate.*

After the speech, the brothers went their separate ways. Tomas remained in Little Falls with an American Legion friend, with news that they had hired on to work in the Minneapolis flour mills. Jonas drove the buggy alone. As he passed through the main intersection of Little Falls, he glanced up at the inscription atop the bank building. The name "German-American Bank" had been chiseled out, but the letters remained visible, a shadowy reminder that the war had changed America.

Soon after Jonas had been cajoled into listening to Ole Hanson, it became Hilma's turn to listen to a capitalizing-capitalist who became fabulously rich by preaching to the choir. On a muggy August day in the summer of 1919, she boarded a train with more than a dozen fellow congregants from the Kalmar Lutheran Congregation for a trip to Minneapolis. The expedition was arranged and subsidized by Hannah Alekson, the wife of banker Henry Alekson, the wealthiest man in Kalmar.

"What Kalmar needs is a revival," she said.

Mrs. Alekson cornered Pastor Hallstrom after Sunday services, interrupting the pastor's conversation with Jonas. A broad-brimmed hat kept her doughy face, offset by brilliant red lips, in the shadows even in the noon-day sun. It was a good thing she was a townie, because her blanched skin wouldn't tolerate the farm sun. She held a prayer book in one hand—along with a dainty silk kerchief that she used to dab her face-- and a purse half the size of a suitcase in the other.

"Where is it, where is that flyer?" she muttered as she scrounged through her bag until she pulled out a pamphlet.

"Here 'tis. Here, Reverend, have a look at this," she said.

Pastor Charlie obliged, but after a quick glance, he handed it back.

"For the good of their mortal souls, the citizens of Kalmar could use a dose of strong medicine," Hannah continued.

Pastor Hallstrom's contorted face said he was unconvinced. Preaching hellfire and damnation was not his style, and he rightly understood her implicit swipe at his own sermons. Jonas smiled inwardly and silently urged his friend to continue the good fight.

Henry Alekson, her balding, bespectacled banker husband nodded to punctuate her points, and the tips of his thin, waxed moustache twitched as he chewed on a cigar (he had the reverence not to light it while on the church grounds). He rocked back and forth on the balls of his feet with thumbs hooked behind suspenders. Pinned to the lapel of his jacket, a curious button depicting a carpenter's square and draftsman's compass begged inquiry, but the banker would only divulge that he belonged to something called the freemasons without further explanation.

Alekson oozed attitude. It seemed he figured to be the local version of banker J. Pierpont Morgan. Well, maybe he wasn't quite that, but where would Kalmar be without his bank? Sure, he swam in a small pond, but he was a plenty big fish. To his way of thinking, he was a nobleman—intelligent, kind, and charitable, but with a mind to sound business practice, and his success was good for the town. Jönsson had long ago learned not to trust the national money trust, and it seemed that his local banker was merely the trust writ small.

"If money is the issue, we'll cover the trip expenses," Hannah said.

Husband Henry stopped nodding and pulled out his gold pocket watch so quickly he nearly broke the chain.

"Time to go," he said, tugging at Hannah's elbow.

"Without proper revival," she continued with a parting shot, "I fear that the offering in the plate on Sundays may shrink."

When she finally pulled away, Pastor Charlie rolled his eyes at Jonas and swore before quickly looking around to make sure no one heard.

"Shit," he said again. "The Aleksons are the congregation's biggest donors, and I hear her veiled threat to withhold their support if'n I don't agree to her extortion."

"Money talks," Jonas replied.

"Ain't it so," the pastor replied with sheepish surrender on his face.

So, it was arranged, and Agnes Hallstrom begged Hilma to accompany the entourage to be headed by Mrs. Alekson. Pastor Hallstrom would attend also, but reluctantly. If the back-sliding congregants of the Kalmar Lutheran Church needed a healthy dose of revival as Hannah Alekson suggested, evangelist Billy Sunday and his travelling road show-- an entourage of two dozen musicians, setup men, advance men, and fundamentalist Bible study leaders--was the man to administer strong medicine.

During Hilma's thirty-six-hour absence, Jonas had his hands full with his three young urchins from two to four years of age. Anders wanted to play cowboys with his younger sisters, but they were only interested in playing house. When two-year-old Signe refused to eat the doughy flap jacks Jonas put before her, she began to wail, "I want Mama." Jonas heartily agreed, and when the Hallstrom buggy appeared on the promontory delivering his wife after their adventure in the city, he was exhausted though he hadn't done a lick of field work.

"Stay for supper," Jonas said.

Jonas was merely being polite, but the Hallstroms said yes, and Hilma was pleased even though the task of preparation would fall on her. The three returnees from the Billy Sunday revival had plenty to say away from the ears of the rest of the entourage. With the addition of the pair of Hallstrom children, the Jönsson kids entertained themselves in and out and chasing all around—Signe did her best to waddle along behind the older kids; Hilma and Agnes busied themselves in the kitchen; and Charles and Jonas checked out the newborn calves and piglets.

After the dishes were washed and dusk settled over the homestead, the children began to nod off, but still the Hallstroms lingered. These four adults ignored the rule against talking politics and religion; indeed, they relished heady conversation with each other. The Jönssons were the only congregants that Charles and Agnes trusted well enough to share true feelings, and the respect was mutual.

As a youngster growing up in Sweden, Jonas only knew an angry and bullying god who looked like the beady-eyed, beak-nosed priest who attempted to manipulate by threatening hellfire. Perhaps because he didn't want to share his patriarchy, Jonas' *fader* wasn't a regular churchgoer, and thus, neither was his family. Pastor Charles was different. He was the clerical image of a different sort of god: human, tolerant, and uncertain. Jonas was uneducated, and Charles had read books and studied subjects that Jonas had never considered; yet they hit it off.

For his part, Jonas knew plenty. Long ago, editor and publisher Teodor Swensson urged him to read newspapers as a means of improving his command of English, and the practice had become a daily ritual. At the close of most days in the Jönsson cabin, Jonas and Hilma spent a quiet hour or two in the glow of a kerosene lantern—Hilma knitting or sewing and Jonas reading.

"Why do you read if it distresses you so?" she would ask.

Jonas would ignore her question, and he would continue to cluck with tongue against roof mouth while shaking his head at the sensationalist press that was less interested in facts than in selling newspapers and stoking the fears of a gullible public eager to find a boogeyman responsible for the frenzy that gripped the nation. *REIGN OF TERROR PLANNED! STOLEN EXPLOSIVES TO BE USED! PLANS FOR WIDESPREAD VIOLENCE AND MURDER! RED PERIL HERE! PLAN BLOODY REVOLUTION!*

Hilma and Agnes joined the men on the porch, and dissection of the Billy Sunday circus was about to begin.

"I declare, husband," Hilma said. "I've never seen such a spectacle. Did you know that Reverend Sunday was once a professional baseball player?"

Jonas shrugged.

"Well, it started simply enough with music while Sunday sat quietly along the edge of the platform. Much as I hate to admit it, the performance by the singers had me going. A man's voice started softly, rising and falling, then higher still. When a mournful chorus answered him, his voice changed, pounding low, powerful, triumphant against the slow, sad chorus. I was shocked when a high-pitched woman's voice wailed, and Reverend Sunday streaked across the platform and slid on his knee like he was stealing a base! I tell you, the riled-up audience exploded."

"I declare," Agnes said, waving her fingers in front of her face in a fanning motion. "You tell it so I see it all again, but it seems so unreal! It frightened me in the moment, but now the absurdity seems laughable."

Pastor Charlie shook his head. Jonas tapped his pipe alongside his rocking chair and tamped in a fresh heaping of Prince Albert. He lit a match and sucked the flame into the bowl.

"Well, he strutted," Hilma continued, "and he screamed, and he jumped, and he ran, and when the crowd was in a frenzy, he started in on sex."

Even in the light of the kerosene lamp, Jonas detected a pink blush on her cheeks as she spoke the word. Agnes giggled, and Charlie's headshaking became more animated.

"I cannot, I dare not repeat some of the indiscrete words he spoke," Hilma said. She took a deep breath and quickly drank down the rest of her glass of water. "It was odd. He teased, and then when he had sparked imagination, he taunted and condemned. His audience allowed him to say the vilest thing because he then turned around and condemned the very image he had created. It was as if he held out a piece of candy and then slapped the hand that reached for it. But they swooned, and they stampeded each other answering his call for repentance at his altar."

Pastor Charlie squinted as if trying to remember which of his congregants went forward and which ones remained in their seats. He cleared his throat, and the others turned to listen.

"The pressure to move forward was immense for Sunday the gatekeeper separated sheep from goats. If you're not with me, you're against God. Subscribe to my view of good and evil or be damned, an outcast, an outsider, one of *those.* Billy Sunday's religion separates and excludes."

"Wait a minute," Jonas said and disappeared into the house. He returned momentarily with four cups and a whiskey bottle.

Charlie smacked his lips at the first taste and leaned back against a porch pole. Hilma took a small sip and began to laugh.

"Dear husband, the best part of the trip was the return train ride. Agnes and I sat next to each other, mocking the evangelist, trying not to let anyone hear. But Evie caught on, and when we realized she was trying to keep a straight face, we all laughed together."

Agnes smiled and nodded.

"I soon had to leave," Charlie said, "and I had to tell these two they were worse than Sunday."

"But you winked at me as you departed," Agnes teased.

"You see Hannah Alekson scowling at all of us?" Hilma asked.

For a few moments, they sat silently, swatting the occasional mosquito. Charlie cleared his throat and the others turned to hear what he had to say.

"He was political, too, you know," Charlie said.

"Really, what did he say," Jonas asked.

"Well, he gave them what they wanted to hear. The audience screeched when he said something like, 'The Bolshevik is a guy with a face like a porcupine and a breath that would scare a pole cat. If I had my way, I'd fill the jails so full of them that their feet would stick out the windows. Let them rule? We'll swim our horses in blood up to the bridles first!'"

Jonas grunted and downed the last of his whiskey before pouring another measure and offering the bottle around. Each of them accepted a little more, and Jonas emptied the bottle into Charlie's cup. Billy Sunday stirred a strange brew: titillating sex talk, altar calls, and rants about Bolsheviks. Whip fear into hysteria and then offer salvation. Jonas thought back to his own recent encounter with a silver-throated orator. Mayor Ole Hanson had stoked the emotions of the 100 per centers by piquing their fears then offering salvation. Instead of the devil and demons: the Red menace. Instead of eternal damnation in the afterlife: hell on earth. Instead of an altar call: the rigid salutes to the flag and the pledge of allegiance.

Pastor Charlie started in again.

"Sunday appeals to our selfish instincts. *Personal* salvation."

He drew out the word.

"He promises heaven, whether that is conceived of as the afterlife or prosperity in this life, but the words of Jesus on the Mount would never cross his lips—blessed are the poor, the meek, the hungry. For Billy Sunday and those who swoon at his every word, empathy is wishy-washy weakness toward the undeserving; charity is merely a means to feel good, to justify one's station, and to draw clear lines of separation between classes."

"Did you see that?" Hilma exclaimed after a shooting star flashed across the sky behind Charlie's back.

Silence settled on the foursome; faces bathed in the wash of stars across a moonless sky. Their conversation was humorous and happy but the circumstances serious and sad.

Summer would soon surrender to autumn, but the unrelenting season of discontent in America would continue, Jonas was sure: capital versus labor, veteran versus non-veteran, Protestant versus Catholic and both against the Jew, and white versus black. Although he was a farmer at heart, Jonas knew plenty about the labor movement. In the long-standing tug-of-war over collective bargaining rights, certain barons of industry relished their chance to smear the labor movement with a broad brush dipped in blood-red paint. The threat of a strike was the chief bargaining chip held by the union, but in 1919, the threat was demonized in the eyes of the public as a conspiratorial plot to establish communism. On these shores, the biggest losers coming out of the war to end all wars were the labor unions, and the papers were full of beatings and arrests.

Charlie again cleared his throat and continued speaking. "*Conversion* is Sunday's watchword. 'If you become like me, if you believe the things I believe, if you repent of your otherness and conform to my norms, then you may join my tribe, but if not, you're damned to hell.' Conformity and certainty are encouraged; dissent and doubt discouraged."

Jonas slowly sucked in a breath of the cool evening air. Charlie could be talking about Tomas and the single-mindedness of the 100 per centers. Ole Hanson and Billy Sunday, and others of their ilk, didn't create the red scare, they merely capitalized on the confluence of circumstances: lingering war fever, the Russian revolution, and a few clumsy bomb-throwing anarchists who provided proof of the great lie that revolution was at hand. Following the war to make the world safe for democracy, black and brown were Red, immigrants were communist infiltrators, liberals and dissenters were un-American, and the 100 per centers were the true patriots. Fearmongering was in season.

Jonas was not an angry man, a wasted emotion in the face of the mean-spirited age. He was cynical, yes, but resigned better described his mood, but he was never disinterested, and these discussions with the Hallstroms nourished him. In a world gone mad, it was refreshing to hear truth.

As the Hallstrom buggy disappeared along the starlit trail, Hilma made sure the kids were tucked in. Discussion was for the mind, but family was for the heart. For now, retreat from the world seemed sage, and raising solid stock—his beasts and his babies—would be his joy and fulfillment.

Thunder rumbled in the west. Jönsson rose to his feet, leaned against the porch pole, and watched the far-off lightning flashes. Hilma cuddled in close, and Jonas put his arm around her waist.

# CHAPTER THIRTY-SEVEN

On December 21, 1919, the winter solstice and the darkest day of the year, Jonas leaned against the burr oak at the end of his driveway with collar turned up and the ear flaps of his red-checkered hat pulled low. He stuffed his mittened hands into the cavernous pockets of his wool coat while he awaited the rural free delivery mail. A few straggler brown leaves clung to the tips of bent and twisted branches, ready to surrender to the next stiff breeze. The forlorn mailbox leaned slightly in a receding drift of grimy gray snow. A foot of snow had fallen weeks earlier but melting and refreezing produced an icy glaze and a sooty layer of dirt. He hoped there was a freshening layer of white snow in the slate clouds that scudded overhead.

Just as he was about to depart, the late-arriving mailman finally appeared and handed over a single letter with a New York City postmark. Jönsson pulled off his gloves and ripped it open.

*Dearest friend,*

*I have been thinking of you much these days. I have heard you are doing well with a thriving family. Is God fulfilling your dreams? I fear he is punishing me for my sins. I jest, for you know I have no illusions of an all-powerful deity, yet I wonder at my fate. Whether it is a wrathful god exacting vengeance for my evil deeds or demons from hell angry for the good I have done, I cannot say. If there is a devil, his name is Palmer, and his avenging angel is Hoover.*

*I wonder if you think of me. I considered writing you*

*when I was first arrested and imprisoned, but I didn't want you to fret or lose faith in our cause, but now that my fate appears hopeless, I thought you should know what became of old Natty Einstein. I'm sure you will not be surprised that I protested the heinous war just past. Am I a pacifist? Perhaps, but I acknowledge the possibility of a just war but remain convinced that this was not such a one. This catastrophic blunder was an imperialist adventure that enriched the capitalists through the blood of the worker—or the farmer, as you may know all too well. Was I a security threat for expressing my views condemning the war and especially the draft? What of the right of free speech?*

*If you still believe in the goodness of America, our adopted home, our beacon of hope, our golden city on a hill—and all such rot—perhaps you will be surprised to learn that our enlightened government considered me an enemy of the state, and I have spent these past eighteen months languishing in federal prison.*

*But that is not the worst of it. Now that the war is over, will I be released, will I return to Duluth, will I return to the life of a humble immigrant thankful for stepping onto these hallowed shores? No. Attorney General Mitchell Palmer, and J. Edgar Hoover, his henchman, have decreed that I am to be deported to Russia, a cruel irony since the Russians are the archenemies of my countrymen in the Ukraine! My crime was to believe in America's greatness-- that speech is free; that all are created equal; that liberty and justice are for all. Or perhaps my sins are fourfold for I am a radical, Jewish, woman, immigrant. Which of these--or is it the sum of all that disqualifies me from the pursuit of happiness?*

*Perhaps it is for the best, and I shall experience the Russian socialist experiment firsthand. Certainly, Lenin and the Bolsheviks can be no more oppressive and unjust than the men who hide behind the skirts of Lady Liberty waiting to ensnare the naïve and hopeful.*

*By the time you receive this letter, I expect to be aboard the S.S. Buford, steaming past Lady Liberty and departing the New York harbor, where I arrived an optimistic immigrant to this land many years ago, but I now depart as a disillusioned victim of the false promise of America.*

*Perhaps God will bless you. If I believed and if I was to pray, that would be my prayer. Perhaps America will fulfill your dreams. The dim spark of optimism that smolders in my heart fervently wishes that it be so.*

*Fondly,*

*Natty.*

Jönsson crumpled the letter before stuffing it into his pocket. He shivered as he began trudging toward the slight sliver of red lingering on the western horizon beyond the cabin. Late that night after the others retired, he pulled out the letter and read it again before dropping it into the glowing embers of the wood stove. He shoved another log onto the fire and disappeared into the bedroom.

# CHAPTER THIRTY-EIGHT: 1919-1920

L ena was a Christmas baby. The midwife couldn't have been too happy about the timing, but she accepted the call without grumbling. After Jonas' family returned from Christmas eve services, Jonas and Gurli turned the sleigh around and returned to town to summon Antonia Maria Sederstrom, the wife of Sven Sederstrom, the livery man who managed the stable on the banks of the creek that sliced through the village.

Maria was one of the few townsfolk without a Scandinavian background, but Sven married her twenty years earlier when he worked alongside her Italian father in the iron mines up north. Her pitch-black hair and olive-skin stood out in the pews of the Lutheran church, and when she crossed herself, she stood out the more. Twenty-five years earlier, the papist piety of Louis Archambault offended Jonas, but he mellowed. If he could fall in love with Natty Einstein the Jew, befriending the Catholic Maria was no big deal. Maria, midwife to his children, boasted six children of her own, some blonde and blue eyed but others dark like her, including Adriana, the oldest, and Federico, the youngest known as "Freddy." A year short of becoming a teenager, Freddy had already begun working for Jonas during busy times on the farm.

Anders and his sisters weren't too happy about baby Lena's interruption of the family's Christmas celebration, but all was forgiven when presents were finally opened a day late. Each child had a gift from their parents, and Tomas lavished expensive toys on his nephew and nieces. Anders received a red wagon and each of the girls received a porcelain doll from

Uncle Tomas.

Tomas had returned from the city with money in his pockets and a button on his lapel proclaiming, "One Hundred Per Cent Americanism" obtained at the inaugural national convention of the American Legion in Minneapolis six weeks earlier.

"This little button is something that makes enemies cringe when it flashes before their eyes," he boasted, parroting lines he had learned at the convention. "Weak-kneed Americans are stronger when a legionnaire is present, and agitators will shut their mouths."

Jonas merely grunted.

"My work in the mills is finished," Tomas reported.

That was all he revealed, but Jonas suspected more. There were bruises on Tomas' hands, and a fading scrape on his face. The newspapers said that secret informers planted by the owners of the Pillsbury and Washburn-Crosby mills had clashed with the union leadership. If Tomas had been involved, Jonas knew it was not on the side of labor for Tomas had boasted more than once that he would be only too happy to work as a strikebreaker and bust a few Bolshevik heads if necessary.

Tomas beamed as he revealed his good news, "I will soon begin work as a deputy sheriff in Little Falls. I will move into an anteroom of the county jail with free rent. The sheriff appreciates a man who knows how to handle a gun."

Tomas pulled out his deputy's badge, which he polished with his sleeve before showing it off.

Almost an afterthought as he was leaving, the younger brother mentioned that he should now be called "Thomas. Thomas Johnson."

"It's the right way to spell it here in America," he said.

Jonas wasn't sure; in fact, he was offended as his younger brother turned his back on his own heritage.

"Don't forget who you are and where you come from," Jonas said.


In May of 1920, Anders would turn five years old, and Jonas intended to continue the ritual of the carving. He wondered whether his name remained visible, etched in the beech tree overlooking the pond back in Sweden, and he checked the carvings in the cottonwood by the creek where he and Tomas had scribed their names in preparation for adding their own sons. He placed a special order with Ingemar Jorgenson, and he had Anders' present in hand well before the birthday. Of course, the gift would be a folding knife with a mother-of-pearl handle. Each evening after the children were in bed, Jonas pulled out the knife and polished the handle while reminding Hilma of the significance of the ritual. She merely nodded and smiled.

Of course, Tomas was invited, but he arrived with an expensive gift: a single-shot, bolt-action .22 caliber rifle. Jonas was upstaged and not pleased. Not only did the rifle exceed Jonas' own gift, but a rifle was too dangerous for a five-year old —even an entry-level .22 caliber model that was useful for target practice or gopher plunking but not for big game. Anders tried to hoist the rifle to his shoulder, but the butt was too long, and the barrel too heavy.

"We'll put this away until you're older," Jonas said as he took the rifle from his son's hands.

Anders scowled.

With the celebratory mood of the birthday party broken, Jonas decided to postpone the name-etching ceremony planned for the creek side cottonwood.

"Who would like to go to the circus?" Jonas asked the children.

It was meant to be a surprise, but the mood needed brightening. Hilma smiled and nodded at him. The next morning, Anders the five-year-old, Olga the four-year-old, and Signe the three-year-old needed no encouragement to finish their breakfast. Even six-month-old baby Lena sensed the anticipation. Hilma led the children in song as Gurli and the Jönsson carriage bumped along the rocky roadway to the Little Falls fairground and the John Robinson travelling circus tents.

Before the show in the big tent, a walk-around. The children huddled close amongst the crowd and the carnival barkers. The girls squealed when the caged lion stopped pacing and glared right at them, but Anders feigned nonchalance. Later, he reached out and grasped his father's hand when a pair of clowns came too close. Olga and Signe beamed as they circled on the merry-go-round, but Anders' affect was one of boredom; the pretend ponies were rather tame compared to riding Gurli.

The big tent was filled with appreciative oohs and aahs as the performance unfolded. The audience eagerly believed the ringmaster's boasts of the "biggest," "most dangerous," "amazing," and "spectacular." The horsemanship of the women in sequins and tights especially impressed Jonas. The clowns frightened baby Lena, if not the older girls, and Hilma hugged her against her shoulder and patted her back.

When the show was over and the crowd filtered out, Anders was curious about the black-skinned men at the fringes, the roustabouts who did the work of setup and teardown.

"Look at those black men," Anders said.

"Don't point, Anders," Hilma said. "It's not polite."

"Who are they?" Anders asked.

"They're just workers," she replied.

"But why are they black?"

"They're n---rs," Jonas said, and Hilma's eyes shot darts.

"Well, what should they be called?" Jonas protested.

Once outside, the family lingered in the shade of a huge oak to allow the crowd to disperse. Impatient Anders soon wandered off.

"Where are you going?" Hilma said as Anders scouted the backside of the big tent. Jonas followed his son, and Hilma trailed with the girls in tow.

"Anders, don't go so close!" Hilma said.

Anders' curiosity led him near an elephant eating hay under the watchful eye of a young black man. Anders stood transfixed. After a moment, the young man extended a twist of hay toward Anders and asked, "Wanna feed her?"

"Anders, don't," Hilma said.

Too late, Anders immediately stepped forward, accepted the hay, and held it gingerly toward the great gray beast whose trunk twisted toward him. He bravely stood his ground as the elephant claimed the hay and shoved it into her mouth.

"Wanna touch her?"

Anders eyes considered the face of the black youth seeking assurance. The young man nodded, and Anders stroked the trunk. He turned to his family, his face beaming with pride.

"It feels like the old saddle, but rough!"

The elephant lifted the moist nostrils at the end of its trunk and sniffed Anders' face.

"The elefunk kissed him," Olga squealed.

"Come Anders, it's time to go," Papa said.

"What do you say to the nice man?" Hilma said.

"Th ... Thank you, n---r."

Hilma stifled a gasp, and the young man knit his eyebrows, glaring into the eyes of the white boy.

"My name ain't n---r," the young man said through clenched teeth, "and it ain't darkie neither. My name is Elmer. Elmer Jackson."

Hilma stepped forward and put her arm around her son.

"Thank you for your kindness, Mr. Jackson. I apologize for my son." She looked down at Anders. "He may need to have his mouth washed out."

"But but Papa said ... "

Hilma glared at her husband.

"He may need to have his mouth washed out, too."


On a Sunday evening a month later with the children tucked in bed, Jonas rocked on the porch puffing his pipe and reading the paper. In late June, the sun was slow to set, and he didn't need the kerosene lantern. Hilma rocked alongside with her knitting needles whirring.

"Sonofabitch!" Jonas suddenly swore. He smashed his favorite pipe onto the porch floor boards, spewing burning ash. He lurched forward and kicked it into Hilma's rose bush before grasping the porch pole for support as he gasped for air.

Hilma watched with alarm, and then her eyes caught the headline on the paper sprawled on the porch. *CIRCUS WORKERS LYNCHED IN DULUTH.*

"Jonas, talk to me," she said.

He wiped his mouth with his sleeve but didn't turn to face her.

"Six negroes were arrested in Duluth, accused of assaulting a white woman."

"Did they? Did they hurt her?"

He shrugged. "The newspaper wasn't clear on that, but after rumors swirled all day, a mob of white men gathered outside the jail that evening, and their minds were made up. They used heavy timbers, bricks, and rails to break down doors and windows to the jail. The police commissioner ordered the police to back off and not use their guns to protect the prisoners."

Hilma stepped forward and placed a hand on his shoulder. With a huge sigh, he turned to face her, and their eyes met, communicating more than mere words could do. Hilma smoothed a lock of his hair that dangled over his eyes.

"The mob pulled three of the men from the jail and convicted them in a sham trial," Jonas continued. "The men were beaten before the mob hung them from lampposts. At least, the governor sent in the national guard the next morning to protect the others."

"Who, who were the men who were lynched?" Hilma asked, but the dread on her face said that she knew.

Jonas' mouth opened, but no sound came out. Hilma picked up the newspaper and read aloud, "The three lynched men were Elias Clayton, Isaac McGhie, and ..." her voice squeaked, "Elmer Jackson."

**********

*Lunch trays remained untouched, and we sat in silence. Eventually, Don moved to the window and stared at the fresh-fallen* snow that glistened in the bright sunlight. Sun dogs haloed the noon-day sun. If you didn't know winter, you might think the weather outside was balmy, but you would be shocked when the icy air pinched your bare cheeks. Sometimes, the brightest winter sun belied the bitterest cold.

"One of my lasting memories is of the circus elephant and the friendly young man named Elmer," I said, breaking the silence. "I remember his flash of anger when I naively called him 'n---r.' Of course, I knew nothing of his lynching. I suppose I heard about the Duluth lynching sometime later—probably in college—but I didn't relate that far-off story with my own experience until Papa told me as much late in his life."

Don returned to his easy chair and drained the glass of water on his lunch tray.

"Papa's humiliation, the deportation of Natty Einstein, the lynching of Elmer Jackson—these were never discussed, but they were in the air we breathed. I don't ever remember a conversation about bullying, intolerance, or racism, but somehow, we knew and learned: equality, toleration, liberty, freedom, opportunity. These grounded Papa's and Mama's trust in America, ideals often honored in the breach, and rendered dearer when abused. They implicitly passed their idealism to their children, even if they didn't overtly preach their beliefs.

"Never thought about it that way," Don said. "When I was a college kid at Gustavus Adolphus in the sixties, I did some civil rights protesting. And, of course, against the Vietnam War. Never considered that my liberal instincts may have been rooted in Grandpa and Grandma's legacy."

Don bit into half a tuna sandwich in white bread, and I pulled my own tray close and began to eat my lunch.

"You know, I was there in Philadelphia in 1948 when Mayor Humphrey helped change the course of civil rights history with a speech to the Democratic National Convention. I thought of Elmer

*Jackson when I helped Hubert write that speech."*

# CHAPTER THIRTY-NINE: 1922

Jonas checked his pocket watch again. He twisted the knob between his forefinger and thumb to wind the timepiece, but it was already tight.

Hilma stood behind Olga, grasping the six-year-old's shoulders and gently swaying, trying to catch the rhythm of the moment. Elsa, the one-year-old toddler, clutched her mama's skirts. Anders chased Signe and Lena around the big oak tree and across the mouth of the driveway to the mailbox; he could have caught them easy enough, but that would have ended their squealing that straddled the line between fright and delight.

Black-headed terns with fantails circled overhead in a late summer farewell to the northland, slowly winding their way to a second summer in the southern hemisphere. The leaves on the burr oak had lost their summertime luster; surely, they were jealous of the nearby sugar maples that gloried in their reds, golds, and yellows.

The Jönssons heard the creaking wagon before they saw it, and Hilma bent over and clutched Olga from behind with her arms folded under her daughter's chin, and her swaying increased. If the child wasn't apprehensive about the first day of school, the mother was.

Sven Sederstrom, the Kalmar livery man, drove his matched pair of gray geldings from his roost inside the wooden cabin perched over the four wooden wheels that would carry the students to school. Befitting his station, he wore a circular-top, billed cap, much like the trolley man's hat

Jönsson once wore. He wore no other uniform, but he buttoned his shirt tight to his chin, adding a measure of formality to his station.

Behind him, a dozen youngsters spread out over eight benches; just the top of their heads were visible through the row of four glass panes on each side of the school bus. A curved roof covered the wagon with a chimney sticking up through the middle along one side. No smoke curled up today, as the coal stove would only be fired up after the weather cooled. In the dead of winter, the tall, spoked wheels would be replaced with wooden skids, and the cozy school wagon would become a sled.

Next to the Hallstroms, the Sederstrom family stood nearest the Jönssons as friends. Antonia Maria, the midwife, and Adriana the schoolteacher, played important roles in the lives of the Jönsson children, and Freddy was a regular on the Jönsson farm when Jonas needed an extra hand. Jonas appreciated the horse sense of the livery man, who also knew a thing or two about human nature. Whether he tended to his horses or the children in his care, he performed in a conscientious manner.

"Hallo, Jonas," Sven said, and he tipped his hat toward Hilma. "Hallo, Missus."

Hilma had a hard time releasing Olga, but Anders clambered up quickly, and turned to cajole his sister, "Are you coming?"

Anders would start his second grade, but this was also his first day in the school bus, and the first day in the spanking new brick building the Kalmar community proudly constructed as a consolidated school for students through the twelfth grade. While the high school was under construction, he had walked daily to his first grade in the one-room schoolhouse just half a mile up the road from the Jönsson family cabin. Even as a first-grader, Anders shined as the brightest among the local farm kids. Twelve students through grade six had been the charge of Miss Adriana Sederstrom, barely nineteen years-old, who taught reading, riting, and rithmetic while reining in the spirited impulses of her handful of students. Miss Sederstrom was the dark-haired, olive-skinned daughter of the livery man and his Italian wife, and she returned to Kalmar after attending the normal school for teachers in St. Cloud.

Even before the school wagon disappeared around a corner beyond the brilliant stand of sugar maples, Jonas' wiped his nose in his hanky before turning to the others.

"Come, come, we have places to go and people to see," Jonas said as he hoisted Elsa onto to his shoulders with her short legs draped around his neck. Her stubby fingers clutched swatches of her papa's gray hair.

Hilma disappeared inside as Jonas hitched Gurli to the buggy. Gurli waited patiently as Jonas changed from his work clothes to his Sunday suit. Hilma also donned her Sunday best. After dropping the three youngest of their children with Evie Jorgenson, Jonas and Hilma made their way to the Farmer's and Merchant's State Bank of Kalmar and an appointment with Henry Alekson.

"Tell me, what collateral can you offer," the banker asked.

When the banker spoke, he removed his wire-framed spectacles, but he would quickly replace them on his face as he listened. Throughout the conversation, he continued this habit—glasses off while speaking; glasses on while listening.

"Well, I could offer next summer's crops," Jonas said.

Alekson peered over the rim of his glasses that slipped down his nose. He twisted the waxed tips of his moustache, which seemed to aid his thinking. He removed his glasses to make his point.

"Not enough. Perhaps drought or locusts or hail will be your lot next year. I shall need a mortgage on your entire farmstead."

Jonas swallowed, but his mouth was dry. Why did he feel the beggar? He needed $2,000 to purchase a four-square house from the Sears, Roebuck, & Company, and he already had more than half of that stashed in socks at home. His farm was coming off a long string of excellent crop years, and the profits had been plowed into purchases of more land, livestock, and implements. His farm was the envy of many, but it all seemed so puny as he sat in front of the condescending banker. Jönsson knew the man to be short, but he sat on a tall chair that heightened his stature and allowed him to look down on the couple who sat on short-legged chairs in front of a massive oak table that served as the banker's desk.

After a moment of silence, the self-satisfied banker spoke again.

"I will loan you $800, not the $1,000 you ask for, but I require a mortgage on your property. If you repay the $800 within five years, the mortgage deed will be ripped up."

Jonas drew a deep breath. The banker's offer would be a hardship, but he could manage, even if he had to sell a heifer or two. He sensed that the banker offered less than asked, not as a matter of financial acumen, but merely to demonstrate his superiority. Out of the corner of his eye, Jonas caught the worried gaze of his wife. He knew she would remain satisfied to make do in their tiny cabin, but she deserved more. His children deserved more, and another was on the way although Hilma did not yet show through her homespun cotton dress.

A month later in the fall of 1922, Jonas led a string of wagons driven by his neighbors to the Little Falls train station to unload a boxcar filled with all the parts pre-cut and numbered for self-assembly according to a book of instructions, of course. With the fall harvest completed, Jonas' neighbors volunteered their labor under the direction of a paid super-intendent. Before long, a square box of a house, two-and-one-half stories high, stood alongside the log cabin with the sod roof. In the basement underneath, a coal-burning furnace radiated heat through floor registers leading to both the first and second floors. Four boxy rooms—kitchen, dining room, living room, and hallway--encircled a center dormer; from the hallway, a segmented stairway with two landings led to four bedrooms above with an attic higher still.

The last step for the family was to move the furniture from the cabin into the big house. Finally, with great pomp, Jonas moved rocking chairs onto the broad front porch. Anders fetched Papa's pipe and tobacco, Hilma carried a tray with cups of steaming coffee and cocoa, and five children bundled in blankets clustered at the feet of the proud parents. Even as the season's first snowflakes gently sifted through the night air before melting on the unfrozen ground, the Jönsson family remained spellbound in time and place.

Just before the Christmas break in the school year, Jonas tied Gurli's reins to a hitching post outside the brick school-house with creaking wooden floors in the hallway and windows that stretched from the radiators all the way to the ceiling. Arriving early for their summoned meeting with Anders' teacher, Jonas and Hilma paused to watch their son dominate the organized child's play in the gymnasium. During recess for the second grade, the mixed boys and girls played a game called "bird." The monitor chose one person to be the bird catcher stationed in the center of the gym with the rest of the students at one end. Each student silently chose a bird's name--robin, cardinal, sparrow, etc. When the person in the middle called a bird's name, the kids with that chosen name would try to fly to the opposite end of the gym without being snared by the bird catcher. Once tagged, that student would join the swelling number of bird catchers in the middle. After a few turns, there were more bird catchers than birds and soon only one bird remained—Anders the eagle--whose quickness and agility allowed him to escape capture even when the whole class chased him.

"Hmm," Jonas said with a nod, but then he glanced at the big clock on the wall. "Come, come, we'll be late."

Miss Adriana Sederstrom had moved from the one-room schoolhouse to the big school as the teacher of eighteen second graders. To the Jönsson parent's surprise, the principal joined the meeting, and it was he who did the talking.

"We're concerned about your son," the tall, thin man who looked much too young said to begin the conversation. His suit coat seemed too tight, and his pants too short. "We're afraid he might get hurt."

Hilma glanced into Jonas' eyes with a mixture of surprise and alarm. She replied,

"Hurt? How will he hurt himself?"

"Well, there's this bully, and he has everyone cowed. Except Anders. Anders stands up to him, but the bully is much older and bigger—he's a sixth grader."

Hilma's eyes spread wide. Suddenly, the scrapes and bruises made sense.

"Yesterday the bully was shooting dried peas at girls on the playground through his pea shooter. When your daughter Olga was hit, Jonas walked right up to the bully, grabbed the peashooter, and snapped it in half. Then, he ran around the playground with the bully lagging behind. Anders runs like the wind, and the bully is rather a clumsy oaf, but Anders tripped, and the bully jumped atop him, and began to pummel him with his fists; even then, Anders fought back, but if the recess monitor hadn't pulled the bully away, it would have been the worse for young Anders."

"I see," Hilma said.

"Who's the bully," Jonas asked, "and what's to be done?"

The principal sucked in a deep breath and wiped his hand across his mouth and down his pointy, weak chin. "I'm not at liberty to say," he said, "but tell your son that it is the teacher's responsibility to enforce order, and he should just walk away—for his own good."

Jonas steamed inside. Someone needed their ears boxed, and he doubted whether the panty-waist principal was the man to do it. Jonas would get to the bottom of this, and the bully's father would get an earful—or more, if necessary.

The look in Miss Sederstrom's dark-brown eyes said there was more to be told, and on the way out, she whispered in Hilma's ear.

"It's Henry Jr."


Nearly a year later, after another bountiful crop and the sale of half a dozen heifers, Jonas appeared in the office of Henry Alekson at the Farmer's State Bank and counted out eight crisp one-hundred-dollar bills, plus a fifty to pay six per cent interest, with two silver dollars back. Jonas remained businesslike during the transaction, and he suppressed a smile when the bespectacled banker stamped "PAID IN FULL" across the mortgage note. The banker seemed non-plussed, if not disappointed, at the early payoff, and he merely removed his glasses and offered platitudes on thrift and pious living. Jonas listened politely, but his stoic face did not reveal his seething resentment.

*Shut your God dammit face, you mealy-mouthed miser. You*

*got your money, and four years early, doncha know! And you better teach your bully boy some respect, or Anders will give him what for! We'll bide our time, but we'll be watching.*

# CHAPTER FORTY: 1924

T he sweet scent of fresh-cut red clover filled the lean-to with life, warmth, and vitality. Gurli's work for the day was done, and her nostrils fluttered, her hooves crunched the straw, her jaws chomped on hay, her ears twitched away a fly, and her eyes flashed affection for her master.

Jonas leaned contentedly on his pitchfork; his task complete. The first crop of hay was in the barn, and not a moment too soon for a June thunderstorm crackled in the west. Federico "Freddy" Sederstrom, the sixteen-year-old hired hand and son of Sven and Maria, rode his bicycle down the road toward town. Jonas had shooed him on his way even though the boy offered to stay and rub a mixture of linseed oil and beeswax over Gurli's tack. He was like that, always looking for another task, another reason to hang around the farm.

"1 ... 2 ... 3 ... 4 ... 5 ... 6 ... 7 ..." Jonas counted from the flash of lightening until the thunder boomed. The light traveled seven miles before the sound followed seven seconds later.

Nine-year-old Anders chewed on a stalk, nodding his head along with his father's counting.
Although he looked the part in oversized bib overalls and a straw hat, Anders was no hayseed, and he disappeared into the four-square house and his bedroom on the second floor to continue reading. He had devoured *The Box-Car Children,* and now *The Dark Frigate*, a pirate novel with nuanced notions of right and wrong, held his interest. Adriana Sederstrom encouraged him in his interest in reading, even though he was no longer in her class, and his summer of 1924 was filled with books. That was all well and good, but Jonas wished that his son took to his farm chores with the same zeal that he showed toward read-

ing. Jonas looked out the driveway and down the road. Freddy had disappeared.

Anders was savvy all right, but he was much more. He was stronger and faster than his peers. He threw harder and hit a baseball farther. He could kick a football near the clouds.

He was of strong character, too. He stood up to the bully, Henry Alekson, Jr., who derisively called Anders, "Underdog," but the insult backfired, and the teachers and students joined in calling Anders by that nickname, but they meant it as a compliment because he defended the bullied. His son's sense of right, and the courage to stand for it, reminded Jonas of Natty Einstein and Charlies Lindbergh, and that was something to be encouraged. It had not been his own lot to be an activist, a leader, or a crusader, but perhaps he had sired a son who could be that person—without the stain that he, himself, carried since that moment in the Irishman's saloon. He didn't often think of his time in Swede Hollow that ended in murder, but it seemed the rest of the world had forgotten entirely, and Jonas no longer feared the lawman's knock on the door. Why, his own brother now sported the badge of the law pinned on his chest.

Soon came the rain, and Jonas stretched out in the hay and slept. And dreamt. The American forgot it was midsommer, but his Swedish subconscious remembered.

*Fader raised the midsommer pole that Mor had covered in flowering clover. The delicious scent curled around him. His Swedish siblings joined hands and danced in a circle around the pole, but he sat apart from the others, a mere child eating his fill of plump, juicy strawberries. The color of the berries matched the crimson bonnet of a faceless dancer, and he rose to his feet to follow the bonnet circling the pole. All else muted gray, and the crimson bonnet glowed. As he came close, the limp of a crippled old man slowed him. The bonnet spun past him again and again, but his reach fell short. Suddenly, the whirling stopped, and the bonnet floated like a butterfly in the breeze and settled at his feet. Bursts of color sparkled around him, and the green clover with pink blossoms swelled and formed a floral archway revealing a naked goddess with skin white as pearls and red hair aflame. Hilma, the twenty-year-old virgin who sailed across the sea to be his bride, stepped through and kissed him as their children danced in a circle around them.*

After the storm passed, Jonas made his way to the kitchen, and he crept up behind his wife who stood at the stove with her back to him. His hands reached around and cupped her breasts.

"Jonas, the children," she said, speaking Swedish, as she pushed his hands away.

Undeterred, he spun her around and leaned her backwards in his arms and kissed her.

"You're an old fool," she said as she smoothed her hair. "But you're my old fool, and I love you." She pecked him on the cheek and winked. "Later."


Four years earlier, Anders' fifth birthday celebration in May had been muted by Uncle Thomas' gift of a gun, and it wasn't until Independence Day, 1920 when Anders carved his name in the trunk of the creek side cottonwood tree, and the tradition continued but with several new twists. The fourth of July in the year of the child's fifth birthday became the day for name carving, rather than the actual birthday, and the girls were included. Truth be told, inviting the girls was Hilma's idea which hadn't occurred to Jonas, but he saw the wisdom of it.

And so, on July 4, 1924, LENA carved her name on the trunk under the column headed by HILMA that already contained OLGA and SIGNE. The column under JONAS included ANDERS, but there were no names under the column headed by TOMAS, even though he had married and had a son of his own. Jonas and Hilma had met his wife only once, on the day of the wedding at the Little Falls courthouse, and they had never seen his baby boy. They didn't even know the baby's name. Thomas hadn't been to the farm, much less the creek side cottonwood, in several years.

After the cottonwood carving ceremony, the family loaded into the buggy to watch the parade down the main street of Kalmar. An honor guard of Legionnaires with rifles on their shoulders followed the stars and stripes carried by a soldier who lost an arm in the war. The butt of the flagpole rested in a pouch in his belt, and his remaining arm held the flag aloft.

Jonas shifted uneasily from one foot to the other. Swedish midsommer celebrated fertility and a fruitful harvest. He remembered Independence Day, the American mid-summer holiday, in Duluth and the iron range where raucous immigrants rejoiced at their participation in the great American experiment in democracy: freedom of expression; freedom of worship; opportunity; self-determination; self-government. As watchers from the far side of the Atlantic, they saw America boldly proclaiming the nobility of the common man based on equal rights.

And so, they came.

If their experience of the reality didn't match the ideal, the ideal wasn't diminished. No, the streets weren't paved with gold. No, American capitalism was an imperfect alternative to the burdens of European feudalism. No, speech wasn't always free--Natty Einstein knew that. The hopeful came, often struggling, seldom succeeding, yet they celebrated the dream of America on Independence Day and proclaimed anew her audacious ideals.

Today, Jönsson sensed a distortion of the celebration; indeed, a revision in the essential understanding of America.

America was becoming less about the nobility of the common man than about military might. Jingoism pretended to be patriotism. The nation already twice remembered the warrior's sacrifice on Decoration Day at summer's start and Armistice Day in late fall. Now, it appeared that the American mid-summer holiday would also be swallowed up by militaristic zeal. True enough, America was born in war and revolution, but it seemed to Jönsson that a confused nation now remembered the battles while forgetting the cause.

And so, Jonas shifted restlessly as the men in uniform marched at the head of the parade.

Following the flag, a community band set the pace, especially a heavy-set man and his oom-pah tuba. Motor cars followed, more this year than last. Hilma enjoyed the quartet of fiddlers who played familiar folk tunes from the old country, but Jonas favored the matched pair of coal black Fresian draft horses owned by a farmer south of town. He was a stranger to Jonas, but others in the crowd grumbled that a German, and a Catholic at that, should have the finest horses around. Gurli had been a faithful servant, but it was high time that Jonas should purchase his own pair of draft horses.

Anders scarfed down more hot dogs slathered in mustard than Hilma cared to count, and the girls delighted in the ice cream cones served up by the ladies of the Lutheran church. Jonas took his scoop of vanilla ice cream atop a slice of apple pie with cinnamon and sugar sprinkled on the crust.

"Such a pretty dress, Signe," Hannah Alekson, the banker's wife, said as she handed a cone to the Jönsson's second daughter. "I remember that from last year when Olga wore it."

Hilma forced a smile and looked for her husband who stood in the shade in conversation with Pastor Charlie.

"I'll see you soon at summer Bible school," Mrs. Alekson said as the Jönsson family moved along.

When the family departed in the fifth inning of the town team baseball game against the nine from Little Falls, Anders protested. He already imagined himself on the pitcher's mound. There would be fireworks in the evening, too late for the Jönsson youngsters, and Gurli pulled the buggy toward the setting sun. Signe, Lena, and Elsa slept on the buggy floor with baby Siri snuggled in her mother's arms. Anders and Olga whispered and giggled in the rear seat.

Here was Jonas' truth, his dream, his ideal, his success—his family. Perhaps the mix of boys and girls could have been better, but he was content. What would life be like without his daughters? If America struggled with her self-understanding, he was clear in his own: husband, father, farmer.

Jonas returned from Kalmar with a fresh stock of newspapers. The political season heated up in July 1924, an election year for president and governor of Minnesota. Jönsson had his fill of politics after he was beaten and abused six years earlier, but that didn't stop him from devouring the newspaper stories.

Everyone expected Republican President Calvin Coolidge to be re-elected, and the latest news increased that likelihood. In a raucous national convention in Madison Square Garden, the Democratic Party destroyed their chances when the leading candidate for the Democratic nomination, Mayor Al Smith of New York City, was rejected by the power brokers because he was Catholic. His principal opponent was the darling of the anti-Catholic Ku Klux Klan. By the 103rd ballot when a nobody was selected as a compromise, the party was irrevocably split, and their chances that fall doomed.

Less than a year earlier, Republican President Warren Harding conveniently died, thus escaping the Tea Pot Dome corruption scandal that was about to rock his administration. Seems some of his cronies he appointed to administration posts accepted bribes to sell oil drilling leases on public lands. The Vice-President, "Silent Cal" Coolidge, ascended to the presidency. Other high-ranking officials, including Commerce Secretary Herbert Hoover and Treasury Secretary Andrew Mellon escaped the taint of corruption and continued to serve in the Coolidge administration that would easily win election in the fall of '24.

Jönsson's interest lay in the statewide politics of Minnesota, but his candidate would also face defeat in the fall election. First, his hero, former Congressman Lindbergh, died suddenly that spring while campaigning in the primary to be the Farmer-Labor candidate for governor. He had been flying around the state, literally, in a small airplane piloted by his son. The Farmer-Labor party had sprouted from the decay of the failed Non-Partisan League of 1918. If the NPL had withered under the lies and exaggerations of the warmongers and capitalists, the cause survived. Jönsson believed, and so did many others, that the mutual interests of farmers and laborers against the big-money bankers and industrialists necessitated speaking with a common voice, and the Farmer-Labor Party filled that niche. Their candidate for governor that year would be a feisty Scandinavian named Floyd B. Olson, who grew up in a Jewish neighborhood of north Minneapolis. As a crusading county attorney, Olson had prosecuted a business alliance and the Klan, and he became the darling of the Twin Cities labor movement.

"By God, Hilma," Jonas said without looking up from his newspaper, "I think this Olson fellow has the gumption to stand up to the men of privilege."

Hilma merely smiled and continued with her knitting. Her younger daughters slept soundly in their beds, Olga read a book, and Anders sat quietly on the steps, whittling with his pearl-handled pen knife. When he finished, he held up the crude shape of a pistol, which his parents ignored.

"It's been a long day, and I'm tired," Hilma said, and she disappeared into the house. Olga followed her.

Anders remained with his father. Jonas rose from his rocker and tapped his curled pipe against the palm of his hand, spewing the ash over the bed of orange day lilies that adorned the sunny side of the house. He buried the bowl in his leather pouch filled with Prince Albert and scooped out a full measure with strings of shredded tobacco hanging over the edges, which he tamped down with his thumb. He struck a wooden match against the porch pole then leaned against it as he sucked the flame into the tobacco.

On this day of independence and the celebration of America, contentment settled upon Jonas the immigrant who answered the call of the new world and received his reward—well, he didn't have a big, red barn yet, but that would come soon enough—and Anders personified all he hoped for.

"One day, this will all be yours," Jonas said.

Anders popped his last licorice jellybean in his mouth as he surveyed the sleeping fields. A whiff of his papa's sweet tobacco wafted past his nose. Fireflies danced over the meadow, and fog clouded the low spots. From the bog near the creek, croaking frogs sang their evensong.

After a brief hesitation, Anders looked at Jonas and nodded, and then he slapped a mosquito.

*********

*I no longer ate with the other residents in the dining hall, and Don was my regular dinner guest. LaDonna became accustomed to delivering a second tray with the evening meal, and Don cleaned his plate, but I barely touched mine.*

*"Gonna eat that slice of banana cream pie?" Don asked.*

*As usual, he downed his dessert and mine as well.*

"I'm sure the first stirrings had already begun," I said. "The world of books caught my fancy more than pride in straight rows of corn. For Papa, sweat on the brow and calloused hands were the mark of a man, but my gaze already lifted beyond the fields of small grains, even if I didn't fully understand it then. That would be a revelation and a reckoning that was still years away."

# CHAPTER FORTY-ONE

When the Great War ended suddenly, post-war fever infected the nation. Although the delirium broke almost as quickly as it began, the soul of America was scarred, like the aftereffects of smallpox. In the fall of 1924, Jonas ruffled his newspaper as he turned the page to follow the words of trial lawyer Clarence Darrow who spoke of the war's lingering effects.

*For four long years, the civilized world was engaged in killing men. Christian against Christian, barbarian uniting with Christians to kill Christians; anything to kill. It was taught in every school, aye in the Sunday schools. The little children played at war. The toddling children on the street. Do you suppose this world has ever been the same since? How long will it take for the world to get back the humane emotions that were slowly growing before the war? How long will it take the calloused hearts of men before the scars of hatred and cruelty shall be removed?*

How long, indeed? Not yet, it seemed. Alongside fresh pock marks, the war fever had blistered the scabs off old scars as well, and the self-appointed healers who treated the festering wounds wore white hoods and burned crosses.

Model-T Fords mingled with the saddle horses and plow horses harnessed to buggies in the rutted street in front of Jorgenson's General Store. Evening chores had been delegated to wives and children while the menfolk had gathered in Kalmar for an important conclave. Even if the suffragists had succeeded in garnering the vote for women just a few years earlier, such nonsense wouldn't carry any sway for this men-only meeting.

Jonas slid off the back of old Gurli and rubbed his hands. Snow flurries carried on a chill November breeze followed him from the farm. He pulled his bad leg behind him as he ascended the exterior stairway to the storage room above the store that sold dry goods and hardware during the day but now served as the den for the inaugural rally of a local chapter of the Ku Klux Klan. Pastor Charlie refused to allow use of the church sanctuary for this unholy gathering. Over Evie's objections and his own misgivings, Ingemar Jorgenson agreed to allow the conspirators to meet in his storeroom on the second floor.

"It would be bad for business if I said no," he said, hoping to persuade himself, if not his wife.

The war-time patriotism of many Swedes had been questioned. What better way to demonstrate their red-blooded Americanism than to join the rising tide of anti-Catholicism that flared again through many parts of the country in the early 1920s, in the latest incarnation of "rum, Romanism, and rebellion." The German Catholics in nearby Stearns County, who were creeping ever closer to Kalmar's Swedish enclave, became handy scapegoats.

Although the Swedes mostly spoke their native tongue in their homes, tonight the meeting room was filled with the finest English the Swedes could muster. Deputy Thomas Johnson returned to Kalmar to speak in favor of forming a local chapter. So did Nils Ahlberg, the mayor, and Henry Alekson, the banker, who organized the meeting.

"How's the wife and family?" Thomas asked, extending his hand to his brother.

"Good." Jonas replied, stretching his arm to shake Thomas' hand. "We're up to six. Five girls and Anders, of course."

Thomas didn't ask the names of the younger girls, and Jonas didn't ask the name of Thomas' son.

"You should come for Christmas," Jonas said.

"Maybe I will," Thomas replied.

Jonas wished to say more to his brother, but the words didn't come, and then Henry Alekson called the meeting to order.

"Attention, attention, please," Alekson said in a raised voice. He pointedly overlooked Pastor Charlie and asked a stranger to offer an opening prayer, someone he called a "Kludd":

"Beneath the cross we glory. We light the cross to remind all who see it that Christ is the light of the world, which shall never fade. Fire destroys the perishable and purifies the righteous. Lord, lift up men who will not flinch when duty calls. Smite the enemy and protect the virtuous."

A chorus of "amens" answered, but not from Jonas or Pastor Charlie.

"We're here to organize and to plan," Alekson began. "Our Christian and American way of life is under siege. Maybe other Klan chapters have a n---r problem in their part of the world, but here in central Minnesota our problem is the God dammit papists who threaten to swallow up the Scandinavian farms and villages."

Alekson glared pointedly at Sven Sederstrom, the liveryman, who stepped forward with eyes aflame.

"In case you fine gentlemen forgot who birthed yer babies, let me remind ya. Twas my Catholic wife, doncha know. What's more, many of yer blonde and blue-eyed brats learnt their ABCs from my dark-haired daughter."

"Calm down, Sven," Mayor Ahlberg said. "No offense intended. We ain't talkin' 'bout yer family. It's those others what concerns us."

"The hell, you say," Sederstrom said with dripping sarcasm.

Alekson chimed in. "It might help if'n yer wife stopped crossin' herself and fingering her rosary beads during our Lutheran services."

"Shit!" Sederstrom stormed out and slammed the door so hard the glass broke.

"Damned thin skin, I'd say," Deputy Johnson said.

Anger roiled Jönsson's gut, but words caught in his throat, and he simply moved away from his brother and toward Pastor Charlie. Jönsson knew the corrosive effects of hatred. He had justified robbing the saloon keeper, in part, because of the Irishman's religion, and now he carried the guilty stain of a murderer, even though he alone knew about it—except for God, maybe. Jönsson also knew scapegoating. He had been abused as a surrogate for the hated Hun simply because he drove the Saxon motor car of an anti-war politician. He knew that intolerance paints with a broad brush, and Natty Einstein now suffered an unknown fate under Lenin. When he thought of Elmer Jackson hanging from a lamp pole in Duluth, he damn near said something to the men gathered above the General Store; he wished he had the gumption; he wished he had the gift of gab to speak truth to his friends and neighbors; he wished his own brother wasn't such a damn fool; but he remained silent.

Scandalous comments bubbled around him.

"Catholic schools teach anti-Americanism!"

"The Pope seeks to take over America!"

"Escaped nuns say that Protestant girls are enslaved for sex!"

"The Knights of Columbus swore an oath to torture and exterminate Protestants!"

The claims seemed absurd on their face, but truth mattered little against prejudice.

"Attention! Attention!" Alekson quieted the crowd. "You know the abandoned schoolhouse on the hill a few miles south of town. From the hill, you can see Catholic farms to the south, and, of course, they can see the hill. That's where we should set our crosses afire."

Most in the room cheered the planning for the cross-burning, but not Pastor Charlie, who did himself proud, at least in Jonas' eyes. Charlie did his best and most courageous preaching ever, but he was swimming against the current.

"Ours is a decent society, and our religion remembers the lesson of the Good Samaritan who comforted the stranger," the pastor began. "I fear that we are unduly fearful, and we shun those we don't fully understand. Worse, we recreate our fellow Americans in ghastly caricatures that heighten mistrust and serve to separate rather than unite. Our parents--and many in this very room--" he said, scanning the lamplit faces of the men in the room," came to these shores to escape religious tests, and I stand on the American promise of freedom to worship as I please, or as you please, or as the Catholics down the road please."

When he finished, the room was silent until Ingemar Jorgenson spoke up.

"Burning a cross on the doorstep to Stearns County ain't necessary. If'n our concern is that the Catholics will cross over and contest with us on our turf, there is a simple solution. We should agree with each other, establish a mutual covenant, that no one will sell goods, and especially land, to any Catholic. If we won't sell, they can't buy."

Alekson glared at Jorgenson who undercut his plans with a proposed compromise. He pushed his glasses tight against the peak of his nose and scanned the faces of the men who nodded at Jorgenson's proposal. Snowflakes swirled through the broken window of the door.

Before Alekson could offer a rejoinder, Pastor Charlie jumped in:

"Let's have a show of hands. Who favors a covenant rather than a cross burning?" The pastor asked, and he immediately raised his own hand.

Jönsson's hand shot up, and so did that of the proprietor-host, Ingemar Jorgenson. Smitty Larsson, the blacksmith, lifted his hand about as high as his ear. Then Willy Peterson, who lived just down the road from Jönsson, and soon nearly every man in the room raised his hand.

There would be no cross burning, and those present signed a hastily drafted covenant. Jonas slipped out of the first and last Klan gathering in Kalmar without signing and without saying farewell to his brother. Although he had voted for the covenant, he really voted against the cross-burning, and he would willingly do business with any man, regardless of religion. He had been dickering with a Catholic farmer south of town who was interested in buying a brood sow from him, and he decided right then and there to accept the German's latest offer.

He muttered angrily all the way home at the crowd but especially at his own timidity. And then, he did something he never did. He prayed.

"Lord, help me to teach my son a better way."

# CHAPTER FORTY-TWO: 1927

Although he hardly slept through the night, twelve-year-old Anders was up at dawn with his father. Today would be a special day, but first the morning chores had to be finished. While Jonas rhythmically tugged on the teats of eight black and white Holsteins, Anders pitched hay into mangers at the front of the expanded lean-to that served as a barn, at least for now, since Jonas had dreams of a real barn, and soon. Pumpa, the orange cat, and her kittens lapped up a dish of warm milk. Eleven-year-old Olga, the second-born of Jonas and Hilma, fed the two heifers that were not yet ready for milking, and a young calf sucked on his mother's teats as she grazed nearby. The daily milk production was more than enough for the family's consumption and Jonas would deliver a pair of ten-gallon milk cans to the creamery in town every morning, returning with a large chunk of ice for the cold closet and whatever else Hilma ordered for the growing family.

"I'm finished," Anders reported.

Olga had already returned to the house. Jonas twisted the cow's teat and squirted milk at his son's face. Anders opened his mouth, but he wasn't as adept as Pumpa the cat, and he wiped the milk on his cheek away with his sleeve.

"Run and get cleaned up, and I'll soon finish," Jonas said.

Each morning, Jonas waited until Anders departed before arising from his short-legged milking stool. With his bad leg, it was a slow and painful process, and he didn't want his son to see.

When all had been completed, Jonas returned to their

Sears, Roebuck & Company four-square house, entering the kitchen through the back door. A dining room comprised the second quarter of the first floor, a living room the third, and the fourth contained the front-entry foyer with a double-landing stairway winding to the four bedrooms on the second floor. The front hallway also contained a door leading down steep steps to a root cellar, a coal furnace whose heat rose through first-floor registers, and a workbench. Grilles in the ceilings of the first floor allowed heat to rise into the bedrooms above, but chilly nights required thick goose down quilts, and the Jönsson family often awoke with frosty breaths. The front door opened to an expansive porch that extended the full width of the front side of the white-boarded home. Facing west, the porch was the place to enjoy the sunset and to worry over approaching storms.

Sisters Lena and Elsa raced in a circle from one room to the next, with four-year old Siri traipsing behind. When her older sisters lapped her, she jutted out her chin and quit chasing. Hilma and the two older girls, Olga and Signe, piled heaps of flapjacks and poured cups of steaming coffee on the long oak table in the dining room. Milk from last evening had chilled in the cold closet, and Anders drained a large glass before digging into the flapjacks smeared with butter and a thick layer of strawberry jam. Anders finished before the others.

"Can we go now," Anders pleaded.

"Do you think Gurli will hitch herself to the wagon?"

Anders dashed out as Jonas winked at Hilma, but she returned a scowl. Before heading outside, Jonas climbed the stairs to the master bedroom, shut the door behind him, and pulled up a floorboard under the bed. A sock lay hidden there. After counting out $300 in ones and fives, he rolled the bills and stuffed the roll into his shirt. There was plenty more in other socks, but the stash of bills needed to grow a bit more before the dream of a real barn would be realized.

After dropping their milk at the creamery, father and son headed toward Little Falls. Anders couldn't stop jabbering, but truth be told, Jonas was just as excited even if he wasn't as exuberant as his son. Upon returning, Anders would drive Gurli and the wagon alone. Jonas would follow behind in a shiny black Tin Lizzy. When Henry Ford's Model-Ts first rolled off the assembly line in 1908, the cost had been $850, but Jonas watched the price drop each year. With Coolidge in the White House and the American economy booming, three hundred 1927 dollars would buy entry into the motoring class of America.

*Aaoogha. Aaoogha.*

Every time Jonas honked on the way home, Anders would turn and grin, but Jonas doubted that the family's new toy would buck up Hilma's spirits.

Never one to mope, Hilma's attempt to mask her sadness failed. She was the pillar of the family. She had departed her homeland young and alone, and she trusted hope, but she was no idle dreamer, and she acted with expectation of results, often nudging a dubious husband forward on their adventure. Her immense vegetable garden reflected her optimism—and her industry. Packets of seeds would one day be soups, stews, and casseroles, but the planting must be timely, and the rows straight and true. Her watering can with a large spout supplemented the rain. She pulled and hoed weeds to prevent crowding out the sun or stealing the nutrients in the soil. She trusted nature to do its part, and she would do hers.

Her buoyancy wavered following Pastor Hallstrom's stunning announcement from the pulpit. Hilma's busyness became rote, absent her normal zest for what each new day would bring. Crooked rows and weeds in her vegetable garden matched the disarray she felt inside. Her best friend, Agnes Hallstrom, would soon depart Kalmar and return to Illinois where Pastor Charlie had accepted a call to a congregation in a small city near Chicago.

Seventeen years earlier, the young women bonded when Agnes brushed the dust off Hilma's freckled face and held her elbow tight as they proceeded up the aisle of the dark sanctuary toward Hilma's marriage to a man she had met only hours earlier. The women shared bicycles, cigarettes, nighties, and suffrage. They had been at each other's bedside when their babies came into the world, and their children had become fast friends and constant companions. Perhaps Hilma felt abandoned, but mostly she seemed lost.

And so, on Easter Sunday, 1927, Pastor Charlie preached his last sermon at the Kalmar Swedish Lutheran Church, followed by pie, ice cream, cards and gifts. When Pastor Charlie and his oldest son drove away in their Ford Motor car, Jonas and Hilma transported Agnes and her suitcases and trunks and younger children to the railroad station in Little Falls.

While Jonas loaded the luggage onto the train under Agnes' supervision, Hilma occupied herself mussing with the Halstrom children: combing hair, smoothing ruffled shirts, and spit polishing dusty cheeks.

"All aboard!"

Hilma jumped.

"Come children," Agnes encouraged.

Hilma slowly turned to face her friend.

"You, you are my sister, my soul, and I can't bear to see you go."

"I know. I know," Agnes said, wiping a tear from Hilma's cheek, and then the tears gushed from both women as they hugged.

"Come, Missus, we must go now," the conductor said.

Although Pastor Charlie was not forced out, and he accepted a new call of his own accord, Jonas and Hilma knew too well that the Hannah Alekson faction had often been a festering thorn in his side. The Aleksons manipulated by withholding their contributions to the operating fund, and therefore the pastor's salary, but gave generously to their favorite projects, like the summer Bible school for children, and Hannah purchased the materials and served as the perennial superintendent, thereby steering the school in the same hellfire and brimstone direction as the Billy Sunday revivals she had eagerly promoted earlier.

On a July Monday morning later in the summer of 1927, twelve-year-old Anders hitched Gurli to the buggy and sat in the driver's seat with the reins in his hands as his sisters climbed aboard. The faithful mare was getting on in years and wasn't used often, but she seemed pleased to be of service for the children. She would pull the buggy to Bible school. Each morning for two weeks, the children of Kalmar would gather for Bible lessons and kitten ball on the grassy lawn adjacent to the church. With the decks cleared in the absence of Pastor Charlie's moderating influence, Hannah Alekson arranged for an earnest young preacher from somewhere down south to lead the daily lessons.

After the first day, Anders argued that it all seemed foolish, and it would be better if he stayed home and helped with the chores. Jonas agreed, but if Anders had to deliver his sisters in the morning and pick them up in mid-afternoon, he might as well stay, Hilma said, and he could watch out for his sisters. After the second day, ten-year-old Signe woke at midnight, screaming from nightmares.

"What's the matter child?" Hilma asked, but she refused to tell her parents what bothered her.

"Something's got her scared," Jonas said.

On Wednesday, the third day, Gurli and the buggy with the children were late returning. Jonas hadn't noticed, but Hilma stood on the front porch watching in the direction of the tall oak that stood sentinel at the mouth of the driveway. Instead of the buggy, a rider on horseback galloped toward the house, and Hilma called to Jonas who came from around back where he and Freddy Sederstrom were shoveling coal into the chute to the basement as Freddie's father, Sven, reined up.

"They've locked the church doors and won't let yer kids and the rest out!" The livery man arrived on his favorite horse, hatless and with windblown hair twisted every which way.

"What? Who locked the doors?" Jonas asked.

"Why, Hannah Alekson, and that God dammit young preacher she picked. They locked the doors and won't let the kids out until they repent, convert, and offer testimony."

Jonas fired up the Tin-Lizzie, and the pair headed back to Kalmar. Sure enough, the doors to the church were locked. Jonas kicked at the door, but it wouldn't budge.

"Here, help me pull up this hitching post."

After pushing and pulling and plenty of swearing, the post exited the ground with a sucking sound, and the men used it as a battering ram. The door soon surrendered to the assault, and Jonas burst into the sanctuary to find weeping children. Anders was up front, pinned to the floor by the joint efforts of the sonofabitch preacher and Henry Jr. with Hannah Alekson wailing at the ceiling, calling upon the Lord to "cast out the demons, cast the demons from this sinner."

When Jonas tackled the preacher, knocking him away from Anders, his son kicked Henry Jr. in the balls, and Jr. whimpered away with his hands holding his crotch. Anders gathered up his sisters, and they rushed outside.

That was the last day Jonas crossed the threshold of the Kalmar Swedish Lutheran Church.

# CHAPTER FORTY-THREE:1928-1929

In the summer of 1928, Jönsson would lose his hired hand, but he would realize his dream of a big red barn.

For a couple of June days while Jonas, Anders, and Freddy Sederstrom cut, raked, stacked, and hauled the first crop of hay, Freddy didn't seem his normal buoyant self. In fact, he was downright brooding. When the last hayrack was unloaded, Freddy mounted one of his father's horses, but before he departed, he leaned forward and rested his forearm on the horn of the saddle. He had something to say.

"Ya been a good boss, Mr. Jönsson, and I 'preciate what ya done fer me, but it's time I made my own way. Shoot, I'll be twenty come fall. Thresher-man Mose Allen is ailin', and he asked me to ramrod his threshing machines this harvest season. I'll be headin' to Nebrasky straight away and won't be done 'til I follow the harvest all the way to Canada."

Jönsson was caught unawares, and the realization that Freddy had grown to manhood had escaped him until that moment, but before he said anything, he accepted the truth of it. Freddy had to pursue his own dream. Jonas stepped forward and stuffed a wrinkled twenty-dollar bill in the chest pocket of Freddy's overalls. Good pay for a good man.

Freddy leaned back in the saddle and scanned the nearby cornfield with green shoots in straight rows. "Hell, Mr. Jönsson, Anders is 'bout my age when I started in as yer hired hand. You'n him will do just fine."

Jonas and Freddy fixed their eyes on the thirteen-year-old

boy.

\*\*\*\*\*\*\*\*\*\*

*"I can still feel Papa's searing gaze after all these years," I said.*

*No longer able to sit in my favorite chair, I spoke from my bed. Don remained slouched in the easy chair that had come to be his own.*

*"He suspected, I'm sure, but he said nothing. Yet, his eyes revealed doubt and disappointment. In that moment, I was sure he wished Freddy could be his loyal son and heir to the farm, because he knew I would not fit the pattern of his plans. He accepted that Freddy must follow his own dream, but he was not yet ready to concede the same for me."*

\*\*\*\*\*\*\*\*\*\*

When it came time to construct the red barn that was the longtime object of his dreams, a mortgage was again necessary; however, Jonas and Hilma drove the Tin Lizzie right past the Farmers and Merchants State Bank of Kalmar and obtained their loan with a ten-year term from a Little Falls bank. Jonas hoped Henry Alekson saw them drive by.

Borrowing money to get ahead was the thing to do in 1928. The booming economy was not for the timid, and the aggressive investor would be the one to succeed.

"The business of America is business," President Coolidge declared. "The man who builds a factory builds a temple."

It seemed that the religion of America was free-market capitalism. Titans of industry functioned as priests, bankers as deacons, and security traders as acolytes; self-interest, winners and losers, and the holy words "supply" and "demand" constituted their creed. Market forces expressed the divine will where the worthy would thrive and the unworthy would fail. Separate the sheep and goats and sacrifice a burnt offering on the altar of the almighty dollar and make a pleasing aroma to the Lord. As mediator of the divine presence, The High Priest, Treasury Secretary Andrew Mellon, preached massive tax cuts and deregulation. Secretary Mellon, already one of the richest men in America, got richer, and so did the other capitalists knocking on heaven's door.

Apparently, farmers weren't on the list of God's elect, according to Coolidge and Mellon. Mellon opposed measures to stabilize the market for farm commodities—thereby aiding the farmer--but when Congress passed a bill over Coolidge's objections, the president vetoed it.

"Farmers never have made much money," Coolidge said. "I do not believe we can do much about it."

Even if the farmer had no friend in the White House, Jönsson couldn't deny the booming economy. He was no wide-eyed speculator, but it sure seemed that the time was right to build the barn of his dreams, even if that meant stretching a bit. So, borrow he did. And, by borrowing just a bit more, a spanking green John Deere D tractor would be delivered after the barn was built.

With the loan in place, Jonas contracted with Henning Henderson to serve as the job superintendent. "Hank" Henderson was known for his thick Swedish accent, which he refused to temper, the ever-present carpenter's pencil that seemed a bodily appendage behind his right ear, and his barn-building know-how. Henderson, in turn, hired three carpenters to handle the joinery and dowling of the post and beam construction. Henderson drafted specific plans in accord with Jonas' dreams.

Henderson shouted instructions and pointed or drew

sketches with his carpenter's pencil. He scurried about in his odd, stalking gait, slouching with long, purposeful steps that carried him quickly from one place to the next. When he got to hammering, the work crew waited until he stopped before asking a question, and even then, his mumble around a mouthful of nails was difficult to understand.

Volunteers stacked wagonloads of Sundqvist sawmill lumber alongside the cleared ground, and small wooden casks held the waiting nails and hardware. A barn raising was old hat for many, and experienced neighborhood volunteers pitched in. Young children watched from a safe distance, and Anders proudly led his buddies in the task of fetching what the workmen needed.

Evie Jorgenson supervised the wives who toiled in Hilma's kitchen. They butchered and fried chickens, sliced the ham or roast beef, mashed the potatoes, baked bread, washed the fresh vegetables from Hilma's garden, and stirred cool lemonade or boiled coffee.

The work filled in nicely between the 1928 planting season and the harvest. Gallon after gallon of red paint soaked into the pine boards, nearly as soon as they were nailed in place. Finally, Henderson the superintendent placed an American flag at the high point of the overhanging peak over a dormer and the second floor sliding door to the hay mow, and all stood back to admire the finest barn in the neighborhood—some said in the whole county. Jönsson was satisfied that he had been wise to borrow a little more to do it right, and he proudly held Hilma close with their children clustered around them. If truth be told, he would have liked his older brother Alfrid back home on the modest farm in Sweden to see what he had accomplished in America. He suspected word got to brother Thomas in Little Falls, but his attitude toward his baby brother was different. There was spite in his heart toward Alfrid, but he grieved that he and Thomas had grown apart. Perhaps Thomas would come to the party to follow the barn raising.

After the neighborhood helped raise the barn, it was time for a barn dance to celebrate.

Jonas crossed the Stearns County border alone, but not without Hilma's knowledge. They had chewed on their decision for several days before he cranked up the Tin Lizzie after he finished lunch and headed toward a certain wooded area in nearby Stearns County. When he arrived at the place, he fiddled under the hood of the Model-T--just for appearances because the Ford was in fine shape; he cast furtive glances this way and that way to make sure he was alone. He still wasn't comfortable, but finally he headed down a pathway through the burr oaks and sugar maples. Sure enough, as he had been told, he came to an opening where the late afternoon sun filtered through, and right in the middle was a single stump with an even-cut flat top. Jönsson hesitated briefly as he checked the tree line in all directions before he pulled out four silver dollars and placed them smack in the center of the stump before wheeling and walking briskly back to the car. He fumbled with the crank and flooded the engine in his haste to get away, but half an hour later, he was on his way back to the farm, arriving in time to help Anders finish with the chores.

The next morning, as soon as the chores were finished, Jönsson returned to the tree stump. Again, he hesitated along the roadway before heading into the woods, but soon he returned with four wide-mouthed glass quart jars with twist covers filled to the brim with Minnesota 13, the finest moonshine whiskey in the land, "stump whiskey," they called it.

All the neighbors who helped raise the barn, and some who didn't, came for the barn dance. Deputy Thomas Johnson failed to appear. Pine Lake Anderson played the accordion, accompanied by Poker Billy Johnson on the nykelharpa he brought with him from the old country. Hilma minded the apple cider, sweet breads, and cheese, and Jonas dispensed the moonshine back behind the barn under an August blue moon. He had a few snorts himself, and Jonas shocked Anders and the girls when he swept Hilma onto the dance floor of the hay mow above the ground floor lined with stanchions for milking cattle; for the evening, it seemed, even his bad leg was healed.

That wasn't all. When he arranged the mortgage on the farm to pay for the barn, he borrowed an extra thousand to purchase a brand new 1928 model John Deere D. When the green two-cylinder tractor with yellow wheels finally arrived from the factory in Iowa, Jönsson hitched up a wagon and pulled the whole family around the neighborhood.

When the November 1928 election rolled around, the precinct of Kalmar voted overwhelmingly for Herbert Hoover, the Republican presidential candidate after Silent Cal chose not to run again. Hoover had been Secretary of Commerce in the Coolidge administration, and the *laissez faire* policies of the Republicans would continue. Treasury Secretary Mellon stayed on.

"We in America today are nearer to the final triumph over poverty than ever before in the history of this land," Hoover claimed in campaign speeches. "We shall soon with the help of God be in sight of the day when poverty will be banished from this land."

Jonas and Anders no longer attended services at the Lutheran church in town, but Hilma remained the mainstay of the choir, and the girls tagged along. After services one Sunday that fall, she brought a flier for Jonas to read that had been promoted by the new minister.

"You won't like this," she said. "Sometimes, I just have to bite my tongue."

The manifesto came from the National Lutheran Editors'

and Managers' Association and opposed the candidate of the Democratic Party, Governor Al Smith of New York, a Roman Catholic. The manifesto claimed that Smith would owe absolute allegiance to the pope and argued that the Catholic Church was hostile to American principles of separation of church and state and of religious toleration.

"God dammit," Jonas huffed. "The pot calls the kettle black."

Hilma shoved the flier into the wood burning stove.

Jonas and Hilma were among the few Kalmar voters for Al Smith, the "workingman's pal," but the Republicans won another landslide election.

Earlier that summer, Freddy Sederstrom had returned to spend a couple of August weeks in the Kalmar community; sure enough, there was steel in the honcho in charge of Mose Allen's threshing machinery, and Freddy earned the respect of the farmers who hired him and the threshing equipment before he moved on to follow the harvest in a northwesterly direction. He turned more than a few female heads as well. Olga, the oldest Jönsson daughter was only twelve, but Jonas couldn't help but wish she was older and courting age.

During the summer and into the fall, Willy Peterson, Jr. from just down the road helped during busy times. Willy was a year older than Anders, but Anders was much taller and stronger. Willy was not the devoted worker that Freddy had been, but he did well enough. With Willy's help, Jonas and Anders managed the fall harvest, especially with the use of the new John Deere.

By the time of the first snowfall, Freddy had not returned to Kalmar.

The blizzard of January 1929 raged for three days. Finally,

a bright sun, haloed by sun dogs, appeared along with a bitter wind out of the northwest. Jönsson had been chomping at the bit to hook a plow onto the John Deere, and he was outside before breakfast, bundled in layers with a scarf pulled over his mouth and hooked over his nose. The pure-white snow squeaked underfoot. Within minutes, ice caked the outside of the scarf where his breath passed through, and white frost dusted his exposed eyebrows, but his exhilaration warmed his insides.

He was a child in a toy store as the green tractor pushed the snow to the sides of the driveway. When he reached the road, he stopped under the oak to check the mail, but he found only a catalogue from the Sears, Roebuck & Company. He dug deep into his layer of clothes and pulled out a red hanky and blew his nose before climbing onto the tractor to head back to the house for a hot mug of Hilma's egg coffee.

He tossed the catalogue onto the kitchen table as he began to strip down. Hilma noticed a letter flutter from the pages of the catalogue, and she carefully sliced it open.

"This is odd," she said.

Jonas worked at pulling his boots off his feet and wool socks.

"The bank in Little Falls has sent a letter. Let me read it to you. 'We hereby inform you that your mortgage has been sold to the Farmers and Merchants State Bank of Kalmar. Your payments shall forthwith be delivered to the attention of Henry Alekson of said bank.'"

# CHAPTER FORTY-FOUR: 1929

One hand guided the steering wheel of the John Deere while the second manipulated the arms of the single blade plow trailing behind. In the spring of '29, Jönsson would spend mere hours turning the soil that occupied him for months twenty years earlier when he walked behind Gurli breaking virgin sod. The two-cylinder engine pounded a steady beat as the flywheel whirred, and he failed to notice the horse-drawn carriage turning into his driveway. Suddenly, he realized that Freddy Sederstrom approached across the fresh-turned furrows still wriggling with earthworms, and he immediately shut the tractor down.

"Freddy, my boy, where ya been all winter?" Jönsson removed his gloves and extended his hand.

"I been holed up in Fargo, Mr. Jönsson, but I come to see if'n I could have my job back."

"Ramrodding a thresher didn't work out, eh?" Jönsson said with a hint of smug satisfaction.

"Well, it ain't that. I made good money, but now it seems I needs to stay put. Ya see, I gots a woman to tend to, and soon a babe." He jerked his head over his shoulder, gesturing toward the buggy.

Hilma had stepped from the porch and escorted a woman toward the house. Even from a distance, Jönsson could see that the woman was plump with child. Jonas and Freddy quickly headed that way.

Freddy's woman was a dark-skinned beauty with black hair wound in a tight bun. Her frightened oval eyes reminded him of the baby racoon that he saw near the creek. She wore a threadbare sweater over a homespun cotton dress that clung tightly to her waist. She dipped her head in a slight bow toward Jonas when he entered the room.

*Hola Señor Jönsson. Me llamo Esperanza.*

With mouth hanging open, Jönsson looked first to Hilma and then to Freddy.

"After the threshing season, I worked for a spell during the sugar beet harvest of the Red River Valley," Freddy explained. "Esperanza and her family are Mexican workers. Easy enuff to see how I could fall for her," Freddy said, draping his arm around her waist and pulling her close. Even in her pregnant condition, she was a petite woman, and she seemed to melt comfortably in the grip of Freddy's arm. "First, I needs a job. With more'n more folks driving automobiles, Pa's livery business ain't got much of a future, and farm work is my fancy anyhow. Once't I get steady work, we'll get hitched."

Jönsson hired Freddy straightaway, and Freddy asked Hilma and Jonas to serve as witnesses for the wedding. The marriage took place before a justice of the peace in Little Falls after the Lutheran pastor turned him down.

"'You crazy? You're a shameless fool,'" the Lutheran pastor exclaimed, according to Freddy's report. "'Mrs. Alekson would have a conniption fit if I presided over the marriage of a Mexican whore,' the sonofabitch said. I wish I woulda slugged him right then and there, but I couldn't strike a man o' the cloth."

"You shoulda popped him," Jonas said, "He sure ain't a godly man, and his black robe and white collar don't mean nothing."

When Jönsson retrieved the Colt six-shooter wrapped in an oiled rag and spun the cylinder, it seemed to be in good working order. Two chambers held live cartridges, and that would be enough. His cold calculation surprised him, and his mind fixated upon finding a new hiding place for the weapon afterwards. Under a floor plank in the old cabin wouldn't do. In the attic in the new house? In the hay mow? The children mustn't discover the gun, but nothing seemed satisfactory.

BANG!

When the bullet hit the mark, he broke down and sobbed. Surely, the red fox who watched from the tree line wondered at the human on his knees with shoulders shaking. Yes, it was for the best he knew, but that didn't lessen his anguish. He felt no guilt, only loss.

He returned to the house before noon. Hilma met him with a hug on the front steps, and they cried as one as they held each other in a tight embrace. At least, he would have hours in which to regain his composure before the children returned from school, and he would have to tell them that Gurli, the family's faithful companion for over twenty years, had gone to horse heaven where she would no longer limp painfully but would forever be a young filly galloping through the butterflies in the meadow. He had delayed his onerous but necessary task until the school year began in the fall of 1929.

He rubbed down the pistol with the oiled cloth. When he finished, he spun the cylinder several times just to see where the single remaining live cartridge would settle.

Soon after the school year began, Jonas and Anders disagreed, and for the first time, the son refused to yield to his father's wishes. Hilma took her son's side, and Anders prevailed. Instead of toiling with his father and Freddy during the fall harvest, the fourteen-year-old freshman would spend his after-school hours practicing with the high school eleven.

"You have always taught me to chase my dream, and I want to be a footballer," Anders said.

"Before play, work. Before frivolity, duty," Jonas replied.

It wasn't merely that Jonas depended upon the labor of his boy. Everyone must pitch in on the farm; that was simply the way of life for the yeoman and his pact with the earth: toil and sweat in exchange for nature's bounty. No, it was more about priorities. Jonas' dream had always been for his son to become a farmer at his side and one day to take his place. As the father, so the son. His son's out-of-character irresponsibility surprised him. Football? The autumn harvest was the glorious climax to the cycle of life on the farm; how could Anders pass that up for child's play? And Hilma? She had always been the family's rock-solid anchor; what was she thinking? His wife and son threatened his fundamental assumptions.

When the first Friday afternoon game rolled around, Jonas pitched wheat-straw alone. And he sulked.

Later, Olga interrupted the silence at the supper table.

"Papa, you should have seen Anders run ..."

Jonas' stern look shut her down.


Jönsson kept the kerosene lantern burning late in the night while reading the newspaper dated October 30$^{th}$, 1929, reporting on the crash of the stock market the day before. The news was both astounding and entirely predictable, Jönsson figured. The stock market speculators and manipulators finally got what they deserved. The corn crop was his best yet, half a dozen fat heifers roamed his pasture, and Henrietta, his brood sow, nursed a dozen piglets suckling on her teats. His socks hidden under a floorboard swelled with plenty of ones and fives, even a few twenty-dollar bills. Hilma and the kids slept peacefully. When he turned off the lamp and knocked the ashes from his pipe, all was well in his world.

On the last Friday of the football season, Jonas invited his son to hear a whistle-stop speech from a fire-breathing politician who was creating quite stir with his progressive vision for Minnesota.

"But Papa, I have a game."

"If you go with me in the morning, I'll attend your football game in the afternoon," Jönsson negotiated.

As a young man, Floyd B. Olson joined the "Wobblies" --the Industrial Workers of the World—the same organization that got Natty Einstein deported to Russia. As district attorney in the Twin Cities, he vigorously prosecuted union-busters, becoming a darling of the laboring men and women in the process, but Jönsson was interested in his ideas of melding the interests of the worker with the farmer. To Jönsson, Olson's Farmer-Labor Party seemed natural and the obvious direction politics ought to take, especially due to the panic that seemed to be spreading after the stock market crash.

True enough, Jönsson had often favored the Republicans, but it was the progressive arm of the party--the wing of insurgent Charles Lindbergh—that held his allegiance. As the Republicans increasingly scapegoated the worker, the immigrant, or the Catholic, progressives like Lindbergh abandoned the Republican Party, and thousands like Jönsson hoped for a champion, a progressive, a liberal, a populist, who would put the people before the aristocrats.

Olson's speech didn't disappoint, and Jönsson was pleased to see the rapt attention his son paid to the candidate. By the end, Anders stood and whistled along with many in the adoring audience. After a mostly silent ride into Little Falls, rich dialogue filled the Tin Lizzy headed back toward Kalmar and the football game. Jönsson chuckled when his son parroted Olson's words, "I am not a liberal. I am what I want to be — a radical." Anders thirsted for more, and Jonas told him about labor battles in Duluth and the candidacy of Charles Lindbergh, and Anders appeared impressed that his father had worked for the campaign and knew Charles Jr. who might be the most famous man in the world right then after his heroic flight across the Atlantic. Of course, Jonas didn't tell his son everything, but Jonas was downright chatty—and giddy.

When Jönsson pulled up in the parking lot of the school, Anders shocked him. "Papa, I think I want to be a lawyer."

The first half of the game was a blur, and Jonas couldn't concentrate on the action. Perhaps it was the second half kickoff when Anders caught the ball and dodged and weaved and then streaked down the sideline for a touchdown when things came into focus. The crowd went wild, and Willy Peterson, the neighboring farmer just down the road, slapped him on the back, nearly doubling him over. Peterson's own son, Willy, Jr. was a squat sophomore who threw a key block.

"Your son is so fast! And only a freshman! That boy is special!"

Exploits on the football field hardly predicted greatness, Jonas knew, and yet ... a lawyer. Maybe a politician. Be careful what you pray for, they said, and he had prayed that his son would learn a better way. That he would be the crusader, the champion for the underdog, the justice worker that he, himself, had never been.

Jonas never missed another of his son's high school football games.

*********

*"That was probably the best day of my life, at least to that point," I said.*

*"What day was that?" LaDonna asked as she interrupted our*

conversation when she stepped into the room with dinner trays. She immediately plumped my pillow that had slid down, and I hadn't thought to adjust it—or perhaps I didn't have the strength.

"I've been telling my nephew about my father, and that was the day that we discovered mutual respect, but you probably wouldn't appreciate respect."

"Shut your mouth, you cranky old man." She spoke in a teasing manner. "What do you know about what I might 'preciate."

"Dear girl, you can't understand what it means when a father and son first see eye to eye."

"Humph," she said with a parting wink as she shut the door behind her.

"I nearly forgot your football days," Don said. "I imagine your exploits on the gridiron opened some doors for you down the road."

"Yes, I suppose so." I replied.

Don missed the true import of that day. Yes, the thrill of lugging a pigskin into the end zone was part of it. Yes, discovering a common passion with Papa for justice politics was part of it. But it was more, much more. That was the day that Papa released me from his dream to allow me to pursue my own. And in that, his dream came true.

"Pastor, you might appreciate a scriptural allusion," I said. "That day was like stepping out of the River Jordan and hearing the voice say, 'Thou art my beloved son. In you I am well pleased.'"

# CHAPTER FORTY-FIVE: 1930

On a blistering August Sunday in 1930, Anders attempted to escape the heat by wading in the creek that flowed through the nearby Tamarac swamp. Hilma and the girls had not yet returned from church services, and Jonas stood alone on his porch worrying about the rows of withered corn. The stalks should have been head high by now and bursting with tassels, but the shriveled stalks barely reached his waist. The second crop of hay had been put up in the barn the day before; what should have taken the better part of a week was finished in a day, and the alfalfa stems with stunted leaves barely filled a corner of the hay mow.

Jonas had spent Sunday morning catching up on his reading. Newspaper pages lay strewn across the porch planks. Seems Senator Smoot and Congressman Hawley figured the deepening depression was the fault of foreigners who exported their goods to America. Many of Jönsson's neighbors agreed; the resurgence of European agriculture in the years after the Great War created keen competition for the American farmer, and the price of farm commodities dropped. Maybe protectionism was the answer as the Smoot-Hawley tariff promised, but it bothered Jönsson that President Hoover signed the bill over the sharp disagreement of leading economists. He hoped Hoover and the Congress knew more than the experts, but he doubted.

An issue of the Saturday Evening Post magazine lay open to an article touting the racial inferiority of the Mexican workers in the United States. Depression was spreading across the land, and President Hoover did what sorry leaders do when faced with prickly problems—he scapegoated. Hoover's call for deportation of Mexicans, even those who had obtained citizenship, became a placebo for the ills of the nation. An anxious populace readily agreed that unclean, improvident, and indolent Mexicans ought to be kicked out. That Mexicans accepted backbreaking and underpaid jobs mattered not; nativists claimed that sending the Mexicans back to Mexico would ease the rampant unemployment on this side of the border and halt the spiral into deep depression.

Jonas recognized poison when he saw it, but he didn't imagine the venom would infect the peaceful hamlet of Kalmar.

When Jonas spied the Tin Lizzy with Hilma at the wheel turning into the driveway, he hustled to clean up the newspapers and hide the Post article. The Sederstrom's were due to arrive that afternoon to celebrate the first birthday of Sven Jonas Hidalgo Sederstrom, the son of Freddy and Esperanza who was named after significant men in the lives of his parents, but Jonas was hardly in the mood to celebrate. He also rued the day of reckoning that would come soon when he would be forced to lay Freddy off, at least for a while.

Olga was the first to reach the porch, and she blurted the news that swirled through the pews, "Freddy, Esperanza, and their baby have fled Kalmar!"

He didn't ask why; he suspected. A rising breeze scattered the newspapers across the field of shriveled corn stalks as he climbed behind the wheel. Hilma anticipated his frenzy and left the car running while sliding to the passenger side. The Ford bounced and rattled and sped faster than it had ever travelled as he pulled the throttle lever to its limit. Before he saw the broken windows, he saw the red paint scrawled on the side of Sederstrom's house: "Mexican bitch." "Whore baby." And then he saw the phrase that wrenched his insides, "America for Americans."

LOST IN THE LAND OF MILK AND HONEY

Three weeks later, Sven shared Freddy's letter with a Fargo postmark.

*Papa and Mama,*

*I feel a coward for running rather than fighting back against the bullies, but sometimes you just gotta do what's best for your own, and Esperanza no longer felt safe—much less welcome—in Kalmar. I know most folks mean no harm, and I can't blame the whole town for the acts of the asses who find courage in a whiskey bottle in the dark of night. Still, Esperanza saw the glances and heared the whispers.*

*Soon I'll be a gringo in a foreign land, for the Mexicans here are packing up and will soon head back to Mexico, even though many in this community have been here for a decade or more. I'll be going with them, and there are two reasons. First, of course, is my wife and child. I figure I wouldn't be much of a man if I didn't accept responsibility for their care and safety. Second, I ain't sure if I care to live in a land what treats folks thisaway. I mean, I heared about the promise of Lady Liberty---"Give me your tired poor folks, wanting to be free"—or sumpin like that, but right now that seems like bullshit, pardon my language, but I'm plenty pissed right now.*

*Be sure and tell Jonas and Hilma how much I appreciate all they done for me. Maybe I can take what I learnt from them and grow coffee beans or whatever the hell they grow on Mexican farms!*

*I'll see ya when I see ya, but I'll always be your loving son.*

*Federico*

# CHAPTER FORTY-SIX: 1931

"A package came for you in the mail today," Hilma said without looking up from the stove. "I opened it."

In a whirl of memory, Jonas' eyes instantly recognized the tiny red pony on the table. After many years, he almost forgot the Dala horse he whittled for Natty Einstein, but he immediately knew that the carving on the table was the one he had given to her.

"Who was Natalia Einstein?" Hilma asked.

She couldn't settle on a cant of her head, which alternated postures in quick, barely perceptible movements, unable to fix upon the comfortable or familiar.

Should he have explained earlier? It never seemed right to remain silent about Natty—or about Ayasha before that—but it never seemed right to say anything, either.

Hilma sat down at the table with a cup of coffee for herself and one for Jonas, signaling she wanted to talk. Her eyes darted from Jonas to the red horse then back to Jonas.

Jonas meekly sat down, uncertain how to speak with delicacy and honesty, but before he spoke, she did.

"I was a young woman, a virgin, when I agreed to be your wife and come to America. You were much older, honest about that in your letters, and I could see the graying hair on the edges in the picture you sent. I guessed there probably were women before me; on our wedding night, your tenderness revealed the truth of that."

She gently stroked the back of his hand.

LOST IN THE LAND OF MILK AND HONEY

"So, husband of mine, know all of that is already baked in the cake, and you needn't apologize or lie."

Hilma reached out her second hand and cradled Jonas' hand between hers. "Read her letter, then tell me about Natalia," she said.

*Dearest friend,*

*I suppose you may consider this my last will and testament. Cancer racks my body, and my time will come soon. I shall scribble this quickly, and then I must swallow more laudanum for the pain, but then my thoughts become jangled.*

*I didn't fare well under Lenin, and I fled Russia soon after my arrival. I made my way to Montreal and then to Winnipeg where I have lived these past ten years and where my bones now rest for I instructed that this letter should not be sent until I passed. Life in Winnipeg has been good … and bad … it has been life. I have written a little for the local labor rag, and you know I have joined a picket line or two.*

*I return the Dala horse to my Swede. I have kept it near as I crossed the sea and back, and it has always reminded me of the kind man that I once knew and loved. I have said my sorrys before, but I repeat them again. You once said you forgave my infidelity. I believed you then, and I believe it still, and your grace will carry me to wherever it is that I go.*

*Here is my last request. I know you will honor it if you are able, but if you cannot, I understand. Will you travel to Winnipeg to retrieve my ashes and carry them to the shores of Lake Superior? You know the place where I wish to rest.*

*With love eternally,*

*Natalia Einstein*

Jonas pulled out his hanky and blew his nose. He took a moment before speaking.

He explained his life as the livery driver for Teodor Swensson and how he met Natty and how she had been a labor organizer who ran afoul of the government that unfairly deported her to Russia. He acknowledged that they had slept together, but it wasn't until he explained her affair with a woman that ended it between them that Hilma appeared shocked.

He wasn't sure if he said too much or too little, but once started, the stories spilled out, and he told of Ayasha his native bride and their son and the fire.

When he finished, he finally took a sip of his coffee that was now cold. Hilma breathed heavy as if she had been running. "My dear, there's more to you and your story than I could have imagined."

They sat quietly for a few moments before Hilma asked, without looking in his face.

"Did you love them?"

Jonas drew a deep breath and sighed. "Yes, of course, I loved them dearly, but that doesn't mean that I don't love you now or love you less."

The slanting beams of the afternoon sun pierced the dust hanging in the air. He squared his shoulders and continued. "You are my heart that pumps life through my veins. You are my soul that enlivens my being. You are my waking and my sleeping, my coming and my going."

Several silent moments passed as Hilma ruminated on all that he said. Then, drawing a deep breath, she moved her face close to his and her moist eyes bore into his own. She placed her palms on his stubbly cheeks and kissed his lips.

"You must go, Jonas. You must go and bring Natty home."

Jonas and Anders rode the train to Winnipeg to tend to Natty's business before carrying her ashes to Duluth. Father and son came to know one another as they journeyed to Winnipeg and back to Duluth. Mourning pierced life's superficialities, allowing deeper conversations. After revealing his prior life and relationships, it seemed conversation--and not merely trivialities about the weather or the crops or Babe Ruth's latest home run total--flowed easier for Jonas; perhaps his son, also, found listening more interesting to a father who spoke of deeper things. Anders learned what Jonas had confided to Hilma, and in a bold moment, Jonas shared his humiliation at the hands of "Americans for America."

When they arrived in Winnipeg, a telegram awaited them.

**I WILL MEET YOU IN DULUTH STOP**

**GIRLS WILL STAY WITH EVIE STOP**

**I LOVE YOU AND I MUST SHARE THIS JOURNEY WITH YOU STOP**

**HILMA STOP**

A pale half-moon glimmered over the eastern horizon. The wreckage of the *Mataafa* had disappeared long ago, but her ghosts danced in the moonbeam sheen atop the swells. Sand oozed between his toes, and sea spray on his face washed away the years since he last walked this shoreline.

"Ashes to ashes, dust to dust," Jonas said as he sprinkled Natty's remains where the waves lapped the sand and rocks. Anders stood a few paces away, but Hilma draped her arm around her husband's waist, her cheeks wet with tears and mist.

Soon after sunrise the next morning, they watched a great ore boat cruise through the ship canal before they crossed over and rode the Park Point trolley to the end of the line and returned. The walls of his cabin overlooking the beach remained, but the roof had caved in. Later, they visited the mansions of the east end before they found themselves walking along Superior Street, where Jonas had driven Teo Swensson's buggy day after day. Electric street cars and brassy sedans jostled with Henry Ford's latest--the model A--but the horse-drawn carriages had disappeared.

Jonas peered up the steps leading into Swensson's newspaper office when the editor himself suddenly appeared--a spry old man--still in a hurry, still worried, still earnestly pursuing the truth.

"Mr. Swensson," Jonas said, extending his hand.

Teo limply accepted the handshake. His face said he knew the man who approached him, but he lacked full recognition.

"Jonas. Jonas Jönsson," the onetime livery driver said, but the wrinkles on the editor's blanched forehead pinched tighter.

"Ole. You may remember me as Ole Jönsson."

"Of course!"

Swensson's handshake suddenly had vigor, and he pumped Jönsson's hand. Jonas introduced his wife and son.

The one thing Jonas had not revealed to son or wife or Thomas or anyone, was the true reason why he had once been called "Ole." "I guess folks thought all Swedes were 'Ole,'" Jonas said as casually as he could manage, "and I never bothered to correct them until I joined up with Thomas on the farm."

"Pleased to know you," Teo said with a slight bow toward Hilma.

"My, aren't you a strapping young lad," he said to Anders, and then he smiled at Jonas. "Your son's a chip off the old block."

It was true, Jonas nodded, but with a hint of surprise in his eyes as if he hadn't noticed before. His son matched his own height of six feet plus, and his angular torso was lean and muscled.

"Your father's strong arms and back helped save lives, don-cha know."

The blank looks on the faces of mother and son encouraged him to tell more.

"What? He hasn't told you of his bravery rescuing the crew of the *Mataafa?*"

Anders stared at his father with wide eyes and a slack jaw and slowly shook his head.

"Why, your father was quite the hero," Teo said. "Come, let us sit in that cafe across the street for coffee and pie, and I'll recount the story for you."


When the family arrived at Duluth's Union Depot the next morning, Hilma purchased tickets with a stopover in Hinckley. They had shared Papa's life in Duluth, and now she insisted they do the same in Hinckley.

When the train whistle signaled arrival at the Hinckley station, Jonas recognized nothing. Even the black scar of scorched pines during their approach to the small city had healed over, and there was little evidence that hellfire once consumed this forest. Tall, straight poplars with silver-gray bark had replaced the great stands of white pine. If the pattern of the streets of Hinckley remained the same, the after-the-fire buildings offered no clues. Even the lumpy mounds of the mass grave where Ayasha and his unnamed son lay buried failed to trigger either remembrance or emotion. Jonas was ready to leave, but Hilma wanted to see more, and they followed the slash in the woods that had been the trail to the lumber camp, but the seasons had washed the ashes away except for a few blackened log timbers marking the walls of the mess hall. Young poplars stuck up like porcupine quills where the roof had once been.

When a loon yodeled in the distance, Jonas' flat affect suddenly disappeared, and his eyes flashed wide with discovery. The loon called him to the place, the bay where Chief Hole-in-the-Lake netted fish, and he plowed through the underbrush to follow the loon's haunting wail. Hilma and Anders followed behind. A thicket had overgrown the pathway, and Jonas felt compelled to burst through the branches that snatched at his clothing and scratched his hands and face. The call of the loon guided him and urged him forward. Suddenly, he stepped into sunlight revealing the clearing worn bare by generations of moccasins, but there was nothing left of the native village; perhaps spirits lingered in the quaking poplar leaves high above the lakeshore.

A black-headed loon swam near, circling on the far edge of floating lily pads, warbling soft and low hoots that seemed an invitation to follow. Jonas waded into the shallow water and paced back and forth following the loon's movements, as if he was ready to plunge into the deeper water, as if the water sprite must be pursued despite the absurdity. No matter the swimmer's speed, or will, or determination, no matter how tauntingly close, the bird would always evade his grasp.

A squeaky chirp from the shore startled Jonas, and he turned to see Anders with lips pressed against thumb knuckles blowing into the sound chamber formed by cupped hands, attempting a shrill cry to communicate with the loon.

And that's when the muddle of joys and sorrows spurted

from his soul. The sadness for all he had lost poured out alongside the gladness welling within for what was now his. Tears of sorrow and shame gushed down his cheeks blending with those of gratitude. He was empty, and he was full.

Hilma and Anders stayed back, and he stood in this moment alone; he had experienced grief of which he could speak but never explain, about which they could listen but never hear.

# CHAPTER FORTY-SEVEN: 1932

W ump!

The familiar sound of foot against pigskin signaled the start of the season, Anders' last as a footballer for the eleven of Kalmar. Jonas clenched his fists and leaned forward as he watched the football tumble toward Anders. His son staggered as he measured the flight of the ball, and then it slipped through his hands, and the opposing team recovered the fumble.

In prior years, Anders had been a man among boys, and he scored many touchdowns as a single wing tailback and recorded tackles in bunches from his middle linebacker slot, but today's game would set the stage for a miserable senior season. The problem was not with Anders, but the big bruisers who had secured the line of scrimmage had graduated, including neighbor Willy Peterson, Jr. Anders the senior was forced to line up behind skinny and untalented youngsters, and he was repeatedly gang tackled as he attempted his sweeps around end or gang blocked as the opposing line mauled the Kalmar defense. Perhaps out of habit, Willy Sr. and Aggie continued to attend the games and sit in the bleachers next to Jonas and Hilma.

"Ooh don't hurt him," Hilma whispered loudly as the opponents swarmed around Anders as quickly as the ball was hiked to him.

Jonas watched in silence, even as his body twisted this way and that as his son attempted to evade the onslaught.

Around the second quarter, Jonas realized he was being

watched by a square-faced gentleman, whose gaze alternated between the field and Jonas himself. The broad-shouldered man looked as if he might have played a little football himself, but that would have been a long time ago as snowy-white hair skirted the edges of his hatless head. The man was a stranger to Jönsson, and apparently to others on the home team side of the field, and his keen interest seemed odd.

Final score: 26-7 for the opposition. The home team managed a single touchdown when Anders returned a kickoff for a touchdown after one of the opponent's own scores. Even with little blocking in front of him, a few shifty moves, a few broken tackles, and then blazing speed into the open field allowed Anders to dash into the end zone with pursuers falling behind. Anders also kicked the extra point. After the final whistle, Anders trudged off the field with a slight limp and dried blood on his jersey. Parents offered condolences to their sons as the crowd filtered into the September afternoon. The four rows of wooden bleachers emptied, but still the stranger remained. As the team slowly separated from the well-wishers and made their way to the locker room, Hilma and Jonas boarded the Tin Lizzy, along with their daughters, to make their way home. Anders knew not to delay; as usual, he would find his own way home to help with evening chores.

With Hilma and the girls tending to supper, Jonas was busy pitching hay into the mangers in front of the stanchions, preparing for the arrival of the milk cows, when he heard a motor car pull into the yard. He peered through the pair of tall sliding doors as Anders stepped down from a vehicle with the stranger at the wheel.

"Papa, this man would like to speak with you. Mama should hear what he has to say as well."

Anders and the stranger headed toward the house. Jonas wiped his hands on his bib overalls and followed behind.

"I'll set another plate," Hilma said to the man in a gray suit coat and tie who still had not uttered a word. "I hope you like fried chicken."

"No, Missus. That would be too kind, and I don't mean to intrude. Plus, I have a long drive back to Minneapolis yet this evening. My name is Bernie Bierman. I'm the new football coach at the University of Minnesota."

It was said that Coach Bierman drove the Minnesota countryside looking for strapping recruits for his team at the University. When he spotted a farm boy, he would ask for directions to Minneapolis. If the boy in the field pointed with a finger, the coach would climb back in his car and drive on, but if the boy picked up the plow and pointed, he would sign him up on the spot. That humorous myth probably developed later after Coach Bierman's many national championships; in any case, that was not quite the way Anders was recruited to be a footballer for the Minnesota Gophers.

Only the *squirt, squirt* of warm milk splashing in metal pails sounded over the lowing of the cattle. Jonas and Anders sat silently on milk stools on opposite sides of the concrete aisle that ran the length of the barn. When the orange cats--there was always at least one known as Pumpa--meowed, Jonas was buried in his thoughts, but Anders teased by twisting his cow's teat and squirting a stream of warm milk in the faces of the feline barn dwellers before filling their pan.

Jonas barely touched his fried chicken after Coach Bierman left, but Anders downed two legs and two thighs and a heap of mashed potatoes, topped off with a wedge of apple pie. It seemed to Jonas that he had grown old while his son had grown into a man, and although Anders was buoyant about his future, Jonas worried.

The drought that scourged the land continued as the depression that began with the stock market crash in the cities crept outward to the farms of the heartland. He sold several heifers and even a productive milk cow for slaughter, but the price was severely diminished with the lack of demand. Farmers were not expanding, only cutting back.

At least, he had cash enough to make the annual mortgage payment earlier that week. The yearly visit to the bank where he was forced to endure the haughty glare of Henry Alekson while he handed over the money was his least favorite day of the year. His receipt of payment was carefully folded and placed with three others in a metal box under a floorboard. He was forty per cent of the way toward paying off the ten-year mortgage note.

Sixty-two. He was sixty-two years of age at his last birthday while Hilma had just turned forty. Although their marriage had thrived despite the age difference, he feared that his bones would soon grow feeble while his bride still danced on youthful legs. For Jonas, November gales swirled, but Hilma picked June strawberries.

How much longer would he be able to keep up with the farm work, especially with Anders leaving for the lights of the big city? He could easily find a hired man; labor was cheap in these tough times, but where would he find the money for wages? He knew, of course, that Anders would leave one day, but now that the coach had offered a place on the Gopher team, that day suddenly seemed near, and Jonas worried at the loss of his son's significant contributions to the farm work. Perhaps his feelings were selfish and outdated, but that didn't stop him from dreaming of a family farm handed from father to son for generations to come.

Perhaps a daughter would marry a farming man, but already sixteen-year-old Olga revealed a yen for a faster life, and

she had taken a job after school working as a part-time operator at the central exchange in the spanking new telephone co-
operative building on Kalmar's main street. The younger girls
were too young to even think about a future.

*Squirt, squirt.* By the time Jonas reached the last stanchion
where Bessie patiently waited--there was always a "Bessie" in
the herd--the ritual of milking had soothed Jonas' anxiety. His
past and his future met in the timeless rhythm of tugging on
the cow's teats with his right hand and then the left—much
like putting one foot in front of the other, and you would follow where life's pathway would lead you. *Squirt, squirt.*

# CHAPTER FORTY-EIGHT 1932-1933

Thomas and Jenny, his wife, and their four city-born urchins piled out their motor car for a visit to the farm and their country-cousins. Not that Little Falls was any great metropolis, but the snooty city cousins thought differently, and it wasn't long before the youngest came screaming to the porch where the adults conversed.

"She stepped in a cow-pie," her oldest brother reported. "It stinks around here."

The year of our Lord, 1932, was another election year, and Jonas paid keen attention to both the local and the national elections. Following the landslide victory of Farmer-Labor gubernatorial candidate Floyd B. Olson two years earlier, Jonas was encouraged that the voters were finally coming to their senses, and another reform governor, Franklin Delano Roosevelt of the great state of New York, promised to do something about the widening depression even as do-nothing President Herbert Hoover merely wrung his hands.

Conflicting visions for the role of government were at stake: Republicans would allow unfettered free market capitalism to run its course, and the government should keep hands off, but the Democrats promised an activist government, and they proposed a "New Deal" that would promote the interests of the common man by creating jobs for the unemployed and regulations for Wall Street and the banks. For the Republicans, the government was the boogeyman, but for the Democrats the government was necessary to rein in the self-interest of business and banking while providing a support net for the worker, the farmer, and the elderly when the free market failed to do so.

The national election was not the reason Thomas paid a visit to his brother in western Morrison County. The long-time deputy had thrown his own hat in the ring in the election for county sheriff. The incumbent announced his retirement and was not running for re-election, and Thomas was a leading candidate to replace his boss, along with another deputy and the Little Falls chief of police.

"I know we haven't always seen eye-to-eye," Thomas said. "But it would be a great help to me, and a comfort as well, if you support my candidacy. People in these parts know you are fair-minded and a man of common sense."

Squeals of fun-making came from the hay mow, the second story of the splendid barn. The city kids learned that farm life wasn't necessarily boring. Upstairs in the house, Anders was alone in his room reading the latest work of his favorite author, a local man from nearby Sauk Centre. Sinclair Lewis had recently been awarded a Nobel Prize. In his acceptance speech to the Swedes, he said, "America is the most contradictory, the most depressing, the most stirring, of any land in the world today."

Hilma and Jenny and the older girls cleaned up after supper, and the Jönsson brothers visited alone on the porch. Thomas chain smoked Lucky Strikes, and Jonas puffed on his Prince Albert pipe tobacco.

In the old country, the sheriff did the bidding of the princes and priests, a lackey of the aristocracy with a heavy heel on the throats of the peasants. If the hired man quit his job, the sheriff would haul him back. If a man spoke heresy against the state-church, the priest would send the sheriff.

Was America different?

He remembered the sheriff who arrested Congressman Lindbergh who spoke against the money trust and for the farmer. The lawman J. Edgar Hoover said Natty Einstein was guilty of sedition—how was that different from heresy? --and deported her. When Elmer Jackson perished at the hands of the Duluth mob, the police commissioner stood by and watched—was that an aberration or a true reflection of the soul of America?

But did it not say something about the audacity of America that immigrant Swede Thomas Johnson dared run for sheriff? Or that Anders would soon attend a great university? Or that his 160 acres would be a magnificent estate in Sweden? His eyes squinted to catch the glint of the setting sun on the windshields of the motor cars parked in his driveway and the sparkling green luster on the John Deere tractor. And such a barn! Perhaps he stretched his finances a bit, but his big red barn would be his pride and joy during his lifetime and would serve his family for generations to come.

Just then, Hilma and Jenny joined the menfolk on the porch, and Hilma brought the letter and photographs received from sister Anna the last Christmas. Anna was the only regular contact with the family back home in Sweden, and Hilma always exchanged Christmas letters on behalf of Jonas and the family.

"Thomas, you must see these," Jenny said. "You must write to your sister with pictures of our children."

The photographs were of Anna's grandchildren. Anna's ten-year old grandson was the image of Thomas at the same age with a mop of blonde hair and a soup bowl cut. His look said he was ready to conquer the world. *Did he chase frogs around a pond? Did he have a pearl-handled pen knife? Had he carved his name in a beech tree?*

Jonas rose from his rocker and stepped to the edge of the

porch. He cleared his throat and attempted to sing, but his voice cracked. Thomas slapped his knee and stepped forward.

"Here's how you do it," he said, but his voice also cracked.

From behind, the sweet song of Hilma filtered out from the porch, over the roses, and on to the red barn where the cattle at stanchions responded with a chorus of moos; how could they resist? *Kulning*. The old way. The Swedish way. The family way.

"I declare," Jenny said. "Aren't you the trio!"

Jonas sniffled, wiped his nose, and slapped Thomas on the back. "Of, course, I'll support you, *Lillebror*," Jonas said. "You're a good man, and you'll be a good sheriff. Tell me how I can help."

March in Minnesota has a split personality, and the weather can't decide if it's winter or spring. On Saturday, March 4, 1933, a couple of inches of overnight snow melted by 10:00 am, creating muddy slop in the driveway and the township roads where the gravel wore thin. The creamery truck was late after getting stuck in the mud earlier in its route to load up milk cans from the neighborhood farms for delivery to the cooperative creamery in Kalmar.

"Alekson closed his bank today," the driver said.

"How so?" Jonas replied.

"Clear across the state, I heard."

Jonas nodded imperceptibly as he drew a deep breath. He was smart to keep most of his well-earned dollars in a sock rather than let Alekson get his grubby fingers on them. He had heard about bank closings in other states as a worried nation began to horde cash.

"Well, we'll see what the new president has to say about that," Jonas said.

"Hell, I guess we will."

Jonas didn't expect FDR to be a miracle worker, but … well, maybe he did expect miracles as milk prices had dropped to such an extent it was hardly worth the effort. Why, he heard that farmers in neighboring Wisconsin had attempted to strike to keep their milk off the market to create scarcity and force prices to rise. A few of his neighbors talked of doing the same but couldn't afford to spill their milk even if the prices were low. Something was better than nothing. Hadn't worked in Wisconsin anyway, but FDR would figure something out.

Franklin Delano Roosevelt had to wait longer than Thomas Johnson to be sworn in. The new sheriff of Morrison County assumed his duties a couple of months earlier. FDR won in a landslide; Johnson eked out a slim victory in a three-way race with barely 40% of the vote. It wasn't until the day after the election when the returns from the western precincts of the county filtered in that Johnson pulled ahead. The support of his older brother tipped the scales.

On Monday morning, Jonas travelled to Little Falls to check on the small deposit he kept in the bank for the odd times when a bank money order or certified check was necessary instead of cash. He also maintained a bank relationship to turn fives, tens, and twenties into hundred-dollar bills to keep his stash of cash-filled socks from becoming overly bulky. Most of his money remained tucked into socks under floorboards. He was surprised to learn that on his first day in office, the president had issued a national order to create a ten-day bank holiday to allow fears of bank failures to dissipate. Well, FDR knows best, he thought. After all, his bank deposit was meager.

Jonas picked up a morning paper, and that evening he read it through. Tucked into a back page, a short article caught his attention.

*Just six days after the German Reichstag burned down*

*under suspicious circumstances, the Nazi Party of Adolph Hitler consolidated its power in a hastily arranged special election.*

Jonas stepped outside for a smoke, but a stiff breeze kept blowing out his matches. Winter wasn't conceding just yet.

# CHAPTER FORTY-NINE: 1934

"Holy cow, look at that golden Gopher run!"

Minneapolis newspaperman Halsey Hall blustered into the microphone, flicking cigar ashes while he described the action on the field. General Store proprietor Ingemar Jorgenson fingered the knobs on the radio as the WCCO broadcast faded in and out. The Gophers and sophomore sensation Andrew Johnson mauled another Big Ten rival on their way to the 1934 national championship. Jonas Jönsson and other menfolk left the farm work for a few hours on Saturday afternoons for the ritual of listening to the radio broadcast of the conquests of the Gopher eleven. Surrounded by worn out sofas and unmatched chairs on the bowed plank floor of the General Store's upstairs, a Cathedral style radio squeaked out Halsey Hall's bombastic play by play pronouncements. Electrical service to area farms was still a couple of years down the road, but townies--Kalmar businesses and residents--boasted electric lights, refrigerators, and radios.

Jonas and Hilma had yet to attend a game in person, but Andrew showed them, and sister Olga, the empty Memorial Stadium earlier that summer. Imagine, over fifty thousand screaming fans packed in to watch Andrew and the other Gopher footballers! Jonas climbed to the top row of the stadium to peer down at the street that ran along the north side of the stadium, the thoroughfare that connected St. Paul and Minneapolis where he had once piloted a gelding pulling a wagon load of Hamm's beer. He remained a long time.

"What's he looking at up there?" Olga wondered.

When he slowly climbed down the steps to return, his glassy eyes seemed to see a faraway place.

Jonas, Hilma, and Olga rode the train to the city to arrange Olga's residence in a tiny room in a private home in the Lowry Hill neighborhood in south Minneapolis. More than her sisters, Olga favored her mother, and that included a pitch-perfect soprano voice, and now Olga would receive professional training at a conservatory of music. Olga also heard a calling beyond a life as a farm wife. Much like Jonas and his son, Hilma lived vicariously through her daughters, and Olga's musical talents would receive the polishing under professional tutelage that had been unthinkable for Hilma herself.

Like his uncle Thomas, Andrew adopted the Americanized version of his name, and Jonas didn't object. The girls did likewise. Although a part of him still pined for a son to take over the farm, Jonas had mostly come around to Andrew's own vision for his future. Jonas listened proudly as Andrew delivered the valedictory at the Kalmar High School graduation just over a year earlier. Hilma subtly passed him her kerchief to dab at his eyes. If his son wouldn't be a farmer, a career as a lawyer was an acceptable alternative. Charles Lindbergh had been a crusading lawyer. So too, Governor Floyd B. Olson. Jonas was sure big things were in store for Andrew.

Andrew promised to return to the farm for summer work after his freshman year earlier that summer, but with the drought intensifying in the summer of '34, there was little for him to do as the crops withered in the fields, and he spent long hours devouring books, especially "whodunits" by Dashiel Hammett, featuring his urbane characters, Nick and Nora Charles. Agathe Christie's series were too continental for Andrew's tastes.

"Father, if I may, I would like to return to the city," Andrew said after just a few weeks.

Jonas was offended. When the rains returned, there would be plenty to do, but in any case, he didn't understand why Andrew preferred the city to the farm.

"Governor Olson will be up for reelection this fall, and I would like to volunteer to work in his campaign."

Jonas supposed that made sense, even if his emotions doubted. In the end, he agreed, and Andrew departed to dip his toes into the turbulent politics of the Farmer Labor Party.

Andrew had attempted to join the Olson campaign earlier during the school year after he heard the governor speak to a packed auditorium. The college freshman lingered long after the speech ended before finding the courage to go to the governor's hotel room to pledge his allegiance. A burly guard sat on a chair outside the doorway to the hotel room. The governor was in the thick of worsening labor unrest, and violence was brewing in Minneapolis.

"You don't want to go in there," the guard said.

"Is the governor already asleep?"

It was only early evening when Johnson went to the hotel.

"Don't imagine he is."

"Well, can I tell him how much I appreciated his speech?"

"Humph!"

The guard smiled, and his belly shook in a silent guffaw.

"Knock on the door if you like."

Johnson knocked, hesitated, and then knocked again.

A shout came from inside the room.

"What the hell do you want? Don't you know I'm screwing my secretary?"

**********

"You're making that up," Don said, smiling and leaning forward in his chair. "You didn't really interrupt the governor in flagrante delicto!"

"It's true," I said, even as I shook my head. "Months later, I became the governor's errand boy, but I never revealed that it was me that knocked on his door that day."

"You promised to tell me about my mother. Why didn't she go to music conservatory like Aunt Olga when she finished high school? Was it money?"

"Yes, by the time your mother was old enough, drought and depression had severely crimped Papa's finances, but now we're getting ahead of the story."

Don sagged back into the plush chair.

"In the fall of '34, I was a sophomore at the University, and your mother was a sophomore at Kalmar High. She was the beauty of the family. Tall and slender like our parents, her auburn tresses were more an inheritance from Papa than from Mama's strawberry blonde genes—not sure where her pure alabaster skin and delicate features came from. She stood straight and proud and allowed her hair to drape down her back."

"I only remember my mother as a stooped woman with hair bound in a tight bun," Don replied.

"By her sophomore year, your mother had taken over for her older sisters at the telephone exchange. Olga was off to conservatory, and Signe got fired. It took some talking from Papa to persuade Otelia Moberg to take a chance on your mother, but she thrived when given the opportunity."

"Why did Signe get fired?"

*"Signe was the eccentric daughter, like the time she followed a spat with her sisters by wrapping herself in a quilt and laying in the hot summer sun. That would show them! Although she may have been intelligent enough, her temperament never allowed her to excel in her studies like the rest of us. Nor did it allow her to retain the job she inherited from Olga as an operator at the Kalmar Co-operative Telephone exchange. Interrupting private telephone conversations and interjecting her own comments just wouldn't do! As Signe entered her senior year at Kalmar High, she had no concrete plans for the future—she bragged she would become an aviator like Amelia Earhart."*

*Don nodded. He knew that Aunt Signe had followed her dream.*

*"Some of my earliest memories are of Mother's church choirs in south Minneapolis," Don said." I was just a tyke clutching at her skirts as she moved from one choir rehearsal to the next. Of course, by then she was a widow following the death of my father in the war."*

*Don leaned forward again as he continued to speak with a faraway look on his face. "Truth be told, I know very little about my father. Mother never spoke about him or his family. The thing I remember most about my childhood was the great sadness that enveloped Mother, especially when I asked about my father. Nor did my aunts have anything to tell me about him, shushing me whenever I would ask. 'Don't upset your mother,' they would say."*

*Don's forehead furrowed as his eyes searched my face. "What can you tell me now? Was he from the Kalmar community? Was he from farm stock?"*

*When I started this conversation with Don, I felt it was time for family secrets to be told, and that would include the truth about Don's father. Just then, the clock on my dresser chimed.*

*"Supper time. LaDonna will be here shortly. I'll tell you about your father in due course, but right now, your mother is only a high*

*school sophomore at this point in the story."*

*Don slowly exhaled.*

*"Patience, dear nephew."*

*K*eep America safe for Americans and the Stars and Stripes the defender of God.

In September of 1936, Jonas Jönsson put his ear up close to his new Philco tube radio and listened to the weekly broadcast of Father Coughlin—a priest, yes, but mostly an uninhibited populist voice crackling with static over the radio waves of America.

*I need not recall for you that both the laboring and agricultural classes of America are forced to work for less than a living wage while the owners of industry boastfully proclaim that their profits are increasing.*

Jonas wasn't sure what to think about the rants of Father Coughlin. Although he agreed with Coughlin's economic populism, he wondered about his unabashed nationalism that tilted increasingly toward nativism. Jonas had agreed with Congressman Lindbergh that America should not enter the European conflict a generation earlier. Lindbergh was right then, and perhaps Coughlin was right now with his America first rhetoric.

*The major portion of our sympathy is extended to our dispossessed farmer, our disconsolate laborers who are being crushed at this moment while the spirit of internationalism runs rampant in the corridors of the Capitol, hoping to participate in setting the world aright while chaos clamors at our doors.*

On the other hand, Germany beat war drums again, and the anti-Jewish screed of Hitler and the Nazis seemed darker and more sinister than the earlier bellicosity of Kaiser Wilhelm. The harshness of Coughlin's "America First" bombast almost made the case for the opposite view.

*Must the entire world go to war for 600,000 Jews in Germany who are neither American, nor French, nor English citizens, but citizens of Germany?*

Coughlin's populist criticism of capitalistic excesses was one thing, but scapegoating the Jews was another thing altogether. Free speech was one thing, but the venom spewed by Coughlin revealed an inner darkness. The priest's nationalistic tribalism descended into nativism and on to shameless bigotry. In the end, he was just another hateful voice shouting "America for Americans," and Jönsson knew only too well where that would lead.

*When we get through with the Jews in America, they'll think the treatment they received in Germany was nothing.*

"Why do you listen to that garbage," Hilma chimed in from the kitchen. "You have enough to worry about without addling your mind with the rants of that idiot."

She was right, of course, and she also doubted the wisdom of spending money for an extravagance in tough times such as these. She was probably right about that as well, but Jonas felt the family needed the diversion the radio could provide. The opera and the symphony expanded the girls' musical vistas beyond their Lutheran hymns, Hilma laughed out loud at the tall tales and wild schemes of Fibber McGee held in check by the steady hand of wife Molly, and Jonas listened to the news while reading his newspapers.

"Come and eat your supper," Hilma called to the girls upstairs and to Jonas in the living room.

Jonas twisted the knob, and the radio went silent. He ate quickly and headed out for evening chores, which didn't take long with his reduced herds. Many of his animals had been sold for cash or butchered. He made sure to finish in time to return to the radio and the president's latest fireside chat.

Once or twice a year, President Roosevelt calmed the nation—and Jönsson--in the throes of depression with a fireside chat over the radio. If the demagogue Coughlin used the radio waves to ill effect, Roosevelt demonstrated the high purpose which this emerging medium could fulfill. Through the radio, Roosevelt quelled rumors and explained his policies with a calming and self-assured tone. If the Congress and the courts failed to appreciate Roosevelt's New Deal policies, the president effectively took his case directly to the people.

Jonas fiddled with the dials as Hilma and the girls gathered. Soon, they heard the voice of the president himself, as if he was there in the living room, speaking directly to them.

> I have been on a journey of husbandry ... I talked with families who had lost their wheat crop, lost their corn crop, lost their livestock, lost the water in their well, lost their garden and come through to the end of summer without one dollar of cash resources, facing a winter without feed or food—facing a planting season without seed to put in the ground ...

> Yet I would not have you think for a single minute that there is permanent disaster in these drought regions ... No cracked earth, no blistering sun, no burning wind, no grasshoppers, are a permanent match for the indomitable American farmers and stockmen and their wives and children who have carried on through desperate days, and inspire us with their self-reliance, their tenacity and their courage. It was their father's task to make homes; it is their task to keep those homes; it is our task to help them with their fight ... In a physical sense and a property sense, as well as a spiritual sense, we are members one of another.

The chat was full of encouragement but short on specifics. Instead, FDR promoted a philosophy of government:

the people united, through their elected leaders, must pull together. Jönsson slept better that night.

The following day, with little real work to do, Jönsson puttered about in the barn until it was time for the mail delivery. He circled wide across his cornfield as if he expected a miracle, and the shriveled leaves and bent and broken stalks would spring upright and green with heavy cobs drooping down the sides. Each footfall kicked up little dust clouds. Thin dust that seemed invisible hung in the air but reddened the sun. When he arrived at the old oak, he wiped muddy sweat from his forehead with his red hanky.

While he waited in the shade, sprawled against the trunk of the broad oak drawing his thoughts in the dust with a twig, he spied a mud turtle with a bright orange painted belly and green head with yellow streaks. The reptile climbed the sloping field toward the high ground where the road passed, no doubt escaping the dried-up marsh and creek that ran along the low side of Jönsson's meadow. Jönsson wondered if the prominent nostrils on the pointy beak smelled Pine Lake, some two miles to the north or if the slowpoke just headed somewhere else, anywhere, nowhere. The turtle moved resolutely, trampling crisp, brown ditch-weeds and leaving scritch marks and a wavy trench in its dusty trail. When the turtle began to cross the gravel road, Jönsson spied a cloud of dust of an approaching motor car, and he rose to his feet and grasped the pokey reptile in the span of his hand between thumb and forefinger. Head, neck and legs jerked back into the shell, and Jönsson deposited the creature safely on the far side of the road. About the time the dusty swirl of Willy Peterson's Chevy truck arrived, the turtle beak peaked out followed by the full head and neck. Humorous eyes blinked twice, then legs flailed in the dust, and the journey continued.

The first thing Jönsson noticed was the missus, Aggie Peterson in her Sunday finest, perched alongside her husband, wearing a tall hat that scraped against the ceiling of the truck cab. The mystery and uncertainty of her new station addled her mind, and she sat stone faced and grim like a widow at her husband's funeral.

"Hello, Aggie," Jönsson said, touching the brim of his straw hat.

She stared straight ahead without acknowledging him.

The engine popped as Willy put her in neutral and jerked on the parking brake, stepping onto the running board, and then onto the gravel roadway. He spit into his dusty palms, rubbed them together, wiped them on his pant legs, and extended his right paw for a handshake, as if sealing a momentous deal.

Peterson had lashed multiple used, bruised spare tires together in the front, and they protruded like a battering ram. The front fenders appeared muscular with canvas bags, filled with who-knows-what, tethered down with ropes. Fresh cut pine boards extended up and over the sides of the pickup box with chair legs poking out between the cracks. The rear of the truck was a clatter of furniture, stacked high on trunks and boxes and strapped into place, hanging over the pine board sides and back. Perched on the top, a cage of squawking chickens tilted ominously toward the side.

"Why'd we stop? Time's awastin'" Gram Peterson's shrill voice from the rear squeaked over the beat of the idling four-cylinder engine.

"Jest sayin' farewell to our good neighbor, Ma," Willy said.

Gram Peterson, Willy's ancient mother, sat on a pair of folded-up mattresses immediately behind the passenger compartment, facing backward toward the family's ice box. The heap of furniture atop the ice box blotted out her view of the road travelled. Her layers of clothing suggested she wore her entire wardrobe, even on a warm September day. The brimmed bonnet tied tightly under her chin shielded her eyes, leaving her sagging and folded facial skin exposed to the sun.

The teen-aged Peterson girls straddled her on either side, and they eagerly stood atop the mattresses to watch and listen to the conversation, thankful for the interruption in their boredom, even as their journey was just beginning. The older girl twisted her braids in her fingers with her mouth hanging open, as if that helped her hear what was said, and the younger one leaned with her chin in her palms, supported by elbows propped on the roof of the cab.

Willy removed his lopsided, broken-billed cap and wiped his forehead with his sleeve. He kept his eyes low and didn't look up into the face of his tall neighbor, due to the small sliver of vanity that remained. He smoothed back his mussed hair with snatches of gray before replacing the cap. Willy wore dirty coveralls under a threadbare jacket that had once been a go-to-meetin' garment. The cloth patches on the elbows didn't match.

"Californey. They say Californey is the place for dried up folks like us."

The Petersons weren't the first family to just pull up and go. Whole families headed elsewhere—California, Arizona, or places unknown, with the sum of their possessions strapped onto the top and sides of the family motorcar. Some men disappeared into the hobo camps.

"Willy Jr. will join us when his summer job with the Works Progress is finished. He'll bring some cash to keep us going."

Peterson's sunken eyes glanced up into Jönsson's face before he stared down the road and to the west.

"Don't know about gas money, though. Only got about a hunnert. I figure we got enough for food and gas for a thousand miles, but Californey may be too far for right now. We'll go as far as we can and then wait for Jr. to catch up."

He was too proud to ask straight away, but Jönsson heard what he was saying. Jönsson pulled out his wallet and removed the sole dollar bill folded there.

"This'll get you a day or two down the road," he said and stuffed the bill into the high pocket of Peterson's jacket.

"Take what you want, if'n you find anything at the home place," Peterson said with his eyes shifting back the way they had come.

Jönsson wouldn't bother to look for he knew what he would find. The boys from town would come and smash the windows, and the bats would fly through. Left-behind cats would prowl around, and if they felt like it, they would chase the mice that stored weed seeds in the corners and shelves and left their droppings in the backs of drawers. A skunk, or maybe a weasel, would take up residence under the porch. The wind would bang the doors, shred the curtains, and rip off a shingle and then another. The once proud paint would slowly crack and peel and fade away under the unrelenting, unforgiving sun. Nails would work their way back out their holes, and the side boards would curl up.

No, it was not something Jönsson cared to see.

Peterson cleared his throat and clambered back behind the driver's seat. The engine popped again as the Chevy creaked and swayed away with the tail pipe spurting a trail of blue-gray exhaust and the smell of hot oil. The last thing Jönsson heard was the voice of Gram singing,

> Waiting for the harvest, and the time of reaping,
>
> We shall come rejoicing, bringing in the sheaves.

# CHAPTER FIFTY-ONE: 1937

T he John Deere tractor was broken, and Jönsson didn't have the money to fix it. He already spent his allotment of drought relief provided by the government. His herd was reduced to a few cows that barely provided milk for the family. Hilma's vegetable garden survived through the daily sprinkling she provided from her watering can with the big spout, but lately the water pressure in the well pump was low.

The mortgage payment was due tomorrow, and Jönsson endlessly counted the rolled bills in his socks to ensure that he had the proper amount. As soon as he assured himself that the money was there, he immediately worried again after the socks were returned to their hidey hole. He promised himself, and Hilma, that after this payment was completed, and the final one due in a year, they would burn the mortgage note and hoist a glass of beer, or two.

When the day arrived for his annual curtsy to Henry Alekson, he cranked up the Tin Lizzy and headed toward Kalmar, with Elsa and Siri in the back seat bound for school. The gathering clouds in the west looked like rain, but it had been such a long time since a real soaker that he doubted his instincts. The spring had been wet enough, and the planting went well, but the sprouting seeds naïvely anticipated summer showers. Whenever rain-heads had gathered that summer, the clouds would spit a few drops before moving on, leaving the corn stalks yearning for a long, cool drink and not merely a splattering that left dusty rivulets on the leaves. After dropping the girls at school, Jönsson entered the bank, ignoring Henry Jr. stationed behind a teller's window and heading straight into the office of old Henry. Soon, the son would replace the father, but not yet, and Junior's icy glare followed Jönsson into his father's office.

Old Alekson looked feeble and not well. He removed his glasses and whispered a greeting. Jönsson watched nervously as the bald, bespectacled man slowly counted the bills and then a second time, and again Jönsson worried he had somehow miscounted even though he had counted and recounted innumerable times.

Five hundred bucks in ones, fives, and tens, plus another sixty bucks for interest. At the time, before drought and depression, borrowing five thousand dollars for a barn, a tractor, and another forty acres had seemed prudent, but now the big, empty barn seemed a prideful folly. One more payment after this one, but he had already scratched and scraped, and there wasn't much left to sell. Even if the drought broke and the rains refreshed the earth, how would he pay for seed to plant? FDR promised help for the farmers, but Jönsson worried.

Beads of sweat formed on Alekson's pasty face, and he gulped a few swallows from a tall glass of water. Jönsson's dry mouth could also use a swig, but he merely licked parched lips.

Finally, the old banker nodded and slipped a piece of carbon paper under the top page of his tablet of receipts and dipped his fountain pen in his inkwell. He meticulously scribed the receipt of payment, dipping the pen in ink after each word. When he finished, he carefully blew the ink dry. He removed his glasses and slid the document over to Jönsson. Jönsson snapped the receipt with relief before scanning it to his satisfaction. He folded it in half and placed it in his shirt pocket with a pat for assurance.

Alekson dispensed with his normal dissertation on thrift and well living, and he remained seated, gently tapping his glasses on his desk as Jönsson departed.

The first raindrops dimpled tiny craters in the dust as Jönsson crank-started the Ford, and by the time he exited Kalmar's main street onto the gravel road toward his farm, the rain was coming so hard he could barely see through the windshield, and he never did shift into high gear. Less than a mile from his driveway, the engine shut down, a nuisance that had been occurring with some regularity. Never mind, he half walked, half ran through mud up to his ankles the rest of the way home, singing a popular song from the radio:

*I'm singing in the rain*

*Just singing in the rain*

*What a glorious feelin'*

*I'm happy again.*

He burst into the house, swung Hilma around, and planted a wet kiss on her lips.

"You old fool," she said with a smile. "You're tracking mud everywhere. Get out of those wet clothes before you catch your death."

"I'll get out of mine, if you get out of yours," he teased, and he took her by the hand and led her up the stairs to their bedroom.

Lightning crackled for more than an hour, the heavens opened, and the rain poured down.

After the storm broke, Jönsson returned to the Tin Lizzy wearing dry clothes and tinkered as the school bus passed by to drop off his kids who waved frantically. He slammed the hood shut and went to the crank at the front. After two attempts, the Tin Lizzy fired on the third try, and he followed the bus toward his driveway. Hilma waited on the porch with her arms around the shoulders of Elsa and Siri. Signe lingered beyond the stoop, but she leaned forward with her face in the doorway.

"Lena called from the telephone exchange," Hilma said in a loud voice as soon as Jonas came within earshot. "Someone robbed the bank."

# CHAPTER FIFTY-TWO

Sheriff Thomas Johnson was there with his deputies. Folks mingled in twos and threes in the street in front of the bank, and the lawmen moved from one group to the next asking what they knew. Some said it was a single hold-up man, either tall or short, but others said it was the mob—probably the remnants of the Ma Barker gang--and would Sheriff Johnson soon call in J. Edgar Hoover's G-men?

Jönsson parked in front of the General Store and joined the proprietor on his stoop under the broad awning that still dripped following the midday downpour. The late-afternoon shadows of the tall building stretched all the way across the street to the beer joint on the far side.

"No shots were fired," Ingemar Jorgenson explained, "but old Henry collapsed from fright."

Jönsson recalled his visit to the pasty-faced banker hours earlier.

"With no physician in town, Henry Jr. rang up the dentist."

Sure enough, Jönsson spied the spindly tooth doctor with slicked-down blonde hair parted in the middle telling anyone who would listen what he knew.

"Heart attack or maybe a stroke," the dentist proclaimed with great aplomb. "He was alive but unconscious when Henry Jr. and I carried him to his Cadillac. Wife Hannah and young Henry departed coupla hours ago for the hospital in Little Falls."

Jonas was late returning home, and Hilma set aside a supper plate while he quickly finished the evening choirs. Then, she warmed the plate in the oven while Jönsson told her what he knew. As he mopped up the last of the plate with a hunk of bread, the telephone jangled, even though it was after hours. Town Crier, Otelia Moberg, told everyone on one party line after the next that the hold-up man was dead, killed when he run his daddy's car off the road in his haste for a getaway. Barely sixteen and from neighboring Todd County to the west, the boy burned up when his car rammed into a tree and caught fire. All the loot, and the bank papers that he had swept into his gunny sack burnt up, too. A passerby discovered the smoking vehicle on the back road not five miles west of Kalmar, but it took a few hours to figure out who it was and what happened.

Jonas dropped the receiver that dangled by a cord from the side of the telephone face and bolted up the stairs. The heap of his wet clothes had disappeared from the corner where he left them, but out the bedroom window he saw them rippling in a gentle breeze on the clothesline out back where Hilma hung them after their noon-day lovemaking. He flew down the stairs faster than he had climbed and nearly knocked over Signe going up. The screen door slammed behind him after he sprinted through the kitchen and out the back door. Feeling in the dark, his fingers found the paper in his shirt pocket. Both the shirt and the paper had dried. Back in the kitchen, he spread the crinkled receipt of payment out on the table. It was still in one piece, but the ink strokes that Henry Alekson had so carefully scribed earlier in the day were now mere smears.

A few days later, Henry Jr., now the bank manager with his father still stroke-stricken and incapacitated, stood on a chair behind the barred teller windows to speak to the assembled bank depositors in the lobby of the bank. He had grown to be a heavy man, but soft and flabby without substance, doughy-faced and sweaty. His plus four trousers over knee-length silk stockings and saddle shoes—better suited for a country club-- seemed especially baggy on his physique. A dapper kerchief peaked from the pocket of his single-breasted, three-button jacket. With daddy not able to say no, it appeared young Henry had splurged.

"Not to worry, your deposits are insured." His manner was not one of concerned assurance but of condescension. "Please line up in an orderly fashion, and we'll help you fill out the paperwork."

Jönsson stood in the rear. He knew all about FDR's Banking Act of 1933 that dealt with thousands of bank failures and financial ruin for innocent depositors by creating the Federal Deposit Insurance Corporation. What he didn't know was the status of his mortgage payment made on the morning of the holdup, and Henry Jr. didn't say much when Jönsson asked him.

A month later, he had his answer when brother Thomas appeared in his sheriff's squad car to personally serve the lawsuit papers that alleged that Jonas and Hilma had defaulted on their mortgage loan, and the Farmer's and Merchant's State Bank of Kalmar pursued foreclosure on the farm.

"It's all bullshit, I know," Thomas said, "but what can I do?"


"All rise."

Jonas and Hilma stood next to their attorney, and Henry Alekson, Jr. stood next to his. The jury filtered in and sat in their chairs. They *suspected* the truth. The Judge *suspected* the truth. The court reporter, and the folks in the seats *suspected* the truth. Hilma and Jonas *knew* the truth. God dammit, young Henry and his lawyer probably *knew* the truth. Unfortunately, Lady Justice is blind, and she could see no proof of payment in the burned-up ledger of bank receipts or the ink-smeared sheet of crinkled paper the defendants had offered as evidence.

Henry Alekson Sr. had been his best hope, but the stroke-stricken man could only stare with vacant eyes at the ceiling from his bed on the second floor of his big house in Kalmar. No words came from his mouth, only drool, and he passed away without speaking a month before the trial. Immediately, Hannah Alekson departed Kalmar and joined her sister in Minneapolis, leaving the bank and the house to young Henry.

All sat down, and then the jury foreman stood up. He mopped his brow with a stained hanky even though the courtroom was chilly. His lower lip quivered as he revealed the verdict.

"We find for the plaintiff, the Farmers and Merchants State Bank of Kalmar," he said and sat down with huge sigh.


Jonas, Hilma, and the girls moved into the upstairs of the Jorgenson General Store and stayed away from the mortgage foreclosure auction. Before moving, they sold the broken-down tractor and farm implements. Pitchforks and shovels. Hammers and saws, even the old axe that had been splitting wood since the first fireplace in the first cabin. Pretty much everything from the barn. They kept most things from the house that Hilma needed and would fit into their new residence. Wood-burning range and oven. Cold closet. Philco radio. Bed frames, springs, and mattresses. Wooden kitchen table and chairs. Beat-up old sofa and living room chairs. Pots and pans, some bought from a drummer on a mule long ago. Dishware. Utensils. Chests filled with shirts, pants, dresses, socks, and underwear. Of course, the Singer Sewing Machine.

Hilma emptied and cleaned her "America chest," and then she refilled it with memories that presently seemed sour but would sweeten with time—like the picture of all six kids sitting atop Gurli and Jonas' courting letters gushing with high hopes for America. Hilma smiled and made a tsking sound as she packed away the picture of her suitor in an ill-fitting rented suit. The bitter with the sweet. In the moment, past remembrances triggered more pain than pleasure, but Hilma knew best, and she packed them away for better times.

At first, Jonas was listless, and he didn't bother to dicker over price, accepting the first offer for this and that, but when it came time to move, he became ruthless, and he sawed down the big burr oak at the mouth of the driveway and burned it up in a bonfire. While the flames leapt high, he returned to the house one last time and searched under the floorboards for an item wrapped in an oily rag.

On an overcast day in May 1937, a German Catholic from Stearns County offered the highest bid at the auction. He purchased the farm with the big red barn and the Sears, Roebuck & Company four-square house. He bought the vegetable garden, the corn and wheat fields, the pasture, and the meadow. He bought the sweat that dripped into the sandy loam and the tears spilled on the carcass of Gurli. He bought the grunts of Jonas and Tomas as they broke the virgin sod, the wails of Hilma as she birthed her children, the squeals of kids playing tag in the hay mow, and the echoes of calling in the cows.

The songbird chorus no longer awakened Jönsson before dawn's light seeped over the land, revealing the inches added to corn stalks. He no longer sifted clumps of soil through his fingers or milked the supple teats of Old Bessie. He no longer rubbed tallow and beeswax on leather harnesses or smeared grease on the axles of the John Deere. The juice of a strawberry plucked from Hilma's patch no longer dribbled down his cheek, and the dust hanging in the hay mow no longer triggered his sneeze. These things were lost, and he was no longer the farmer: no longer the breeder or the butcher, no longer the tiller, planter, cultivator, harvester or gleaner.

But then, who was he?

Jönsson lost possessions, standing, and reputation, but

these were small things compared to the loss of identity. He lost the farm, and he lost himself.

# CHAPTER FIFTY-THREE

Drought rocks surfaced and sand bars fingered into the waterway, but the big river kept on flowing. Currents changed, and fish swarmed in the deep pools, but the big river kept on flowing. Backwaters and tributaries dried up, but the big river kept on flowing.

Each day during the summer and fall of 1937, four men from Kalmar, Jönsson among them, rode together to toil for the Works Progress Administration constructing park buildings on the former Lindbergh farm on the west bank of the great river just outside Little Falls. Hilma urged him to take the job, despite his inclination to brood, and they needed money to live.

Of course, most people thought of Charles Junior, the brave young pilot who captured the adulation of the world ten years earlier, but Jönsson remembered Charles Senior because he challenged America to live up to her own ideals. Lindbergh's lineage included the policies of Floyd B. Olson and the Farmer Labor Party and Franklin Delano Roosevelt and the New Deal. Lindberg also created the space that allowed Charles Jr. to grow and expand and spread out and reach new horizons as the son of a Swedish immigrant, even if the son was now making a fool of himself with his adoration of Germany, Hitler, and the Nazis.

Jonas made no claim to accomplishments like Lindbergh, far from it even if his own blood had dripped in the dusty street of a southern Minnesota town; nor was it likely that his own son would achieve the fame of young Lindbergh, but Anders—Andrew—had big things in store, Jonas was sure. And, of course, Olga the soprano would never achieve the status of Jenny Lind, but she was a Swedish nightingale in her own right, and she would soon perform in the finest venues of Minneapolis. Signe departed the boring streets of Kalmar for the energy of Minneapolis, but Jonas and Hilma weren't quite sure where her destiny might lead. Lena graduated high school and worked full time at the telephone exchange because Otelia Moberg was ailing. Lena would love to follow Olga to conservatory, but the money wasn't there, not now. Elsa and Siri would soon finish high school, and the depression hadn't dampened their enthusiasm for bright futures. His children would be Jonas' legacy.

Jonas spent his daily lunch break eating Hilma's sandwiches on the riverbank where he and Tomas visited with lawyer Charles Lindbergh two decades earlier. Jonas flung a big pine branch into the flow back then, and the river whisked it away. Had the limb reached the sea, or did it snag somewhere in the rocks, on a sand bar, or behind a man-made dam?

The WPA park project was therapy for his soul. He relished working with his hands, and the pay kept food on the table in the spacious apartment atop the General Store of dear friends Ingemar and Evie Jorgenson. Hilma helped in the store, especially because Evie suffered from arthritis, while Jonas spent his days on the bank of the Mississippi just southwest of Little Falls.

The work crew spread out with different tasks to transform the Lindbergh farm into a state park. Jonas supervised construction of a walking bridge over Pike's Creek at the south side of the Lindbergh property, assisted by Tony Sikora from the eastern end of Morrison County.

Tony was still a boy: lean, short, with skinny arms lacking man muscles. His movements were jerky and quick. He arrived each day with a gunny sack slung over his shoulder filled with work gloves, a hammer, his lunch, and a rain slicker with an open slash across the back. No hat covered the thick mop of oily black hair slicked behind his ears. He wore a faded jacket with rips at the shoulders on the backside that said a larger man than Tony had previously filled the coat. Knees threatened to poke through faded blue jeans. Beneath a smooth face, a few stray whiskers masked a weak chin.

He seemed to have no intuition for the work to be done, but he dutifully followed the instructions from the man who was old enough to be his grandfather, and there was a mix of curiosity and respect in his eyes at the crippled old Swede who sometimes had difficulty rising from the grassy bank of the Mississippi. The eyes said what Tony's mouth dared not speak —that this low-paying job was for young men just starting out and not for someone like Jonas who should be home rocking a grandkid on his knee and sipping a mug of cocoa.

Jonas' days at work were good, and evenings listening to the Philco with his family were passable—he followed the light-hearted fluff of Jack Benny, but he stopped listening to the news or reading his newspapers. He stalled before turning down the lights and climbing into bed because he knew that disillusionment, regret, self-reproach, and anger would find him in the murkiness between wake and sleep.

Jonas had always been a quiet, private man, but now even more so, and he seldom ventured from his sanctuary above the General Store. When he did, he heard words of encouragement and support. He wasn't the only industrious farmer who had failed, but that didn't lessen his embarrassment or his resentment. What was more, the townsfolk suspected Jönsson's truth and young Henry's lie, and the Kalmar Bank suffered because those who could do so took their business elsewhere.

If healing requires forgiveness, Jonas was not likely to recover quickly. Forgiving young Henry for the disruption in the lives and dreams of Jonas and his family—all for a measly $560 —was unthinkable. That Henry's rash lie also jeopardized the prosperity of the Kalmar Bank was hardly consolation or just punishment.

Once again, fate would intervene. Did justice prevail? Or mercy?

Jonas held the old Colt revolver lightly in his hand.

Five of the cartridges had been fired long ago, but the sixth and last spent shell reeked of freshly fired gunpowder. Sprawled on the bedroom floor of the big house built by his father, the naked body of Henry Alekson, Jr. stared with unseeing eyes and a gaping hole in his chest. Sheriff Thomas Johnson was called, and he made the arrest.

In the winter of '38, Slightly more than a year after losing the farm, Jonas Jönsson was back in the Morrison County Courthouse.

"Will the defendant please rise," the sonorous voice of the clerk of court reverberated through the Morrison County Courtroom, bouncing off the tall stained-glass windows and shaking the spittoons placed strategically around the cavernous room, or so it seemed to Jonas Jönsson, the murderer who had escaped capture for nearly fifty years but who now faced justice. A wooden rail, the "bar," separated the lawyers and participants from the crowd that filled the gallery and spilled out the back door and into the hallway. Sheriff Thomas Johnson sat in the front row next to Jonas' own family.

In a squeaky voice that contrasted with the booming exclamation of the clerk, the silver-haired judge in a black robe spoke next.

"Jonas Jönsson, you have been charged with the murder of Henry Alekson, Jr. How do you plead?"

"Guilty, your honor."

"Does the defendant have anything to say before I pass sentence?"

"No, your honor.

"I hereby sentence you to life in prison."

Hilma gasped, and the girls sobbed. Twenty-three-year-old Anders sat grim-faced. Jonas had pleaded with the family not to come, but they ignored his command.

For sixty-eight-year-old Jonas Jönsson, life in prison might not be long.

# CHAPTER FIFTY-FOUR

**"Y**ou must go now. The poor man needs his rest."

*The night shift arrived at my nursing home, and LaDonna shooed Donald out.*

*"Let him stay just a while longer," I said. "I have more to say."*

*I wasn't used to being overruled, but LaDonna would have the last word.*

*"Come back in the morning, Sweetie," she said with a light tap on Don's shoulder. "Visitors were to be off the floor an hour ago."*

*"Tomorrow is Christmas eve, Uncle Andrew," Donald said as he donned his overcoat. "I'll be heading out in the morning for a drive to Wisconsin. I'll be spending Christmas week with my daughter and grandkids."*

*"No," I said sternly as LaDonna plumped my pillow and checked my oxygen. "I don't have much time, and I must tell the rest."*

*Perhaps Donald expected my telling of Papa's story to end with the trial, but the critical part of the story was yet to be told. At ninety-nine years of age and just a week short of the new year, I felt panicky that I might not finish the story. My death was near, but there were truths yet to be told.*

*"I'm sorry, Uncle Andrew. I must go, but I'll see you in a week on New Year's Eve."*

*I jerked the oxygen cannula from my nose and sat straight up. "No, not yet you mustn't go. There is more to tell, much more."*

*Too late, the door closed behind him. My New Year's resolution was to stay alive, at least for one more visit with Don.*

*For a long week, I willed my heart to beat, my lungs to breathe, and my mind to remain alert until Don returned, but as the week passed, I almost lost my resolve. Maybe it would be best if I would pass on before Don returns. Have I revealed enough? Will the rest of the story be too much? How will Don handle the truth of the night that Alekson was killed? Perhaps it would be best if the truth dies with me, I wondered, but when New Year's Eve rolled around, I was still among the living, and Don returned as promised.*

*I took that as a sign.*

*"There was another person in the room that night when Uncle Thomas arrested Papa," I said as I began my New Year's Eve conclusion to the story.*

*My gnarly fingers clutched Don's jacket and pulled him close to better hear my squeaky voice, barely a whisper.*

*"It was a snowy Christmas eve in 1937, and I was home from law school. All of us were there to open a few simple gifts and share a joyous supper: Olga, Signe, Lena, Elsa, and Siri. Papa was happier than I had seen him since … well, since he lost the farm. Oooh, the scents that wafted around the rented residence over the General Store! From one corner, a fresh-cut and trimmed spruce with a star on top, and in the kitchen, Mama was in her glory setting a fine table with a bone-in smoked ham, green beans, sweet rice covered with cranberries, buttered lefse, ginger pepparkakor, cinnamon kanelbulle, and eggnog."*

*I paused and looked at the Christmas wreath hanging on my nursing home door. Despite the oxygen cannula in my nose, I think smelled fresh cut spruce.*

*"I always loved Mama but seeing her afresh in this place and not the familiar farm kitchen allowed me to realize how much I appreciated her. She was still a young woman then, not yet fifty, and*

*more beautiful than ever. I remembered her nightly ritual—when we were young--of letting down her long tresses and allowing the girls to share one hundred brush strokes, but now her cinnamon-colored hair was cropped short. I knew that the faded Christmas dress under her apron was not new, nor was the sweater she would wear after the cooking was done, but that mattered little to her."*

*"More than anything, her hazel eyes revealed the inner strength that carried the family—and Papa—during hard times and especially then. Her gaze was steady, resolute, compassionate, and assuring. She knew, and accepted, that she was the rock of the family, and if she could bear up, then so could the rest of us. Her strength was our strength, and she was our fortress where we found safety and sanctuary."*

*"I remember her that way also," Don added. "I saw Grandma's spirit lifting my own mother as a widow with a child. When Mother sunk low, Grandma was there to bolster her up. When Mother was weak, Grandma was strong."*

*"Late in the evening," I continued, "Papa stayed home alone as Mama and the schoolgirls departed for the candlelight service at church, and Olga, Signe, Lena, and I went out for a drink with friends."*

*I released his jacket and pointed at a water glass. I sipped and swallowed with difficulty. After a few deep breaths, I invited Don in close again with a beckoning finger, and I continued.*

*"When we returned after a couple of hours, Papa was still awake, sitting in the dark, waiting for the safe return of his children, like he had done so many times before. I didn't see him at first, but I knew he was there because I smelled his pipe smoke."*

*"'What's wrong?' Papa asked, snapping on the light. 'Where's Lena?'"*

*Don lurched back. He had been calmly listening, but the mention of his mother caught him off guard. His eyes widened, and his* breathing quickened.

"Olga and Signe were weeping, and Papa didn't see me slip out again. Earlier, at the tavern bursting with merry makers, I realized Lena had departed our table and hadn't returned."

"'She went to the lady's room, but that was a while ago,' Olga said."

"'She's not there,' Signe said a moment later."

"I asked around, and the barkeep said he saw her leave with the banker a while ago. 'She didn't look none too happy, but I figured it warn't my business,' he said."

"That's when I brought Olga and Signe home to Papa before leaving to find that sonofabitch and Lena."

Don was in distress. There was paradox in his eyes, not **wanting** to hear more but urgently **needing** to learn the truth. His eyelids clenched shut but immediately opened wide.

"I found them alright. When I broke through the kitchen door of Henry's big house, I heard her screams from the bedroom, and I dashed up the stairs. I pummeled him where he lay, and he cowered under the covers. Your mother gathered up her ripped clothes, and quickly dressed."

"Please, I need a drink of water," Don said, stumbling to the table and spilling half the pitcher as he filled a tall glass and chugged it down quickly, nearly choking.

Again, I reconsidered telling the rest, but Don returned to my bedside and insisted. "I'm ok," he said running his fingers through his hair and leaning in. "Go on, damn it. Don't leave me hanging."

"'Run home,' I said to your mother. 'I'll ring the sheriff.' I called the sheriff's office, and Uncle Thomas arrived shortly before Papa. Your mother was hysterical, and it took some time for Papa to figure out what happened and hurry over to the banker's house. It was me who stood in the corner when Uncle Thomas arrested

Papa."

Just then, LaDonna, the night nurse, appeared at the door.

"My Lord, what are you two up to," she asked, pushing her pink-rimmed glasses back on her nose.

I grit my teeth and pushed her away when she attempted to smooth my hair. "Don't fret over me, and please leave the room. God damn it, LaDonna, give me ten minutes," I pleaded. "Leave us alone for ten minutes."

LaDonna offered a squirrely smile, and Don escorted her to the door, assuring her that it was ok to leave us alone for just a few minutes more.

"Are you alright, Hon?" she asked Don.

I'm sure the agitation on his face alarmed her. He shut the door behind her, and he returned to my bedside.

"So, Grandpa shot the bastard who assaulted my mother, and that's why he went to prison—not because Alekson cheated him out of the farm."

Don appeared calmer, and again I hesitated to tell the rest.

"Not exactly," I said.

"Before Uncle Thomas arrived, and Papa a few minutes after that, Alekson asked if he could get dressed, but as soon as he exited his bed, he lunged at me with a knife, and I shot him. Shot that son-ofabitch dead with Papa's skunk gun."

Don's mouth dropped.

"You?"

My head nodded slightly; I smiled; and I licked my dry lips with a thick tongue. My confession was nearly complete.

"When Uncle Thomas and Papa arrived, I explained what happened."

"'Self-defense,'" Thomas said, looking at the knife lying next to the body. 'Mebbe there'll be a trial, mebbe not, but I don't think you need to worry.'"

"That's when Papa took the pistol in his hands and looked it over. He handed the weapon to Tomas and placed both his hands gently on the shoulders of his baby brother and looked him straight in the eye."

"'We must be clear-eyed about this,' Papa said. 'How will this look to a jury? Shall we place poor Lena on the witness stand? Guilty or innocent, Andrew's future is tarnished. If the full story comes out, Lena's life is also smeared. Arrest me, and I will confess. Tomas, dear brother, do this for me. I had my reasons to want the man dead, and people will believe I did this, and my offspring can stay out of the story. Lena and Anders were never here. I'm an old man, and life holds little for me except my son and my daughters. My children are my life. My children are my future."

"I protested, of course. 'It is my deed,' I argued to Papa and Uncle Thomas, 'and I shall bear the consequences.'"

"'No!' Papa replied, voice rising. 'This shall be the last instruction I give you, my son, and I ask that you honor your father in this.'"

"And then Papa did something he had never done before in my hearing—he quoted scripture. 'Thou art my beloved Son, in whom I am well pleased.'"

"Papa drew a deep breath, lifted his chin, and said calmly, 'I am a murderer, and you are not.'"

"Ding! Ding! Ding! The pinball machine I played earlier at the tavern exploded in my head with flashing lights and clanging bells. Thoughts and emotions caromed off bumpers and flew every which way. Tilt! Tilt! In that surreal moment, Papa revealed the full story of Swede Hollow and a broken leg, of an Irish saloon keeper, and why he came to be called 'Ole,' and I listened in stunned silence. My *jangled consciousness could not respond."*

*When I began telling this story, Don learned of the death of the saloonkeeper, and he was confused because the whole family only knew that Papa went to prison for Alekson's death. Now, hopefully, it all came together and made sense.*

*I gestured for water, but I could only manage a few sips. I sucked in a couple of breaths and continued as quickly as I could, but my energy was waning rapidly.*

*"I saw strength in Papa that I didn't know was there. And resolve. And purpose. And confidence. As he poured out his life's tribulations, he found meaning in all of it, that the whole of his life pointed to this moment of sacrifice in which he saved me, and Lena, and the family ... and himself. In preserving our chance at the American dream, he realized his own."*

*"Papa finished with an emphatic statement, 'Allow justice to finally be served!' Uncle Thomas' face turned ashen. Perhaps he had long suspected there was more to Papa's story before he tracked him down in the Duluth hut, but now he had no time to think, to ponder, to mull it over. He had his sworn duty to uphold the law and to let the evidence speak."*

*"'But, but Jonas, don't, please don't ask this of me,' Thomas stammered."*

*"A single tear trickled down the sheriff's cheek."*

*"'Lillebror,' Papa said softly, wiping the tear away. 'Lillebror.'"*

*"That's when Uncle Thomas broke down in sobs, and he hugged his big brother close, and then they both hugged me before Thomas clasped handcuffs on Papa's wrists."*

*My breathing slowed, and a few silent moments passed. I placed my bony fingers on Don's hand and peered into his eyes, but he remained dumbstruck, still processing my revelations. I had one more shocker to share.*

*"You have heard my confession. I'll take communion now. Please offer absolution, and, if you are able, forgive me for killing your father."*

Don's face blanched, and he rose to his feet and moved to the window, but the Cardinals were long gone. He started to turn toward me once but halted. He pressed his arm against the glass and cradled his head in the crook of his elbow. His whole body shook as he sobbed. Finally, he faced me, wiping his nose on his sleeve.

"The fucker deserved it," he said.

He arranged his communion set, and with tears in his eyes and halting voice, he stammered, "The Lord bless you and keep you; the Lord make his face to shine upon you and be gracious to you; the Lord lift up his countenance upon you and give you peace. Amen."

Pastor Don's hand jerked as he made the sign of the cross on my forehead. For the first time in days, I felt at peace, and my final breath would come soon. But, if I had found my peace by revealing the last chapter of the story, I disturbed Don's, and he fumbled closing his communion set and spilled wine over my bed sheets. The blood of Christ.

# EPILOGUE

This is Pastor Don speaking. With the passing of the Judge, I became the oldest living descendant of Jonas Jönsson, and the mantle of storyteller now rests upon my head. The Judge was buried on a frigid Thursday the second week of January 2015. A few stray snowflakes settled on the casket and didn't melt, and I wished I had worn a hat for the graveside prayers. Earlier, funeral goers filled the cavernous cathedral of Central Lutheran Church, tucked between the downtown confluence of freeways and the Minneapolis Convention Center. The Governor and both United States Senators headed the long list of dignitaries.

Coming to grips with the Judge's story of Grandpa Jonas, which in the end turned out to be my own story, is an ongoing process. My Illinois birth certificate now made sense; when mother realized she was pregnant following Alekson's rape, Grandma sent her to live with Pastor Charlie and Agnes near Chicago, and the made-up story of my father's demise in the war became family mythology. Henry Johnson, the name listed as my father on my birth certificate, never existed, and that upset me.

My anger at not knowing the truth hopped around. First, it settled on my mother for *not* telling me; then, it fastened on Uncle Andrew because he *did* tell me, but I never resented him for what he did. Eventually, I internalized it as self-loathing. The blood of the family nemesis courses through my veins. I am the spawn of the evil that befell Grandpa Jonas, my mother, and the rest of the family. I'm not sure that I'll ever attain closure, but I'm working on it.

I better understand the burden my mother bore believing that her father's imprisonment was for exacting justice against *her* rapist, but I don't believe she knew the full story. I still don't know if Grandma Hilma knew the truth about the sacrifice Jonas made for the good names and futures of his beloved children, but I think it was his secret, known only to his brother and son, and now to me.

There is one last chapter to be told.

Uncle Andrew never married. With his father's imprisonment, he became the head of the family, and he accepted the responsibility for supporting his mother and younger sisters —at least until they could make it on their own. His first paycheck as an assistant attorney for the City of Minneapolis paid for Grandma's move to a south Minneapolis apartment, and he continued to pay her rent from that point forward. I know he helped my mother with groceries and my school clothes.

Meanwhile, his career advanced.

Mayor Hubert Humphrey persuaded Uncle Andrew that he could better serve as a crusading lawyer on the home front rather than in the military during the Second World War; I'm sure Uncle Andrew also felt the pressing responsibility of family. Uncle Andrew was there when Humphrey forged the lagging Democratic Party and the passionate Farmer Labor Party into formidable opposition for the Republicans, and he served as prosecuting attorney when Mayor Humphrey scrubbed the Minneapolis police force clean of mob influence. He served as counselor to the mayor's Committee on Human Relations that fought racial and religious discrimination in Minneapolis. He helped write Humphrey's "bright sunshine of human rights" speech to the 1948 Democratic National Convention that marked the first salvo in the emerging civil rights movement, and he continued to serve as Senator Humphrey's *aide-de-camp*.

In 1955, DFL Governor Orville Freeman appointed Uncle Andrew to be the Chief Justice of the Minnesota Supreme Court. At that time, the forty-year-old prosecutor would begin a long career as Minnesota's preeminent judge. Only a few family members and close friends, including the gregarious Senator Humphrey, observed the swearing-in ceremony in the governor's office. They waited a few minutes because Hilma was late arriving from the south Minneapolis apartment that Uncle Andrew provided all those years.

Before long, she appeared in the governor's office pushing a wheelchair. On the second Sunday of every month for seventeen years, Hilma had visited Jonas in Stillwater prison, and now he was home. Senator Humphrey immediately jumped to his feet and vigorously shook the hand of Andrew's eighty-five-year-old father, recently paroled from Stillwater prison where he had been a model prisoner and editor of the prison newspaper. The first year had been the roughest, but another inmate, a French-Canadian who dominated the prison social structure, looked out for him. Pete Archambault, Grandpa's erstwhile nemesis, became his protector.

I met my grandfather for the first time soon after that swearing in of Uncle Andrew, and so did the rest of his grandkids.

Highway 169 to St. Peter was still wet following a morning shower as Uncle Andrew piloted his red and white 1955 Chevy Bel Air toward the rich farmland of Nicollet County. Miles of black pavement dried quickly as the sun peeked out. By the time we stopped for gas, only white, wispy puffs floated across an azure sky.

I squeezed in back with Grandma Hilma and my mother; Grandpa Jonas sat in the passenger seat. Grandma Hilma glowed. Every little thing pleased her. She laughed at jokes, bubbled with remembrances, and hummed during breaks in the conversation. The strawberry hair of her youth had ripened into a rich auburn, now arranged in an elegant bouffant with a flip just above the neck following a recent perm. Cherry red lipstick seemed just right.

Mother, too. I don't remember so many smiles as during the car ride that day. In the weeks since the prison released Grandpa, her dour expression sometimes receded, and this was such a day. She sat up straight seated next to me, and it dawned on me that she was a tall woman. Knowing what I now know, I can see that her father's imprisonment was a crushing burden that was now lifting.

Grandpa said little the entire journey, but his head jerked this way and that as his eyes soaked up a generation of change since he had been a free man. Fast automobiles on the highway, monstrous tractors in the fields, and tall silos in the farmyards. Yet, the corn still tasseled, and the Minnesota River along the roadway still meandered on its journey.

Before long, we turned off the highway and onto a gravel township road. After a few wrong turns, we found the freshly mowed lawn of a prim farmstead. Siri and her husband lived on his family farm that had been homesteaded by his grand-parents, expanded by his parents, and now served as the home place where Siri raised her own farm kids. In the shade of the elm trees that lined the driveway, my aunties, their husbands, and my cousins cheered Grandpa's arrival. He clenched his teeth to maintain composure, but I saw his chin quiver.

I sat at the grownup's table while my younger cousins squirmed around card tables set up on the porch, drinking down their cherry Kool-Aid before the serving dishes were passed. At gatherings such as these, Aunt Olga's husband, a Lutheran pastor, typically said grace, but before he could start, his wife piped in.

"Excuse me, Hon," Aunt Olga said as she rose to her feet.

"This is the first time we've been together in decades. The first time ever for some of you, but we're missing someone. You kids never got to know Aunt Signe. She helped keep America safe in the war as a pilot who transported planes from aircraft factories to bases. She was a member of the Women Airforce Service Pilots, known as WASP, and these women freed up male pilots for combat duty. She died in a plane crash in 1944. She was the most adventurous of us, and ..." Olga's voice tailed off, and she convulsed in tears.

Over the muted sounds of sniffling, which the younger kids didn't understand, Grandpa Jonas stood up, with assistance from Grandma. Before saying anything, he blew his nose, and then he cast his eyes around the room to make eye contact with each of us. The words wouldn't come, his chin trembled, and he simply nodded emphatically as tears flooded down his cheeks. He slumped down into his chair, and the rest of us rose, clapping our hands.

Wiping a tear from his eye, Olga's husband said, "I can offer no prayer better than what has been said and unsaid, so I will simply start, "Come Lord Jesus, be our guest ..." and we all joined in the familiar table prayer. Siri, her husband, and their kids made the sign of the cross at the end.

After second helpings of roast beef with mashed potatoes and brown gravy that spilled onto the candied carrots--followed by juicy slices of watermelon and a seed-spitting contest--Siri's husband and ten-year-old son, Jonny, escorted Grandpa on a tour of the barn, and I followed along. Grandpa moved nimbly with the aid of a spanking new diamond willow cane.

An orange cat curled around Grandpa's leg. "Pumpa," he said, reaching down and scratching the back of the cat's head. Outside again, Grandpa leaned on a freshly painted board fence, surveying the fine herd of Holsteins.

"Which one is Bessie?" he asked.

Jonny glanced at his father with a confused expression.

"Why, that one is Bessie. How did you know there was a 'Bessie'?"

Grandpa Jonas lived another five years in the south Minneapolis apartment that had been Hilma's home for many years —a convenient location for grandkids to come and go—before he passed away quietly in his sleep. Following Grandpa's funeral, Uncle Andrew pulled me aside.

"Papa asked me to include you, as his first grandson, when we spread his ashes," he whispered in my ear.

And so, on a fine June day in 1960, fresh off my college graduation from Gustavus Adolphus College near Siri's farm, we sped north along Highway 10 in Uncle Andrew's long and low-slung Cadillac DeVille with big fins. Uncle Andrew allowed me the thrill of driving while he sat in back with Grandma. Bees buzzed in the clover that nearly reached our knees as we walked across a meadow toward a woodlot with a creek running through it. Halfway down the gentle slope, Grandma stopped. She cupped her hands at the sides of her mouth and called with a clear voice.

*Ah hoo. Wee hodee do. Ah hoo. We hoo. Wo wee!*

Cattle moved to the barbed wire fence at the near edge of a pasture and watched us with curiosity.

Following a rainy spring, the high water in the creek splashed and gurgled as it meandered through the tamarack swamp. We each took a turn shaking Grandpa's ashes into the flowing waters.

The cottonwood was certainly taller and broader than when Tomas had encouraged Grandpa to carve their names there; later, Hilma and their children added their own etched signatures. The decades' old scars had filled in, but the names were still legible. Grandma Hilma wept softly as she traced the names with her finger.

"Add your name," Uncle Andrew said, tossing me Grandpa's pen knife with a mother-of-pearl handle.

# ABOUT THE AUTHOR

## Rw Holmen

Except for four years while an under-
graduate at Dartmouth College and two
years in the Army, Obie Holmen has
resided in Minnesota his entire life. His
Scandinavian great-grandparents immi-
grated to central Minnesota late in the
nineteenth century. Although this novel
is not autobiographical in any sense, fam-

ily anecdotes and personal experiences colored the storyline.

Army service interrupted college, including a tour of duty as a
Ranger conducting small team reconnaissance missions in the
mountains and jungles of Vietnam.

After Dartmouth, it was on to law school at the University
of Minnesota, followed by a career as a civil trial attorney in
St. Cloud. Other vocational and avocational pursuits included
studying with the monks of nearby St. John's Abbey and University School of Theology and founding a Caribbean Travel
Company.

Obie and his wife, Lynn, recently celebrated their fiftieth wedding anniversary. They boast three adult children, all currently
residing in Minnesota, and two grandchildren.

# BOOKS BY THIS AUTHOR

## A Wretched Man: A Novel Of Paul The Apostle

This novel characterizes Paul as a flesh and blood human with inner passions and emotional turmoil. What was the "thorn in the flesh" that tormented him? Journey with Paul on his pilgrimage. Shiver with him around a mountain campfire, breathe deeply of the aromas wafting through a teeming marketplace, sway with the veiled Temple dancers to the melodies of the harp, savor a tangy goat stew in a tumbledown hut in a nameless hamlet. Along the way, you will witness the birth pangs of Christianity.

## Queer Clergy: A History Of Gay And Lesbian Ministry In American Protestantism

A finalist for a Minnesota Book Award.

This work of non-fiction chronicles the journey of progressive Christian denominations as they moved from exclusion to inclusion of LGBTQ persons.

## Gonna Stick My Sword In The Golden Sand: A Vietnam Soldier's Story

A bold, dark, and intense retelling of the Vietnam experience.

The author refers to Golden Sand as "autobiographical fiction."

True incidents serve as inspiration for the book, but the stories are told with literary embellishment. The author served with K Company, 75th Infantry (Rangers) in the central highlands of Vietnam in 1969-70, and he was twice awarded a bronze star for valor in combat.

## Wormwood And Gall: The Destruction Of Jerusalem And The First Gospel

A finalist for a Midwest Book Award.

The Great Roman-Jewish War was a watershed moment--no, more than that, an apocalypse in which the end of the world seemed near--not only for the Hebrew people, but also for emerging Christianity, and this novel remembers this oft-forgotten setting for an early, important chapter in the history of the church. Amid death and destruction, the dispirited remnant of the followers of Jesus, who had been awaiting the return of their crucified messiah for four decades, needed encouragement and words of hope. In response, an unknown person compiled the good news narrative that has come to be known as "the Gospel according to Mark."